Feat of Clay

Mary-ellen DeLeon

Published by Mary-ellen DeLeon, 2014.

FEAT OF CLAY

First edition. June 17, 2014.

Written by Mary-ellen DeLeon.

Dedication

Thank you to my friends and family for without your belief in me when I had none of my own, I would not have had the courage to share what I write. Gracious thanks to my Mom who taught me by example. From her I learned some of the most important lessons in life. You are my greatest gift. I hope I am at least half the parent you are.

Thank you to the ladies of CTales and all the other places where I read other's stories and shared some of my own work. Your encouragement means more than you will EVER know.

Special thanks go to: Nic of Ficland. Your writing inspired me beyond words. DRC-PLT who always told me I was worth more. White Onyx who told me to be strong and that I deserve to be happy. You go girl!

Thank you my darling daughters. Juliana, my earth angel, who crawled in my lap over and over again forcing me to quickly save and close my laptop because she was too young to read certain scenes. And to my dear Angel Maggie who could fly before she was born, you have touched my soul in ways only you and God can understand.

And lastly, thanks to all the wonderful writer websites that I combed through to find grammar lessons, marketing skills, and other tools I needed to begin a quest to publish my works.

This story is one of my more recent efforts to delve into the mystery genre. I hope you enjoy the ride. So much went into the writing of Feat. Mitch was inspired by my grandmother who sometimes does not remember my daughter's name or what grade she is in but always gives her a smile and a hug. Madge is a combination of all the wonderful nurses and other staff who assist in the care of the elderly. Their kindness, compassion, and patience overwhelm me. They don't get the credit they deserve.

Chapter One

When Brighton walked into the pub all he wanted was anonymity. The week had been long, filled with meetings and court appearances. He was tired of defending scum bags even though his win record was close to one hundred percent. This particular Friday, he wanted to be no one.

He was wearing a worn pair of jeans, a plaid shirt, and a baseball cap pulled down just enough to cover his clover eyes. The sound of his favorite boots walking on the hardwood floor made a few heads turn. Brighton opted for a stool at the bar, one which had a vacant spot on either side.

"Scotch neat," he said to the bartender.

Brighton took his first gulp and welcomed the burn as if it would wash away the week's ugliness. A few moments later, he felt a presence next to him, yet he did not acknowledge the body. He took another smaller sip and pulled a fifty out of his wallet.

"Keep it coming," he commanded, slamming the bill down.

"Yes, sir."

Harmony Blake's week was a disaster. Pretending to be something you're not was never easy when the role was the exact opposite of who you were. In addition, on Tuesday when the director had instructed her to fall over a child's toy and land in another actor's arms, the stunt did not go off as planned. Harmony's face had come in contact with the corner of an end table. She had a huge welt that makeup could not cover until Thursday. All of her scenes had to be shot from her bad side until then.

"Jack and ginger," she said.

The bartender mixed her drink and placed it on a napkin in front of her. She took a sip through the tiny straw.

"Fuck it."

Harmony tossed the straw aside and guzzled at least half the drink.

"Keep it coming," she repeated.

Brighton snickered.

"What?"

In response, he shook his head.

"Was your week as bad as mine?" she asked.

"I don't know what yours was like so, I would not care to speculate on whose week was worse. Mine was pretty bad."

She noticed the Rolex on his wrist and the diamond and onyx pinky ring.

"You don't look like you belong here."

"Neither do you."

"You haven't even turned your head."

"In my line of work, you need to know what you can't see."

"And what line of work is that?"

"It doesn't matter."

Harmony was silent for a bit. She decided he was not there for small talk. She didn't really feel like talking anyway. Yet there was something about him. Although his clothes told her otherwise, this man beside her was polished and refined. He even had finely manicured fingernails, and his cologne was obviously expensive. He was not at all the type to be in a dive. It was not a place she frequented either.

Finally, she could hold her tongue no more. "What are you doing in a dump like this?"

"I could ask you the same question."

"I have a date with Jack," she said raising her glass. "He always keeps me warm and satisfied."

Brighton lowered his voice. "Can Jack make you scream?"

Quietly she replied, "Can you?"

The bartender filled both of their glasses. Brighton downed his scotch and turned so he was directly facing Harmony. He extended his hand.

"Brighton Clay."

She put her hand in his. "Harmony Blake."

"That's a beautiful name. It suits you."

She blushed and poked the brim of his hat so she could see his eyes. Her own widened.

"You have the most incredible green eyes I have ever seen. No wait, they're more hazel. OK, maybe they're aqua with gold flecks. Damn, are they reflecting your shirt? They seem to change."

He laughed. "My mother always said they change with my mood."

"Oh, and what is your mood right now?"

He leaned closer and said, "Intrigued."

Thirty minutes later they were in a hotel room. Her lips enveloped him and a deep throated moan escaped his lips. It had been months since... His fingers tangled in her hair. He thrust deep and hard into her yearning mouth.

The two spent three hours exploring every position and using each piece of furniture in the room. When they had exhausted all other possibilities, they attacked each other in the shower.

As Brighton dressed, Harmony said, "I don't expect you to call. This was a one-time thing. I don't have time for a relationship."

"Works for me."

Saturday morning Brighton woke up feeling the effects of alcohol and a night of passion. After a long hot shower to ease his aching muscles, he headed to the kitchen. He whipped up a protein shake and made some multi-grain toast. He sat at the dining table and turned on the morning news. Brighton opened his crossword book and was thinking of eight letter word for unhinged. With his ballpoint he wrote, d-e-r-a-n-g-e-d.

"Meat handler," he said aloud knowing no one was there to hear. "Ah, butcher."

A story came on the television that made his ears perk up. As he took a sip of his drink, he looked at the screen. He spewed protein shake all over the puzzle.

Several minutes later, Brighton composed himself enough to find his cell and dial.

"Jason, I need a lawyer."

Jason got out of bed and walked to the window. "Clay, you are a lawyer."

"No, I mean, I think I may be a suspect."

"OK, it is seven o'clock on a Saturday morning. This had better not be one of your twisted jokes my friend or I'll come over there and beat your ass until you can't sit for a damn week."

"Turn on the channel seven news."

Jason found his remote and turned on the news.

Harmony Blake was one of the stars of Sands of Time. She had been on the show for three years and sources say she was up for a leading role in the next action flick. She left behind a seven year old son.

"What does Harmony Blake have to do with you, Brighton?"

"We spent last night together. I left her in a hotel room around eleven pm."

Ms. Blake was found three miles outside the city on the side of the road by a passerby. There are currently no suspects in the case and police are baffled.

"Jesus, Brighton. Please tell me she was alive and well when you left."

"She was Jason, I swear. She may have been a bit sore but she was definitely alive."

Ms. Blake was so badly beaten that identification was difficult. She was last seen leaving the studio after shooting an episode of her current daytime drama.

"Do not talk to anyone without me there. Do you hear me?"

"I know the drill, Jason. I'm a fucking defense attorney."

"Exactly, and you will be raked across the coals on this if word gets out that you were with her whether you did it or not. And God forbid they lock you in a cell with someone you failed to get off."

"Tell me about it."

A female voice asked, "Jason, what is it?"

Jason said to his wife, "It's nothing, Molly. Go back to sleep."

"Then stop swearing and hang up the phone," she replied sleepily.

Jason exited his bedroom and walked down the long hall to his kitchen.

"Was she in your car? How did you meet?"

"We met at O'Reilly's Pub. She followed me to the hotel in her car."

"Good, there's no evidence in your car, good. Did you leave anything at the hotel?"

"Other than a shit load of bodily fluids?"

"This is no time for jokes, Brighton."

"I'm not joking. It was like we were in a damn porn movie. She had skills like you would not believe."

"Shit, I don't need to hear that."

"Jason, you have to help me. I swear on my mother's grave I had nothing to do with her death."

"I believe you, man. The question is, will a jury?"

"There is no evidence. No one at the bar knew me. I had never been there before."

"Good, that's all good. Damn. What the hell is up with you and women?"

"What the hell is that supposed to mean? She left me, remember?"

"Yeah and I was there to pick up the damn pieces. I'm coming over."

"Why?"

"Because I want to see your face when you tell me you had nothing to do with this," Jason admitted.

"Do you really think I could beat the shit out of a woman I just met?"

"Remember what my wife said when she first met Lydia? You're ex looked just like Harmony Blake."

"Fuck you," Brighton said and hung up the phone. He did not want to be reminded of HER.

The bartender at O'Reilly's contacted the police and said that he had seen Harmony with a man on the night she was killed. His description of the man was vague at best. He told the police what the man was wearing and that he had light brown hair and wore a Rolex. A sketch artist was called in and the drawing was plastered on the local news.

"Brighton, did you see the sketch on the news tonight?"

"Yeah, good thing I had the cap on, right? That doesn't even resemble me."

"Maybe she was with someone else earlier or she went back after your romp?"

"Could be."

"OK, well, don't say anything to anyone about where you were Friday."

"Jason, you don't have to treat me like one of your defendants."

"Yes, I do. Attorneys make the worst clients, trust me. Lay low and do not go back to O'Reilly's... ever!"

"Yes, boss."

"I am not joking."

"Why do you always think I am joking?"

"Because you are a sarcastic jerk, that's why."

"And still, you keep opening yourself up to my witty remarks," Brighton laughed.

"Shut the fuck up and stay away from all women for a while."

"That I am not going to do. I'll give it a couple of weeks but after that all bets are off."

"Are you ever going to settle down?"

"I tried that, remember? It didn't exactly have a happy ending for me."

"It barely even began, Clay."

"Good night, Jason. Go make love to your wife."

Chapter Two

Two weeks passed and Brighton felt as if he were in the clear. He talked to Jason about coming forward to tell the police he'd seen her. As they sat in a private booth at a bar outside the city, Jason instructed him otherwise.

"Maybe you think you'll give them some sort of lead but trust me, anything you say can and will be used against you and that is not just a quote. It is a damn fact."

"I know that Jason. Stop treating me like an idiot." Brighton pushed his glass back and forth on the table.

"You are not an idiot. You are a potential suspect whether you did it or not. You are also my client and I will talk to you as I see fit. Otherwise, go talk to some other attorney. Maybe you could go tell the prosecutor. He'd love to hear your little tale of fucking some chick who winds up dead."

"You know, if we were not friends I swear your ass would be in a sling right now," Brighton said as he downed his second scotch of the evening.

Jason retrieved a couple of twenties from his wallet. He slapped it on the table and said, "Go home. Alone. Don't pick up any strays. I gotta get home to Molly."

"Take your money back. I got this."

"Save your money, Clay. You may need it to pay for my services."

As soon as Jason left, Brighton raised his glass signaling to the waiter for another refill. His mind went back a year when Jason had thrown him a bachelor party. Although he had gotten completely wasted that night, he recalled quite clearly the stripper Jason had hired. She had raven hair much like his bride to be and absolutely no tan line. That night he had promised himself he would confess to his wife on their wedding night the crimes he had committed with the stripper. OK, so it was only her going down on him; but still, he was about to get married; and the thought of having secrets from his wife did not sit well in his heart.

The day after the bachelor party, Brighton tried to ignore his pounding head as he stood waiting for her to walk down the aisle. He waited. People started to whisper. He waited some more. Then the maid of honor called him with her finger to the back of the church. He half expected to find his bride saying she had forgotten something and could he stall the ceremony.

"Brighton, Lydia isn't here. I called her cell and it went straight to voice mail. There's no answer at her place either."

"She's probably stuck in traffic."

"The limo driver is waiting outside her apartment building. He hasn't seen her."

Brighton swallowed hard. "She wouldn't..." He shook his head. "I talked to her last night just before the party. She said I love you."

"I don't know what to tell you."

Brighton pushed past her. "I'm going to the apartment. I'll call you as soon as I know anything."

He dashed to his Mercedes. He drove way beyond the speed limit. He saw the limo parked outside.

"I'm sure she will be right out," he said to the driver as he rushed toward the front door. Unwilling to wait for the elevator, Brighton ran up three flights of stairs and banged on the door to her apartment. A moment later he remembered the key. He unlocked the door and shoved it open. Her wedding dress lay on the bed. Brighton called Jason.

"I think she's gone. She left everything. Her dress and veil are here." Brighton sat on the edge of the bed as tears began to fall. "Why would she do this? She told me she loved me just last night."

"I don't know, my friend. Did she leave a note? Check your phone and email."

Jason waited a minute.

"There's absolutely nothing. I don't get it."

"I'll make some excuse to everyone. I'll come get you. Stay put."

"I'm going for a drive."

"Brighton, no, don't. You shouldn't be alone right now."

"I'm not going to do anything stupid."

"You left yourself wide open for a wise crack; but considering the circumstances, I'll let it go."

"I'll call you later, Jason."

Brighton's mind came back to the present as he looked at his empty glass. Then, he noticed her. A dark haired woman sat opposite him in the booth.

"You look like you could use some company," she purred.

"No thank you."

"We can just talk, Honey."

"I am not your Honey."

Brighton reached for his wallet. He pulled out a twenty.

"Are you insulting me with that?" the woman asked pointing at the money.

"It's not for you. I told you I am not interested."

Brighton flagged down the waitress.

"How about we have a little quickie in your car?"

Brighton grabbed the bill that Jason left and handed both to the waitress.

"That should cover everything."

"Why thank you, Sir. Do come again!"

Brighton glanced back at the table to make sure he hadn't left anything. He saw the dark haired beauty stand and step in his direction. He held up his hand and shook his head.

"I can make you forget your troubles," she teased.

Brighton walked out of the bar alone.

Brighton spent the weekend at the brownstone working on the library, removing the old shelving and replacing it with stained wood. He didn't turn on the television or radio. Instead, he listened to music from his college years, recalling some of the good times.

Sunday afternoon, Lydia walked back into his mind. He wondered where she was. She had disappeared off the face of the earth. The police investigated finding was no sign of foul play. Yet Lydia had left everything including her purse, credit cards and checkbook. Nothing was missing from her apartment.

Brighton had paid the landlord two months' rent on her place in case she decided to come back. When the time was up, he packed all her things and put them in storage. One year later, her things remained in the tiny unit still untouched. Once in a while he debated donating everything to charity. He still hoped one day she would return.

Monday, Brighton walked in to the office cheerily greeting the receptionist.

"Good morning to you too, Sir. Attorney Campbell would like to see you in his office. Shall I bring you some coffee?"

"I can get my own coffee, Marilyn. If Jason comes looking for me, tell him I'll be there in a few."

Brighton dropped off his brief case and suit jacket in his office. He stopped by the kitchenette and poured coffee into his mug. When he arrived at Jason's office, his friend was on the telephone. He waved to Brighton, signaling him to enter and close the door.

"Yeah, Tom, I'll be there at three. Order something to eat. No alcohol. I need your head clear when we talk."

Brighton took a seat opposite Jason's desk.

"Absolutely. Listen. I have to go. My second favorite client just walked in."

Jason replaced the receiver in the cradle. He looked at Brighton.

"Please tell me you did not pick up some hooker on Friday after I left."

Brighton's mouth dropped open.

Jason's eyebrow popped up.

"One approached me. I turned her down and walked out of there."

"Saturday morning, they found a brunette hooker beaten to death much like Harmony. I talked to a friend of mine on the force. They're thinking serial killer. Both women had signs of rape. Both had similar features. And," Jason paused and grimaced. "Both bodies were cleaned with bleach. He said it was poured down their throats mostly likely just before death and injected into other places as well."

"Jesus Christ."

"It's not looking good from where I'm sitting Brighton. If you did do this, tell me now. We can plead insanity or something."

Brighton closed his eyes and shook his head. He sighed deeply then looked at his longtime friend. "Jas, you have known me for how long now? Do you really think I would beat the life out of a woman then try to hide the evidence by making her swallow bleach?"

Brighton stood and began to pace. He ran his hand through his hair. He rubbed the back of his neck.

"Fuck, this has to be some odd coincidence. I barely talked to that hooker. I said 'no' like three times then walked away."

"Either that or someone is watching you."

Brighton stopped dead in his tracks at regarded his friend. "You don't think..."

"Think about it. Two similar looking women were killed in the same fashion right after coming in contact with you."

"This doesn't make sense. I'm a defense attorney, not a prosecutor. I get the bad guys off. Do you think some victim of one of my clients went nuts and is killing women I talk to? Does that seem likely to you?"

"No, it doesn't make sense. What does make sense about serial killers, Brighton?"

"I hate to think there's some psycho killer out there murdering women because of something I did or didn't do. We should go to the police with this."

Jason shook his head and leaned forward. "No, you are not talking to anyone about this but me. Let the police come to you if they find anything. Otherwise, just keep your big mouth shut."

"But Jason, if I can stop this guy..."

"Maybe this was just a coincidence. For now, pretend like nothing out of the ordinary is going on. That is my legal advice."

For a few weeks, Brighton pretended that nothing unusual had happened in his life. Eventually he began to believe it. There were no other reports of women he knew being beaten and left for dead. The topic was not discussed. Life had returned to normal once more.

One of the partners saw Brighton in the kitchenette one afternoon. "Hey Clay, a bunch of us are going to Centerfolds tonight. You game?"

"Who else is going?"

"All of the guys and Monica wants to join us too."

Brighton grinned and shook his head.

"C'mon, you need a night off. Come check out the local talent and get a good buzz on. Maybe you'll even get lucky and get a lap dance."

"OK, fine, I'll be there."

"Great, bring lots of singles," Brad joked.

An hour after Brad's invitation, Jason stopped by Brighton's office.

"I heard you're going to Centerfold's tonight. Do you think that's wise?"

"Close the door," Brighton commanded.

Jason did as he was told then he sat lazily in the chair adjacent Brighton's desk.

"Things have quieted down."

"Sure they have, but why would you stir the pot?"

"Because the rice is starting to get sticky."

"OK, if you insist on going, I'll drive you and take you home. That way if any bodies are discovered tomorrow morning, you'll have an alibi."

"You just don't want me getting laid. What will Molly think about you going to a strip club?"

"I'll tell her it's a business meeting."

"Who are you kidding? You just want to watch Monica flirt with the chicks, and you're using me as an excuse."

"It's every man's fantasy, isn't it? Monica is drop dead gorgeous, brilliant, and she loves to...."

Brighton put his hand up to stop Jason from continuing. "OK, you can drive. But don't tell me at eleven that you got to get home to your wife so you can relieve your aching groin."

Jason laughed heartily.

Brighton went home after work, showered, shaved, and put on dress slacks and a button down shirt. Jason arrived promptly at seven.

"Molly decided to go to her mom's for the night. I'm a free man," Jason announced.

"That ring on your finger says otherwise."

"I'm not that free," Jason remarked.

"Did you eat?"

"Nah, did you?"

"Let's go grab a steak then hit the club."

"Who's buying?"

"You pay for dinner; I'll get the cover charge at Centerfold's."

"Pay cash."

"No one is following me, Jas. I would have seen something by now."

Jason said, "I still think you should be careful for a while. You never know when something is going to come back and bite you in the ass."

"I'm going to be the one biting tonight."

Jason and Brighton went to their favorite steakhouse and had their fill of fine food. Brighton had a bottle of a local micro-brew. Jason decided to be designated driver in case something did happen.

"You can have one with dinner, Jas. The club is not that far away. You'll be sober by the time we head home."

"I'm not taking any chances. I want to be totally coherent tonight."

"You're a real killjoy; you know that. Nothing is going to happen. You should chill out."

"I don't know why you're not more concerned, Clay."

Brighton leaned a bit closer to his friend. "Let's drop it. I don't want to discuss this here."

Later at Centerfolds, the guys from the firm were seated around the right corner of the stage. Brighton and all the others had a few drinks and things were getting a little raunchy. Monica was stuffing bills in every girl's G-string as they waltzed by. Monica was one of those women who could be completely business-like at work. She was intelligent and knew her way around a courtroom. She also knew how to let loose and have fun and that particular night was no exception.

A brunette wearing little more than a black thong sauntered to the corner of the stage. She stopped in front of Brighton. She turned her back to him, spread her legs wide and bent over, peering at him between her knees. Brighton leaned forward and licked his lips. She straightened and glanced over her shoulder at him. There was something about the way her eyes sparkled that reminded him of Lydia.

Without warning, Brighton jumped up and headed for the men's room. Jason followed him. Once inside, Jason looked around to make sure they were alone.

"Are you OK?"

"She looks like Lydia."

"Every dark haired woman looks like Lydia to you, Clay."

"I need to get out of here."

Jason frowned. "Sure, I start to have a little fun and you go all 'I shouldn't be here' on me."

"You saw the way she... I am not getting set up again."

Jason nodded. "OK, let's go. I told Molly I would call when I got home anyway."

On the way out, the brunette stepped in front of Brighton.

"Leaving so soon?"

"Yeah, um, long day, I have to get home."

The woman held out a card. "Call me. I'd like to give you a free lap dance."

Brighton kept his hands in his pants pocket. "You're very beautiful but I'm taken."

She eyed at Jason.

"Oh, fuck no, not like that," Brighton said.

She tucked the card in Brighton's waist band. "When you're not taken, call me."

Brighton and Jason both watched as she walked away.

"Fuck she is one hot piece of ass," Jason growled.

"Tell me about it. I'd like to act out the entire Kama Sutra with her. Let's get going before I chase after her and do something I'll regret."

"I bet she tastes like honey."

"With a mix of bourbon."

The first thing Brighton did when he woke up Saturday morning was check the local news. The final thing he did before bed was watch the late night news. He did the same on Sunday.

"Thank God. No dead bodies," he said as he turned off the television and settled in for the night."

Chapter Three

The week was especially busy for Attorney Clay and he spent the majority of his time in the courtroom. His skill and cunning made the vilest murderers seem like playful kittens accidentally killing unsuspecting mice. He could twist a juror's opinion to suit his needs. Still, his work was not easy and all the conniving was taxing.

He returned to his office late Friday afternoon, tossed his jacket on the sofa, and fell into his leather chair. After a long deep exhale, Brighton sat up and punched the buttons on his phone to retrieve his messages. He listened haphazardly, taking minor notes and saving any important messages. He took a cursory glance at his email, deleted any spam, and replied to a select few.

Brighton took another long deep breath and decided he needed a release. He had kept the stripper's card never intending to use it. He withdrew the card from his wallet and ran his fingers over the embossed print. He dialed.

"Cecelia Demure, you know what to do," her voice cooed.

"Brighton Clay. I met you last Friday at Centerfold's. Call me."

He hit end then cursed himself for being abrupt. "Damn, I didn't leave my number."

Brighton locked up his desk, pulled on his jacket and grabbed his briefcase. Just as he stepped into the hall his cell buzzed.

"Speak to me," he said without glancing at the caller id.

"Brighton, it's Cecelia. I'm sorry I didn't pick up. I didn't recognize the number."

His pulse raced. "Hey, how are you?"

Cheerily she replied, "I'm awesome. How are you?"

His lips curled. "You are awesome. I happen to be exhausted but hungry. I know it's almost seven but if you haven't had dinner..."

She cut him off. "I'd love to. But I have to be at work at ten."

"There's a great Italian place just down the street from Centerfold's. I can pick you up or meet you there. It's close enough to work so we won't have to rush."

"Sounds perfect, I'll be at the restaurant in thirty."

"OK, see you then."

Brighton went back into his office and collected a fresh dress shirt from the bottom drawer of his desk. Since his home was farther from the office than the gym, he opted to go to the later for a quick shower. Always being prepared was one of Brighton's quirks. He kept a travel kit in his trunk which included toiletries, a clean pair of boxers, and several condoms.

"You're late," he said with a smirk as he held out her chair, "but you look incredible."

"I am only two minutes late."

"In my line of work, if you are less than five minutes early to a meeting, you are late."

She took the cloth napkin and placed it in her lap. "So is that what this is? A meeting?"

"It is certainly not a chance encounter."

"I suppose not, but I'm not a client either."

"If my clients looked half as beautiful as you, I would never leave the office."

When she blushed, he leaned forward and whispered, "Every head turns when you enter a room."

"Oh, you are a charmer, aren't you? Perhaps I should have kept my distance."

"By the time the sun comes up, we will have been much closer than this," he said gesturing to the space between them.

"And what makes you think I want to be that close to you?"

"You're the one who initiated by pointing that fine ass of yours at me last week. Did you think I wouldn't take you up on that offer?"

"When you ran to the men's room I wondered."

Brighton saw the waiter approach. He sat back, leaned one forearm on the table, draped the other across the back of his chair, and placed his right ankle across his left knee. To Cecelia, he looked incredibly comfortable in his own skin.

Before the waiter could speak, Brighton asked for the wine list and ordered calamari. His eyes did not leave his date for a second. The waiter nodded and disappeared.

"How do you know I like seafood? Maybe I'm allergic to it," Cecelia teased.

His brow lifted as he asked, "Are you?"

"Thank God, no I am not. I love seafood."

"And you love to tease, don't you?"

"It's helpful in my line of work."

The two stayed at the restaurant talking for nearly three hours. Cecelia told him she was studying to be a physician's assistant, and working at the club was a way to pay the bills. She wowed him with her intelligence and witty humor. He was captivated. He could listen to her speak for hours and never tire of her melodic voice.

Out of the blue he asked, "Have you ever thought about singing?"

"What? Oh gosh, no, I can't carry a tune. What made you ask that?"

"You have a lyrical speaking voice. I thought perhaps you might sing as well."

"I only sing when I'm in the shower," she mused.

He smirked and whispered, "Maybe someday you'll let me listen."

"There you go again, Mr. Clay, trying to charm the pants off of me."

"Is it working?"

"Oh," she muttered. "Speaking of work, I have to get going. Are you coming?"

"Not yet."

Cecelia's insides were aflame.

Brighton signaled for the check. He took a quick peek then tossed two hundreds in the folio.

"Shall we walk? It's a beautiful night."

"I don't want to have to walk back to my car alone later."

He put his hand on the small of her back urging her toward the door. "You won't be alone after work."

"You're being presumptuous."

"And you're scrumptious."

Their fingers interlaced as they exited the restaurant.

"Maybe later I'll give you a taste."

"My mouth is watering," he breathed in her ear.

Watching Cecelia dance that night was completely different than the previous Friday. For one thing, her eyes locked on his several times. He felt like he was being taunted in a most delicious way. Second, he knew when her shift was over, he was going to take her in every position possible. Her body would be his to do with as he pleased. She would surrender to his will. In turn, she would experience the most erotic pleasure she had ever known. With each beat of the music, Brighton's arousal grew. He needed to get her alone and soon or he would surely explode.

On the walk back to their cars, he acted with nonchalance. She was cool, nearly standoffish. He opened her car door and she slid in.

"Follow me," she demanded.

Once inside her apartment, neither could hide their desire. Clothing flew. Lips brushed flesh. Teeth grazed skin. Hands roamed everywhere. The air filled with pleasured sounds.

"I've wanted you since the first moment our eyes met," he admitted. He scooped her up and asked, "Which way?"

"Last room on the left," she purred.

Her spacious apartment had three bedrooms. He briefly wondered why. The thought left him as he tossed her on the mahogany four poster bed in her room. He buried his face in her as she squealed with delight.

Cecelia placed her head on his chest. She could feel his heart pound and his chest heave as he tried to regain composure. Brighton stroked her hair.

"Fuck, that was..."

"...Earth shattering."

"Mhm."

She looked up at him and asked, "Are you staying?"

"That's up to you."

She put her head back on his chest and replied, "At least stay until you can stand without your knees buckling."

"That might be a while."

Brighton stayed until after breakfast on Saturday morning.

"I have to get to the office and clean up a few things. Are you working tonight?"

"Actually, I have plans." She saw the look in his eyes and added, "My sister is in town. We're having a girl's night out."

"Have fun," he said brushing his lips against hers. "I'll call you tomorrow."

"I'll look forward to it."

He kissed her and said, "Bye."

"Bye."

After another kiss he said, "I have to go."

"So go," she laughed.

"One more."

When their lips separated again, Cecelia shoved him away. "Enough." She patted his behind and shooed him out the door.

"Fine, I'm going. Call me when you get home tonight," he told her as he stood in the hall outside her door.

"What if it is late?"

"I don't care if it's three am. Call me."

"Demanding, aren't we?"

He leaned toward her and she put her hand up. "Go before I make you stay."

For the next three weeks, Brighton was walking on air. He went to Centerfold's every night Cecelia was there. He sat center stage and watched as other men drooled over her knowing that he would be the one escorting her home.

The case Brighton was working on was neither high profile or complicated. This gave him a chance to enjoy normal working hours. Evenings when they weren't at Centerfold's, he would take her to dinner or clubbing. He claimed he didn't dance, and the first few times he let her go on the dance floor alone while he watched. They always ended the evening at her place. More than half the time, Brighton spent the night.

Memories of the two murdered woman nearly disappeared from Brighton's conscious mind. Occasionally on nights he spent alone, Harmony would enter his dreams. He would wake in a cold sweat and wonder what had really happened to her. Then he would push the thoughts back and tell himself it was over.

One Saturday morning Cecelia asked, "Why don't we ever stay at your place?"

"My house is too far and I am working on the brownstone; it's a mess."

Ce sipped her orange juice. "I highly doubt it is that bad, Bri. You are always well groomed and impeccably dressed. I don't see you living without some semblance of order." She wiggled her eyebrows and added, "I think you're trying to hide something. Maybe you are a serial killer and you are grooming me to be your next victim. Or perhaps you've got a wife and kids, a whole other life."

Brighton sighed. She couldn't read the look on Brighton's face.

"What is it?"

"I was engaged. As a matter of fact, I was standing at the altar waiting when her maid of honor signaled to me. My fiancée disappeared without a trace. I had purchased the brownstone so we could live together. She hadn't moved out of her apartment yet. She left no note. She took nothing."

As he spoke, Cecelia moved closer to him. She sat in the chair near him and took his hand in hers.

"I'm so sorry. I didn't mean to pry."

He shrugged and let out a small laugh. "You remind me of her in so many ways, Ce." He gazed into her eyes and ran his index finger along her jaw line. "Lyd had a beautiful smile like yours. She made everyone around her happy. She became my world." A single tear slid down his cheek and Cecelia brushed it away. "Then she was gone."

"And no one ever found her?"

He shook his head. "There was no evidence of foul play. If someone had taken her, it had to be someone she knew and trusted. The lock on her door was intact and she lived on the tenth floor. No one could have broken in."

"Was her car still there?"

"Yup, everything was as it had been. All her jewelry, clothes, electronics, even her purse was in its place."

"What about her family? Did they have any idea where she might be?"

"Her parents own a house in Montreal. The watched it for six months and Lydia never showed up. Her brother lives in France and he claims not to have seen her. If she did fly anywhere, she did so under an assumed name because there was no record of her at any airline. The police checked. It was almost as if she never existed."

Cecelia tilted her head. "Did she ever meet any of your friends?"

"Of course she did," he said with agitation coloring his tone. "Do you think I imagined her?"

"I didn't say that Bri. I'm sorry. Please don't be upset with me. It's just so strange."

Brighton took a deep breath. "Next weekend we can stay at my place and I'll make you dinner and breakfast."

Cecelia placed a gentle kiss on his cheek. "I'll bring a change of clothes and my riding crop."

Brighton pulled her into his lap. "Who gets to wield it?"

"We can take turns."

"Let's practice," he said just before covering her lips with his.

"Clay, I'm taking you out to lunch," Jason said as he stepped into Brighton's office on Monday.

"What's the occasion?"

"Do I need a reason to take my best friend out to lunch?"

Brighton regarded his friend. "Something is up; that I can tell. You are grinning from ear to ear. You must have gotten laid last night."

"And this morning, but that is not why I'm smiling. You'll have to wait until lunch." Jason waved as he left the office.

Brighton spent the remainder of the morning working on his billing and some paper work. He had a meeting with his client in the afternoon and was due in court the following day. He wanted all his ducks in a row. By noon he was ready for a break. He pulled on his suit jacket and headed to Jason's office. His friend was just stepping into the hall.

"How does steak sound?"

"Excellent," Brighton replied.

"Shall we walk?"

"Damn, you are in a good mood. You never walk. Are you going to tell me now?"

Jason shook his head as they went down the hall to the elevator. "When we get to the restaurant, I'll tell."

"So something is amiss."

"I wouldn't exactly say amiss."

"You have piqued my curiosity."

The restaurant was only a few short blocks from the office. Jason had made a reservation because they were usually busy on Mondays at noon. The two men were seated almost immediately and Jason asked the waiter for champagne.

"Oh, not for me, Jas, I have a meeting this afternoon."

"Fine, Friday you and Cecelia are coming out with Molly and me so we can celebrate properly." Jason looked up at the waiter and said, "Just water for now." He turned his attention back to Brighton. "You cannot tell anyone yet. We're keeping things quiet for now."

Brighton had a feeling he knew what Jason was going to announce.

"How far along is she?"

"About fourteen weeks, how did you know?"

"You have that 'I'm about to be a daddy' look about you. Congrats, man. That's awesome."

"We've told the grandparents. No one else knows." Jason poked at his silverware as he spoke. "Oh, except one of her friends knows too. So do not say anything at work. We want to make sure this one sticks."

"How is Molly feeling?"

"She's tired and horny as hell."

"TMI, Jason."

"What can I say? It must be the raging hormones. She was like that last time too, although she had wicked morning sickness. We're hoping that her not having it now is a good sign that the outcome will be different."

Brighton lifted his water glass. "Here's to a happy healthy pregnancy and a bouncing baby boy."

Jason tapped his glass against his friend's. "Thanks. A girl would be just as good. I don't care either way."

"A son could carry on the Campbell name."

Jason shrugged. "If this pregnancy goes well, we'll probably try again anyway. Having one of each would be good."

Brighton nodded. Jason saw the sadness in his eyes.

"Maybe Cecelia will be the one."

"I'm not sure I want to put myself in that position again."

The waiter came and took their order. When he left, Jason said, "I highly doubt that anything like that would happen again. Women just don't evaporate without a trace. Lydia must have had cold feet and..."

"Jas, what if something happened to her?"

"You can't think like that. Besides, the investigator said there was no evidence of foul play. Maybe she planned it all along. Maybe she had a hidden identity."

"But why wait until our wedding day to vanish. It just doesn't make sense." Brighton shook his head and took another sip of water. "Nothing about it makes sense. I call her brother once a month. He has never heard from her. Not one of her friends or family members knows anything."

"Witness protection? Maybe her cover was blown."

"You've been reading too many murder mysteries."

"Why would I have to read about murder when we live in that world every damn day?" Jason half joked.

"Touché."

When Brighton returned to the office, he called Cecelia. She said she was supposed to work Friday, but she would see if someone could cover for her.

"Excellent. Are you coming over tonight?"

"Absolutely, you promised to make me dinner."

"And you're going to be dessert."

"I'll stop by the store and get some whipped cream."

He growled into the phone. "I gotta go. I'll see you later, Babe."

Friday after work, Brighton went home, showered, shaved, and put on one of his best suits. He locked up and headed out to pick up Cecelia. When she opened the door, his jaw nearly came unhinged. The metallic violet dress she barely wore was sensuously revealing.

"Damn, you look good."

"Thank you. You look pretty fine yourself."

He bent his arm and said, "Shall we?"

Cecelia slipped her hand into the crook of his elbow. "Where to?"

"GILT," he told her.

"Wow, what are we celebrating?"

"Jason's wife is pregnant. Don't ask about it though. They're not telling anyone just yet. About six months ago she had a miscarriage."

Cecelia nodded thoughtfully. "That must be hard."

Brighton held the passenger side door open and watched her slide in. She always moved with grace. Part of him wanted to spend the night pleasing her until she begged him to stop. He let out a low growl just before closing the door. Brighton took a few deep breaths as he walked around the car. He was hoping to curb his appetite for her. When he took his seat behind the wheel, and she put a hand on his thigh he sighed.

"Save that thought for later," she purred.

"You make it hard to wait especially when you're dressed like that."

"Let's not order oysters tonight. I don't think I would be able to control myself."

He growled again and she giggled.

GILT was one of the most expensive restaurants in the city. They had an extraordinary wine list. Jason and Molly were in the lounge. Jason extended his hand to Brighton yet his eyes were glued to Cecelia. When he released his friend's hand, Jason pulled Cecelia into a hug and kissed her cheek.

"You are almost as beautiful as my wife." He stepped back and introduced the two women.

"It's nice to meet you Molly. I love that dress. Burgundy is a good color for you."

"Thank you, Cecelia. I love your dress too although I'm afraid I would never have the confidence to wear it," Molly said. "You wear it with elegance."

Cecelia smiled politely.

"Ce, what would you like to drink?"

"You chose, Bri. You're better at wines than I."

Knowing that the wine list at GILT was extensive, Brighton asked the gentleman behind the bar for his recommendations. While Brighton was ordering, Molly spoke with Cecelia.

"Jason tells me you are studying for your PA."

"Yes, I am. I worked as a receptionist in a pediatrician's office for a while. I watched the nurses and doctors work and decided I wanted to help people. I'm not sure what kind of doctor I'll work for yet. I'm still debating. What do you do?"

"I'm an accountant."

Brighton handed Cecelia a glass. She took a delicate sip.

"Mm, nice choice."

Twenty minutes later, the four were escorted to a table in the main dining area. The two women sat at adjoining sides of the square table set for four. The men sat opposite their ladies.

The menus at GILT changed seasonally. Being summertime, the selections included preserved melon, turbot, and charred summer squash. As the small group of friends reviewed the menu, they decided to all try different dishes. Once their order was placed, Cecelia glanced at the intriguing French architecture.

"This place is absolutely stunning." Cecelia looked at Molly and asked if she had been at the restaurant before.

"No, I haven't. I've heard good things about the food. I always wanted to come. This seemed like an occasion to splurge."

Jason and Brighton talked shop while the women got to know each other. Although Brighton was listening intently to Jason, he was keeping an eye on Cecelia. She was artistic and clever in her speech. His eyes moved to her lips and he yearned to press his to hers.

Cecelia felt his heated gaze from across the table. Slowly she wrapped her foot around his calf. He tried desperately not to release the moan lingering in the back of his throat. He wondered if he would always feel so captivated by her.

About half way through the meal, Brighton's cell buzzed alerting him of a text. He looked at the phone under the table.

She's pretty

He glanced at the number. Since it was unfamiliar, he assumed it was a miss-dialed number. Cecelia glanced at him and he shrugged.

The waiter reappeared and asked if anyone was interested in dessert.

"Oh, absolutely," Molly said. "We'll take one of each and four forks."

While the waiter stood in disbelief, Cecelia said, "I think we are going to be very good friends, Molly."

"What are you waiting for?" a grinning Jason asked the waiter. "She gets what she wants."

"Yes, Sir. Right away Sir."

The four of them laughed as the waiter scurried away.

Molly leaned back. "Oh, I don't think I can eat another bite."

"Mm, that strawberry rhubarb dessert was the best. I've never had anything like it."

"Everything was excellent," Molly said. "Thank you, Jason."

"Yes, thank you for inviting me as well," Cecelia added. "If you excuse me, I need to visit the ladies' room before we leave."

Both Brighton and Jason stood.

"I'm going to tag along."

Jason kissed his wife's cheek as she passed. "Don't be too long, babe."

"Don't worry, Jason. I'm not too tired to thank you for dinner properly once we get home."

Cecelia looked at Brighton and said, "What she said," tilting her head toward Molly.

As the two men sat, Jason said, "I guess we're both getting lucky tonight." He waited until the ladies were out of earshot before adding, "I think I'm going to keep her pregnant. She can't keep her hands off me. She had her foot in my lap all night. I'm about to burst."

"Uh, that's a little too much information, my friend."

"Aw, c'mon, I bet you're waiting to rip that dress right off of Cecelia. Damn she looks yummy."

"Hey."

"What? I can look. Hell, Molly points out babes for me to check out all the time. She always said as long as I keep my hands to myself I can drool all I want."

Brighton laughed heartily. "You are one lucky bastard."

"And look at you? Do you know how many men in this place would give their right arm to be with Ce? She just oozes sex. I bet she could make a corpse ejaculate."

"You're sick."

"I prefer unique. And you can't tell me I'm wrong. I don't know how you can let her dance half naked in front of other men though. That would drive me nuts."

"It won't be forever. Besides, it's kind of a turn on knowing I am the only one she lets play in her garden."

"Damn, did you just say 'play in her garden'? You are so whipped my friend."

"And you're not. 'She gets what she wants,'" Brighton mocked. "You'd buy Manhattan for her if she asked."

"I guess we're both just puppets for our women, huh?"

Brighton raised his glass. "I'll drink to that."

They were barely inside the door of Cecelia's apartment when Brighton covered her lips with his and peeled the dress off. He could not get enough of her nor her of him. Her hands were quickly undoing his slacks and pushing them down along with his silk boxers.

"Don't ever wear that dress again," he growled.

"I thought you liked the way I look," she purred between kisses.

"I've been hard all damn evening."

"That's not the dress's fault."

Cecelia lifted her right leg to his hip. Brighton seized the back of her left thigh and pushed her against the wall just outside her bedroom. She gasped as he thrust into her deep and hard. At first his moves were frantic. He forced himself to slow the pace. His gaze locked on hers.

"Do you know what you do to me?"

She released the lip she did not know she was biting to respond. "Can't you tell you have the same effect on me?"

"Mm, yes," he hissed.

Cecelia mewled. Brighton loved that sound. Her sweet music could drive him wild with lust. Still, he maintained a gentle rhythm wanting to enjoy the feeling of her walls around him and being the cause of her pleasure.

"Bri, I'm falling." The softness of her expression and the sparkle in her eyes told him what she meant.

"I'll catch you," he whispered then pressed his lips to hers.

They spent the night and the following morning reveling in each other. Just after eleven am, they lay wrapped around each other. Brighton kissed her shoulder and stroked her hair.

"I want us to be exclusive," he breathed in her ear. "Not that we aren't already, but I want you to know I have no desire to be with anyone else, Ce."

"Nor do I. You're all I ever want. You're all I'll ever need."

Chapter Four

It had only been a short few weeks yet Brighton and Cecelia were head over heels in love. Brighton no longer went to the club every night she danced. In the beginning, he wanted to make his presence known to her and the men who watched. In a way, he was staking his claim on her. The need to be there lessened as his trust in her grew.

Neither uttered the "L" word. Yet each could see it in the other's eyes. In the throes of passion, their eyes would lock and that little four letter word would hang between them.

For Brighton, it was too soon after Lydia's disappearance. Although it had been a year, the grief was still in his heart. He often wondered if the incident with the stripper at his bachelor party might have been the issue. Still, Lydia could have said something to him. He never thought she was the type of woman to run away, most especially from her family.

Brighton called Lydia's brother once more.

"Have you heard from Lydia?"

"Brighton, she's gone. You need to get past this and live your life. I have. And don't call my parents either. You'll just upset my mother."

Brighton nodded. "You're right." After a brief pause he asked, "I still have all of Lydia's things in storage. Should I give them away?"

"I think you should. Hanging on to her clothes and other paraphernalia is useless and, to be honest, a bit disconcerting."

Brighton knew he was right. Lydia was not coming back. There was no sense in holding on to material things. Brighton called Molly and asked if she knew anyone who would be interested in Lydia's personal affects. She agreed to sort through everything with him and decide what should be donated or simply disposed.

One Saturday, Brighton told Ce that he had plans.

"Oh, OK," she said with a touch of disappointment.

He decided to tell her the truth. "I'm going to a storage unit filled with Lydia's things. Molly is helping me."

"And you'd rather I not be there."

"No, it's not that. I didn't think you would want to..." He looked down.

Cecelia put her hand under his chin and lifted his head.

"I know this will be difficult for you. If it would help, I'll be there."

Jason went to the storage unit along with Molly. He did not want her lifting any heavy boxes. Brighton stopped at the office and signed out the key. Jason had volunteered his SUV so they would have room to pack everything. They drove from the office to the unit. Brighton could feel his heart rate quicken as he unlocked the garage-like door and pushed it up.

The musty smell from dormant items hit their senses and each of them took a step back. Brighton had labeled everything and suggested they start with the clothing. Pieces were separated into categories. Some articles were brand new while others were well worn.

"I know of a shelter for women of domestic violence that would love to have some of these things," Molly said as she held up a silk blouse. "Some of those women leave their homes with only the clothes on their backs."

In the corner of the storage unit stood a chest of drawers. Jason opened the top drawer. "You should sell some of this jewelry, Clay. I bet you could make some nice change with this," he said holding up a diamond pendant.

"I don't want any money," Brighton informed him. "If you want it, take it."

Jason tucked the bracelet in his pocket and Molly glared at him.

"What?"

"Bri, why don't you sell the jewelry and you can donate the money to charity. Or what about the annual auction in the fall? You can donate the items to that."

Brighton agreed that would be a better idea.

"What else is in here?" Jason asked as he pulled open the next drawer. "Everyone stop. Do *not* touch a thing."

In unison, they all asked why.

"Cecelia, take Molly home in the SUV." Jason backed away from the bureau as if he feared something inside would jump out at him.

"What is it Jas?" Brighton demanded side stepping his friend.

Jason put his arm out in front of Brighton. "Get out of here. Trust me."

After the women were in the car, Jason and Brighton stood outside the unit.

"What the hell is going on?"

"We have to call the cops this time, Bri."

"Why? What's in there?"

"I think you should get in your car and wait for the cops. I don't want you in there."

Brighton pushed past his friend and went back into the unit. Without touching anything he peered into the open drawer.

"Jesus."

"Only answer yes or no questions. If they want more, I'll do the talking. Remember, you're their first and only suspect at the moment."

Brighton rubbed the back of his neck. "I haven't been in that storage area for months. Someone must have broken in." He looked directly at his friend and said, "You do believe me, right?"

With honesty, Jason replied, "I have three trains of thought. One says you are damn stupid putting trophies of your victims in a storage unit with your damn name on the agreement."

Brighton opened his mouth to speak and Jason put his hand up.

"Or two, you are fucking ingenious leaving evidence and then inviting us to witness the recovery of said evidence. Or three, you have no idea how those..." Jason swallowed hard, "...things got in there and you are innocent. I prefer to believe the last of the three."

"But you're not sure," Brighton said weakly.

"I'm sorry, Bri. It just does not look good from where I'm standing." Jason paused and straightened his spine. "But I will defend you with my life."

The door to the interrogation room opened with a bang and two detectives entered. They sat opposite Jason and his client.

Detective Shaw spoke first. "We understand the storage unit was rented under your name, Mr. Clay."

"Yes," Brighton replied.

"And you have rented the unit for nearly a year."

"Yes."

"When was the last time you were there?"

Jason put his hand on his friend's arm. "Are you charging my client with something?"

The two detectives glanced at each other.

"We're charging him with at least two counts of murder."

Brighton's breath caught in his throat. His heart raced.

"On what grounds?" Attorney Campbell questioned.

"We found seven severed fingers in his storage unit. No one else had access. The key had to be signed for."

Brighton started to shake. Anger pooled in his belly and his adrenalin surged through him like flames. He pursed his lips to control his thoughts from leaking out in words.

"Someone could have broken in," Jason explained.

"We've requested a search warrant for your home," Detective Brooks told the suspect. "Is there anything you care to tell us before we find it?"

"I have nothing to hide," Brighton said through gritted teeth. "I did not kill anyone."

"How do you know Harmony Blake?"

Brighton tried not to show any emotion. Jason spoke up immediately.

"What does an actress have to do with my client?"

"Listen," Shaw said still addressing Brighton. "We know your fiancée disappeared on your wedding day. The body was never found. The fingers we found were in varying states of decay. Is one of them hers?"

Brighton's hands curled around the edge of the table between him and the detectives. "What kind of a sick bastard do you think I am? I'm a fucking defense attorney."

"That is all the more reason to suspect you, Mr. Clay. You know your way around the law. You've defended murderers successfully. You've used that knowledge to go on your own little killing spree starting with Lydia Moliere. Where did you hide the bodies?"

Brighton was furious. He pushed the chair back, and his attorney stopped him from rising. "Don't," Jason scolded.

Detective Shaw suggested, "Listen to your lawyer, Mr. Clay. You're already in deep. You don't want to add assaulting a police officer to the charges."

Brighton took a deep breath and said, "I had nothing to do with Lydia's disappearance. Someone is out there killing women and trying to frame me for it. You have no evidence to support your arrest."

"We have enough to search your dwellings and keep you over night, Mr. Clay," Detective Lawson explained. "Seven fingers were found, and I have two dead bodies with missing fingers. The unidentified digits are in varying states of decay. The coroner estimates the detachment of some to be from several months to over a year in age. We are contacting Lydia's family to see if we can identify one of the fingers as hers. When we do, you won't be able to dig yourself out of the hole you're creating."

"I know the law and my rights, Detectives. This meeting is over. I need to confer with my counsel in private."

"We decide when the meeting is over, Clay," Detective Shaw sneered. "If you confess and tell us where the bodies are, this will go a lot easier on you."

Through gritted teeth, Brighton hissed, "With all due respect, your tactics will not work on me. When I am done filing a charge of false arrest, you won't be able to show your face in this precinct."

"Is that a threat?"

"Not at all, it is a promise."

"Brighton," Jason admonished.

As he sat back in the hard wooden chair, a look came over Brighton's face that Jason had never seen before. His eyes were wild and the vein in his neck was throbbing. It was as if Brighton Clay were using every ounce of energy not to physically lash out at the detectives. In that moment, Jason Campbell wondered if the man sitting in the chair next to him was the real Brighton Clay or perhaps he had misjudged this person all along.

Cecelia and Molly had left the storage area before the police arrived and Jason had not told either of them what he had found in the drawer. Hours later when Jason arrived home, Molly put her arms around her husband.

"What's wrong? Where is Brighton?"

As he hugged Molly, Jason looked over her shoulder at Cecelia who was standing near the living room sofa. "I think the two of you should sit. I need a drink."

"I'll get you something."

Jason sat in the wing-back chair near the hearth. He put his elbows on his knees and rubbed his face.

"Jason, what is it?"

He grumbled something inaudible then looked at her. He stood and began to pace. Molly returned with a tumbler full of amber liquid.

"Where is Brighton?" Ce asked.

"He... Oh, sweet Jesus, I should have called the damn cops weeks ago."

"OK, you're really scaring me Jason. What the heck is going on?" Molly wanted to know.

Jason let out a long sigh. "They think he killed seven people."

Both women gasped.

"No, no, that can't be right Jas. We have known Brighton for years."

Jason shook his head. He paused a moment to down his drink then continuing walking the length of the room back and forth.

"There were body parts in the drawer."

"Body what..?" Cecelia said. She had heard him but her brain did not comprehend.

"Fingers to be exact. I shouldn't be telling you this." He stopped suddenly and looked at Cecelia. "I'm afraid you might be the next target. Whether Brighton did this or not your life is in danger. You should leave town and do *not* tell anyone where you are going. I have friends who can set you up in a safe house."

The contents of Cecelia's stomach churned.

Molly put her arm around Cecelia's shoulder. "Jas, you're talking like a crazy man. Brighton did not kill anyone. Someone must have broken in and planted those things there."

"I hope you're right. Regardless, two women that Brighton came in contact with recently turned up dead the following morning." He stepped in front of Ce, sat on the edge of the coffee table, and put his hand on her arm. "You need to get lost. If he didn't do this and someone is framing him, he might go after you. And if he did..."

Cecelia got to her feet. She stomped a foot on the floor to emphasize her words. "He did not do this and I am not leaving him just when he needs me the most."

Jason looked up at her. "He told me to protect you, Cecelia. I'm doing what I have to do. With any luck I'll have him out on bail soon but still, you need to disappear."

"No, no I will not," she stomped again.

"Can she stay with us?" Molly asked.

Jason addressed his wife although his eyes remained on Cecelia. "Oh hell no, Molly. I am not putting you in danger, especially not now."

They all took a deep breath. The air in the room was heavy.

"I have a sister upstate. I can go there."

"No you can't. If someone is trying to frame him, they know everything about him <u>and</u> you." He stood and looked directly at her. "I think whoever is killing these women killed Lydia too."

Cecelia's head was spinning. She could not believe Brighton was the type of man to take the life of another human being.

"I want to see him, Jason. I'll go wherever you want me to but I have to see him first."

"I'll make arrangements. Tonight you can stay here. I'm sure Molly has something you can wear. Tomorrow we can go to your place and get some things. I'll make a few phone calls and set something up for you."

Tears welled in Cecelia's eyes. "I haven't known him for long but I know he is not a killer, Jason."

Sunday morning Jason went to see his client.

"How are things going?"

"How the hell do you think they're going? I feel like a caged animal. You have to get me out of here soon or I will go insane. The food sucks. I am in here with the same type of scum I've represented. I cannot take this any longer."

"It's one more night, Bri. Monday morning I'll be here to take you home. You can do this."

Brighton was wringing his hands. "OK, OK, I can do this. Have you found out anything? How is Ce? Does she hate me?"

"She wants to see you."

"No, um, yes, I don't know. She's in danger. I can't risk it. But I need to see her. I need to tell her face to face that I did not do this."

"She believes you didn't kill anyone. She didn't want to go anywhere at first. I had her spend the night with us. I'd let her stay, but with Molly...."

"I know; you're right. I don't want to put Molly in danger either. Jas, we have to figure out who did this. Money is no obstacle. Get the finest PI in the city and find out what the hell is going on, OK?"

"I'm already on it, Bri. I was up all night making phone calls. Luckily, the DA likes you. Everything has been kept under wraps. The news reports are only saying there is a suspect in custody. Your name was not mentioned at all."

"That's probably because I'm a defense attorney, and the powers that be don't want the general public to know someone right under their noses might be a serial killer. Shit. Why me? Who the fuck is doing this?"

"I don't know my friend, but we will get to the bottom of this. And now that you're an official suspect, I can get information on the murders. I am going to scan those reports with a fine tooth comb. There has to be something they missed or something that I can use to prove you didn't do it. Whoever this guy is, he knew enough to wash away evidence with bleach. Still, maybe there were traces left behind, a spot he missed or a stray hair, something."

Brighton nodded. His mind was working overtime. He was thinking of his other murder cases and the tricks he used to get others off. It was a whole new ballgame when you were the suspect.

"Are you listening?"

"Hm, yeah, listening. Pull my cases files on Thurman and Sheffield. I have some ideas, and I bet they won't let me in the office until this is cleared up."

"You're probably right on that. I'll call Nick and let him know what's going on. He can steer your case work to me."

"Yeah, do that."

The guard cleared his throat and pointed to his watch.

"I have to get going. Hang tight, Brighton. Tomorrow morning I'll see to it you're at the top of the list. Hopefully we'll get a judge that likes you. I'm getting Cecelia set up in a safe house. Maybe tomorrow afternoon you can see her briefly but then she is heading out of town until this guy is caught."

"Thanks, Jason. I don't know what I would do without you."

"You'd hang."

Brighton was released on bail and his passport was confiscated. Jason took him home. The brownstone looked like it had been hit by a windstorm.

"Jesus, they left no stone unturned," Brighton said putting one of his chairs upright.

"The good news is they found nothing linking you to the murders."

"That wasn't luck, Jason. I didn't do it. How could they find anything?"

"Someone could have planted evidence. Perhaps this guy doesn't want to get caught yet. He's going to string us a long for a while."

Brighton flopped down on the sofa. "Seven," he grumbled.

Jason shook his head. "Why he waited until number five to kill someone who knew you is quite curious."

"Maybe he didn't. Maybe when they find the other bodies, they will be women I knew. Maybe even..."

Brighton didn't want to say it. Lydia could have been one of the victims.

"Go take a shower and I'll start picking up in here. Once you're cleaned up I'll take you to my house for something to eat and you can talk to Cecelia."

"I'm surprised she wants to talk to me at all. We haven't known each other all that long."

"Perhaps it's because Molly and I trust you."

Brighton stood and headed up to the master suite. His room was torn apart just like the rest of the place.

"Well," he said to himself. "I guess I'll have plenty of time to clean up since I can't go to work."

As he washed off the stench from spending two nights in lockup, Brighton scanned his mind for suspects. No one in particular stood out. If Lydia had been the first victim, maybe it was someone they had both known.

"Could it have been an old boyfriend?" he wondered aloud.

He dressed and returned to the living room. Jason had put all the furniture in place and was in the kitchen putting things back into drawers and cabinets.

"Leave that," Brighton told him.

Jason stopped what he was doing and looked at his friend.

"Let's get out of here. I'm going to be spending too much time here as it is."

When Cecelia saw Brighton she immediately threw her arms around him.

"Oh, Bri, I'm so sorry this is happening. Jason is going to clear this all up. Then you and I can be together."

Brighton was overcome by a rush of emotions. His knees were weak at the realization that this might be the last time he would see Cecelia for a long time. Finding the murderer could take months.

"I missed you so much." He leaned back and gazed into her eyes. "It's not safe for you to be seen with me. Jason said he is going to set you up in a safe house. Have him get you a disposable phone. That way at least we can talk, and no one can trace the call."

"I don't want to be away from you when you need me the most."

Jason and Molly were in the kitchen to give their friends some privacy.

"Listen. Whoever is doing this is watching me. He saw that hooker proposition me. Even though I left her at the bar, he killed her. He is out to get me and is willing to kill anyone in the process. I don't want that happening to you. I couldn't live with myself."

"I'll be careful. And I am sure Jason will watch out for me."

Brighton pulled her close once more burying his face in her neck. "I don't want to let you out of my sight."

"Then don't. Let's run away to some place where no one can find us."

"I can't do that. I have to find out who is doing this and put a stop to it." Brighton looked into her eyes again. "I may not have killed those women, but I am responsible for making it stop."

"No you are not, Brighton. That's the police's job. Your job is to stay safe so we can be together."

Molly made lunch for everyone. Shortly after that, two burly men came to take Cecelia to a safe house. Brighton did not want to let her go, yet he hid his desire to keep her near him.

Jason introduced his associates to Cecelia.

"Dominic is my cousin. Sal is his friend. We go way back."

Dom grinned. "Yeah, Jason used to be a bully before he went all smart on us."

Ce glanced at Brighton. She felt a little more at ease knowing he was familiar with the two men who would be protecting her.

"Take care of her," he said to the men with his eyes fixed on Cecelia. "She means the world to me."

"We will," Sal replied. "Ain't nothing gonna happen to her while we are watching her."

"Yeah, we got her covered, Clay. And once they prove your innocence, we'll bring her back to you unharmed."

Brighton left a gentle kiss on her lips and said, "I'll see you soon."

"I hope so."

From the front porch, he watched as Ce slid into the back seat of the car and they drove away. He stood motionless for several minutes even after the car was out of sight. He felt his world slowly falling apart. He thought of his house on the island and considered going there for a while until things were wrapped up. Yet the dominate side of him, the one that wanted revenge, told him to do whatever was necessary to catch the person responsible for wreaking havoc on his life.

He went inside and asked Jason, "What's the plan?"

"Plan for what?"

"How are we going to find this guy?"

"WE are not going to do anything but make sure you are never alone. If another body shows up, I want you to have an airtight alibi."

Brighton's hands tightened in to hard fists in his pockets. "Jesus, Jason, I need to do something. I can't just sit around and wait for this bastard to kill someone else."

"You have to keep your nose clean, Bri. Trust me."

"Trust me is all I ever hear from you. I need action. I need a plan."

"Let's go to your place and clean up. Maybe in the process we will find something the cops didn't. After all, he must have been watching you. Perhaps he even broke in and left something behind or he took something and it will give us a clue to his identity."

Brighton nodded and his fists unclenched. "Good. At least I will be doing something."

Jason suggested Molly come along. "I don't want you out of my sight either," he said pulling his wife closer.

"I can go to my parents' house," she suggested.

"That's not a bad idea," Jason agreed. "While we're at Brighton's you can book a flight. At least if you're in Florida, I'll know you're out of harm's way." He patted her backside. "Go pack a bag. We'll get you the first plane out."

"Oh, so now you're rushing me?"

He kissed her check. "Honestly, my heart wants to keep you by my side, but my head says you'd be safer farther away. Besides, you're mom wants to dote all over you and the little one."

As Molly went upstairs, Brighton said to Jason, "I'm sorry about all this. You shouldn't have to be separated from your wife."

"Don't worry about it, Bri," Molly called from the top of the stairs. "I was wearing him out anyway."

Brighton smiled and hollered back, "TMI, Molly."

In a low voice, Jason said, "I'll have more time to concentrate on your defense if she isn't around. Not that I won't miss her. She's one hell of a distraction."

"I guess neither one of us will be getting any until this thing is solved," Brighton sighed.

Jason patted his friend on the back. "I'm going to go help her. Stay put."

Brighton paced the living room. He rubbed the back of his neck, shook his head, and came close to punching the wall. Never before had he felt so trapped. He wanted to kill the source of his anxiety but he knew that would only cause him more trouble. Since the arrest on Saturday, he had been searching his memory wondering who would have the motive to frame him. Who would want him locked up?

He also wondered about the other women who had been killed. Only two bodies had shown up yet there had been seven severed fingers. The thought of Lydia being one of the women made his heart ache and his blood boil.

"Are you ready?" Jason asked as they descended the stairs.

"Yeah, let's go. Do you think I can go to the house on the island? I'd like to make sure everything is in order there."

"It is probably as messed up as the apartment. The search warrant included both your residences and your office."

"Shit. Did anyone say anything to you?"

Jason opened the car door to let Molly get into the back seat. "I told them I was your legal counsel and as such, I could not say anything. They get it."

"Thank God it hasn't been all over the news."

Jason closed the car door. He continued to talk as he placed Molly's bags in the trunk and proceeded to the other side of the car. "They don't want a city wide panic. If they had enough to be sure you were guilty, they probably would have publicized it more and bail would have been substantially higher. They don't want to say they made an arrest, let you go, and have another body pop up."

Brighton flopped down in the car. When Jason got in, Brighton asked again if they could go to Long Island.

"I want to get Molly off to her mother's first."

"I'm calling the travel agent right now," Molly said as she dialed her cell.

"Tell her I don't care what airport or airline, I want you outta here."

"Thanks, Jas."

He looked at his wife in the rear view mirror. "I love ya babe. I don't want anything to happen to you or our bun."

"I know, Jason. I was just teasing."

By the time they arrived at the brownstone, Molly had a confirmation on a flight later in the day. The three of them cleaned up and began to put everything back where it belonged. Jason told his client to make a list of everything that was missing so he could compare it with the list of evidence taken by the search team.

"And let me know if something is here that wasn't before. This guy knows an awful lot about you. Check for bugs too."

"Bugs?" Molly questioned.

"The listening kind, babe," he explained.

She nodded as she folded some clothes that had been strewn over the bed. She pulled open a drawer.

"Don't lift anything, Molly."

"I'm not an invalid, Jas. I can put clothes away. Yuck, maybe we should clean the bureau first. There's all this dust over everything."

"They printed the place."

"I guess they wanted to be thorough."

Brighton noticed a number of his possessions were missing including his laptop. They had gone through his desk and taken his flash drives as well. It seemed like all of his clothes had been searched, but none were taken.

"There's a box missing from the closet shelf."

"What was in it?"

"There were pictures of Lydia and me, our wedding bands, and the tennis bracelet I bought her as a wedding present. I guess I should have put the jewelry in a safe deposit box."

"I'll get it back for you. They have no reason to keep that stuff."

Brighton looked at Jason. "Do you think they'll test the stuff that was in storage to see if they can find a DNA sample of Lydia's to match to the..." He swallowed hard, unable to say the word.

"They probably will, Bri. At least that way you'll know she didn't just disappear."

"I don't think that will make me feel any better especially knowing what this bastard does to his victims."

Jason breathed a sigh of relief once Molly boarded the plane to Florida.

"That's one less thing I have to worry about. Are you up to stopping at the precinct? I want to get a list of things they took from your residences."

"Yeah, I'd like to see that list myself. I want to know why they hell they took that box."

"I was thinking the same thing."

As they walked into the building thirty minutes later, all eyes were Brighton. The whole police force knew he was a suspect in the murders. The head detective on the case was reluctant to share any information.

"Look, I'm Mr. Clay's attorney, and we have the right to see what you have on my client."

The man grumbled as he pulled out the evidence list.

"Please make a copy for me."

He griped once more and unenthusiastically lumbered over to the copier. Jason waited until they were outside and in his car before he began to skim the paperwork.

"They didn't log any rings or bracelets. There are a few photos mentioned, but it doesn't say what the pictures were."

"One of the cops probably pocketed the jewelry."

"There's another alternative."

Brighton and Jason looked at each other and simultaneously said, "Someone else took them."

"I need to see which pictures they took. I had one of my parents in my office that I don't remember seeing."

"Do you want to go back in?"

"I can't stay in the car alone, remember?"

"Right, c'mon, as long as we're here we might as well get a look now."

Chapter Five

"There's something you're not telling me, Bri." Jason said as he handed his friend a mug. They were sitting in the kitchen of Brighton's place.

Brighton ran his finger down the list of confiscated items for the fourth time. "Hm? Oh, I was just wondering why the hell someone would want a picture of my parents. I mean, Mom passed away years ago and the old man is in a nursing home. He doesn't even recognize me when I visit half the time."

"You rarely talk about them anymore. How's the old man doing?"

"Physically he is healthy as an ox. He'll probably outlive my kids. Mentally," Brighton shook his head, "he lost it when Mom died. Sure, the dementia probably would have happened anyway, but losing her broke his heart."

"How did they meet?"

"What does that have to do with anything?"

Jason took a long drink of his coffee. "Someone took their picture. Maybe this has something to do with them somehow. Did anything happen when you were a kid?"

He looked down and his cup. "You know he isn't my birth father, right?"

"I assumed that since you have a different last name."

Brighton sighed. "My mother was only nineteen when she got pregnant. The guy gave her money to get an abortion. She refused. Luckily, her parents were supportive and helped her finish school. I stayed with my grandmother when my mother was either working or in class. She met Mitchell several years later. I was about four. After they were married he adopted me."

"And you have no other siblings?"

"When I was ten my mother miscarried. They never tried again after that."

"So you don't remember your parents having any enemies? You didn't piss off anyone in college? None of that?"

"My mother was a grade school teacher, and my father was a principal. Everyone loved them both." He pushed his mug back and forth on the counter. "I'd talk to my father, but I doubt he'll remember much. My mother's parents moved to Scottsdale ten years ago. I doubt they'll know anything."

"Still, I think we should investigate all leads. And it would be better for your family to hear what's going on from you rather than some headline."

Brighton agreed. He called the home to check on his father first. The nurse said he was having one of his better days.

"I'll stop by after dinner time."

"OK, but don't come too late."

"I won't, Rosalyn. I know his routine."

After he disconnected the call, he dialed his grandparents' home.

"Oh, Brighton dear, how are you? It's nice to hear from you."

"How are things in Scottsdale, Grandma?"

"It's warm and sunny like every other day. When are you coming for a visit?"

"I'm not sure I can get away any time soon," Brighton replied rolling his eyes. "Look, I have some unpleasant news. This is not an easy thing to say so I am just going to jump in. There have been two confirmed murders here recently."

Mrs. Clay interrupted. "Oh, Brighton, you live in the city. That's not news."

"Well, not usually. The thing is," he took a moment to find the right words. "They think I had something to do with it. I met both of the women the night they were murdered. They found some evidence in the storage unit where I kept Lydia's things."

Mrs. Clay gasped.

"I didn't do it; I swear."

"Oh, dear, I know that. But why would anyone want to make people believe you did it?"

"That brings me to my point. Someone took of Lydia as well as one of Mom and Dad. I was wondering if you could think of anyone... Was Mom or Dad in any kind of trouble? Did they have any enemies from a long time ago?"

"Oh dear God, no. Mitchell is a marvelous man. All the parents and students loved him. He was wonderful to your mother. He loved you as if you were his own."

"I know that, Grandma. I'm just grasping at straws; I suppose."

"Could it be one of your past clients, Brighton?"

"I don't know. I'm looking into that as well. Jason is helping me. We have a private investigator checking leads."

"Why don't you come and stay with us for a while until things blow over?"

"I can't leave the state."

"So you're a suspect? Were you arrested?"

"Yes, I was. Jason got me out on bail."

"I always liked that boy."

Brighton could not help his lips from curling. "We're both grown up now, Grandma."

"Apparently so, Brighton, but not too grown up to call me, right?"

"No, Grandma, I'm not too grown up to call. I'll try to talk to you more often once this mess is settled. I promise."

"OK, Brighton. Take care of yourself and let us know how you're doing."

"I will." He hung up and glanced at his friend. "Nothing."

"It was worth a shot."

"Let's finish getting this place together. I assume you're coming with me to see my father."

"Like I said; I'm not letting you out of my sight except to shower."

Rosalyn, the receptionist at the nursing home, greeted the men with a smile as Brighton signed the visitor's log. "Mr. Daniels will be so happy to see you. He doesn't get many visitors."

Brighton tilted his head. "Have there been other people stopping in to see my father?"

"There were a couple of detectives who stopped by on Sunday. They told me they were old friends. Check with Madge."

"Anyone else come in?"

"Not that I am aware of but I am only here in the evenings."

Brighton's lips curled and he leaned over the desk. "I don't suppose you could check the log and see if anyone else has dropped in recently."

Because of his proximity, the woman was flustered. "I, um, I can check. Stop by the desk on your way out."

"Thanks."

As the two men walked down the hall the woman fanned herself and watched until they turned the corner.

The wing of the home where Mitchell Daniels lived was for people with Alzheimer's and other forms of dementia. The doors remained locked and a pass code was needed to enter. Brighton punched the code into the keypad and the door unlatched. As they entered, a woman said she needed to get out.

"Mrs. Levine, how are you?"

"How do you know my name?"

"It's Brighton. My father Mitchell lives here," he said as Jason closed the door.

"I need to get out. My sister is waiting for me."

"I'm sorry, Mrs. Levine. I can't open the door once it's been closed."

She grumbled as she turned to walk down the hall.

"God bless the people who work here," Jason said quietly. "I don't know how they do this all the time."

"It's not easy."

They found Mitchell in one of the common areas talking to Madge. They were both laughing at something. Madge saw Brighton first and stood from the chair.

"Brighton, it's so good to see you. How are you?"

After a quick embrace he replied, "I'm well Madge. Thank you. How are you?"

"My cheeks hurt from laughing so hard. Mitch has me in stitches. I'll let you have some private time."

"I'd like to talk to you before we leave."

"Sure thing, I'll be around," she said as she exited the room.

"Hey Dad, how are you?"

Mitchell saw his son and leaned to the side looking beyond both his visitors.

"Where's your mother?"

Brighton sat in the chair Madge had occupied moments before.

"She couldn't come, Dad."

Mitch moved closer to Brighton his son and whispered, "Good, because I don't want her knowing about Madge. The woman has a thing for me. She's always asking if I need anything, she brings me food, and makes sure I shave. If it wasn't for your mother, I would definitely take her home."

Brighton suppressed a laugh although in a way, he was saddened that his father could not remember that his wife had passed.

"She is one hot ticket, Dad."

"She sure is. But I would never cheat on your Mom. She's all I ever needed."

Brighton blinked back his tears. "So how are you doing?"

The older man shrugged. "I can't complain. I won at bingo last week. I took your mom out to dinner and bought her a dozen roses. She was all over me."

"That's a little too much information Dad."

"You're in college now, Bri. It's no secret that your parents have sex."

Brighton glanced at Jason.

Mitchell followed his eyes. He tipped his head in Jason's direction. "Is this your new roommate? I bet he steals all the chicks from you."

This time, Brighton let himself chuckle. "Yeah, he does, all but one."

"Oh, yeah. You got a girl?"

"Her name is Cecelia."

"What happened to Lydia?"

Brighton swallowed hard. "We broke up."

"Damn. She was a nice girl, so smart and pretty."

The three men talked for a while. Brighton tried to jog his father's memory about old times. Although Mitchell shared a few stories, none of what he revealed seemed pertinent. Brighton could tell some of what his father disclosed was conjured up from the older man's vivid imagination.

Brighton decided not to tell his father what was happening in his life. He knew Mitch would not remember. His short term memory was all but gone. What he did recall was usually spotty at best.

When Madge returned to the room, Brighton asked his father if he had any visitors.

Mitchell looked at Madge. "Um, your mother stops by."

"Anyone else?

He shook his head.

"There were two detectives here on Sunday Mitch, remember? They were asking questions about your son."

"Is my son in trouble?"

"No Dad, I'm not."

"Who are you?"

"Dad, it's me, Brighton."

Mitchell's eyes widened. He shook his head. "Nope, Brighton hasn't been here in months. He's at school."

Brighton sighed.

"Hey, Donna, why don't you let me take you out to dinner tonight with the boys."

"Mitch, you already had dinner," Madge told Mitchell.

"Are you sure?"

"Yes, Mitch, I'm sure."

"OK, well, next time our son stops in with his friend, we'll take them out."

Brighton ran his hand through his hair. "I should get going, Dad. I'll see you next week, OK?"

"Who are you?"

Out in the hall, Madge asked Brighton if he was in trouble. He nodded as a reply.

"What did the detectives want with my father?"

"They were asking all sorts of questions about you and Lydia. Your father was in and out. Most days he thinks you're still in school. It was confusing to the police. They asked me if he had any visitors, how often you came, and if I had overheard anything. I plead patient confidentiality. I know that's for doctors. They said they'd come back with a warrant if I wasn't cooperative. I told them they could check the visitor log, but I would not tell them what Mitch and I discuss. Most of it is useless anyway."

Brighton hugged Madge. "Thanks for taking such good care of him. He looks great."

She laughed. "He chases all the women around. The problem is that he doesn't remember their names. Then again, they don't remember his half of the time either."

Madge saw guilt and grief in Brighton's eyes. She lightly touched his arm.

"He's doing well, Brighton. I know you didn't want to just put him in a home, but it is nice here. Trust me; there are many places that don't treat their patients well. This isn't one of them. He's happy even when he isn't in the present."

They embraced once more. The men stopped at the front desk to retrieve the information promised by the receptionist. She blushed and batted her eyelashes. Brighton was charming to her yet he felt no connection. He was thinking of Cecelia.

After leaving the convalescent home, Jason suggested they stop by the office.

"I had some of your case files pulled. We can take them back to your place and go through them. Maybe we'll find something."

Brighton nodded and continued staring out the window. Although it was night, the city lights were bright and people were bustling by on the sidewalks.

"We'll figure this out, Clay."

"What do you think Ce is doing right now?"

"She's probably thinking about you. I'll call Dom. I told him to pick up a cell for Cecelia like you asked."

"Where did they take her?"

"They took her out of the city, somewhere safe. They have connections."

"So you don't know where exactly."

"No, I don't. I thought it would be best that way."

Only a few lights were on in the office building when they entered. They went straight up to the fourteenth floor. The office was eerily quiet with only the after-hour's lights illuminating the halls. There were two boxes of files on Jason's desk. Brighton flipped through the folders quickly.

"Looks like only the most current files are here. It's a place to start."

The two men spent the next few days combing through files. There didn't seem to be many likely suspects.

"What about Pierson?"

"He's locked up."

"He could have connections on the outside."

Bri shook his head. "I don't think he fits. He raped his girlfriend once. He isn't a serial offender."

"Yeah, you're right? Perkins?"

"He is still in jail too. Although, if he were out, I would say he was a prime suspect. He is definitely a psychopath. Knew he was guilty the moment I took the case. He liked to torture his victims."

"Didn't he threaten you?"

"Yeah, when he was hauled out of the sentencing hearing he hollered something at me like 'You'll pay for this.' But with all his crimes, he's not getting out ever," Brighton said emphatically.

"Again, I think someone in jail might have friends on the outside."

"Not Perkins. He was a loner. He had no friends and none of his relatives would even testify on his behalf."

"I guess we keep looking."

Jason spoke with the investigator daily. He discussed everything with Brighton. Jason talked to the police as well. No one seemed to be able to find anything connecting the murders to someone else.

Brighton called Cecelia several times a day. He would ask what she was doing and if Dom and Sal were treating her well. She told him she had been reading a lot and shopping online. She would have things delivered to her house, and one of the guys would pick the items up.

"You shouldn't do that, Ce. What if one of them is followed?"

"It's OK, Bri. We have moved twice this week. They are very good at what they do."

"I miss you, Ce. Please don't go falling for one of them."

"I won't, Bri. I miss you too. Sometimes I wish you could sneak over so we could spend a few minutes together."

"I would like nothing more, trust me."

It was Friday night and she asked him what his plans were.

"Jason and I are going to grab a couple of steaks. He suggested we take a break from the case files. He thought maybe some time away from the investigation might do us some good."

"He's probably right. Besides, with the police and the PI checking into things, you should step away for a bit."

"I wish I could have dinner with you instead of Jason."

"Soon we will be together again, Bri."

Brighton hoped Cecelia was right. After he hung up, the two men went out to their favorite steakhouse. Jason told his friend he had talked to his wife and she was doing well. Her mother was enjoying her company. They talked about anything except for the current situation. After dinner, they went back to Brighton's place. They played chess, smoked cigars, and had a couple of beers. After two games, they watched an old action flick. Then Brighton told his friend he was turning in for the night. They locked up the brownstone and Jason retired to the guest room. He took with him the keys to his car as well as his client's keys.

At three am, Cecelia's eyes fluttered open. The men had moved them to a small apartment where she had her own room. It took a few minutes for Ce to remember where she was. She had been in a very deep sleep and dreaming of Brighton.

"Hey, beautiful."

"Mm, Bri? What..?"

He put a finger to her lips. "Sh, I don't want to wake the guys, I needed to see you."

He spoke barely above a whisper. His breathing was ragged.

"How..?"

"Sh," he repeated then pressed his lips to hers as he knelt by the bed. "I missed you so much."

"You smell like cigars and bleach."

He pulled back the covers, and Cecelia shivered slightly.

"Mm and you smell like sex. Have you been cheating on me?"

"I was dreaming about you."

When he slid into bed next to her, Cecelia realized he was wearing only his briefs. He gently pushed her back and moved over her, pressing his pelvis into hers.

"Make love to me," she pleaded.

He lifted her nightie. Ce tugged at the waistband of his underwear. He pushed them down just enough to free himself. He pinned her arms over her head with one hand then thrust into her. Cecelia surrendered to him. He moaned at her readiness. He pounded relentlessly into her. Before Cecelia could catch her breath it was over.

"Thanks, beautiful. I gotta go before they find me here."

"Can't you stay for a moment?" she asked as he climbed out of bed.

"It's not wise."

She sat up. "Is that all you came for? A quickie?"

As he pulled on his jeans he bent down and placed a kiss on the top of her head.

"Go back to dreaming of me."

Her eyes filled with tears. "Bri, please."

He slipped on his untied sneakers and grabbed his jacket. Without another word, he exited the room and made his way downstairs.

She ran to the window hoping to see his car drive off. She stood there for several minutes then realized he must have parked away from her line of sight. She curled up under the covers and wondered if what she had experienced was a waking dream. Maybe he hadn't really been there. She closed her eyes and inhaled through her nose. The scent of bleach and cigars remained.

Cecelia got up and pulled on a robe. She made her way to the living room and saw Sal sound asleep on the sofa. She wondered how anyone could have slipped past him. She went to the other bedroom and saw Dominic was asleep as well; yet as soon as she closed the door and turned to go back to her room she heard his voice.

"Cecelia? Is something wrong?"

She poked her head back into the room.

"Either I had a very vivid dream or Brighton knows where we are. I think we should move again."

"Where's Sal?" Dom asked as he rose from the bed.

"He is asleep on the sofa."

"Start packing. I'm not taking any chances."

She nodded. Dom followed her down the hall. He tried for several minutes to wake Sal. Finally he resorted to tossing a glass of ice cold water at him.

Sal shook his head violently and wiped his face with his hands.

"What the fuck, man?"

"We're moving." Dominic thought it highly unusual that Sal was sleeping so deeply. He had always been a light sleeper.

"Why? What happened?"

"Just get your things together and we'll talk on the way."

The three of them drove until the sun was up. They stopped to get something to eat then returned to the car. Sal asked Dominic where he was planning to go.

"The cabin," was his only reply.

Sal nodded.

Cecelia watched the scenery go by. She thought about her visitor and a strange feeling came over her. Maybe it wasn't even Brighton. She felt nauseous at the idea of perhaps being with the perpetrator. Could it have been?

Dom glanced in the rear view mirror. "Are you OK?"

"Not really," she admitted.

"It's going to be all right, Ce. Where we're going, no one will find us. Trust me."

Chapter Six

Brighton called Cecelia twice during the day on Saturday. Each time, the call went to voice mail. He left a simple message saying he loved her and asked her to call when she had a moment. By sundown he was worried.

"Jas, could you call Dom and ask him how things are going? I'm worried about Ce."

"Maybe they took her shopping or something. She's been away from home, and she didn't pack a lot. She probably ran out of clean clothes."

"I guess. But even if she was shopping, she would have picked up the call, don't you think?"

Jason shrugged. "Dom would have called me if anything was wrong."

"Unless he is unable to," Brighton added.

Jason dialed Dominic's cell and Dom immediately picked up.

"What's up boss?"

"How is everything going?"

"Good. I'm not staying on the phone long. In case someone is tracing the call. We moved at three am."

Jason took a few steps away from Brighton and lowered his voice. "So everything is fine," he said for Brighton's benefit.

"He's listening?"

"That's good."

Dominic took his response as a positive.

"Ce told me either Brighton paid her a visit or she had a very realistic dream. I didn't want to take any chances. I have to go."

The called disconnected yet Jason continued to talk. He nodded his head and said, "That's what I told him. Did she buy out the store?"

Brighton breathed a sigh of relief. "Let me talk to her."

"Yeah, sure. Just tell her to call him when she has a minute. I'll talk to you soon."

"Wait," Brighton said just as Jason hit end. "Why didn't you let me talk to her?"

"She was in the shower. I guess she had a long day of shopping with the guys. He said she was turning in early."

"I don't get it. Why doesn't she want to talk to me?"

"Give it a rest, Bri. She probably needs a break."

"A break?" he repeated. "I haven't seen her in days." He began to pace. "We don't talk more than a few minutes at a time. I miss her. She said she misses me."

"Calm down. I'll get you a drink."

"I do *not* want a drink. I want to see her." He moved closer to Jason. "You know where she is. Take me to her."

"I don't know where she is. They moved again."

"Why? Did something happen?"

"The less you know, the better you both are. Now, let me get you a drink. You need to calm down."

Brighton grunted in frustration then flopped himself down on the sofa. "You're right. It's better off if I don't know where she is. Knowing would only get me into trouble."

Just after nine that evening, Brighton's cell rang. He glanced at the caller id and, although it was an unfamiliar number, he assumed it was Cecelia.

"Hey, beautiful, how are you?"

"Exhausted, I did not sleep well last night. Then we spent the afternoon shopping. How did you know it was me?"

"It was a lucky guess. Jason tells me you moved again. I figured they might have gotten you a new cell as well."

Cecelia hesitated. "Yes, Dominic thought it would be best."

"I'm not going to ask where you are. All I need to know is that you're safe."

"I am, Brighton. Dom and Sal are taking very good care of me."

"I miss you so much."

Cecelia decided not to mention what had happened the night before. If anyone was listening in on the conversation, no one needed to know he had paid her a visit.

"I miss you too, Bri. Listen, um, I hate to do this but Dom says I can only stay on for a couple of minutes. I love you."

"I love you too. I'll call you..." He heard the dial tone and sighed.

With all of his electronics in the hands of the police, all that remained was his television and the new cell he had purchased. He checked his email. There was nothing but spam. He tossed his cell aside and walked down the hall.

"Jason," he called through the door. He waited a moment. The door opened and he saw his friend on the phone. He waited in the doorway.

"I love you too, Molly. Give your mom a hug for me. I'll talk to you soon."

Jason hung up and placed his phone on the nightstand.

"What's up?"

"I feel like I am a prisoner in my own home. I need to do something."

"Tomorrow we'll go check on your house on the island. I bet there is a mess to clean up."

"Let's make sure we check the attic. When I moved my father to the home, I packed up some of their things and put them away."

"Why didn't you tell me that before? There might be something we can use."

"I honestly do not think my parents have anything to do with what is going on. It has to be something I did."

"Regardless, we should examine everything. Get some sleep. We'll leave early in the morning."

Brighton started to walk away then looked back. "Are you sure Ce will be safe with those guys?"

"Absolutely, I would trust Molly with them."

Jason's words made him feel a little better. Still, he could not stop worrying about her.

Sunday morning at five, the two friends were on the road with coffee and a supply of food for lunch. It was nearly a three hour trip as the house was near the tip of the island. They planned to spend whole day. Who knew what kind of mess the police had left after their visit?

There was police tape over the front door. Brighton let out a long sigh as he pulled it off. The lock on the door had been broken.

"We'll have to take a ride and get a new handle before we head home," he said to Jason without looking at him.

The house was in even more disarray than the brownstone. They cleaned in the living room and worked their way around the first floor. After lunch, they tackled the second floor. Brighton thought they would leave the attic for last and pack up any boxes to bring back to the city to examine their contents.

By dinner time, most of the furniture was back in place, clothes had been put away, and there was barely a sign that anything had been disturbed.

"Shall we attack the attic?"

"Lead the way," Jason said with a gesture toward the ceiling.

The access to the attic was in the walk-in closet of the master suite. Brighton positioned a step ladder directly below the door. When the molding around the opening creaked and a few paint chips and some dust fell, he thought the police hadn't found the door. The edge of the opening aligned with the middle of Brighton's chest when he was on the top step of the ladder.

"Pass me up the flashlight. I have a light hooked up but I can't see it from here."

He placed the flashlight in his waistband and hauled himself up and into the attic. He found the fixture and turned on the light.

"How does everything look?"

"Like no one has been up here for months," Brighton hollered down. "Are you coming up?"

"No way man, I don't like heights or ladders. I'll stay down here and you can pass down whatever you want to take."

"You know; it just occurred to me. I had a key in my desk to a safe deposit box. My parents had some documents in there. Most of it was insurance and shit like that. Should we spend the night and hit the bank in the morning?"

As he spoke, he moved a couple of boxes closer to the opening. One by one, he carefully handed them to Jason.

"How come you just thought of that now?"

He shrugged. "There's been so much going on in my head I can barely think straight anymore. And I miss Ce."

"You're not the only one not getting any," his friend complained.

"I'm not talking about sex, Jas. I just miss being with her."

"It's only been a week. Things will get back to normal as soon as we find out who the hell is doing this. How many damn boxes are up there?"

"Only one more of consequence I think. The rest is just stuff I couldn't part with."

"You're too damn sentimental."

Brighton lowered himself down on to the top of the ladder. Jason suggested they pile the boxes in the living room, pick up something for dinner, and buy a new lock and handle for the front door.

"So we're spending the night then?"

"Yeah why not? I'd like to get a look at those papers in the safe deposit box. Maybe there is a beneficiary to a life insurance policy or some other strange information that may lead somewhere."

Brighton rolled his eyes as he lifted a box. "You're not thinking Mitch had a secret lover or something, are you?"

Jason chuckled. "If he did, he wouldn't remember."

Later in the evening, the two sat in the dining room with papers and other items they had taken out of the attic. Brighton pulled out an old photo album. There were pictures of him, his mother and his grandparents when he was a baby. He smiled sadly looking at his Mom. He missed her.

At the back of the album there was a sealed envelope. "My darling boy" was written on the outside by his mother's hand. He used a letter opener to get inside. The envelope contained a letter and a picture of a baby. He began to read.

My darling B:

My arms ache as I write this letter. Even after spending only a few hours with you, I am deeply in love and wish circumstances were different. The thought of losing you weighs heavy on my heart. Although my family has offered their support, I cannot see how I can possibly keep you and give you the life you deserve.

They are coming tomorrow to take you. I wish there was another way. Perhaps someday we will meet again and I will be able to explain why I have made the decision to give you up. I hope your new family treats you well.

You will always be in my heart.

Your loving mother, D.

Tears streamed down Brighton's face.

"What is it?" Jason asked.

"My mother was going to give me up for adoption. I guess she changed her mind." He wiped the tears away with the back of his left hand as he held out the letter for Jason to see.

"Wow, are you sure this is about you?"

"The date at the top is my birth date so it has to be."

"Hm, that is strange. Wouldn't she have tossed the letter once she knew she was keeping you?"

Brighton snickered. "She was even more sentimental than I am. I guess that's where I learned it from."

Jason leaned has back against the table and crossed his arms. "Do you think the adoptive parents would have been ticked off? I mean, it sounds like the paperwork was all set and all that was left was to hand you over. Do you think your grandmother would know what happened?"

Brighton glanced at his watch. "She might know but I think it is too late to call her."

"It's earlier there," Jason reminded him.

"Yeah but I just want to sit on this for a bit. Maybe I don't want to know."

Jason patted his friend on the back. "OK, buddy, you can call her tomorrow."

The following morning, they packed everything into the SUV. Over the next three hours, Brighton could think of nothing but the letter he found. He was anxious to talk to his grandmother. Watching the scenery go by and seeing people on their way to work seemingly without a care was not helping the feeling in his gut.

"After I make that phone call, I want to go see my father again."

Jason glanced at his client for a second. "If he knew anything, the chances of him remembering are..."

"I know. I figure since he thinks I am in college, maybe the older memories are still there. Perhaps I can stir up some old feeling and get him talking."

"Do you think your mother would have told him you were almost adopted?"

"My mother was big on honesty." He cleared his throat. "Well, she always said she was. Now I am not so sure. I don't know how she could have kept this from me. She told me everything else."

"It was probably too painful, Bri. And since you weren't actually adopted, why tell you?"

"I suppose."

Once the SUV was unloaded, Brighton went into his room and dialed his grandmother's number.

"Darling, how are you?"

"I'm OK. I've been going through some of Mom's old stuff. And, um, I found something."

"Well, I am sure whatever it is, you can sell it or dispose of it however you like."

"No, it was nothing like that. I was looking through an old album and an envelope fell out. She had written me a letter on the day I was born."

"Oh?"

"Did you know about the adoption?"

"Brighton, I hear your grandfather calling. We were just on the way out the door. I'll talk to you soon."

When he heard the dial tone, he stared at the telephone in disbelief. He dialed again and the call went straight to voice mail. He flopped back onto the bed in frustration.

Ten minutes later, Jason tapped on the door.

"Yeah, come in."

"So? Did you find out anything?"

"She hung up on me."

"What?"

Brighton sat up. "She said they were just leaving and hung up."

After dinnertime on Sunday, Jason took his friend to see his Mitch. Brighton's father was still in the sitting room talking to another man. He looked up and saw the two younger men approaching. He smiled and stood to hug his son.

"What are you doing here? Don't you have some girl to chase after?"

"I heard you're the lady chaser around here Dad."

Mitchell glanced around. "Sh, I don't want your mom knowing."

He gestured to his father to sit. "So how are things going?"

"Good, good. Your mother and I just had dinner. Not sure why she likes coming to this place but I do what she wants. You know how it is. Keeping the woman you love happy makes life easier."

He grinned at his father, trying to hide the sadness he felt seeing Mitch the way he was. He swallowed past the lump in his throat.

"How old was I when you met Mom?"

"You were three, no, closer to four, and quite the handful. The first night your mother let me come to the house to meet you, she had you all dressed up. You shook my hand like a man then glanced at my watch. You asked if you could wear it then proceeded to tell me how it worked."

Jason choked back a laugh. He could picture a young Brighton being very mature for his age.

"You were very bright and inquisitive. You wanted to know what I did for a living and how much money I made. Your mother scolded you for asking."

When Mitch talked about his adopted son as a little boy, he seemed like his old self again. It warmed Brighton's heart to hear his father talk of the past. Mitch treated him like he was his own flesh and blood.

Taking a chance, the younger man asked straight out, "How much do you know about the adoption?"

"Oh, you were ten when I adopted you. Your mother insisted you keep her last name. I'm not sure why. It hurt at first but I would have done anything for her. She was gorgeous back then and very convincing."

"Did Mom ever tell you she almost put me up for adoption as a baby?"

"Where did you hear that?" Mitch asked with a raise of his brow.

"I found some old paperwork."

"Maybe you didn't read it right. Your mother would never have given you away. She told me the doctor's thought you may have suffered from a lack of oxygen when you were born. She said she knew they were wrong because you were miles ahead of the other children at day care. I could tell by your diction and vocabulary that you were intelligent beyond your years. Speaking of which, how is school going? You're a sophomore now, right?"

"No, Dad, I graduated a few years back. I'm a defense attorney now."

"Are you sure? It doesn't seem possible."

"Yes, Dad, I am sure."

"Oh, so how is that girl you're dating? What was her name? Rachel?"

"Rachel and I broke up junior year."

"Oh." Mitch rubbed his temple. "Why don't I remember that?"

Brighton patted his father's shoulder. "It's OK Dad. As long as you remember the important things, I think you're doing just fine."

"Like your mother's birthday?" he asked with a huge smile. "I'm getting her a new car. She's going to love it."

"That's great, Dad."

"Brighton, your father needs to get ready for bed," Madge said as she entered the sitting area.

Mitch leaned close to his son. "Hopefully she'll give me a sponge bath. She's hot. Do you know her name?"

Bri laughed and then looked over to the nurse and said, "OK Madge, I guess Jason and I will be going."

"Madge," Mitch said nodding as if hearing her name for the first time. "I'm all yours I guess."

Brighton called his grandmother the following morning hoping she would have time to talk. The call went directly to voice mail. Frustrated, he asked Jason to call the private investigator. The two men sat in the office at the brownstone with the phone on speaker as Jason dialed.

"Johnson," the detective answered.

"Nick, it's Jason Campbell and I've got you on speaker phone with Brighton here."

"What can I do for you?"

Brighton chimed in, "I need to find out if I was put up for adoption as a baby."

"What would make you think you were?" the man asked as he began to make notes.

Brighton read the letter to Johnson.

"It has my birth date at the top and she said I was only a few hours old. I am assuming the adoption either fell through or she changed her mind."

"Let me see what I can find out. Where was your mother living at the time?"

Brighton answered all of Johnson's questions and the investigator told Jason he would get back to them.

Three o'clock Monday afternoon, Brighton's home phone rang. Not too many people called on the land line anymore so he was tempted not to answer. Something told him to pick up the phone.

"Brighton, do you think you could pick me up at La Guardia?"

"When?" he replied to his grandmother.

"I just landed so as soon as you can."

"Why didn't you tell me you were coming?" he asked as he waved across the room at Jason. "Get the keys," he mouthed gesturing toward the door.

"I have to talk to you and I couldn't do it over the phone."

"We're on our way."

With the afternoon traffic, the drive to the airport took longer than expected. An odd feeling swept over Brighton and he was anxious to see Mrs. Clay. He wondered if his question about the adoption was the catalyst to his grandmother's last minute flight. She didn't like flying and he knew that.

With her hand on her upset stomach, Mrs. Clay was waiting patiently outside the terminal. A Mercedes pulled up and her grandson stepped out. She opened her arms as he approached.

"Oh darling, it is so good to see you." After a warm hug she looked him over. She shook her head with a smile. "Your mother would be proud of the man you have become."

"Even though I am a suspect in a series of murders?" he asked dryly.

"Oh dear, I know you didn't do it. You couldn't have. You don't have a bad bone in your body. Now, put my bag in the car and let's go grab dinner. I know it is a little early but I am famished."

"You're staying with me at the apartment, right?"

"If that is all right with you."

"Well, Jason has been staying in the guest room. I'll change the linens and you can make yourself at home there."

Jason had popped the trunk and Brighton dropped his grandmother's suitcase in.

"Where will Jason sleep?"

"Don't worry about me, Mrs. Clay," Jason said as he opened the door for her. "I can crash on the sofa. How does Italian sound for dinner?"

"Wonderful, Jason, thank you."

The conversation during dinner remained light. Brighton was tempted to ask questions about the letter yet he wanted to do so in private. It was more than difficult to hold his tongue. Jason kept Mrs. Clay occupied with discussions of the weather back home and such. When the waiter returned to take their dinner plates, he asked if anyone wanted coffee or dessert.

Mrs. Clay glanced at her grandson and replied, "I think we are all set."

Upon arriving at the brownstone, Jason told them he would go to the guest room to change the bed clothes and prepare the room for Mrs. Clay. Brighton was glad Jason had the compassion to let him have some privacy. Brighton looked at his grandmother. He could tell by her posture that she was deep in thought. He gave her a moment before he asked why she had come.

"The letter you found," she took a deep breath and continued, "Donna did not write it to you."

Brighton tilted his head like a puppy trying to understand.

"Your mother had twins. We tried to contact your father. If he had come back and taken responsibility, perhaps she could have kept you both. She knew we would have a hard time supporting her with one child but two? It would have been next to impossible. She agonized over the decision."

Brighton felt his heart sink. It was one thing to think he had been put up for adoption. The emotions that overwhelmed him were unexpected. Inside he always felt something was missing in his life. Now he knew why.

"It was difficult for her to choose. You were both beautiful babies. Brent was born first. He was the stronger one. We knew that right off. You were blue when you arrived and it took several minutes for the doctor's to get you to breathe. I think that was the reason she chose you. The pediatrician thought that you might have suffered from the lack of oxygen and Donna was afraid the adoptive parents would be... She knew she would take care of you no matter what happened.

"Luckily you turned out fine. We knew there could not have been brain damage when at two you were reading and," she chuckled, "you could talk your mother into doing anything. You were such a chatterbox. Your grandfather said you could charm the heat out of the sun."

"I remember him saying that when I was older," Brighton said with a nod. "Do you know what happened to my brother?"

"I am not sure if his parents kept the name Brent. The adoption was closed. Your mother wanted to be able to contact him but there are laws, and she never met the adoptive parents. She knew very little about them."

"Do you know if they lived nearby?"

"I have no idea."

"I need to know more. Do you have any of the records? She must have signed something from the agency. Or did she use an attorney? Anything you know would be extremely helpful."

"Why do you need to know? Maybe his parents never told him about you."

"Gran, for all my life I felt like there was something missing. Even when I was with Lydia, I felt incomplete. Now I know that there is someone out there with whom I have a bond. I need to find him."

"I, um, I brought an envelope with the agreement in it. Maybe you can call the attorney if he is still practicing." She sighed. "Please, Brighton. Think about this before you try and contact him. What if he has no idea that he was adopted? You might disrupt his life."

"What if he has been looking for me, Gran? I have to do this."

"The paperwork is in my suitcase." Mrs. Clay stood. "I'll give it to you tomorrow. I want you to think about this first. OK?"

He stood and hugged his grandmother. "I will. Now, let's give you a quick tour and let you get settled."

Chapter Seven

Monday morning, Brighton woke up just as the sun was peaking over the horizon. He went down to the kitchen and started a pot of coffee. Jason began to stir on the sofa as the aroma wafted through the air. He padded into the kitchen to find Brighton leaning against the counter.

"So, have you made a decision?"

"I have not changed my mind. I am going to find my brother."

"What if he is the one who..?"

Brighton put up a hand to stop his friend. "He's not. There is no way. I am not even going to think that."

Jason poured a mug of coffee and swallowed a large gulp.

"OK, let's think this through. There is someone out there killing people and trying to frame you. He knows a hell of a lot about you. Who else could get close enough to you to find out these things? And the clincher my friend, is that whoever is framing you took a picture of your family. Who the hell else would do that?"

"I refuse to believe my brother could do this."

"He may be your brother biologically but you know absolutely nothing about him, Bri. Don't let your emotions get in the way of the truth. Get the paperwork from your grandmother and we'll give it to the PI. He can find your brother and at least figure out if he could have been involved."

"I promise to keep an open mind, Jas."

"That's all I ask."

Thirty minutes later, Mrs. Clay came down fully dressed carrying a large manila envelope in her hand. She held it out to her grandson. "Do what you think is right."

He gave her a hug before taking the envelope. "Thanks, Gran. You know, whatever I find, it does not change the way I feel about Mom. She did everything for me and I know giving up my brother was difficult. I don't think I ever said thank you for supporting her and allowing her to keep me."

"Oh darling, I wish we could have kept you both."

They hugged once more. "I love you Grandma."

"I love you too."

"How long are you staying?"

"As long as you want me, I'll stay. I'd like to see your father while I'm here if that's all right with you."

"I am sure he would be happy to see you."

"Do you think he'll remember me?"

"He can remember things from a long time ago. It's the more recent stuff that he forgets."

Jason cleared his throat. "I'm going to go home for a while. Do you think the two of you can manage to stay out of trouble?"

"Are you sure you should leave me alone with a beautiful young lady?" Brighton said with a huge grin.

Mrs. Clay laughed. "You always were a charmer. We'll be fine, Jason. I bet you could use a break. And while I'm here, you can sleep in your own home. I can watch my grandson."

"I think it would be better if Jason spends the nights here. I need an alibi in case... Well, I'm not sure the police would take my grandmother's word that I have been behaving."

"He's right, Mrs. Clay. It's better that I'm here at night." Jason turned his attention to his client. "I'll be back soon. If you want, you can take her to see your father. Then we'll meet back here. If you decide to look into that," he said pointing to the envelope, "we can drop it off later today."

Brighton tossed the information to Jason. "You take it. I don't want to look at it. Let Johnson find him."

Jason nodded and left the kitchen.

"Dad, I brought someone to visit."

Mitchell stood and opened his arms. "Mom, it's so good to see you."

Brighton's heart warmed at his father's words. Mitch always referred to Mrs. Clay as Mom.

"Hello Mitch, you look good. How is life treating you?"

"I can't complain. I wish my son would come see me more. He's so busy chasing co-eds," Mitch chuckled. "Have a seat. I'll have Donna get us something to drink."

Madge smiled and held her hand out to Mrs. Clay.

"Madge, this is my grandmother."

"Yes, I remember. How are you Mrs. Clay? You look fabulous."

"Oh thanks Madge."

Mitch looked at Brighton for a moment then back to his mother-in-law.

"Um, since when do you call your daughter Madge?"

Mrs. Clay smiled softly to her son-in-law. "It's a game we play." She patted his hand. "I can't get over how good you look. My daughter must be taking good care of you."

"I'd like to tell you how she takes care of me but that might be a little TMI as the kids would say."

They all laughed although Brighton felt his cheeks flush. His father was much more direct since the onset of his dementia. He was not ashamed of or embarrassed by anything. Still, his old world values would not let him discuss such details with his mother-in-law.

"How come you didn't bring Carl with you?"

"He had a golf game with some retired pro. Carl and his golf, you couldn't drag him away from his clubs."

"You tell Carl he shouldn't let his beautiful wife drive here by herself. Some old coot here might snatch you away."

"Oh, Mitch, please. I bet if you weren't my daughter's husband you would be the one stealing me from Carl."

"You bet cha!"

Brighton and his grandmother stayed at the home for nearly two hours. They talked about old times and when Mitch was courting Donna. Brighton heard all new stories. Later, Mrs. Clay explained that some of the details were a little mixed up.

"You know," she said as they pulled out of the driveway, "your father looks amazingly well. Anyone who didn't know the family might think he was fine. He looks so happy."

"He is most of the time. Then he gets this look on his face like he knows he is missing something but can't quite figure out what it is. A few months back he went through a bad spell. He had gotten a bit... I'm not sure how to say it. Angry, maybe? Easily agitated? Anyway, they adjusted his medication and things evened out. Madge said that happens sometimes with dementia patients."

"At the moment, he looks terrific. It's a blessing he thinks Madge is Donna. He doesn't have to remember the grief."

He reached over and took his grandmother's hand. "I miss her too, Gran, but we still have each other."

She smiled and held his hand to her cheek. "I wish you lived closer."

"Once all this stuff blows over, I'll come see you more often."

"I've heard that before," she said trying hard not to be sarcastic. "I mean, you have a life Bri. As long as you are safe and happy, I can't complain."

"I am happy. Did I tell you I was seeing someone again?"

"You are?" Mrs. Clay beamed. "You must let me meet her while I am here."

"Um, you can't. Jason has her under protection. We were afraid whoever is framing me might go after her. I don't even know where she is. We talk on the phone, but they change her number so the calls can't be traced."

"Your life has become quite complicated. It will get better; I promise. This will all go away and you will have your happily ever after."

"I hope you're right."

Instead of driving back to the brownstone, he took his grandmother through the city. He pointed out a few hotspots then took her shopping on Fifth Avenue. They looked in a number of store windows and Mrs. Clay reminded her grandson that she did not see the need to wear lavish clothes. She dressed impeccably but simply.

"Your grandfather and I do go out once in a while but it is usually to the early bird specials," she laughed. "He's not cheap; he likes to come home before it gets dark."

"C'mon; let's go in here," Brighton said gently nudged her into Tiffany's.

A saleswoman greeted them saying if they had any questions to let her know.

"Thank you, Melinda. I think we'd like to browse a bit."

With a nod and a wink, she retreated although she kept her eyes on Brighton.

Mrs. Clay and her grandson looked into several of the glass cases. She reminded him she did not like expensive things. Mrs. Clay stopped at the display of Jean Schlumberger designs. Her eyes lit up. Brighton gestured to Melinda.

"Is there something you would like to see closer, Miss?"

Mrs. Clay looked at Brighton.

"Go ahead. It costs nothing to look."

"I'd like to see the rose gold earrings and pendant, please."

The saleswomen gingerly retrieved the jewelry from the display and held it out for her customers to get a better view. She tilted it side to side ever so slightly to emphasize the way the light twinkled off the round diamonds offset in a rose gold X formation.

"This is a magnificent set. You have superb taste."

"We'll take them."

"Oh, Bri, I couldn't. You should be buying these for your girlfriend, not your grandmother."

"OK, fine. The pendant is yours. I'll bring Cecelia back at another time to get her the earrings. They are exquisite."

"Marvelous," the saleswoman beamed. "I'll wrap that up for you."

While Jason had some time alone, he called Dom.

"There's been a development of sorts." Jason explained the recent discovery. "I have a feeling Cecelia might have been visited by Brighton's brother. Don't tell her, not yet. It will only upset her. I would however, keep your eyes and ears open and move if you have to. Don't let her use the same cell phone for more than a few calls. I don't know how he found her but he did."

"Sal and I are taking turns sleeping. One of us is awake at all times. She won't get any further visitors; you can trust me on that."

"Good, keep it that way. I don't want her being the next victim."

"Understood."

"So, how was your day, Mrs. Clay?"

"It was wonderful, Jason. How kind of you to ask. My favorite grandson bought me this lovely pendant."

"Gran, I'm your only...." Brighton stopped himself.

"It is delicately beautiful as are you, Mrs. Clay."

"I'm not sure which one of you is better at bullshitting," she laughed.

Brighton's eyes widened having never heard his grandmother use such language. She grinned and patted his shoulder.

"Now, why don't I go to the kitchen and see if I can whip up something for you boys."

"You don't have to do that Gran."

"Oh but I want to. There is nothing like a good home cooked meal to make all the bad stuff easier to deal with."

The following morning, Jason received a text from Dom.

We're moving again. Front desk had a package for Ce. Earrings from Tiffany's

"Damn it," Jason said aloud.

Brighton looked over his coffee at Jason. "What is it?"

"Nothing, it was just one of those stupid texts you get from spammers."

Wednesday afternoon, Mrs. Clay was packing her suitcase. Although she had wanted to spend the week with her grandson, he thought it would not be wise. They had discussed it Tuesday evening at dinner.

"Bri, I feel safe with you and Jason around. I highly doubt someone is going to come after an old lady like me."

"First of all, you are not old, Gran. And second, I don't know how this guy thinks. I haven't told you everything because I don't want you to worry, but he has done things and been places. He is out to get me no matter who gets in his way. I'd rather I knew you were home with Gramps."

She reluctantly agreed.

Brighton stepped into the guest room Wednesday and asked his grandmother if she needed any help.

"I'm fine Brighton. I have to tell you, the pendant was quite enough. You didn't have to sneak out and by me a Tiffany's scarf as well."

"What? I didn't..."

Mrs. Clay touched the butterfly scarf that she had placed around her neck. "It is absolutely beautiful."

"Take it off," he said gruffly. "I didn't buy that for you."

"But it was in the dresser between my clothes. I thought you had hidden it there."

"Jason!" Brighton hollered.

His friend came running up the stairs two at a time.

"What is it?"

"Did you buy that?" he asked pointing to the scarf that Mrs. Clay had dropped on the bed.

"Why the hell would I..? Oh shit. He was here?"

Mrs. Clay felt ill and Brighton caught her before her knees crumbled beneath her.

"Call the cops. I want them here. I want them to print the whole damn place and look for listening devices and cameras," Brighton demanded.

Jason was already on his cell calling the PI.

"I'll have Johnson come over too."

Luckily, one of the policemen was a friend of Jason's. While the other officers swept the brownstone, Jason's friend escorted

Mrs. Clay to the airport with Brighton. Jason stayed behind to talk to the PI and supervise the investigation.

"I don't understand how someone could have sneaked in and put that with my clothes. He must have known I was staying with you. Is he stalking you?"

"Yes, Gran, I believe he is. This guy is getting into my home and hurting the women I come in contact with. Now you know why I need you to go home."

Mrs. Clay's hands were trembling. "I'm worried about you, Bri. Why can't you stay with your grandfather and me until they catch this madman?"

"Because they think I am the madman."

"That is utterly ridiculous."

"Tell that to the DA. I think he wants me to fry."

"Don't say things like that, Brighton," Mrs. Clay scolded.

Once at the airport, Brighton and the officer waited until Mrs. Clay passed through security. On the way home, Brighton broke down in the car. He felt his world crumbling. How could a person break into his place without being noticed? Could it be someone he knew, someone he trusted?

The police were still searching the apartment when Brighton returned. He looked at everyone suspiciously. He watched their final steps. He eyed Johnson. He even considered that his best friend might be a possible suspect. He ran his hand through his hair then shook his head.

"What's going on, Bri?"

"Are they done upstairs?"

"Yeah, I think so."

"I'm going to go lie down."

"I'll make sure everything gets cleaned up."

Brighton retired to his room. He flopped down on the bed and put one arm over his eyes. In his mind, no one could be trusted. Well, possibly there was one person in his life he could call. He grabbed his cell and dialed.

"Bri, how are you?"

"You sound nervous."

"We're on the road again."

"What happened?"

"Someone left me a pair of earrings from Tiffany's. Didn't Jason tell you?"

As far as Brighton was concerned, this was one more reason to suspect Jason. "Oh, oh yeah, he did. Sorry, I forgot. There's a lot going on in my head." Brighton lied about knowing to protect Ce. "I miss you so much."

"I miss you too"

"Call me in ten minutes."

Cecelia knew why. Being on the phone too long was not a good idea. She waited then dialed.

"Dom said you had a visitor."

"Yes, my grandmother came to see me. It seems my mother was keeping a big secret."

"Do you think it could be your brother who is doing this?"

Brighton swallowed hard. "I don't know what to think anymore. I am breaking my head trying to figure out who would want to frame me so badly that they would want to frighten my grandmother." He paused for a moment then added, "Please take every precaution. I'm really worried about you."

"I'm worried about you too, my love. I'll call you in ten minutes."

During the next few minutes, Brighton began to wonder if Cecelia was involved. He got up and started to pace.

"No," he said out loud. "There is no way she has anything to do with this. Jesus, I think I am going insane."

When his cell rang once more, he jumped.

"Hey so um, when this is over, you and I are going to go to some deserted island and leave the world behind. How does that sound?"

"Like a dream come true. I can't wait to be in your arms again."

"I really do love you, Ce. Remember that."

Cecelia lowered her voice. "Brighton, why are you talking like that? You know I love you too."

"I know you do. I am just lost and confused and I swear I am about to lose my mind."

"I'm in the car with Dom and Sal." She lowered her voice further. "I'll call you later when I get a minute alone. There is something I need to tell you."

"All right, I'll talk to you then."

Nearly an hour later, there was a soft knock on the bedroom door. When Brighton responded, Jason stepped into the room.

"They found listening devices and cameras. We figure they were put in while you and I were at the house on Long Island because they had done a sweep when they executed the search warrant."

"Jesus."

"Hopefully, this guy will stay away from your grandparents. If it is your brother, they're his family too."

Brighton sat up. "If it is my brother," he repeated as with a roll of his eyes.

"Did you have another suspect in mind?"

"I'd rather keep that to myself."

"You think I had something to do with this?" Jason asked with a mixture of anger and hurt. "We have been friends for years. You introduced me to Molly, for God's sake."

"Let's just say I am keeping all options open like you suggested."

This time it was Jason who paced the floor. "You have got to be kidding me, Bri. I would never..."

"Jas, the scarf was left while my grandmother was resting on the sofa and I was in the office. And you could have placed the equipment while I was sleeping any day since I have been home."

"OK, that is true but still, Bri, I swear to you..." Jason stopped dead in front of his friend. "...on the life of my unborn child, I have nothing to do with this."

"I believe you as much as you believe I didn't kill those women," Brighton said bluntly.

"Fair enough. If you don't trust me then perhaps you should find someone else to babysit you so no other bodies pop up." Jason turned on his heel and headed for the door. Before he exited the room, he glanced back at the man sitting on the bed. "I'm not sure I recognize you anymore, Brighton. The old you would never have suspected me."

"You're right, Jas. I'm sorry. This whole thing has got me running circles in my head. I have my own list of suspects. Maybe Lydia isn't dead. Or maybe her family has something to do with this. It could be my brother. It could be you or Ce. Fuck, maybe all of you are involved and this is some sort of gaslight deal. You're all trying your damnedest to drive me to the brink of insanity."

Jason returned to his friend's side and placed a hand on his shoulder.

"I am losing it, Jas. Perhaps I shouldn't tell you that but besides you and Ce, I can't trust anyone." Tears fell and he swiped them away with the back of his hand. "And there is still the possibility that the person doing this is someone we haven't even thought of yet. All I know for sure is that we have to end this and soon."

"We will figure this out, my friend. I think right now you need a diversion. Let's go grab something to eat and we can forget about his for a while."

"I don't want to go out," Brighton sighed. "I want some time alone."

"I'll be downstairs if you need me."

Brighton spent nearly two hours alone in his room. He wrote a list of potential suspects and motives. By the time he finished, his head was ready to explode. He went to the bathroom and found a bottle of pain reliever. He downed two pills with a glass of water. He heard his cell ring and dashed to answer it.

"Hi Bri."

"Hey beautiful. How was your day?"

"Are you alone?"

"Yes, I'm in my room. Jason is downstairs."

She sighed. "There are a few things I need to tell you. I don't think Jason has told you everything."

He took a seat on his bed. His heart rate increased along with his suspicions about his best friend.

"I don't know if he thinks he is protecting you."

"I have known Jason since college. I never thought he was the type to keep secrets. Maybe there is a side of him that I don't know that well."

"He didn't say anything about the earrings, did he?"

"No, he did not. I'm sorry I lied earlier. I was afraid it would scare you."

"Receiving a gift is nothing compared to what else has happened."

Brighton cleared his throat. "Did you know that the earrings you received were part of a set? I bought the pendant for my grandmother and I had told the saleswoman I would come back for the earrings to give to my girlfriend."

"How can he get so close to you without you knowing?"

"It gets worse. When she was packing, my grandmother found a Tiffany's scarf in the clothes she had put in the bureau. He was here and in the guest room."

"She must have been scared out of her mind. Is she all right?"

"I sent her back home. I called the cops and they found surveillance equipment. It hadn't been there last time the police were here."

"There's something else you need to know. Do you remember that Saturday when you called me a few times and I didn't pick up?"

"Yeah, you spent the day shopping."

"Actually, we only picked up a few things. We spent a good portion of the day on the road. I, um, I thought I had a dream that you came to see me. It was so real. The more I thought about it... I thought it was you Bri. I'm sorry."

"Ce, you can't control your dreams."

"Well, um, it turned out it wasn't exactly a dream. It took me a bit to realize but someone came to my room. It was dark. He sounded just like you. I should have known. You always wear boxers."

"Wait, what? You..?"

"I'm so sorry. He was so much like you, his hands, his lips, his..."

"Are you telling me you had sex with some stranger?"

"I told you, Brighton, I thought it was you!" she whispered angrily.

"Brent."

"Your brother?"

"Yes. More and more I am thinking he is the one who is trying to frame me. I don't know his motive but it makes perfect sense, Ce. Especially now."

"I'm sorry."

"Ce, I think you should be here with me. If you were with me twenty four seven, I wouldn't have to worry about you. If he found you not just once but twice, there is a high likelihood that he will locate you again. Wouldn't it be better if you were by my side?"

"Dom and Sal would tell Jason I was coming and he would tell them to keep me here."

"Then we need to make a plan. Hang up. I'll get a prepaid cell tomorrow and call you. I love you, Ce."

"I love you too."

The following day, Brighton and Jason went to get groceries. While at the market, Brighton sneaked away from Jason and purchased a prepaid cell phone with cash. He tucked the cell into the inside pocket of his jacket.

When they returned home, Brighton called Ce from his house phone.

"Have Dom take you to buy another cell. Do *not* give anyone the number. Call me on my old cell and hang up. I'll call you from the prepaid phone I bought today."

He hung up.

Cecelia called his cell later that evening and hung up as instructed. He immediately returned the call.

"Hey beautiful."

"So what's the plan?"

"We're going to have to find a way to ditch your guards. If I walk in there, it won't be good. And I have to get rid of Jason too."

"Do you think he is involved?"

Brighton thought for a moment. "I hope not. I am not excluding anyone until I know with absolute certainty."

"So what happens when we're together? Do we run off somewhere?"

"I wish we could, Ce. But this trouble will follow me. I have to stand my ground. At least if you're by my side I can be sure you are fine. I won't let you out of my sight. I'll handcuff us together if I have to."

"So I guess we'll be showering at the same time," she purred.

"If that's what it takes to keep you safe, I'll suffer through it," he teased back. "Damn, I miss you so much."

"We'll be together soon."

"In the meantime, keep your eyes and ears open. I'll let you know when I am coming to get you. I promise I won't just sneak in your window."

"Good, if someone does sneak in here again, I *will* cut their dick off."

"Then I'll definitely warn you ahead of time. I'd like my manhood to stay attached."

"Me too," she admitted.

Over the next few days, Brighton mapped out a plan. He did not speak a word to anyone about retrieving Cecelia. He was afraid if he told anyone, things would turn out badly. Brighton had told Ce she would not have much notice and to be prepared. He never asked where she was. She began to wonder how he would find her. She considered telling Dom or Sal but surely they would tell Jason. She knew whoever was framing Brighton had to be close.

As a precaution, Dom decided to uproot his client again. This time, the three of them moved into a suite in a hotel just outside the city. The rooms were on the second floor. There were sliding glass doors leading out to a balcony in the main living area and the in larger bedroom.

"Cecelia, I think you should take the smaller room. There is only one door and a small window. You'll be safer."

Ce frowned. "I am feeling more and more like a prisoner, Dominic. I doubt this guy is going to sneak in here again. He can't be that bold."

"I'm not taking any chances."

She huffed and disappeared into the tiny bedroom. She waited until Dom was settled and Sal had left to pick up dinner before calling Brighton.

"We've moved again. Dominic takes his job very seriously."

"I promise, Ce. I will find you. I don't want you worrying. It's going to be soon, my love."

"I'm not unpacking. If he asks, I'll tell Dom I want to be prepared in case we have to move on short notice again."

"I can't wait to put my arms around you," he sighed.

"I love you, Bri."

"I love you too, beautiful. Sleep well."

"I'll be dreaming of you."

Three days later, Ce was half asleep when her cell notified her of a text.

Outside R U Alone

Dom asleep Sal awake Tiny window How do I no its U

Trust me Can U climb out Short drop

Will U catch me

Absolutely

Will drop my bag first

Leave it

A second later, Cecelia sent a text saying the window was not the kind that opened.

Give me a sec

He waited somewhat impatiently and afraid to reply in case she had gone into the living area. He heard the click of a latch. Looking up, he saw Cecelia step back from the French doors then turn. He moved out of the shadows. She breathed a sigh of relief knowing she had made it past Sal without him noticing.

"Some bodyguard," she whispered.

She saw him waiting for her. Carefully, she stepped over the railing. Shaking her head and taking a deep breath, she pushed off the balcony. He caught her, lowered her feet to the ground then covered her lips with his.

Jason fumbled for his cell. His eyes blinked at the clock. Three thirty it flashed. He hit the accept button.

"She's gone."

"Who the fuck is this?"

"Dominic, asshole!"

Jason jumped out of bed and ran down the hall flicking the light switch as he passed it. "Shit, Cecelia?"

"Yeah, she's gone and she took nothing with her. Well, her purse is missing but everything else is still here."

As he flung the door to the master bedroom open he yelled, "How the fuck did she leave? Did someone take her? Bri, wake... Shit, he's go..." Just then, Jason saw the light glowing from beneath the bathroom door. He barged in.

"Jesus, Jas, what the..?" Brighton spouted as he wrapped a towel around his waist.

"He took Cecelia."

Brighton seized the cell from Jason.

"You were supposed to protect her. What do you mean he took her? How the hell did that happen?"

"I'm sorry, Mr. Clay. Sal noticed the door to her bedroom was ajar. He looked in and she was gone."

"Are you sure someone took her? Maybe she just got sick of you two moving her around so much. Jesus. Did you call her cell?"

"I never took her latest number. I was with her twenty-four-seven. Never thought I needed it."

Brighton tossed Jason's phone at him and went to retrieve his own. He dialed a number and put the cell to his ear. A second later, Jason put his hand on his friend's arm.

"The cell phone is still in her room."

Brighton felt his knees buckle. He dropped the cell as he flopped on the bed.

"Dom, call the police. I want them to scour every inch of that hotel and talk to every God damned employee there."

"Understood." Dom disconnected the call.

"You told me they'd protect her, Jason. Now she's gone." Tears streamed down his cheeks.

Jason sat next to his friend on the bed. "I know but this guy is good. He has eluded the police; he gets into places without being seen; he knows everything you do and everywhere you go. He's like a damn ghost."

"Or a best friend," Brighton muttered.

"Jesus, Bri, we're not on that again, are we?"

"No, no, I trust you." He stood and walked the length of the room. He ran a hand through his still damp hair. "So what do we do now? I cannot just sit here and do nothing especially now that he has Ce."

"I'm going to call Detective Shaw then Johnson. I swear to you, Bri, I won't sleep until we find her."

Four hours later, Brighton and Jason were at the precinct. Detectives Lawson and Shaw were questioning them in the disappearance of Cecelia Demure.

"My client was home all evening. There is no way he was involved in Cecelia's abduction."

"Are you sure he didn't sneak out while you were sleeping?"

"I am absolutely positive. He turned in early. I was down in the living room until nearly midnight. When I went upstairs he was sleeping. I saw him in the bed."

"You checked in on me?" Brighton asked with surprise cracking his voice.

"I check every night." Jason turned his attention to the detectives. "I have been with Mr. Clay every damn day since this whole mess began. There was only one time I left him, and that was when his grandmother was in town. He has not been alone once in days."

The two policemen looked at each other.

Shaw addressed Jason. "How do we know the two of you aren't in this together? Maybe the two of you get off watching each other rape and kill women."

Brighton's hands tightened in his lap. Blood rose to his face. He had to keep his composure. Jason's fists were clenched and ready to beat some sense into the two detectives.

He sat in front of the television itching to get out and feed his desire. He flipped through the stations to see if he could find something to take his mind off his need. Then he saw a news story. Anger and frustration built inside him. Joined with the aching arousal in his loins, his emotions drove him out of his living room.

He pulled on nondescript clothing and gathered his tools. After packing the trunk, he said good-bye.

"Can't I go with you?"

"Not this time you can't. They're getting too close."

"I hate being left behind."

"You'll manage."

After he was gone, his partner in crime watched his car speed off.

"I am not staying here like a sitting duck."

The police released Brighton and Jason. They had nothing connecting the two men to the disappearance of yet another woman. Until they had something concrete to go on, the police had no choice.

Jason and Brighton rode to the brownstone in silence. Not a word was exchanged until they were inside.

"I know what you're thinking, Jas. You are wondering if I had enough time to get to Cecelia. Perhaps I did have the time but I did not kidnap her."

"This completely sucks because that means he has her."

"How do we know she was actually taken? There were no signs of struggle. The only thing she took was her purse. She even left the cell she just bought. What if she felt she would be better off alone?"

"Or what if she's trying to find her way back here?"

"Exactly. Like I said, she probably got tired of being with those two goons."

"What if Brent has her?"

Brighton shook his head. "I can't think that way. It... It just hurts too much. I can't lose her."

"Then let's get serious and do something. I'm calling Johnson to see if he found anything."

Before Jason could retrieve his cell the home phone rang. Brighton picked it up.

"I got something. I think I found your brother or at least where he is staying."

"Where?"

"I called the police. They're on their way to his apartment right now. I'm not telling you where it is. You should stay put until you hear from either the police or me."

Brighton looked at Jason. "Johnson thinks he found where Brent's been living."

"I knew I was paying him good money for a reason. Where?"

"He's not giving it up. He sent the police."

Johnson said, "I'm waiting outside the building. Will call you when we find something?" He disconnected the call.

Forty minutes passed. The waiting was taking a toll on their friendship. Adrenalin and anxiety were a powerful mix and before long, each began questioning the other's actions. Jason wondered why Brighton wasn't more torn up about the disappearance of Cecelia. He thought more and more that his friend could have been involved. Brighton had similar thoughts. What if Jason had been divulging information to Brent? Why would Jason turn on him like that?

"I'm going to call Molly. I need someone to talk to."

Chapter Eight

After Jason left the room, Brighton picked up his cell and sent a text.

The reply text said, *What's going on?*

PI thinks he found Brent. Waiting for more info R U OK?

I'm fine Miss U

Miss U too B safe

When the land line rang again, Brighton nearly jumped out of his skin.

"Yeah."

"No one is here but we definitely found where he's been staying. The cops found some empty bleach bottles, woman's lingerie, and some other evidence. There were more digits in the freezer."

Brighton nearly fell into the chair. This was good and bad news.

"Did they find any evidence that he took Cecelia?"

"They are still combing through the place. One of the officers talked to me but would only give me limited information. I think they are afraid I'll tell you too much. Where is Jason?"

"He went upstairs to call his wife."

"Don't leave the apartment. And stick together."

"Why?"

"Call it a hunch. From what I've been able to gather, he hasn't been gone long. I think he's looking for another victim. You need to have a solid alibi. I'm going to head over to your place."

"We'll be here."

Brighton sent a text.

Brent not at apt

There was no reply, and Brighton began to worry.

Brighton texted to a different cell.

If I confide in U Swear not to tell Jason?

I think I no what UR going to say Trust me I'll do anything I can to help

A moment later, Jason came down the stairs. Brighton filled him in on the details.

"So we still don't know where Ce is?"

"The police have no idea. According to Johnson, they found nothing of hers at the apartment."

"He could have her hidden somewhere."

"Don't even think that, Jas." Brighton turned away from his friend. Hiding something from Jason was more difficult than he anticipated. "I have to remain optimistic otherwise I'll go insane."

"I understand, buddy. We'll find Ce and get this guy."

When the private investigator arrived at the brownstone, he was bombarded with questions. Jason knew Johnson was holding back. He assumed the police had only revealed partial information. Still, he surmised Johnson knew more than he was letting on.

Brighton's cell buzzed. He peaked at the text and the edge of his lip curled.

"Who is it?"

"My grandmother is checking up on me," Brighton lied. "So what do we do now? Brent is on the run and Cecelia is out there somewhere with no protection."

"Honestly, I think we should wait it out until the police locate Brent. Brighton, I know you are getting frustrated sitting here doing nothing but it's better than you going off half-cocked and maybe ending up dead."

"If anything happens to Ce, I'd rather be dead."

"Don't talk like that," Jason admonished. "No one else is going to die." He was watching his friend closely. He wondered why Brighton was intently deleting items from his cell.

There were no news reports that evening about the discovery made by the private detective. Johnson told his clients he felt the police wanted to keep it quiet. The following morning however, there was a story of another body found. The report did not reveal the identity of the victim. Jason called the precinct.

A few minutes into the call, Jason covered the mouthpiece and said to Brighton, "It wasn't Cecelia."

Brighton breathed a sigh of relief and ran his hand through his hair. He continued to fidget as he listened to Jason talk.

"So it had to be him then. Everything was the same including the missing finger?"

A moment passed and Brighton saw Jason nod. The murder was definitely the work of Brent, if he in fact was the actual killer. Brighton's mind was reeling. How could his brother turn into such a monster? Was he working alone or in conjunction with someone? Could Jason be feeding Brent information, planting things, and assisting Brent in his plot to frame Brighton?

Jason disconnected the call and looked at his friend.

"This one was worse than all the others. I think this guy is pissed off."

"You mean more than before?"

"I'm going to be honest, Bri. I think Cecelia took off or someone helped her get away from Dom and Sal. I think she is hiding somewhere and the killer is ticked because he had every intention of making Ce his next victim."

"And on what exactly are you basing this theory."

"For one, you are not as broken up about Ce's disappearance as I thought you would be. The night Dominic called you put on a good show for me. You wanted me to think you had no idea she was missing. But you did, didn't you?"

Brighton avoided Jason's eyes. "I have no idea what you are talking about."

"See, you can't even look at me and say that."

"I..." Brighton hesitated. Jason was going to find out eventually so Brighton decided there was no time like the present to reveal his secret. "I know where she is but I am not telling you or anyone else. He was getting too close despite everything your goons were doing. I sneaked out that night leaving a pile of pillows under the covers. I knew you had been checking up on me. You don't trust me anymore and that's killing me. We have been friends too long not trust each other. I got Cecelia and sent her somewhere safe. I'm not saying where in case that bastard somehow got back in here and planted more listening devices."

"So when you came out of the shower you had just gotten back?"

He nodded.

"Jesus, what if another woman had gotten killed that night? You took a huge risk, my friend," Jason said punching his friend's shoulder.

He rubbed the spot on his arm. "It was worth it to make sure Cecelia was safe. I lied to her and told her I was bringing her here to keep her close. I knew that was not a good idea. So I sent her away. I purchased a prepaid cell which has not left me since the day I bought it so there is no way anyone knows the number. Our calls and messages can't be traced. And I delete all history so if something does happen, no one will find out where she is."

"Well thank God Cecelia is safe. I hope you didn't do something stupid and send her to your house on the island or worse... to your grandparents' house."

"I would not put them in that kind of danger. Especially now," Brighton added. "I think Cecelia's disappearance made him run out and kill that other woman. He is probably pissed that he wasn't the one to get to Ce."

"This guy is one sick bastard. My cop friend said this one was worse than the others. This one suffered."

"Which is all the more reason I am glad Ce is out of reach and why we need to catch this guy whether it is my brother or not."

"You should not have followed me."

"I hate sitting here alone. Besides, I came up with this plan; I should get some of the fun."

He pulled her into his arms. "You just like hearing them scream."

"I'll admit, it does kind of turn me on," she said with a raise of her brow. "I do have a question."

"Yes, my love," he said before biting her soft pink flesh.

"When you fuck them, does it feel as good as when you fuck me?"

"Nothing feels as good as when I fuck you, my dear."

"Good answer. Now back to the plan. I think we need to bump things up a bit. Just because his new girlfriend is MIA, doesn't mean we can't hit him where it hurts the most."

She let out a tiny whimper as he continued to gnaw on her neck.

"Part of me was thinking we should go after Molly but she's way too sweet not to mention in fucking Florida. We could go after Jason," she mused. "Or maybe..."

He looked up at her with curiosity.

"Maybe we could drive him to the edge if Lydia showed up."

"How the hell are you going to do that? What are you going to do? Show up at his house and say, 'Here's Lydia'," he said in his best Jack Nicholson impression.

"Not quite, my darling. He'll see her from a distance, chase after her, than she will disappear. If it happens enough, he'll think he's going insane."

With a hard smack to her bare backside he asked, "You love to torture poor Brighton, don't you?"

"Hell, yes."

Chapter Nine

A few days later, Jason was standing at the deli counter in the market. Brighton had gone to produce to pick up a few items. He was selecting a few ripe tomatoes when a scent captured his attention. He glanced over his shoulder and watched a woman walking away; her stature and gait was similar to Lydia's. He shook his head telling himself there was no way it could be her. The woman's hair was corn silk blonde, not brunette as Lydia's was. Brighton picked up a few more fresh vegetables then caught up with his friend. He said nothing to Jason about the woman he saw.

"They had some really nice eggplant."

Jason lifted a brow at Brighton. "And you expect me to eat that?"

"Hey, I make a damn good eggplant parm."

"Put some veal in it and maybe I'll give it a try."

"I'll go see if they have any cutlets. I can layer it between the slices."

As Brighton walked away, Jason called after him. "Just because I'm staying at your place doesn't mean I have to eat what you cook."

Brighton simply waved over his shoulder at Jason.

Several minutes later, the two men were in line waiting to have their purchases tallied up so they could head home and have dinner. Brighton's nose was once again tickled by the familiar scent and a melancholy smile swept over his features.

"What is it?"

"There's a woman here that is wearing the same perfume Lyd used to wear. I bought it for her."

"You're hallucinating, my friend."

Brighton's eyes followed the sweetened air, and he saw the woman once more. As she rushed by, she tucked a lock of hair behind her ear. Her profile was so familiar it made Brighton's heart flutter.

"There she is," he whispered with a tilt of his head.

Jason's head turned but the woman vanished through the door.

"Yup, hallucinating."

"Shut up."

A few days later, Brighton was standing with his coffee cup looking out the front window. He had woken early hearing a truck pull up across the street. He was watching as furniture was moved into the place diagonally across the way. What caught his attention were not the items from the truck but the woman who seemed to be telling the movers what to do.

"What cha watching?"

"She's moving in."

"Who?"

"The woman who looks like Lyd."

"I thought you got over this when you met Cecelia. Every woman looks like Lydia to you."

"But this one could be her twin. And she wears the same scent. Her gestures, the way she incessantly tucks her hair behind her ear, it's all just like Lyd."

"Looks like she broke her hand," Jason said noticing the cast covering the woman's wrist and hand.

"Yeah, I wonder how that happened."

"Maybe she was packing and fell or something."

"Mm."

Jason took a sip of his own coffee. "Is she alone?"

"Appears to be. Either that or whoever she lives with is working. Maybe she took the day off to supervise and he couldn't."

Jason nudged his friend. "Why don't you go say 'Hi' and pull her pigtails?"

"Fuck you."

"You look like a love sick puppy."

Brighton walked away from the window.

"Even if that was her, you're with Ce now, remember?"

"Yeah, I remember Jason. And I love Ce. You're probably right; I'm hallucinating.

A few days later, Brighton talked his friend into a trip to the gym. He thought it would be a way to clear their minds so they could take a fresh look at the information they had about Brent. Before leaving home, Jason called the PI and made arrangements to meet for lunch.

Brighton ran on the treadmill for forty minutes. He hit the weight room and then sat in the sauna until the strain from working out began to fade. As he stepped out of the heat, he saw her in the hot tub. She had her cast covered arm out on the side wrapped in a towel. She glanced at him, blushed, then downcast her eyes.

Brighton squatted down near her. "I haven't seen you here before. You just moved in across the street from my place."

"Oh," she said without looking up.

He extended his hand and introduced himself.

She daintily put her right hand in his. "Melissa." She looked up for a second or two.

"It is nice to meet you, Melissa. Are you new to the city?"

"Yes, my fiancé and I moved here from Coopersburg, Pennsylvania."

"I've never heard of Coopersburg."

"It's near Allentown. Not many people have heard of it. The population is less than three thousand." Her eyes continued to avoid his.

"Well, if you need any help adjusting to city life, just let me know. I'd be glad to help you and your fiancé get acquainted with New York. I'm sure it is quite different from Coopersburg."

"Thank you. I'll discuss it with him."

"I promise; I'm not trying to pick you up. I'm very much in love with my lady friend."

She nodded slightly.

"I'll see you around then?"

"I suppose you will."

Brighton stood. "Have a good afternoon, Melissa."

Her eyes scanned slowly up his body as she replied, "You as well."

Brighton took two steps back before turning and heading to the men's locker room. Jason was just coming out of the shower.

"Had enough?"

"She's in the hot tub."

Jason shook his head. "Don't tell me you talked to her."

"I said hello and asked where she was from."

"And?" he asked with a raise of his brow.

"Her name is Melissa. She and her fiancé are from some small town in PA."

"See, it's not Lydia. Are you happy now?"

"This is going to sound incredibly odd."

Jason laughed maniacally.

"Do you think Lydia could have had a twin?"

"If she did, don't you think you would have known?"

"I didn't."

"Not every family has some long lost sibling, Bri. There is no way Lydia had a twin."

"Hm yeah, I guess you're right. I'm going to hit the shower, and then we can catch up with Johnson."

Over lunch, Brighton asked the private investigator if he had checked into Lydia's disappearance. Johnson explained that someone had seen Lydia leave her apartment with a young man.

"To my knowledge, the police never found any witnesses," Brighton said.

"I tend to get people to talk. The cops ask questions. I interrogate. My source said she was threatened bodily harm if she talked to the police."

"Who saw Lydia leave?"

"I can't tell you."

"Seriously?" Brighton fumed. "We are paying you to find this stuff out and you can't tell me?"

"Look, she was very adamant about not telling you or anyone else. She practically begged me. I could tell she was scared."

Brighton glanced at Jason then back to Johnson. "Did she say Lydia was under duress?"

The detective nodded. "I think Brent took her. That's my opinion. She said Lydia addressed the man as Brighton and he shoved her against the wall and instructed her not to say anything to anyone. Then Lydia stepped back like she was afraid. Still, she went with him."

Brighton rubbed his left temple.

"I'm not sure if you were told," Johnson continued, "but one of the fingers was definitely Lydia's. I think she may have been his first victim."

Brighton's eyes flashed up. "Why the hell did you not tell me this before? I'm going to fucking kill that bastard with my bare hands."

The vein in Brighton's neck pulsated.

"Bri, you need to calm down. We need to stay focused. You cannot bring her back. Once we find this bastard, we have to get him to tell us where he hid the bodies. Those families need closure. And so do you."

Brighton gritted his teeth yet agreed with his friend. "Fine. Do we know where he is? There must have been some trace of him?"

Johnson shook his head. "Your brother has changed his name so many times. He has several aliases including all the proper false documents to cover his tracks. That's why the police had a hard time finding him. I get below the surface," the investigator bragged.

Brighton held up his hands. "I don't want to know how you do that."

"It's better if you don't," Johnson admitted flatly.

Jason asked what their next move was going to be.

"Brent has not been back to his place. No one has. I figure he found another place to hide. I have eyes on the streets. Someone will spot him. And when they do, I am not waiting for the cops to show up. I want this guy as badly as you do."

"I highly doubt that," Brighton grumbled.

Later that evening, Cecelia called Brighton.

"Hey beautiful, how are you?"

"I miss you terribly."

"I miss you too. We are going to get this all cleared up soon and we can be back together. What have you been doing?"

"Enjoying the spa and shopping. I love being someone else. No one has any expectations of me. And... I met someone."

"Um, what do you mean?"

"Oh, not like that. I mean I met another woman. She's a writer and came for some peace and quiet. We met in the spa. We're going to dinner tomorrow then to a club. And don't worry, I am all yours. We're just going to blow off some steam. I won't let anyone buy me drinks."

He breathed a sigh of relief as she spoke. "Thank God. You had me worried. Is this woman a famous writer?"

"She has a few best sellers, but she writes under a pen name so no one here knows who she really is."

"Good, I don't want you hanging around with someone well known. You need to be as anonymous as possible."

"I know, darling. I'm being careful."

"Hang up."

Five minutes later he dialed her number.

"Do we really have to hang up every few minutes still?" she asked. "I mean, no one has either of our numbers, right?"

"I'm not taking any chances, Ce. I love you. I don't want to lose you. I couldn't survive that."

She sniffed.

"What's wrong?"

"I think that is the sweetest thing you have ever said to me, Bri. I love you too, so stay safe, OK?"

"I will. We will be together soon."

"I wish I could believe that. My bed is cold without you."

"Ditto, my love."

Chapter Ten

"I don't think you should be getting quite so close to Brighton, my love."

"Why is that, darling? Are you afraid I might fall for him?" she asked.

"Eventually he might figure out your game," he replied.

"He is not as intelligent as I am. If I think he is putting the pieces together, I will back off." She spritzed her neck with some of the perfume she knew Brighton liked.

"He's a fucking attorney, Babe. He has to be smart."

"He speaks intelligently but he lets his emotions lead him when he is not in the courtroom. He wears his heart on his sleeve. He still misses the woman he almost married. I can tell by the way he looks at me. And I've seen him eying women who look like the Lydia he knew."

"Remember, he has that private dick and his lawyer friend working to find us."

She shook her head. "No, they are looking for you. They have no idea you're not working alone. There were no traces of me in that apartment the police searched." She knew if Brighton found out she was involved, she could talk him out of believing she had anything to do with the murders. She knew he would believe she was taken under duress, and she did not want her partner to know that.

"Are you going out again?"

"Yes, one of us has to get food and supplies. And you can't leave. Someone will spot you."

"I hate being caged like an animal."

She tilted her head and glanced at him from different angles. "I have an idea."

"No offense, Jas, but I'd really like to do something alone for a change. Can't I just go to the market by myself? It is broad daylight and I'll be back in less than an hour."

"Fine, go, but do not come crying to me if someone who resembles Lydia ends up dead tomorrow morning."

"Thanks, you are so uplifting at times."

"I'm sorry Brighton but I do not want you out without an alibi. As your attorney, I have to protest."

"Duly noted."

Brighton pulled on his jacket and headed out to the local grocery store. As he strolled down the aisle, a familiar scent tickled his senses. His smile grew and he followed his nose two aisles over. She was speaking with another woman. Melissa caught his eye and smiled. Her friend's back was to Brighton. He moved down the aisle with purpose.

"Hello, Melissa."

Her friend turned and, placing her hand to her chest, gasped, "Oh my."

Embarrassed by the woman's reaction and taken aback by her appearance, Brighton swallowed hard. She had chocolate brown eyes and dark straight hair that sat on her head like a wig. She wore heavy makeup and Brighton wondered if perhaps she was hiding less than perfect skin.

"Bea, this is my friend and neighbor, Brian."

"It's Brighton," he corrected.

"Oh, I'm so sorry," she feigned embarrassment. "I should have remembered such an unusual name."

"That's quite all right, Melissa. I'm sure you have met quite a few new people. How are things going?"

"I'm doing well getting everything organized. Things are falling into place."

Brighton nodded and glanced at Bea.

"Bea is an old friend of mine. She came up to help me out."

"So your fiancé is still away on business?"

"I'm afraid so." She looked down and added, "It's been a bit lonely." She touched her friend's hand and said, "Until Bea joined me."

"How long will you be in the city?" Brighton asked Bea.

The woman cleared her throat. "Oh, I'm not sure yet. I suppose as long as Missy needs me here."

Brighton was surprised at the deep tone in her voice. His eyes drifted to her neck which was concealed by a silk scarf.

"If you ladies don't have any plans for the evening, why don't you come over for dinner? My friend Jason and I would love the company."

"Um, I'm not sure, Brighton."

"Awe, c'mon, what could it hurt? If you don't like the food or Jason, you live right across the street. You can bow out graciously and I'll understand."

"What do you think Bea?"

"I think it is a marvelous idea as long as your friend Jason is as cute as you are, Brighton," Bea chortled.

"I can't believe you agreed to this," Melissa said as she reapplied his makeup. "What if Brighton figures out who you are?"

"Oh please, he isn't that bright," he mimicked.

"And what was with that laugh? Women do not chortle like that, at least not the intelligent ones. You need to tone down the femininity."

"I'll do my best, Babe."

"Jason is smarter than Bri. He worked his way through law school. He didn't have everything handed to him. If they ask you any personal questions, be very careful what you say. Make it plausible. And I think you should pretend to be older. It would help compensate for the heavy makeup and deep voice."

He grimaced as she plucked at his brow.

"I should have waxed your brow and upper lip."

"Maybe you can do that next time."

"There won't be a next time. We can't take that chance."

"Oh, so you can pretend to be someone you're not but I can't?"

She lifted his face and stared into his eyes. "I am better at acting than you. The contacts, wig and makeup may hide who you are to a certain extent, but we cannot let them figure out our ruse. If they do, this is over."

"I'll behave and speak only when spoken to."

"Good. Now stand up and walk around. I want you to get used to those shoes. You walk like a guy in his girlfriend's pumps."

"Because I am," he reminded her. "Why do I have to wear a skirt anyway?"

"It hides your junk, jackass."

"Couldn't I just wear a long sweater or something?"

"Trust me. I know what I am doing."

"You know, you treat me like this was all your idea from the start."

She stepped closer to him and put her arms around her neck. "Who is the brain behind this plan, huh?"

"We are, my darling. I set the parameters; you just filled in the blanks."

She raised a brow. "I think you should learn your place. You wouldn't have made it this far without me and you know that."

"I would have done things a little differently had you not convinced me to let you take part."

She brushed her lips against his ear and whispered. "You wanted me the moment you saw me. Had I not played along you would have killed me, no?"

His lips parted to answer.

"Had you not been so easy to seduce, I would have been your first victim; I know that; you can't deny it, my darling."

He exhaled as he felt the heat of her breath on his neck. He knew she had changed the rules the minute he felt her lips the day he walked into her life. There was something undeniably sexy about her and the thought of stealing her away from Brighton fueled his desire to make his brother's life a living hell.

"Don't think too much, my love," she teased. "You might hurt your favorite organ."

He growled, "You make me so damn hot when you take charge."

"Cool your jets, big boy. We are going to dinner, and I do *not* want to explain why my friend Bea keeps grabbing her crotch."

"You have got to be kidding me," Jason said as he watched Brighton prepare dinner. "You actually invited them into your home? What do you really know about this woman? Can you trust what she told you?"

"There is something about her, Jas. I need to be near her. I have to get to know her."

"Do you think Cecelia would like you getting this close to another woman?"

"It's not like that," Bri insisted.

"Look me in the eye and tell me you have no romantic notions about this woman."

Brighton paused. He inhaled deeply then lifted his gaze to meet his friend's. "I love Ce. Nothing has changed regarding her. I need to know more about Melissa. I know it's farfetched, but maybe she is connected to Lyd. I need to know how."

Jason sighed. "Fine. But don't make a habit of inviting her here. And if she winds up dead because she came in contact with you, I promise not to say I told you so."

"Thank for that," Brighton replied with attitude.

Jason stared into Bea's eyes as he handed her a glass of Merlot. Beatrice held his stare as if they were having a contest to see who blinked down first.

"Thank you, Jason," Melissa said as she took the other glass from him in an attempt to break the eye contact between the two.

"You're quite welcome. So Bea, you're from Cockeysville too?"

"Coopersburg," Melissa corrected.

"Oh, right, Brighton told me. And what do you do there?"

"I work for a museum part time. What do you do?" Bea asked with an edge to her voice.

"I'm a defense attorney."

Bea smiled yet kept her eyes locked on his.

The proximity of the two was making Melissa nervous. "So you work with Brighton?" she interjected.

"That's right," Jason replied his gaze immovable.

Brighton returned to the living room. "Dinner is coming along." He noticed the tension between his friend and Melissa's. "Why don't you two have a seat?"

Several seconds passed before Jason and Beatrice stepped back and moving at the exact same moment.

"Do you two live together?" Melissa asked.

"Temporarily," Jason said, continuing to size up Bea.

Bea sat uncomfortably on the edge of the sofa. Jason remained standing.

"And you work together as well? I'm not sure I would want to spend that much time with anyone."

"It's not easy," Jason growled.

"Hey."

"What Bri? I miss my wife and my private time. You're not the easiest person to live with."

"I don't do bed checks on you, Jas."

"He bed checks you?" Bea laughed. "How sweet. Do you think he'll sneak out with his friends and get into trouble?"

"Something like that," Jason replied.

"How long have the two of you known each other?"

"We went to the same law school," Brighton explained. "We were both chasing after the same girl. Jason won. But I found someone better in the end."

Butterflies erupted in Melissa's stomach. "She was one lucky woman."

Brighton tilted his head and regarded Melissa. He couldn't explain why he felt so drawn to this woman. He wondered if she was connected to Lydia in some way. Each time he met Melissa, he noticed something else that reminded him of Lyd. Maybe it was true what people said. Everyone has another person who could be their twin.

"Brighton?"

"Hm?"

"For a minute you looked like you were a million miles away."

"I'm sorry. I have a lot on my mind. Why don't you all go into the dining room? I'll put the salad on the table and we can start with that."

Jason eyed Beatrice's backside as she walked into the dining room. He shook his head. "Bri, can I help you with anything?"

Brighton knew his friend was not interested in helping. Still, he said, "Sure."

As soon as they were in the kitchen, Jason stepped close to Bri and whispered, "That is not a woman. Did you see the way she walks? Her hands? And you must have noticed that voice."

"I don't judge. Maybe she is just a very masculine woman."

"I want to rip that scarf off his neck and prove to you he's a man."

"Don't."

"I didn't say I would. I sure do want to though."

While the men were speaking in the kitchen, Melissa was telling Bea to watch what she said. "Jason is on to you. I'm positive. I told you Jason was smarter than Bri. And what is up with all the macho staring each other down."

"You told me not to be too feminine."

"Jesus, you go from one extreme to another. Knock it off or I am sending you home."

Before Bea could answer, Jason burst through the door between the kitchen and the dining room. He placed the salad bowl in the center of the table. Brighton was behind him carrying a dish filled with Chicken Cordon Bleu.

"I'll be right back with the roasted red potatoes and glazed carrots. You can go ahead if you want."

Jason served the salad and then the meat. Instead of continuing to question Bea, he decided to observe her quietly. Brighton returned and dished out the carrots and potatoes. The conversation during the dinner was light and general. Brighton talked about the city and all the culture it offered. He also told Melissa about the nightclubs and fine dining establishments. Bea interjected a few words here and there, yet for the most part she did not interact.

When Brighton suggested they move to the living room for coffee, Bea confessed she was tired and was ready to go home.

"Maybe we both should go. We can do coffee another time."

"I'll walk you ladies across the street."

"That isn't necessary, Brighton."

"I know but it is the gentlemanly thing to do."

Melisa smiled demurely and agreed to have Brighton escort them home. When they arrived at Melissa's door, Bea thanked Brighton for a lovely evening and went inside.

"I'm sorry that Jason and Bea didn't seem to get along."

"It's all right. You didn't do anything wrong. Bea is... I'm not sure I should tell you this." Melissa bit her lip. She looked up at the brownstone behind her and saw the light go on. She turned her focus back to Brighton.

"Bea is actually my brother. He... she is uncomfortable in her body. She's considering changing. I asked her to come to New York to see if she would be happier being someone else. You know, try being a woman on for size before he makes a final decision. I mean, physically changing your body is drastic and permanent. There are so many things to consider. Not to mention the fact that our parents are totally against it and said they would disown him if he had the surgery."

"I have to admit Melissa; I thought there was something about Bea that didn't fit."

"Does it bother you?" she asked timidly.

"Why would it? There are many people who want to change something. Some changes are more dramatic or unusual. But who am I to judge?"

Melissa touched Brighton's arm. The heat emanating from her shot through his body.

"Thank you for understanding. I love my brother. All of his life he has pretended to be something that my parents wanted him to be. I told him it was time to live his life the way he wants to. I am glad this doesn't change anything between us. I could use a friend in the city."

"Anytime you need anything, Melissa, I'm a phone call away."

Her hand remained on his forearm as she took one step closer and looked into his eyes. "There are moments I feel so alone, even with Bea here. It is hard for me to talk to her about some things. I feel like I can trust you. Maybe it is your kind eyes."

Melissa leaned up and kissed his cheek. "Thank you, Brighton. You've made me feel a little less alone."

Brighton cleared his throat. "You're welcome Melissa. How soon will your fiancé be joining you?"

"I'm afraid he won't be. He called me earlier today. He, um, met someone. I guess he's known her for a while and she traveled with him for business on several occasions. One thing led to another and..." A tear slid down her face. "I'm sorry. I have to go." Melissa turned and ran up the steps into her building.

Brighton stood frozen. In less than five minutes, Melissa had confessed so much. He ached for her. He put his hand over the spot on his arm where she had touched him. He looked up at the windows and released a heavy sigh.

A few minutes later, Brighton found Jason in the kitchen cleaning up.

"Bea is her brother."

"I told you she was a man. No woman is THAT masculine. Why was he in drag?"

Brighton relayed Melissa's story including the break up with her fiancé. Jason listened, taking in all the information and pondering. He could see the attraction his friend had for Melissa.

"Bud, you need to back off. If you really love Cecelia, stay away from Melissa. She is messing with your head."

"I know you're right, Jason. But she is all alone in a new city."

"She isn't alone, Bri. She has her brother here. Maybe he is a little unique, but he is her brother."

"She said she can't talk to him about some things."

"That is not your problem, my friend. We need to get this murder accusation off your back and move on with life. Bringing another person into the mix will make things more complicated. Trust me."

"You're right. I have enough issues without making things worse. I'll stay away from Melissa."

"Good, now help me clean up this mess."

"Oh hell no," Brighton said as he grabbed a long neck out of the fridge. "I cooked; you clean." He laughed and exited the kitchen.

Chapter Eleven

Brighton had not seen Melissa for several days. He had stayed away from the front windows of the brownstone. He and Jason shopped at a different market. They had dinner either at home or they went to the outskirts of the city to dine. Brighton knew he had to avoid Melissa; his friend was right about that.

One morning, Jason received a call from his wife.

"Jas, I'm scared. I'm having contractions. They're not regular. The doctor here said not to worry but I can't help it. I need you."

"I can't leave Brighton alone, Molly."

"Then come with him."

"I wish I could Babe but he can't leave the state."

"I need you Jason. You have to choose: your wife or your friend."

"Let me see what I can do."

Jason made a few phone calls. After making arrangements, he spoke with Brighton.

"I need to go to Florida. Molly is having contractions off and on and she's scared. If this wasn't our first, it might not be so bad but I have to go."

Brighton began to protest. Jason put his hand up to stop him.

"I called Johnson. He is going to stay with you. There is no one else I would trust."

"Fine," Brighton grunted. "I hate having to be babysat."

"It is for your own good, my friend," Jason said patting his friend's shoulder. "My flight leaves tonight. Johnson should be here within the hour. I'll take a cab to the airport. Call me if you need anything. I don't know how long I'll be. I may bring Molly back." Jason hesitated for a moment. "I don't want her having the baby without me."

"I get it, Jason. You should be there with her. Don't worry about me."

"Thanks. I have to go pack."

The following morning, Brighton was up before the sun. He made coffee and stepped outside to grab the paper. The air carried a slight chill yet he decided to sit on the stoop and read the paper. He needed some quiet alone time. Although there were lights on in neighboring homes, there were not many cars on the street.

He found the sports section and read a couple of articles. He checked the forecast then opened the calendar pages. He paid no attention to the world around him as engines started and vehicles pulled away from the curb. People walked by and a few said, "Good Morning." One person seemed to move close and pause for a moment.

"Good Morning, Bri. How are you?"

The voice sent warmth through his body.

"Hello Melissa. I'm well. How are you?"

She sat next to him and bumped her shoulder against his. "I can't complain. I am going on an interview today," she added excitedly. "It's nothing special, only a receptionist position but I'll be happy to be working again. I need something to do since the jerk isn't coming back."

"Where's the interview? Maybe I can put in a good word for you."

"Oh no, I don't want you to do that. I want to get the job on my own merit."

"Good for you. Stand on your own two feet."

"That's right. Say, what are you doing tonight? If I get the offer, do you want to do dinner?"

"With you and Bea?" he asked.

She shook her head. "Just you and I. You can leave Jason home too."

"He left last night for Florida."

"Oh really?" Melissa said although she already knew. "Maybe we can have dinner here at your place?"

"I have another friend staying with me."

"Hm, so you don't like to be alone. Well, maybe you can send him to the movies or something."

Brighton could not stop his lips from curling into a smile. "Call me when you get the offer and perhaps we can make some sort of arrangement."

"Deal," she said bumping into his shoulder again. "I have to go. I just stopped to say hello. I'll call you when I get back, K?"

"K."

Brighton watched the sway in her hips as she made her way across the street. He felt that familiar tug in his jeans and scolded himself.

"Cecelia. Cecelia," he thought in an effort to take away his desire for Melissa.

Later in the day when Bri told Johnson he was going out to dinner with Melissa, the detective balked.

"I don't like that chick. I've had my eye on her. Where are you going?"

"I'm debating whether I should take her some place popular or quiet. I know I need to stay out of trouble, so I thought a more public spot would give me more a better alibi. Then again, who would know what happens after I take her home. Maybe we should go to a restaurant where no one knows either of us."

"Or I could follow you," Johnson suggested.

Brighton wasn't fond of the idea of being watched. Still, he agreed knowing that at least if any bodies showed up, he might be questioned but wouldn't be tossed in a cell.

Brighton took Melissa to an Italian restaurant that was not well known yet not exactly obscure either. The clientele were local people who were mostly middle class. He figured he would not run into any of his work friends or anyone who knew Lydia.

They sat across from each other at a table that could sit four. Brighton ordered some fried calamari and they nibbled on the appetizer until Melissa had chosen her entrée. He waved to the waitress who promptly took their dinner order and brought another round of drinks.

"I'm glad we grabbed a cab," she said. "Now we can drink and not worry about driving home." She took a sip of her pear Martini. "This is lovely. You should try it."

"I'll stick to my scotch." He downed half of the single malt liquor. "Care to tell me where you will be working now or is it still a secret?"

"I don't want to jinx it. They said I was one of two applicants that they're considering."

"Do you know anything about the other person?"

Melissa took another drink and licked her lips. "She's a woman, that's all I know."

"Is your brother planning on staying in New York long?"

"He is scheduled to go home soon. He wanted to make sure I was all right staying by myself. It's a bit scary but I've already made a few friends in the neighborhood."

"Is it anyone I know?"

"The bag boy at the market asked me out."

"The red head who looks like he's about twelve?"

"Yup, that's the one. I swear he must still be in high school."

He laughed. "I hope you let him down easy."

"I told him in five years if I am still visiting the same market and not involved, he could take me out to dinner."

"You didn't!"

"I did; I swear. He is very sweet."

"Sweetness fades."

"It didn't with you."

"Thank you but you don't know me all that well," he said with a wry smile.

"I'm trying, Brighton but you are holding back. Is it because of your girlfriend?"

"That's a good part of it. I'm also in some trouble right now. I'm not sure being around me is wise."

Her voice cracked as she asked, "Oh, what kind of trouble?"

"I can't say."

"So it's something illegal?"

"I'm sorry Melissa; I can't talk about it."

The salads arrived and the two sat quietly eating until their main courses were served. Then Melissa blurted out, "Are you planning on marrying her?"

He replied with a simple, "Yes."

"She is one lucky woman," Missy whispered.

He touched her hand. "You will find someone when you least expect it."

Her eyes froze on his fingers as they brushed against the back of her hand. She hadn't wanted to admit it but she still had feelings for him. She wondered if things would have been different, if Brent hadn't shown up that day and told her what happened. Would things have turned out differently?

Brent was waiting up for her. He asked how her evening was.

"It was pleasant."

He seized her by the wrist. "Did you fuck him?"

"No," she said without making eye contact.

"But you wanted to."

She didn't respond.

He pulled her even closer and covered her mouth with his. He kissed her ferociously. Her knees weakened. Brent stole her breath. She was putty in his hands. Brent bent her over the sofa and took her fast and hard.

"Has he ever made you feel like this?" he sneered. "Has he?"

"No, oh God," she whimpered.

"You love how I fuck you."

Other than his name, the next string of words passing her lips was indecipherable. Brent knew the effect he had on her, and he wasn't afraid to use her just as she used him. They both had reasons to get even with Brighton. Their anger had grown into hatred which became a bond stronger than anything either had experienced before.

That night, she found sleep difficult. She tossed and turned, remembering the day he had walked into her life. She was preparing for what she thought would be the happiest day of her life when there was a knock on the door.

"Bri, what are you doing here? Why aren't you dressed? You're not supposed to see the bride before the wedding."

He looked her over with a wicked grin etched on his face. He stepped into her apartment and kicked the door closed. Without a word, he pulled her into his arms and pressed her against the door. Lydia didn't protest. In fact, she undid the robe she was wearing and let him take her. When he was satisfied, he stepped back.

"Damn, you are even more beautiful close up."

"Wha..? Brighton?"

He laughed manically. He put his hand to her throat. "Your sweet Brighton is not what you think he is. He is a cheating, lying bastard."

"You're scaring me," she choked out as his grip tightened.

"You know what he did last night? He let some tramp suck him off."

"What, no, not Brighton. Who are you?"

"I'm the better half of the egg, the half that our mother gave away."

Her voice shook as she spoke. "What do you mean?"

Brent explained to Lydia how he had been given up for adoption, abandoned by his mother, thrown aside like a broken toy. Then he told her about the bachelor party and the hooker. She asked for proof. Brent had been following his brother for months. He was working as a waiter the night of the party and managed to get a video with his cell of the hooker giving Brighton a lap dance.

"That doesn't prove he let her touch him."

"Trust me; he did. I talked to the whore after."

Lydia was confused, shocked, and angry. "I want to talk to her. I want to know what happened."

"Fine. Then come with me. When you realize what a pig he is, you'll want to get as far away from him as you possibly can."

She sat up in bed and ran her hand through her hair pushing the thoughts back where they belonged... in the past.

"Brent, wake up."

"Urgh, what time is it?"

"Two am. C'mon. We're changing the plan."

Saturday morning, Johnson woke up groggily. Moments later he remembered he wasn't home. A strange feeling overwhelmed him and he recalled a weird dream. There was something over his mouth and nose making it hard to breathe. He fought to no avail. Now that he was awake and fully coherent, Johnson grabbed his cell and dialed.

"Detective Shaw," the voice on the other end responded.

"Johnson. I know you identified one of the fingers as belonging to Lydia. Were you able to decipher when the digit was separated?"

"As a matter of fact, it not as far back as we thought it would be. Hold on, let me pull the report."

Chapter Twelve

Johnson jogged down the hall as Detective Shaw told him that the finger which matched Lydia's DNA appeared to have been detached from its host only a few months ago. "The coroner said there was no way it was a year old."

"I have a real bad feeling about this." Johnson burst through the door to Brighton's bedroom only to find an empty unmade bed. "Stay on the line," he told Shaw. Johnson looked in the master bath and no one was there. He dashed down the stairs and looked in every room calling out his client's name. He even looked on the front stoop.

"Brighton's gone. Damn it. I had what I thought was a dream last night about someone smothering me with a cloth soaked in something."

The breeze made by him closing the front door hit a piece of paper causing it to skate across the floor. Johnson picked up the note and read over the phone.

You let your guard down Detective. You should sleep with one eye open.

"Son of a bitch. So it wasn't Brighton," Shaw admitted.

"Nope, never was. And now the killer has him. You'd better step up your game Shaw or Brighton will be the next body at the morgue."

Johnson disconnected the called and dialed another number. Groggily Jason answered, grumbling about the hour.

"They took Brighton right from under my nose. I think they knocked me out. Called Shaw already. I am sure they will have a crew here to dust and will find nothing."

Jason's mind immediately focused as he bolted upright. "Damn it, I knew I shouldn't leave."

"It gets worse, my friend," Johnson headed back up to Brighton's room. "I think Melissa was actually Lydia. The finger they found had been separated only a short time ago. Now we know why she had the cast. It was to hide her missing digit. And I would bet money that her brother was actually Brent. That's probably why he was covered in makeup and dressed in drag."

"Jesus. Any clue as to where they might have gone?"

"None. They left a note." Johnson read the note to Jason. "I bet they made themselves a key one of the times they were here. They sneaked in and took care of me first. They probably drugged Brighton as well. There is no way he would have gone without a fight."

"Damn it," Jason repeated. He could hear Johnson rummaging around.

Molly sat up and rubbed Jason's back. She heard only half of the conversation yet it was enough to make her worry.

"At least we know Cecelia is safely tucked away somewhere. No one but Bri knows where she is. Did they take his cell phones?" Jason asked.

"I cannot find either of them."

"Shit. Then they know her new cell number and we don't. I am heading over."

"No," Molly begged. "Let the police handle this."

"She's right, Jason. Stay with your wife. The last thing I need is for them to take you too. The cops and I will find Brighton and get these two murderers locked up for good."

"OK, but keep me in the loop. I want to know your every move."

A short while later, the crime scene investigators were at the brownstone. They dusted for prints and looked for clues. Two officers were sent to canvas the neighborhood. Two more went across the street and found the apartment where Lydia and Brent had been staying. The rooms were also printed and evidence was collected.

Brighton struggled to wake up his mind. He could tell by his position that he was not in bed. The ropes around his wrists dug into his flesh. His ankles were bound as well. He muttered something.

"Wake up, Bri Bri," he heard a voice singing. "It's morning."

A moment later the sting of a hand connecting with his cheek made his eyes flash open.

"There you are," Melissa sang.

Brighton blinked. The woman before him had Melissa's hair and stature yet she had removed all makeup and facial prostheses.

"Lyd... Lydia?"

She laughed manically. "I'm surprised you remember my name you cheating bastard. I bet you remember the feel of that whore's mouth on you though."

"Ce is not a whore!"

"I'm not talking about that bitch. I'm referring to the bachelor party."

"What? How did you..?"

"I have my ways."

In an effort bring his mind to full awareness, Brighton shook his head like a wet dog. "I was going to tell you but you disappeared. Is that why you left?"

"You were going to wait until our wedding night to confess your infidelity?"

"Lydia, please, it meant nothing to me."

"That's what you said about that wench Rachel."

"That was completely different. You and I had only been together two weeks. We had gone out what, three times?"

"It didn't matter at the time, but then you let that whore..." Lydia turned away from him. "Once a cheater..."

"Lyd, it wasn't like that."

"Fuck you," she said and left the room slamming the door.

Brighton checked his surroundings. He was in an old abandoned warehouse, of that he was sure. He had no idea where it was located. He was tied to a wooden chair tightly enough so it would be difficult to escape. His stomach growled. He felt exhausted from the effects of the drug and lack of sleep. He was trying to process what had happened.

Thirty minutes later the door swung open. Brent eyed his brother as he skulked around the chair. Brighton remained quiet, pretending to be unaffected by his presence. Brent rounded his twin several times before speaking.

"What do you have that I don't?"

"A soul," he sneered.

Brent back handed his brother.

"Maybe our mother looked into your eyes and saw the emptiness there."

After the next blow, Brighton tasted his own blood. Brent stood directly in front of him. He took a gag from his back pocket and tied it around his victim's head. He pulled out a cell phone and redialed the last number on the recent calls list.

"Ce, darling, how are you?"

Brighton's eyes narrowed and he tried to holler her name. The cloth in his mouth prevented his voice from being heard over the phone.

"Good morning, Bri. I'm well. How are you?"

"I miss you. I want you here with me."

Brighton writhed in the chair nearly knocking it over.

"Come back to New York."

"Is it safe? Did they find Brent?"

"They found Brent. He wasn't involved. Someone had stolen his identity and committed the murders."

Brighton rocked the chair until it fell over. Cecelia heard the crash.

"What was that?"

"It was nothing, my love. I've been pacing and I wasn't looking where I was going. A chair toppled over." Brent kicked Brighton. "If you're here with me, you'll be safe."

"Why don't you come get me? I would feel better about coming home if I traveled with you."

"You know I'm not allowed to leave the state, darling."

"So you are still a suspect?"

Brent grimaced. She was being difficult. "Just come home, darling. I want you in my bed."

"Will you make the arrangements?" Cecelia asked. She knew if it was truly Brighton on the line then he would know where she was.

"I'm..." Brent was trying to think quickly. "Yes, I will. I'll call you later with the details. I can't wait to hold you in my arms once more, Ce. I've missed you terribly. I'd better hang up now. I love you."

"Ditto," she replied.

He hung up and laughed. "She is almost as gullible as you are my dear brother." Brent turned on his heel and exited the room. Just before he closed the door he looked back at Brighton. "I'm going to make love to your girlfriend then tear her limb from limb."

Brighton fought back the tears as hard as he tried to escape from his bindings. With his ankles tied to the legs of the chair and his arms behind him it was useless. He twisted his arms trying desperately to free his wrists now bleeding from the tightness of the rope.

What seemed like hours passed before he saw or heard anything. Brent and Lydia were standing outside the door. He heard a few words most of which were curses. Apparently Lydia was not happy with Brent calling Cecelia and telling her to come back to New York. The voices stopped and moments later they stepped through the door.

"Pick him up," Lydia demanded.

"Why? He deserves to be on the floor."

Lydia glared at him.

"Fine."

Brent righted the chair along with Brighton. Lydia pulled over a second chair and sat in front of their captive. She reached out and touched his cheek. "I'm sorry. Does this hurt?"

"No," he said, "not as much as you disappearing on me."

Somewhere deep inside Lydia a piece of her remembered the love she had for him. Then she remembered the lies. The day after Brighton had proposed, Lydia's best friend Rachel showed up at her apartment. Lydia had called her earlier to tell her about the engagement.

"Are you sure you want to marry him?" Rachel asked her friend taking a sip of the tea Lydia had made for them.

"Why wouldn't I? He's smart and hot and he has a great future ahead of him."

"As your best friend, I have something to confess, Lydia. Maybe he told you already and you have made peace with it; I don't know. But marriage needs to be based on trust. There should be no secrets."

"What are you talking about?" a wide-eyed Lydia asked.

"I slept with Brighton."

"What? When?"

"It was months ago. You two had just started seeing each other. I didn't mean for it to happen. I would have told you sooner, but I had no idea things were getting so serious."

Lydia confronted Brighton later that day. He had openly admitted his indiscretion and she immediately forgave him. When Brent showed up on their wedding day and said Brighton had been unfaithful once more, something inside Lydia snapped.

Brighton's voice brought Lydia back to the present.

"I never meant to hurt you, Lydia. Rachel was a mistake; I told you about it and you forgave me. And I was stupid to let that woman at the party near me. Once we were married, I would have never..."

She slapped him again to stop his babbling.

"I don't want to hear any more excuses. I'm going to let Brent have his way with Cecelia. You can watch. And when he's done, I will cut your heart out and stomp on it like you did to mine."

Brent stood a few feet behind Lydia. He was practically drooling in anticipation of taking Cecelia in front of his brother.

Brighton begged, "Please Lyd, if you ever loved me, do not touch Cecelia. She is innocent. She did nothing wrong. Punish me but don't hurt her."

"Stop whining you poor excuse for a man." Lydia stood and put a hand to his throat. "Do you know how easy it is to kill a man and get away with it? Brent taught me everything I needed to know." Her grip tightened. "We could take your life right here and now then vanish and no one would be able to prove it was us. You think our other victims suffered? You haven't seen anything yet."

Lydia released him and he coughed in an effort to catch his breath.

"Lydia," he croaked. "Tell me something."

"What?" she snarled.

"Does your family know you're alive? Do you know what you put your parents and your brother through?"

For a moment, Brighton thought he had gotten to her. She looked like a doe in headlights. Then the blood drained from her face and any warmth in her heart dissipated.

"Don't try to trick me, Bri Bri. They don't give a shit about me. They were happy to marry me off so I would be out of their hair."

"That's not true, Lyd, and you know it."

"Fuck you and your lies, Brighton."

"What happened, Lydia? What did Brent do to you?"

Lydia glanced over her shoulder at her accomplice. Then she grinned maniacally at Brighton.

"He showed me how to have fun," she sneered.

Chapter Thirteen

Cecelia paced her room for over an hour. There was something about the call from Brighton that bothered her. She could not explain the feeling; it was just something in her gut. She hadn't heard back from him and was wondering if he had made plans for her to come home. She dialed his cell.

"Hey Babe. How ya doin'?"

"I'm well. Have you taken care of the arrangements yet?"

"I'm working on it. I'm trying to make sure you have a safe trip. Can you find out the fax number to the hotel? That way I can fax you the information."

"I can do that. How's Molly doing?"

"She's fine. Why do you ask?"

"Jason must be pacing like a caged animal."

"I wouldn't know, Babe. He went to Florida."

"Oh, right, you told me. Maybe I'll call Molly to check on her."

"No, um, don't call. Jason is with her. I am sure she is fine. No need to bother them. Listen, I have to go. Call me when you get that fax number, OK sweet cheeks?"

His response made Cecelia sure there was something not quite right.

"Absolutely. I love you."

"We'll be together soon, Babe."

"Oh, and Bri, there's something I need to tell you."

Brighton heard and felt his stomach growl. What was worse, his bladder was stretched. He knew if he waited long enough, his body would absorb any fluid it could to survive. He just had to wait it out. No one had entered the room in what seemed like hours. He felt weak and his muscles ached from being stuck in the same position. All he could think of was Ce.

The door burst open.

"My dear brother, you did not tell me you were going to be a father."

Brighton hid his surprise. "You never asked."

"It's very interesting, the timing of it all." Brent laughed. "Are you sure it's yours? After all, she did let me fuck her."

Brighton's hands fisted behind him. "When Cecelia called me the morning after your visit she asked why I had been off my game the night before. I guess you are not as gifted as I am."

Brent grabbed him by the throat. "You are in no position to be throwing insults at me. I could take your life in seconds."

"Do it. Just leave Ce alone," Brighton choked out.

Brent considered his brother's words, tightening his grip. When his hand opened, Brighton coughed, trying to catch his breath.

"Seeing you squirm while I fuck her again would be much more satisfying than taking your life now."

Jason hadn't heard from Johnson. He had no idea where his friend was. He was concerned about Cecelia. And on top of all his other worries, Molly was still having intermittent contractions and had started spotting. She was put on bed rest. Her mother was taking care of her. All Jason could do was sit and wait. It was driving him crazy.

"I'm sorry about all of this, Jas. I shouldn't have made you come here. Maybe Brighton wouldn't have been taken if you were there."

"Don't think like that, Molly. If I had been there, maybe they would have kidnapped me as well. I'm where I should be, with my family," he said taking her hand in his. "I love you, Molly. You are the center of my world."

"I love you too, Jason."

"When all this is over, we are going to go home and live happily ever after. I promise."

"I'm with you through good and bad. As long as we are together, nothing else matters."

"So what did you find?" Johnson asked Detective Shaw.

"Not a whole heck of a lot," the policeman replied. "The only prints in the place were yours, Brighton's and Jason's."

"This is very strange since Brent and Lydia were at the brownstone for dinner once. Sure they were in disguise but fingerprints don't just disappear."

"Maybe they were careful not to touch anything but the dinnerware. We didn't dust everything in the kitchen."

"Did you find any evidence across the street?"

"We found Lydia's prints there as well as another set. We don't have Brent's fingerprints on file. We did find some DNA that appears to be his."

"Damn it."

"There's something else. We found the identity of two other victims. One was a Rachel Greenly. We did some checking and she was friends with Lydia. They had a falling out two days before the wedding. Three days later she told her family she was flying to LA with a friend. She never arrived in California. They found her car in a ditch but no body. We matched her DNA to a missing person's database."

"And who was the other victim?"

"Marsha Willis was her name. She worked at the firm as a temp for three months. She filled in for Clay's secretary who was on maternity leave at the time. She left the firm about a month before Lydia disappeared."

"Did they find her body?"

"Yeah, off the Jersey shore. It took us a while to put everything together. We started searching for Jane Does with missing fingers. Marsha popped up; we sent a request for the DNA and bingo."

"Well whoever the other two fingers belong to, you can be sure they are dead and that they are somehow linked to this whole mess. It is obvious now that Lydia and Brent were trying to frame Brighton by killing women he had come in contact with. Too bad they were not smart enough to leave more evidence leading to Brighton. Not sure what Brent's beef was other than being put up for adoption. Lydia was obviously after any woman who showed an interest in Brighton."

"She is one sick bitch."

"I can't argue with you there. Keep me informed, Detective. I have my men poking around. I'll let you know if I find anything."

"Wake up," she said shaking him. "Wake the fuck up."

Brighton's eyes came into focus. "Wha..?"

"Your girlfriend is dumb as shit, ya know that?"

"What did you do to her?"

"Nothing yet, lover. But she gave us the fax number to the hotel in Connecticut. Brent is going to drive up there and bring her back." Lydia ran her hand up and down Brighton's thigh. "I can't wait to see you watching him fuck her. She'll think it's you and be all, 'Oh I love you Brighton.'" Lydia laughed.

"Cecelia will know it's not me."

Lydia leaned in close to his face. He could feel the heat emanating from her. "She didn't know last time, lover."

"It was dark; she was half awake; she had no idea I had a twin. Now she knows. There is no way she will think he is me."

"Hm, we shall see, dear Brighton," she mocked stroking his cheek. She leaned in even closer. "I think she is as easily fooled as I was by a Clay brother."

"Seems like you were fooled twice. Brent has gotten you to do some terrible things, Lydia."

"He has forced me to do nothing."

"Then you are not the Lydia I knew."

"That is for damn sure. I am wiser, stronger, and more fit that that old girl was." She straightened and looked him over. "Hm, I'll be back shortly, darling."

Brighton's mind was reeling. Could Ce be pregnant with his child? Could it be Brent's? Did anyone know where he was? Johnson and the police must have figured out who took him. He felt so weakened by lack of food and water that he began to see images that were not there. He saw Cecelia, his mother and father, and other people he knew. He saw a light shining but no window or other light source for the glow.

Lydia was not gone for long. She came back with a bottle and an unmarked paper bag. Lydia sat across from him and opened the bottle which was labeled Spring Water.

"Drink this," she insisted putting the bottle to his lips.

He turned his head. "No."

"You will die here without water. I cannot have that happening, at least not yet."

"I have to go to the bathroom."

"Pee on yourself. I don't give a damn."

"Are you afraid if you let me stand that I'll overtake you?"

"Fuck you. There is no way you could get away from me."

"Then untie my ankles and take me to the bathroom."

"And then you will drink?" she asked.

"Yes."

"Fine."

Lydia put the bottle on the floor. She unbound his legs. She directed him toward the door staying several steps behind him.

"You are aware that I not only have the gun but that even if you should knock it from my grasp, I can still kill you with my bare hands."

"At this point, it would be a blessing. I'm too weak to fight," he lied. He knew if given the chance to escape, his adrenalin would kick in, and he would fight with every ounce of energy he had.

Lydia smirked as she told him where to go. Once he had relieved himself, she took him back to the spot he had been in for over 28 hours. On the way to the bathroom and back, Brighton took mental notes. It was definitely an abandoned warehouse. There were small windows up near the ceiling and large bay doors in the main part of the building. The office they had kept him in had been cleared of all furniture except a few chairs.

He returned to his seat. Lydia held up the water and he drank. She put the cap back on and picked up the bag from which she retrieved a sandwich. She pulled off a piece and held it up.

"Eat."

He knew he needed the food so he took a bite. Then he said, "Water," and she gave him another sip. As he ate, she began to tell him what happened on the day of their wedding.

"I thought he was you at first. He is remarkably similar. His voice, the way he carries himself, all of it was like you. It wasn't until his hand was at my throat that I began to wonder. He told me about that whore. I didn't want to believe at first. Then I remembered Rachel."

"That was a mistake, Lydia. And I told you about it. You forgave me."

"I was stupid. You would have cheated on me again. You proved that."

"What happened at the bachelor party was nothing, Lyd. I was going to tell you about it. I was drunk, not that it's an excuse. Still..."

"You cheated before that."

"You and I had only gone out a few times. Rachel meant nothing to me."

"You knew she was my friend, Brighton."

"Not until after."

Lydia shook her head and got to her feet. "Regardless, you are a pig. A cheating lying pig." She walked around the chair eying him. "And I took care of Rachel."

"What do you mean?" he asked with wide eyes.

"She was my first. I was a bit nervous but once I got started, I couldn't stop. The rage was..."

He could see the excitement in her eyes as she rounded the chair once more. She was thrilled by her kill.

Her voice turned cold as she continued, "...intense and I felt so alive. It was as if I found my calling," she said walking away from him. She was in her own little world, lost in the memory of the first time she saw life drain from someone's eyes.

Brighton wondered what happened to the sweet Lydia he fell in love with. Sometime between the moment she met Brent, and now she had lost the person she was and become evil and bitter. Surely there must be something more to the story. A woman does not run off on a killing spree just because her fiancé cheats.

While Lydia rambled on, Brighton was thinking of a way to escape. She had not rebound his feet. He could run. Still, his hands were tied. How could he fight if she caught up to him? He wriggled his hands, trying desperately to break free. When

Lydia moved behind him, he froze. She didn't seem to notice him anymore. She was lost in thought.

For several minutes, he watched and worked to free himself. At first, the ropes seemed to tighten. Once he let himself relax and concentrate he felt them loosening. "Only a few more twists," he thought.

Chapter Fourteen

On his way to Connecticut, Brent imagined nailing Cecelia in front of his brother. It was one thing to take her that night when she thought he was Brighton. To actually rape her in front of him would be the ultimate pleasure. Several times during the trip he rubbed his crotch.

He pulled into the lot at the hotel to call Lydia.

"I'm here. I won't be calling you again until we're back in the city. How is my dear brother?"

"He's annoying as hell but fine. I fed him. I didn't want him starving on us before we had the chance to torture him a bit more."

"I'll be back soon, Babe. Then we can play."

"I'm tingly all over. And I mean ALL over."

"I'll take care of you when I get back. Don't you dare take care of your needs with him!"

"Not to worry, Brent, I have no desire to touch that pig. Get back soon, OK?"

Lydia went into the warehouse office. "Your brother is about to pick up your lover."

"I told you to leave her alone," he snapped.

"And just what are you going to do about it?" She ran her hand through his hair. "You're not exactly in a position to defend her are you?"

"I don't understand, Lydia. What changed you?"

She put her hands on the arms of the chair and leaned down within an inch of his face. "YOU happened. You cheating bastard."

"That can't be the only thing."

She slapped him and yelled, "Shut the fuck up. You really know how to piss me off."

As she turned to walk away, he felt the ropes on his wrists begin to give. He had been working them for hours. If he could shift his thumb, he might be able to break free.

"I'm going to go set up. I have a few things to do to prepare for the main event."

"Please, Lydia," he begged. "Please don't hurt Cecelia. She's carrying my child."

"Yeah, Brent told me about that. How do you know it's not his?"

"I just know. Please. Let her go."

"I'll consider your request." Lydia stepped outside the office then stuck her head back in. "No."

Brent approached the desk. Cecelia had not given him the room number. When he asked the clerk for her room, the gentleman simply nodded, clicked a few keys on the computer, and then said "Room 1707. Take the elevator to the seventh floor, turn right. It's at the end of the hall."

Brent grinned wickedly as he pushed the button for the seventh floor. The door closed and he rubbed his crotch once more.

"Down boy, you'll get what you want soon enough."

The door opened and Brent stepped into an empty hallway.

"A quickie wouldn't hurt, I suppose. It's better than driving back with a raging hard on. I bet Cecelia will be game."

Brent tapped on the door. "Ce, it's Bri."

When the door opened, Brent saw no one. He eagerly stepped inside expecting Cecelia to bounce out from behind the door wearing nothing but a smile.

Lydia had been pacing for nearly an hour. She ran her hand through her hair. She chewed her lip. Her gut was telling her something was wrong. She dialed Brent's cell. Voice mail answered.

Brighton jumped as Lydia stormed into the office.

"What the fuck are you doing?"

"What the fuck are you doing?" he repeated.

She walked back and forth in front of him. "He should be back by now. It's been hours. How the fuck long does it take to drive to Connecticut and back?"

Brighton's heart sped up. "It depends on the traffic, the time of day."

"Shut the fuck up. I wasn't asking you."

"Then who the hell were you asking? There's no one else here."

Lydia grabbed him by the shoulders and shook him. "Don't you think I know that?"

The chair almost fell over and the force with which she shook him was enough to pop his thumb out. He had been working his hand and finally it was starting to come free.

"Just a bit more," he told himself, keeping his expression blank.

"Maybe he got to Cecelia and decided to leave you stuck with me."

"What? That lying bastard. All men suck." She returned to pacing. "When I get my hands on him, I swear on my mother's grave, he is going to pay. I'll kill him, Cecelia, and then you. Fuck you all."

Brighton got one hand free and loosened the rope a bit further to release his other hand.

"He never loved you."

"Love? What do you know about love?"

When she turned away from him he yanked hard. He was glad she had not rebound his ankles. He lunged for her, catching Lydia by surprise. With his right arm around her neck, he grabbed her left hand and forced it behind her back between them.

Lydia hollered a stream of obscenities as Brighton struggled to get her to the ground.

"I don't want to hurt you Lyd, but if I have to I will."

"Fuck you!"

He fought with every ounce of energy he had. The adrenalin surge was intense yet she was stronger than he remembered. Lydia ran the heel of her shoe down his shin and stomped on his foot. The pain was searing. His vision blurred for a second yet he did not lose the grip he had on her.

Once he had Lydia face down on the concrete floor he placed his knee on the small of her back. With his large left hand he was able to hold both her wrists. She squirmed and eventually bucked him off. Lydia scrambled to her feet and took an offensive stance.

"You cannot win, lover. I'm stronger and more agile than you."

"Perhaps," he snarled.

They stalked each other looking for the right move. Brighton saw the fury in her eyes. She was not the Lydia he knew. Something wild had taken over her. She was a woman possessed by her own demons and willing to destroy anything or anyone that got in her way. He backed toward the door. Escaping the room and locking her in seemed cowardly but what choice did he have? He had no weapons. She knew the surroundings; he did not.

When Brighton neared the door, Lydia charged. At the last possible second he moved aside and she flung herself against the wall screaming more vile language.

"I'm going to fucking rip you limb from limb," she growled through gritted teeth. "Then I am going to cook your organs and have them for dinner."

The thought made him sick yet it also clicked in his mind. His hand landed on her throat. She clawed at his arms. Brighton pulled all the strength he could muster and squeezed. His awareness heightened his desire to survive. When Lydia tried to knee him, he avoided the blow.

Lydia began gasping for air. Her eyes rolled up. The fight seemed to drain from her body. Brighton released her and she fell to the floor in a heap.

"You may have learned to fight but your bitterness and anger got the best of you, Lydia."

She was still alive. He could see her chest rise and fall as he pulled her limp body away from the door. He retrieved the rope and began to tie her hands. Still paying close attention to her, Brighton was able to avoid her leg as she swung it up in an effort to knock him down. Her strength had dissipated.

Brighton bound her wrists. He grabbed the rope that had once kept his ankles tied to the chair. Lydia tried to scoot away from him. She was hissing like a wildcat. There was a small voice in Brighton's head that urged him not to injure her further. He hushed the voice as he seized her ankles. He fastened her ankles together. Brighton stepped back for a moment watching Lydia act like a trapped animal. Then he exited the room and locked the door from the outside.

The main part of the warehouse had some old equipment left behind. He spotted a backpack on a table. He rifled through it and found a cell phone. He dialed Officer Shaw's number. The call went to voice mail. Brighton dialed zero for an operator.

A woman said, "Hello."

"I need to speak with Detective Shaw. It's an emergency." As Brighton spoke, he headed for the nearest exit.

"I'll give you his supervisor."

A second later the captain answered.

"This is Brighton Clay. I have Lydia here in a warehouse. I have her tied up but I am not sure how long the rope will hold out." Brighton spotted a few signs on the buildings nearby and told the detective everything he could see.

"We'll be right there. Stay put."

Brighton disconnected the call and dialed another number.

The hotel room door slammed shut causing Brent to jump and spin around.

"Freeze!" Detective Shaw hollered pointing his gun at Brent's chest.

"What the hell?" Brent questioned with his hands spread out.

"Turn around and put your hands on your head?"

Brent tried to hide his anger over being duped. "What's going on? I just came to pick up my girlfriend."

Johnson stepped out of the bathroom and leaned against the doorjamb. "We know it's you, Brent."

"I'm Brighton. I don't know where Brent is but I'm sure he's with Lydia. The two of them are trying to frame me."

The officer cocked his weapon. "Put. Your. Hands. On. Your. Head."

"I'd do it if I were you, Brent. Shaw has been aching to bring someone in on this case and if it means he has to kill you he will. And," he added pulling out his own weapon, "if he doesn't, I will."

Brent obeyed the officer. "OK, don't shoot."

As Brent was being cuffed he asked, "What am I being arrested for?"

"Kidnapping, attempted kidnapping, six counts of murder, and we are going to add anything else we can think of later."

"I didn't kill anyone. She did it. All I wanted to do was stop the wedding. It was her idea to frame my brother. I had nothing to do with it."

"Yeah right, a woman convinced you to go along with a plan to kill other women and frame your long lost brother," Johnson scoffed. "We'll see what your partner says when she hears you blamed her for everything."

"I swear to you; she's evil. She said she would make me suffer a long painful death if I didn't go along with her."

Detective Shaw interjected, "I'd keep your mouth shut, Clay," then proceeded to recite his rights.

Johnson rode up front in the squad car. He dialed Jason and told him they had taken Brent into custody. He asked if Jason had heard from his friend.

"No I haven't. Do you think Brent will tell you where they have Bri?"

"After he tried to convince us that Lydia was the culprit, he clammed up. He's just sputtering in the back seat. Once we get him in an interrogation room, maybe we can get something out of him. At least we know Cecelia is safe. I'm glad she knew enough to call you before giving any information to Brent."

"She's a smart woman."

"That she is, my friend. I'll call you once we get to the city."

"OK, man and thanks for everything."

"It's not over yet, Jason, not until Lydia is behind bars too."

"Hey, beautiful. How is Connecticut?"

"Brighton? Is that really you?"

"Yes, my love, it is really me. Lydia is tied up. Last I heard Brent was on his way to get you. Too bad you sent him on a wild goose chase."

"Seriously, did he think I was that dumb?"

"When he said he was driving to Connecticut to get you, I was relieved he would be nowhere near where you are. So, um, are you really pregnant?"

"I was just trying to gauge his reaction."

"Oh, thank God," he sighed.

"What exactly do you mean by that?"

"I'm sorry that came out wrong," Brighton admitted running his hand through his hair. "All I meant was I wanted to be with you every step of the way when we have our first baby. I love you, Ce. I didn't want you to go through that alone."

"Good save, Bri," she laughed. "Now, when can I come home?"

"As soon as I know Lydia and Brent are incarcerated. I hear the sirens. I have to go. I'll call you later, OK?"

"You'd better. I love you."

"I love you too, Ce."

Brighton's body ached from being in the same position for too long. It suddenly hit him how exhausted he felt. His foot throbbed. Her nails had left trails of blood on his arms. His head pounded and his vision blurred. He put one hand on the side of the building for support.

Two cruisers arrived and the uniformed men took Lydia out of the warehouse screaming and cursing at Brighton. He wondered what had really happened to her. She had changed so much. He pitied her as they shoved her in the back of the black and white.

"You must be Brighton Clay," one of the officers said.

He nodded.

"We'll have to take you downtown for a statement. Do you need medical attention?"

"I'm fine. I'd like to make sure she is locked up before doing anything else."

The man opened the back door of the second cruiser and Brighton slid in. He was tempted to lie down. He watched as the man rounded the vehicle and got behind the wheel.

"Detective Shaw is on his way back to New York with the perp in custody. He tried to tell Shaw he was you. It is a damn good thing Cecelia knew he wasn't you. She is one smart cookie for giving him a fake location. Where is she anyway?"

"Not in Connecticut," was all Brighton would admit. No one would know. He was going to keep her hideaway a secret just in case. He gazed out of the window. "She is safe; I spoke with her. Once I know Brent has been handled, I'll bring her home."

"Is Jason still in Florida with his wife?"

Brighton looked up into the rear view mirror.

"What's going on?" Molly asked her husband. "You look like a kid with a new toy."

Jason stepped into the bedroom where his wife had spent her time as of late. "Johnson called and said they captured Brent. They are en route to New York."

"That is great news," she said patting a spot on the bed. "Cecelia was smart to call you before revealing her location. Has anyone heard from Brighton?"

Jason sat on the edge of the bed and took his wife's hand. "Not yet but I assume now that they have Brent they will find Brighton soon. Brent tried to claim he was Brighton. When that didn't work, he claimed Lydia was the master mind and committed all the murders."

"Can we go home, Jason? I love my mother but she is getting on my nerves."

"We will have to talk to the doctor first. I'm sure you can't fly. At least if we're driving, I can stop any time."

"It's a long drive to New York; I know. Still, I'd rather be in my own house. I miss our bed."

Jason leaned over and kissed his wife's forehead. "I know darling. Let's see what the doctor says, OK?"

"Can we call him now?"

"It's late, babe. Get some sleep. I'll call him first thing in the morning."

"Lie down with me?" she pleaded.

Jason slipped into bed and pulled his wife close. He wondered where Brighton was. He waited until Molly was asleep and then sneaked out of the room. He went outside and called Cecelia.

"Hi, Jason. How is Molly?"

"She's OK for now. She wants to go home."

"I do too. Brighton said he wanted Brent and Lydia put away before I come home."

"You spoke with him?"

"He called me from another cell. He said she was tied up and the police were on their way. That was hours ago. I'm surprised he hasn't called you."

"He's probably at the precinct giving a statement."

"I hope so. He sounded tired. I'm tempted to head back to New York."

"I think you should stay put. If Molly and I are going home, I'll let you know. I don't want you back in the city alone."

"Brighton will be there."

"Wait until you hear from one of us, OK?"

Cecelia reluctantly agreed.

The following day, Molly's doctor said she could travel if they stopped along the way. He did not want her driving or sitting up for too many hours. Her mother complained about them leaving at first. Molly explained that she wanted her own doctor to deliver the baby. Eventually her mother came around.

Jason planned a route with three overnight stops. The first day of driving home was uncomfortable for Molly. For the morning leg of the trip, she sat in the front seat holding Jason's hand and trying to hide her nervousness. They stopped for a quick lunch and to stretch their legs.

"Why don't you sit in the back for a while?" her husband suggested. "Maybe you can get some sleep."

"All I have done lately is sleep."

"Are you sure this is a good thing? I mean, traveling back to New York."

"I'm fine, Jas. I can do this. I want to be home."

Jason pulled out a blanket and two pillows that his mother-in-law had insisted they take with them. Molly settled into the back. Jason turned on the music player in his cell and put on some soft jazz. Before long, Molly had drifted to sleep.

Jason used his Blue-tooth to make a quick call to Cecelia.

"We're on our way to New York."

"How is Molly?"

"She is sleeping at the moment. We should be home in about three days. If I were alone I would drive right through but she's not supposed to sit up for long."

"I'm worried, Jason. I haven't heard from Brighton."

"I'll call Johnson. Hang tight."

Jason disconnected the call. He was concerned as well. It wasn't like Brighton not to call. Something was definitely wrong.

The detective picked up the call before the second ring. "I'm on it. The NYPD hasn't heard from Brighton. He was supposed to be brought in for a statement but he never made it there. The officer that picked him up was a recent transfer. I don't know how the fuck this happened. Lydia is a psychopath and they brought her to the hospital. They had to sedate her. She was acting like a wild animal. Brent said he knows nothing about who took Brighton and part of me believes him."

"Jesus."

"We'll get him. In the meantime, if you talk to Ce, tell her to stay put."

"I just spoke with her. I'll relay your message. Find him, Johnson. That's what I'm paying you for."

"At this point, Jason, I'd do it for free. I want these people locked away for good. Whoever is helping Lydia is probably just as sick as she is. And I'll be honest with you. I think Brent may have been telling the truth about her being the one who was intent on killing those women. He may have played a role but she was pulling the strings all the time."

"She must have had some sort of psychotic break. She used to be very sweet."

"Not anymore, my friend. Not anymore."

Chapter Fifteen

Molly slept until Jason stopped for the night. They checked in to a hotel, had dinner, and spent the rest of the evening relaxing. He did not tell her about Brighton. He was afraid it would only add to her stress. He toyed with the idea of turning back and keeping her in Florida. He knew she would be pissed if she woke up and they had returned to her parents' house.

"Are you having any contractions?"

"I had a few in the car but they were very mild. I think the bed rest is helping."

"Tomorrow we will be passing through Virginia. Do you want to spend a few days at the beach?"

She smiled remembering their honeymoon. "Although that would be lovely, I really want to be home." She gazed into his eyes for a moment then added, "Are you trying to avoid being in New York?"

"No, why would you ask?" he said turning his face to the television.

"You're hiding something from me. I can always tell. I'm not going to ask what it is because I know you'll give me some line of bull."

He had to smirk at her comment.

"I love you. And I love that you're protecting me and the baby." She rubbed her belly as she spoke. "I'm going to pretend everything is fine and just pray that it is."

He kissed the top of her head. "Get some sleep, my love. We have another day of driving tomorrow."

When Jason had called Cecelia the second time, he told her everything and explained that he had not told his wife. Ce agreed to keep his secret. On the next day of their journey home, Molly asked if Jason had talked to their friends.

"I talked to Ce yesterday."

"I miss talking to her. It seems like months since we chatted."

Jason sighed silently. "Do you want to call her?"

"I'd love to."

"Look in contacts," he said handing his cell to his wife. "She's listed as CD."

Molly flipped through, found the number and pressed send.

"Hi, Jason. Is everything OK with Molly?"

"It's fine, Ce."

"Oh, Molly, how are you?"

"I'm hanging in. I assume Jas told you we were driving back home. The doctor said I couldn't fly. It isn't the best way to go, but soon I'll be sleeping in my own bed."

"Well, tell Jason not to drive too fast. It's better to get there safely."

"He is being very cautious and sticking to the speed limit." Molly lowered her voice and added, "So unlike him."

"Hey, I heard that," he laughed.

"So how are things where you are?"

"The weather is beautiful. Sometime you and I should take a trip out here and leave the boys at home."

"I don't know if I'll be doing that any time soon, Ce. I'll have a little one to think about."

"Hm, true, and Jason will probably use any excuse not to change diapers."

Molly giggled.

"What is she telling you?" Jason wanted to know.

"Nothing dear," Molly replied.

"Other than being stuck in a car, how are you doing really?"

"I'm fine; I told you. It's more annoying than anything else right now. I was a bit scared at first but the contractions have slowed and there is no more spotting. As soon as we hit the New York line I am calling my doctor to make an appointment. I want him to check me out. It's not that I don't trust my mother's doctor, but he handles woman well past their childbearing years."

"I'm glad you are heading home then."

"I can't wait," Molly admitted.

"So, do you know what you're having?"

"We're waiting to find out."

Cecelia nodded not knowing what else to talk about without mentioning Brighton. Molly was the one to break the silence.

"I'm going to let you go Cecelia. I'm sure you have some shopping or reading or something to do. I hope we can get together soon, you know, the four of us. It was so fun to have dinner together."

"I would like that very much, Molly. Take care of that little peanut, OK?"

When Molly got off the phone, she stared out the window. She had heard Jason's second phone call to Cecelia. She knew Brighton was missing even though both Lydia and Brent were in custody. That meant there was at least one other person involved. She sighed heavily. Jason reached over and took her hand in his bringing it to his lips.

"Are you all right, my love?"

"I just wish everyone was home and safe."

"We will be soon, Molly. I promise."

She turned her head toward him. See knew it was a promise he meant, yet he might not be able to keep.

"How are you feeling today?" the psychiatrist asked Lydia.

She squirmed in her bed and mumbled something.

"You have to speak clearly for me to understand."

She would have made an obscene gesture had her hands not been tied down.

"I cannot take the restraints off unless you promise not to injure anyone. You bit the nurse."

She smiled wickedly.

"Lydia, I'm here to help you. Nothing you say to me will go outside these walls."

"Pf-ft."

"OK then, I'll just sit here for the hour. I have nothing to do and I get paid either way."

The doctor watched as Lydia's eyes darted around the room as if she were trying to figure out how to break free. Being in restraints was an issue. If she could just get word to...

"Tell me what you're thinking."

"Do I get to make a phone call?"

"This isn't jail. If you promise to behave, I can have someone hold the telephone for you."

"I'll behave," she replied rolling her eyes. "But keep that male nurse away from me. Men suck and that includes you."

"You've been accused of killing women. You expect me to send a female nurse in here?"

"I haven't killed anyone. I have been in this hell hole for a year."

"No, Lydia, you've been here for less than twenty four hours."

"You're lying. All men lie."

"Who would you call?"

"My husband. He must be worried about me. I'm sure he filed a missing person's report by now even if it only has been a day."

"Who is your husband?"

"For a doctor you sure aren't very smart. It must be listed in my file."

"It says here you are single."

"But... let me call my husband."

"What is his name?"

"Brighton Clay."

A female nurse and a female security guard entered Lydia's room. The psychiatrist remained in his seat. The security guard stood at full attention just inside the door. One of Lydia's wrist restraints was removed and a telephone was placed on a rolling tray beside her bed. The nurse backed away as soon as Lydia's hand was free.

"Is it really necessary to have all these people listening to my private conversation?"

"I'm afraid it is, Lydia. You are under arrest for several felonies."

"Of what am I accused?"

"We discussed this earlier. You killed six women."

"What? Why would I do that?"

"I don't know."

"Well my husband is a defense attorney. He will know what to do."

Lydia picked up the receiver and dialed a number.

"Oh, Brighton, thank God you are there. Please come get me. They have me locked in some psych ward and I am being accused of murder. Please help me."

The person on the other end of the line disconnected the call. She dropped the phone. Crocodile tears immediately burst forth from her eyes, and she sobbed like a child whose favorite toy had been taken away.

"What happened, Lydia?" the psychiatrist asked as he gestured for the phone to be removed.

"He hung up on me. My husband hung up on me. This is a total nightmare."

"Lydia, you are not married. Brighton was your fiancé but you disappeared on your wedding day. That was over a year ago."

"I... but... he..," she stuttered in disbelief. "I remember him coming to see me the morning of the wedding. I was taken aback when I opened the door to see him standing there. It seems like just yesterday. Where have I been?"

"I apologize but my time is almost up. I'm going to order some tests, blood work, CAT scan, etc. I'll be back tomorrow to talk." He stood and approached the bed. Carefully he took her free arm and replaced the restraint.

"Wha... what are you doing?"

"It's for your own safety, Lydia. Someone will be in to attend to your needs."

"You're leaving me? I can't be here alone. I'm frightened." Her voice sounded like young girl who was afraid of the dark.

Was Lydia a gifted actress, confused sociopath, or pure evil?

"You will be fine, Lydia. There is an officer standing outside your door. Get some sleep."

"I have to go," the man told his captive audience.

Gagged and securely fastened to a metal table, the victim could not respond.

"You won't escape this time. You won't ever make it out of this room alive."

Chapter Sixteen

Brighton's eyes flashed open. He turned his head about an inch or two either way. He was fastened tightly to a metal table, stripped down to his boxers and covered with a raggedy blanket. It was not enough to stop the chill from creeping into his bones. From what he could see, he was in a basement. There were no windows in his line of sight. The walls were gray concrete. There was a workbench along one wall with woodworking tools hanging above it.

Brighton had no concept of time. There was a light source somewhere in the room. It seemed man-made, not from outside. It shed no clue as to what time of day it was.

He thought about the officer that picked him up from the warehouse. Brighton had studied him in the rear view mirror until his eyelids had begun to droop. His body was drained from lack of food and restful sleep. His muscles ached from the fight. The next thing he remembered was waking up in that cold room unable to move. There was no way to escape.

On the second day of their trip home, Jason and Molly avoided talking of Brighton. Molly did not want her husband to know she had overheard him talking to Cecelia. He had not wanted to put his wife under any more stress.

Jason waited to make two phone calls until later in the afternoon when he believed his wife was asleep in the back of the car. The first number he dialed was Johnson.

"Anything yet?" he asked.

"Lydia is a psychotic bitch."

"Tell me something I don't know."

Johnson switched the telephone to his other ear and pulled out some notes. "The psychiatrist said Lydia thinks she is married to Brighton."

"What?"

"She actually called someone and told the doctor her husband Brighton hung up on her. I think she dialed a random number. And that transfer cop is still missing. We're sure he was in on the whole thing. Maybe he was in contact with Lydia and when Brighton attempted to escape, he was alerted somehow. He was at Brighton's when the search warrant was executed. I'm thinking he was the one that planted the bugs."

"So she has someone on the force in her pocket. How the hell did that happen? She must have some strange sort of effect on men. Maybe Brent was right and Lydia was pulling the strings all the time."

"I am thinking that more and more. The psych doctor thinks she may be faking the whole psychosis."

"At this point, I would not put it past her." Jason was worried for his friend. "Do we have any leads on where the imposter cop took Brighton?"

"Detective Shaw thinks he can't be far, not with Lydia in the psych ward. If she's calling the shots, then this other guy is probably sitting tight. And she is the one with the grudge as far as we know."

"Yeah, as far as we know," Jason repeated with a roll of his eyes. "I'm thinking this rogue cop is the one who has been planting everything like the scarf and the presents to Ce. There is no way Brent or Lydia could have been doing it, not without someone recognizing them."

"Like you and Brighton recognized them when they were in the freaking room with you?"

Jason gripped the steering wheel tighter. "They were in disguise."

"She was almost his wife and he couldn't tell it was her?"

"He had been seeing her in every woman since she disappeared. When he said Melissa reminded him of Lydia, I figured it was the same old thing. He wanted her to be alive, to be OK."

"I get your point. Still, she is a master mind for sure and she has boys at her beck and call. That is evident." Johnson thought for a moment. "There must be others she has manipulated. Someone at work?"

"I can't think of anyone at the moment, but when I get back to the city I'm going to the office to nose around. I bet somebody there came in contact with Lydia since her disappearance too. I could see her trying to cause trouble for his career."

"Good, snoop around. Let me know if you find anything. I'll review the list of people in and out of Brighton's house: the cable guy, telephone repairman, and any person who has been at his place over the past year."

"Keep me posted on that. I'm going to give Ce a call and update her."

"How is she handling all this?"

"Hard to tell on the phone but I know she is concerned for Bri."

"I'm glad you told her to stay put. There is no telling what is happening with Brighton, and I don't want any more victims of this crew."

Cecelia paced in her room. She was afraid to leave so she ordered room service. When the food came, she told the waiter to leave it outside the door. She ate half the meal for lunch and the other half for dinner. She hadn't seen anyone since she realized Brighton had been taken again. When her cell rang her nerves jumped and her stomach tightened.

"Brighton?"

"I'm sorry, Ce, it's Jason."

She sighed. "I didn't even look at the caller id. I was hoping..."

"I know Ce. We haven't found him yet but Johnson is going through everything again. We're retracing and reinspecting every bit of information we have."

"It may already be too late."

"Don't think that, Cecelia. We will get him back."

"You can't promise me that. No one can."

"OK, Brent, tell us your version of the story one more time. What made you want to frame your brother for murder?"

Detectives Shaw and Brooks were questioning Brent Clay again. Although the attorney advised his client against talking, Brent was singing like birds in spring.

"In the beginning, I wasn't out to frame him for anything. I only wanted him to know what it felt like to lose. He had everything he ever wanted dropped in his lap. I had to struggle at everything: school, work, women. I was nineteen when I went in search of my birth parents. I found my grandparents first. When I called, my grandmother hung up on me. I showed up at their house. She knew almost immediately I wasn't him and told me not to interfere.

"'Your mother is happily married, now. Please do not take that away from her,' she had said. Like she assumed I would ruin my mother's life. All I wanted to do was know why she gave me away. Anyway, I let it go for a year or so. I began looking again and found out about Brighton so I started following him."

Brent ran his hands through his hair and leaned back in the hard wooden chair. "It seems crazy now, although not as crazy as Lydia."

"What made you go after Lydia?"

He sighed. "She was beautiful, intelligent, and a little bit wicked," he smirked. "I caught the two of them fucking in an alley one time. Neither knew I was there but man she howled like a banshee. As I watched them, I knew I had to take her from him. Initially I was going to go to her apartment, pretend to be him and elope with her, tell her I wanted to avoid the ceremony and then later reveal who I was. She figured it out too soon.

"When I told her what happened at the bachelor party she freaked. We took off and over the next couple of days she went from being angry to psycho bitch. She killed her friend Rachel. I had absolutely nothing to do with that. She brought back Rachel's finger and put it on ice. That thing was in our freezer for months."

"OK, so it was her. You've told us that. She cooked up the plan to frame him. There must have been others involved. How did you manage to sneak the scarf into his place and put it with your grandmother's clothes?"

"I didn't do that. I'm not sure who did. Lydia would disappear from time to time. She also had a cell phone that I never touched. She got calls once in a while and she would leave the room. I have no idea who it was."

The two detectives exchanged glances. This was something new.

"You never picked up a call accidentally, maybe when she was in the shower?"

"Never, she would take it into the bathroom with her. I complained about it a few times and she would fire me one of those killer looks."

Brent continued to spill out information and both Shaw and Brooks took notes. In addition, they were recording the entire confession. Brent told them about the other victims. He even revealed how they were chosen and as much as he could remember about their identity.

"So you and she killed seven women together."

"I told you. I had absolutely nothing to do with Rachel. That was all her. As far as the others, I helped her capture them."

Brent's attorney put his hand up and told his client not to admit to anything else.

"Look, I don't want to get blamed for what she did to those women."

"You were there, Brent. In your own words, you helped her capture them. Harmony was raped. You are just as guilty as she is."

"Maybe I am, but I am not as sick as she is. She cut them up, made them swallow bleach. It was..." Brent choked.

"And you stuck with her through it all," Shaw said. "You never once walked away."

"She would have killed me. I was playing her game."

Brooks interrupted, "I'm not buying it. Not one bit."

"That's enough," the attorney said. "He's given you what you asked for. You know how it started. You have the information on the victims. What does he get in return?"

"We'll discuss it with the DA."

Chapter Seventeen

Molly and Jason were on their final leg of the three day drive to New York. She was happy to be close to home and looking forward to sleeping in her own bed. With Brighton still missing, Molly's excitement was fleeting. She wanted him home and safe and she was worried about Cecelia being on her own with no one knowing where she was.

"Are you going to call Ce when we get to the house?"

"You can call her now if you'd like," her husband said.

Molly picked up his cell phone and dialed. Cecelia answered almost immediately.

"Jason?"

"No, it's Molly. We should be at the house in about two hours."

"That's great. How are you feeling?"

"Exhausted and I am ready to stop moving. I feel like I am on the run. How are you?"

"Bored and lonely," Ce admitted. "I want to come home but I'm afraid."

"I know. But I am sure they'll find Brighton soon."

Jason reached over and interlaced his fingers with hers. He breathed a sigh of relief. He hadn't wanted Molly to worry. Now that she knew, part of the weight of the situation lifted.

"Did Jason tell you?"

"I kind of figured it out. He forgets I sleep lightly."

"Has he heard any good news?"

"Hold on; I'll put you on speaker phone." Molly hit the button. "Ce wants to know if you have any good news."

"I wish I did. We have no idea where Bri is. Lydia is still a psychopath. Brent swears Lydia was the one to kill all those women. And we have no idea who else is involved in this whole scheme."

"I'm scared, Jas. I'm here all alone. I don't know who I can trust. I have not left my room in three days."

"Do you want me to send someone to get you?"

"Is there someone you trust?"

"I could have Sal and Dom pick you up?"

"That worked out well last time," she said sarcastically.

"That's all I got," Jason admitted. "I don't trust the damn cops. Johnson is too busy looking for Brighton. And I have to stay with Molly. She can't take anymore travel."

Cecelia sighed. "I'm going home to my parents. I can't stay here anymore. I'll travel under the alias Brighton set up for me. No one will know."

"What if someone is watching your parents' house?" Molly asked.

"They're after Brighton, not me. The only reason I was in danger was because they were framing Brighton. Now that they have him, there is no need to kill innocent women."

"Ce, you're assuming these people are thinking logically. If Lydia was calling the shots, there is no telling what they'll do to get her out."

"But that is exactly my point. Their two main objectives right now are getting her out and keeping Brighton trapped. They won't be following me."

"If you think you can go safely, Cecelia, I won't tell you not to go."

"I'll keep away from anyone who looks suspicious. And I know how to defend myself."

"Be careful, Ce," Molly begged. "I don't want to lose a good friend."

"I'll call you when I get to where I'm going."

Cecelia already had a plan. She had been thinking of leaving. She called the front desk and asked them to call for a car to the airport. She was going to get the first flight out to anywhere then find a way home.

When the Campbells arrived home, Jason told Molly to lie down. He unpacked their bags then made a few phone calls. He checked in with Johnson first. Then he called the office. When he got off the phone, he made an appointment with Molly's doctor, and he peeked in on her.

"I'm going to go into work for a little bit. There are some things I need to check out."

"I'm coming with you."

"You should rest."

"Do you want me to be her all alone?"

"Not really, but..."

"Did you call the doctor and make an appointment?"

"Tomorrow morning at nine," he said.

"OK, then, let's go to the office, pick up something to eat on the way home, and I'll spend the rest of the evening right here."

"It sounds as though you have made up your mind."

"And you know I won't change it so let's go."

He kissed her forehead. "C'mon. I'd like to show off my pregnant wife."

Thirty minutes later, Jason and Molly stepped off the elevator.

"Attorney Campbell, Molly, oh it is so good to see you!" the receptionist beamed as she came out from behind the desk. She put her arms around Molly then pulled back. "You are absolutely glowing, Molly. How are you feeling?"

"I'm happy to be back in New York."

The receptionist looked at Jason. "How is Attorney Clay holding up now that those awful people are in custody?"

"He's as well as can be expected," Jason lied. The fact that Brighton had been re-abducted had not been released to the press.

"Tell him we all miss him."

"I'll do that. I'm going to have Molly lie down in my office. Please don't let anyone disturb her."

"Not many people are here at the moment. I'm leaving in a few minutes myself. It's after five."

"Oh, right, good, then we will have some peace."

Once Molly was settled, Jason sat as his desk and went through his messages. While driving, he had little time to check in so there were a large number of emails and phone messages. One email announcement caught his eye. Molly saw the look on her husband's face.

"What is it?"

"Flatley got partner."

"But I thought you and Brighton were up for that."

"We were."

"Who is this Flatley guy?"

"He came from Dunham and Burke in LA."

"So he just started here?"

"Yes, about two weeks before the first..."

A light went off in Jason's mind. His wheels were turning.

"You don't think?"

He glanced over at her. "It is a distinct possibility."

Jason grabbed the receiver and dialed a number. "Mark, it's Jason."

"You're back in New York? Since when?"

"We just got back this afternoon. How the hell did Flatley get partner?"

"I meant to talk to you before the formal announcement but... with Brighton being accused of murder he was taken off the list. And... well... you haven't been around much. You're tied to his case so..."

"Jesus, man. You could have told me sooner."

"I know; I should have."

"I thought we were closer than that."

"It was a business decision, Jas. Don't take it personally."

"Fuck you. Fuck this whole damn firm. Brighton and I are going to open our own damn firm and you'll see what we can really do."

"I'm going to ignore the fact that you cursed at me because I'm not in the office."

"Fuck you," Jason repeated and hung up the phone.

"Jason..."

"Don't Molly. Brighton and I both deserved that position."

"There was nothing you could have done. I know you, Jason. Friends come first. You had to help Brighton. I bet right now you are thinking that you would not have done anything differently."

"Actually, there is one thing."

Molly sat up and tilted her head.

"I knew about the first killing. Not Rachel but the one we thought was the first. Brighton called me. I told him to keep his mouth shut, that it was just a coincidence that he knew the woman. I knew he didn't do it. But if I could change anything, I would have taken him to the police right then." Jason rubbed the back of his neck. He dropped his head forward and back then turned it side to side. "I should have taken him to the station right then and there. Sure they would have arrested him, interrogated him, but we would have avoided the next murder, and maybe we would have found out about Lydia sooner."

"Stop second guessing yourself, my love. Let's just concentrate on the now. If Flatley did have something to do with this, how do we trap him?"

"*WE* don't do anything. I'm going to call Johnson and let him know. But not here. Who knows if my phone is bugged?"

Molly covered her mouth and glanced around the room. Jason nodded and neither of them spoke another word about their suspicions until they had returned to his car.

"If this Flatley guy was involved in framing Bri, I bet he bugged your office too. Now he knows we know."

"If he's listening at the moment. I need to call Johnson."

Jason called the detective and told him what he suspected.

"I'm on it. And, well, there's some bad news."

Jason barely slept that night. He paced the living room. Cecelia called at six in the morning.

"I'm at my destination," she said. "I don't think anyone followed me and I'm safe."

Jason told her everything that happened the previous night including the news that Johnson had shared.

"They'd better find out where they have Brighton soon," he said. "I'm going to the office today to snoop around some more."

"Be careful, Jason."

"I will. Trust me."

Jason took Molly to the doctor. Luckily, the doctor reported that mother and baby were in good health. He agreed she should remain on bed rest for the remainder of her term. It would only be a few weeks yet the doctor wanted to be cautious.

Molly insisted she go to the office with her husband.

"After that, I promise to stay in bed for the rest of the day, but I don't want to be alone in the house."

The law firm was abuzz with activity. Everyone took a moment to welcome Jason back and greet his wife. Once inside his office, Jason closed the door and pulled the blinds closing out the people walking in the hallway. He told Molly to lie down, and he went to work checking for listening devices. When he found a bug on his desk he pointed it out to his wife. He put a finger to his lips. He thought it would be best to leave it there and report it to the police.

They had been in the office for nearly an hour when there was a light tap on the door. Jason rounded his desk and opened the door only an inch.

"Hey, bud, how are you?"

In a low voice Jason said, "I'm well." He opened the door further and stepped into the hall. "My wife is resting. What can I do for you, Howard?"

Howard remained stoic as he asked Jason how Molly was doing.

"She's fine," Jason replied gesturing down the hall. The two men walked toward an unoccupied conference room.

"How was Florida?"

"Hot."

"I bet. So everything is going well the pregnancy?"

"Yes."

They moved inside the room and Jason closed the door.

"Why all the one word answers?"

"I hear congratulations are in order."

"Yeah, well," Howard Flatley replied rubbing his temple. "I had no idea they would chose me over you or Brighton. You've both been here longer but with everything going on I guess..."

"It was a business decision," Jason said trying to keep from slugging the younger man.

"So are there any leads on Brighton?"

Jason raised an eyebrow. "What do you mean?"

"I heard someone else was arrested so I assumed they have a good case."

"I suppose."

"What are they doing to find Brighton?"

"I'm not at liberty to discuss the case."

"If they have the killers, then there is no case for Brighton, right?"

"There are matters I have to attend to. It's not completely over yet."

Flatley reached for the door. "Let me know if you need any help. Mark turned the Lawson case over to me."

"The last thing I need is help from you, Howard."

"I'm sorry you feel that way, Jason." Flatley dropped his voice and added, "You'll be sorry too."

Chapter Eighteen

Once Cecelia was safely settled at her sister's house, she decided to call Jason. She had lied to him about going to her parents' house. She trusted no one.

"Ce, how are you?"

"I'm well, Jason. Safe and sound. Have you heard anything about Brighton?"

Jason hesitated. "Well, I did find some interesting information."

Cecelia waited. Jason sighed.

"OK, here goes."

He told Cecelia everything that Johnson had said the last time they had spoken. He left the bad news for the very end.

"What do you mean she escaped? I thought she was being watched. How could she get out?"

"She obviously has the connections, probably someone on the force in addition to the fake cop who took Brighton from the warehouse."

"You have to find him, Jason. They're going to kill him."

"Believe me, Ce. I know that. Johnson has people sweeping the city."

"But he could be anywhere."

Brent had given the police a few leads which turned out to be useless. Still, a few patrol cars were sent to check some of the places where Brent knew Lydia had stayed while in New York. Nearly forty eight hours after Lydia's escape, one of the patrols called into the station reporting seeing a person who looked like Lydia getting out of a cab in the an area of low income housing not far from the warehouse where she had been captured. Immediately, Detectives Shaw and Brooks were notified and Shaw called Johnson.

Shaw pulled up next to the patrol car. The officer gestured toward the house.

"She went in the gate and around to the back."

"Are you sure it was Lydia Moliere?"

"Absolutely sure, Sir," the young officer replied.

Two more patrol cars arrived. Detective Shaw exited his car and gave all of the others directions.

"They have at least one hostage. Let's make sure no one gets away this time."

Johnson stayed in front of the house. He waited as the seven policemen surrounded the building. Two broke down the front door while two entered through a side door. The others went behind the house.

Several minutes passed and Johnson remained at attention in case anyone tried to exit the dwelling. He was itching to get inside yet he let the police do their job. People began to step outside their homes and congregate in the street. More squad cars, paramedics, and an ambulance arrived and the police held back the crowd asking them to return to their homes. The medics remained in their vehicles.

When several gunshots rang out, the onlookers scurried in various directions, some covering their heads. Johnson did not flinch. He was sure by the sound that the shots were deep inside the dwelling. An eerie quiet spread through the air as if everyone held their breath. Time seemed to stand still. The silence was broken by a blood curdling scream and several more guns shots.

Two officers emerged from the side door supporting a weakened Brighton between them. One of the men had given Brighton his jacket. The medics grabbed their gear and hooped out of their vehicle. One of the ambulance personnel pulled out the gurney.

Shaw and Brooks exited the building next with another man in custody. Johnson wondered where Lydia was until he heard Shaw tell someone to call for the coroner.

"She's dead?"

"No, one of her other minions is though," Shaw replied. Then he looked at one of the paramedics and said, "There's one still alive in there but take care of Brighton first."

The two medics glanced at each other. Since there were two more medical personnel, the paramedics ignored Shaw and headed for the side entrance of the house.

"She's not worth it," Shaw called after them.

Brighton lifted his head. "How badly is she hurt?"

"She'll live to stand trial; I'm sure."

When his eyes finally fluttered open the first vision he saw was Cecelia. She smiled and caressed his cheek.

"Well hello there," she whispered. "How are you feeling?"

"Better now that I see you. How long have I been out?"

"Over twelve hours," she told him.

"Lydia?"

"She's still in surgery last I heard."

"Brent?"

"He's still locked up."

"God you look amazing."

"You look like hell," she joked.

"When can you take me home?"

"The doctor said as soon as you are up and have something to eat."

"Screw the food." Brighton groaned as he sat up. "I want to be home in my own bed next to my beautiful soon to be wife."

"What?"

"Marry me."

"Brighton, you have just been through an incredible ordeal. You don't know what you're saying."

He took her hands in his. "I know exactly what I am saying, Ce. I have been away from you for too long. All I could think about was what I would do without you. I never want to think that way again. I want you by my side every morning when I wake up and every night when I go to sleep."

Tears formed in her eyes. "I love you, Brighton."

"I love you too, Ce. What do you say? Will you marry me?"

"Yes, with all my heart, yes."

The first thing Brighton did when he arrived home was call his grandmother. He had spoken with her at the hospital yet only briefly. He and Cecelia were sitting on the sofa when he dialed Mrs. Clay's number.

"Hey, Gran, I'm home."

"Oh, I am so glad dear. How are you feeling?"

"Much better now. I'm sitting here with my fiancée."

"What? You're getting married? Oh, I am so happy for you. When do I get to meet her?"

"Do you want to talk to her now?"

Cecelia shook her head with widened eyes.

"Sure," Mrs. Clay replied.

Brighton covered the mouth piece. "It's OK, Ce. Just say hello."

She swallowed hard as she took the receiver from his hand. "Hello Mrs. Clay."

"Hello, Dear. It's a pleasure to speak with you."

"It's nice to talk to you as well."

"Brighton speaks very highly of you. He told me you are studying to be a physician's assistant."

"Yes, I am." Cecelia glanced at Brighton who wore a broad grin.

Ce and Mrs. Clay talked for several minutes. Then she gave the phone back to Bri. He said his good bye and promised to call and even visit more often. As he placed the receiver down, Cecelia asked what he wanted to do.

"Fuck my fiancée."

Ce fanned herself. "Oh my. Are you sure you're up for that?"

Brighton took her hand and pressed it into his crotch. "What do you think?"

"Mm, should we go upstairs?" she asked moving off the sofa.

Brighton pulled her into his lap. "I can't wait that long."

Their lips crashed together. Hands began tugging at clothes. Yet a few minutes later, they were interrupted by the doorbell.

"Fuck."

"Hold that thought," she said as she pulled away. "Get rid of whoever it is."

Brighton zipped up his jeans as he approached the door grumbling. He threw the door opened ready to argue with whoever was on the other side.

"Um, it looks like we're interrupting something," Jason said with a smirk, holding a six pack in one hand and a pizza in the other. "But Molly wanted to see you."

Jason's wife looked down and stepped back. "I'm sorry Brighton; we can come back."

"Don't be ridiculous. Come in." Brighton grabbed the beer from his friend then stepped back to let the visitors enter.

Cecelia heard the voices and straightened her clothes. Although she wanted nothing more than to take Brighton upstairs and show him all she had missed while being away, she knew he could not turn down his friends.

"Ce is in the living room. You might want to give her a sec."

"I'm fine, Bri," Cecelia said stepping into the foyer. "I thought you were on bed rest, Molly."

"I needed to see for myself that Brighton was alive and well. I insisted Jason bring me over, and of course we had to bring food."

Cecelia slipped her arm into Molly's and the two went into the living room.

"Sorry to... man, go put a shirt on or something," Jason said with a mix of humor and annoyance.

"Hey, it's my house. You don't like what you see... leave."

"Listen, when you're all settled and ready to go back to work, we need to have a long chat."

Brighton took the pizza from Jason. "I'm not sure I want to go back to the firm."

"Good, we're on the same page." Jason smacked his friend on this shoulder.

"I haven't talked to Ce, yet but I'm thinking of moving out of the city. There are too many memories here. Too much shit has happened. I want to start fresh."

"Let's talk about this later. For now, we'll just enjoy some food and relax. Tomorrow is another day."

"You got that right. And thanks, Jason. For everything you did. Without you, I..."

"Aw, shut the hell up. Go get some plates."

"I thought they would never leave," Brighton groused as he returned to the living room. To his surprise, Cecelia was not there. He noticed one pump a few steps away from the sofa. The second shoe was closer to the stairs. A smile spread on his lips as he followed the trail Ce had left for him. Halfway up the stairs, he picked up her blouse and from the very top step he retrieved her bra.

He was about to reprimand her for haphazardly tossing her apparel around but the sight of her naked form sprawled across his bed halted his words. She noticed the dumbstruck look on his face and raised an eyebrow at him.

"What was it you wanted to do to me before we were so rudely interrupted?"

Within seconds his lips were on hers as he frantically removed his jeans. The anticipation was almost too much to bear. Too many days had passed. Too much time had been wasted. He needed her more than anything he had ever wanted before. Yet just as he was about to enter her he pulled back panting.

"I love you, Ce." He took a quick breath and added, "I want to make love to you, but I also want to fuck you so hard you won't be able to stand."

"There is nothing stopping you from doing both."

"Mm, I think slow and easy first."

He brushed his lips against her nipple causing her to shiver. He circled it with the tip of his tongue then gently suckled until the flesh firmed in his mouth. Cecelia's fingers tangled in his hair.

"I missed you so much," she purred.

His left hand cupped her right breast. He rolled her nipple between his thumb and forefinger. He took his time as he traveled south using every ounce of self-control. His body ached for her. His groin was on fire. He felt dizzy from her scent as he neared her center.

Brighton ran his tongue up her slit then blew on her damp flesh. She trembled again. Her desire was as overwhelming as his. Their eyes locked as he began to savor her sweet elixir. She whimpered and bit her lip. Each time she neared climax, he would retreat for a moment leaving her walls throbbing with need.

"Brighton, please..."

"Please what, my love?"

"Now. Inside. Me."

"Patience, darling. If I can wait, so can you."

"Mgh, you love teasing me."

"Oh yeah."

He latched onto her tender swollen bud and she cried out, "Oh, oh God, Bri."

This time, he did not stop. He sucked hard and long until she was writhing and making those sweet sounds of pleasure.

When he felt she was at the peak of ecstasy, Brighton moved over her. He took both her wrists in one hand and pinned her arms over her head. He thrust into her fast and hard then froze, completely filling her as they rode out her wave together.

When her body began to relax, Brighton started to move. His hips rocked gently at first. Then his movements quickened becoming near frantic as he searched for his own release. He had held it for so long, his climax nearly eluded him.

Then it hit like a tidal wave of pleasure. The power of his orgasm stole his breath. He could not form words, not even a thought. His head fell back. His lips parted. And a long guttural moan escaped his throat.

Moments later, he collapsed on to her breathing heavily. Several minutes passed before either could utter a word.

A few hours later, Ce woke up completely entangled in his limbs. She smiled. There was nowhere she would rather be. His breathing suggested he was asleep. She tried not to move yet her body ached. Before long, she could not resist the need to stretch. He grunted and tightened the hold he had on her.

"Bri?"

She waited a few more minutes and then wiggled free.

"Huh?"

"You were practically suffocating me, Bri."

"I was? I'm sorry," he mumbled rolling onto his back. "I... I must have been dreaming."

Cecelia turned on her side to face him and propped her head on her elbow. "Are you all right?"

He blinked, pushing back the images of his dream. "I will be."

She placed a hand on his abdomen and scooted closer. "Can I do something to make you feel better?"

"I'm sure you can think of something."

When the sun came up the following morning, Brighton suggested they go out and have some fun. He did not want to go to the office nor did he have any desire to stay in a place where someone had been monitoring his every move. He had been cooped up and tied down for way too long.

They strolled down Fifth Avenue and stopped in a few stores. Brighton spoiled Cecelia and bought her some new clothes, shoes, and some accessories. Several times she insisted he did not need to buy her anything.

"Get used to it," he told her. "You're going to be my wife soon and I plan on giving you the world."

"All I need is you."

"You have me." He pulled her into his arms and whispered, "Every. Inch. Of. Me."

"Save that thought for when we're alone."

Brighton looked around the boutique. "Go see if anyone is in the dressing room."

Just after one, they visited a local bistro and ordered some food to go. They enjoyed a picnic lunch on a bench in Central Park. After they ate, Cecelia suggested they return to her apartment.

"Maybe you could stay at my place."

He stopped walking for a second and looked at her. "You're asking me to move in with you?"

"Why are you surprised?"

He grinned and squeezed her hand. "Let's stop by my place so I can pack a few things."

Brighton packed two suitcases and a garment bag while Cecelia put all his toiletries in a small duffel. Brighton also took his recently returned laptop and briefcase. By three thirty, they were at Cecelia's apartment. All of his clothes had been put away and his personal items had found their place.

He sat on the edge of her bed. Ce put her hands on his shoulders and sat astride him. "I don't have much food in the fridge. Do you want to go grocery shopping or have something delivered?"

"Let's get Chinese and eat naked on the bed. We'll go grocery shopping in the morning."

"I like the way you think."

"Then I have something else I want to discuss."

"What's that?"

"I have to talk to Jason before I make any plans, but I am not going back to the firm. I think we're going to start our own business. The thing is; I don't think I want to stay in the city. I know you have school and your job but..."

Cecelia put a finger to his lips. "First of all, screw the job. I can get a job anywhere. As far as school, I'll be done in December. That's only a couple of months. Where were you thinking of moving?"

"I have the house on Long Island. It's a better place to raise a family. I'm sure Molly would like to move to a quiet neighborhood."

"That sounds lovely," she said caressing his cheek.

Brighton tucked a lock of her hair behind her ear. "So when do you want to get hitched?"

"I'm ready when you are."

"Doesn't it take like a year to plan a proper wedding?"

"I don't need a big expensive wedding. I would be happy spending a weekend in Vegas and going to one of those cheesy little chapels."

A look of surprise swept over his features. "What about your family? Wouldn't they want to be there?"

"Probably but they'll get over it. And we can always have a big get together with all our friends and family later."

"Hm. That might work."

Cecelia placed a soft kiss on his lips. "So I finish school. We fly to Vegas at the end of December and get married. Then we can have a huge party at your house on Long Island and invite our families. And you and Jason can scope out a location for your new firm."

"That sounds like a plan. But you missed something."

"What?" she asked with a questioning look.

"When do we start planning our family?"

Her left brow popped up. "Now?"

He answered her with a kiss.

Chapter Nineteen

One of the doctors at the hospital had given Brighton the phone number to a psychiatrist. The doctor said he may experience symptoms of post-traumatic stress due to being kidnapped and held hostage. For a few days Brighton considered calling. He was restless and often times would wake in the middle of the night and pace.

"Maybe you should go see someone. It couldn't hurt."

The following day he called and made an appointment.

Brighton turned in his resignation effective the end of the year. He decided he could use the time to clean up any lose ends and keep an eye on Flatley. In the back of Brighton's mind he was sure the younger attorney was involved in framing him.

Now that he was staying with Cecelia, Brighton moved most of his personal items into her apartment. Some of the furniture he had sent to his house on the island. Other items he donated or sold. It was bittersweet closing the door on the brownstone for the last time. He had worked had to make it his own. He had to admit he felt bad for Lydia. He had loved her at one point. That had not changed. It was painful to think she had been so disturbed by his actions.

One day on his lunch break, Brighton made a trip to a store downtown. When he returned to the office, he made reservations at one of Cecelia's favorite restaurants. Then he called the florist. Before leaving work, he called his fiancée.

"Put on that royal blue dress and silver heels. I'm taking you out to dinner."

"What's the occasion?"

"I love you."

"Seems like a good enough reason. Do I have time for a quick shower?"

"Absolutely."

She was ready when he came home with a dozen long stem roses.

"They are lovely, Brighton. Thank you. Let's me put them in water before we go." She pecked him on the cheek and went into the kitchen for a vase.

At the restaurant, they had to wait a few minutes for their table. Brighton led his fiancée into the lounge and they each enjoyed a glass of wine. A short while later they were escorted to a private table away from the busiest part of the dining area. The wine steward approached and Brighton ordered a bottle of champagne. The steward gave a polite nod and back away.

"What is going on?"

He smirked. "Why are you so suspicious?"

"Roses? Dinner at my favorite spot? The champagne? And that look in your eye? You are definitely up to something."

He leaned a little closer and said, "I am definitely up."

She kicked off a shoe and slid her toes up his legs until they settled at his groin.

"Hm, well, that is nothing new. But you're spoiling me and there must be a reason."

"I love you. I don't need any other reason."

"Fine," she pouted removing her foot. "Don't tell me. Just don't expect to get any tonight."

"Oh, you're going to withhold sex? Won't that hurt you as much as it pains me?"

"Damn it."

He leaned back casually and let his eyes take her in. "You're beautiful."

The wine steward returned, popped the cork on the bottle of champagne, filled their glasses and disappeared.

Brighton lifted his glass. "To us."

She tapped her glass to his and took a sip.

"So how was your day?"

"Uneventful. How was yours?"

"Productive."

The waiter came and Brighton ordered one of Cecelia's most loved dishes and a steak for himself.

"I love the way that dress brings out the color of your eyes."

"You're making me nervous."

"Am I?" he grinned. "Moi?"

"Yes, you."

He glanced around the restaurant. It was crowded yet the other diners seemed to be in their own little world. He stood, moved closer to his fiancée, and dropped to one knee as he removed a small black velvet box from his jacket pocket.

"I know I already asked and that you said yes but I wanted to do this right. I love you Cecelia. You are my reason for..." He closed his eyes and paused a moment. He opened his eyes and gazed into hers. "I knew you were something special the first time I saw you. With everything else going on, I was afraid to get close to you. I could not get you off my mind. We were meant to be together. Ms. Cecelia Demure, will you marry me?"

He flipped open the Tiffany box with his eyes still fixed on hers. He removed the ring from the box and took her hand in his. A two carat round diamond flanked by two perfectly colored round sapphires were set in platinum. The simple setting was perfect to set off the sparkle in the gems.

"Oh, Brighton. It's beautiful."

"Not nearly as beautiful as you, my love."

"I love you. And my answer has not and will not every change. Yes, I will be your wife." She leaned down and kissed him. Then in his ear she purred, "Are you sure you want to have dinner or would you rather go home and take this dress off of me slowly?"

"Oh, we are having dinner, my darling. You will need all your strength tonight. We're not going to be getting much sleep."

Molly and Cecelia were having lunch in a small cafe in little Italy. They had spent the morning walking and window shopping.

"That ring is absolutely stunning."

"Thank you, Molly. I have to say I was actually surprised he got down on his knee. I mean; he'd already asked me. I figured we might go pick out my ring together. Brighton just called me from work and said he was taking me out to dinner."

"Jason made me a picnic lunch and proposed to me in Central Park Zoo. It was totally unexpected."

"That's sweet."

Molly took a long drink of water. "I think after we eat I should go home and lie down. I feel like my ankles are starting to swell."

"I'm sorry; we should have stopped sooner."

"It's OK. The doctor said since I was no longer spotting I should get up more. I guess I overdid. Are you still talking about getting married in Vegas?"

"I think so. I don't want a big wedding. To me it is a waste of money. The ceremony really doesn't matter so much. In some ways, I feel like we're already married."

"My mother would have killed me if I didn't have a huge wedding with all her friends. I would have been happy going to a JP. My parents paid for everything so I didn't complain."

"Once we move to the island, we'll have everyone over for a party."

"Have you seen the house?"

Cecelia shook her head. "Have you?"

"It's beautiful. It has five bedrooms, two and a half baths, a huge yard, and a double garage. The back half of the yard is fenced. Brighton always said when he got married he was going to move there to raise his family and he was going to get a couple of dogs."

"Hm, I thought moving to the island was something he had recently decided."

"Oh no, he had always planned to move out of the city. Although I think he was going to work at the firm and spend the weekends on Long Island. He was in line for partner. I don't think he would have given that up if things had worked out differently."

"So Lydia had been to the house?"

"I think so."

"Did he have it built with her in mind?"

"Don't start second guessing things. Brighton loves you, maybe even more than he loved Lydia. To be honest, there was always something strange about her. In public she was sweet as cherry pie. There were times when she talked to me and no one else was around that I thought maybe she was a little nuts. Now I know I was right."

Cecelia tilted her head.

"It wasn't anything specific, not that I remember," Molly continued. "She had an odd way of looking at life. She was suspicious of others, most especially Brighton." Molly shrugged. "Anyway, that's all over with now."

Cecelia put her fork down. "Let's get you home so you can put your feet up. You look like you could use a rest."

"OK. It was nice getting out of the house for a while without Jason fawning all over me. Thanks, Ce."

A few days later, Brighton arrived home before Cecelia. He found a note on the kitchen counter.

"There's a casserole in the oven and a salad in the fridge. Please turn the oven off at 5:45. You can eat without me. I should be home by six thirty. Love, C."

He checked the clock then flipped off the oven. Brighton went to the bedroom and stripped then headed for the shower. It had been a long frustrating day. He ran into Flatley several times. And later in the afternoon, one of the older partners had stopped by Brighton's office.

"We're very sorry to lose you Brighton. You were a shining star here."

"Then why was I passed over for partner?"

"If you were on the committee, would you have made someone like you partner with everything that was happening?"

"Why not choose Jason then? I would rather he have it then some newbie."

"Jason is an excellent attorney. He doesn't bring in the new business like you do. People like him well enough but you are like a magnet."

"Then maybe you could have waited until all this was resolved. Why promote some... You know what? It doesn't matter at this point." He stood and rounded his desk. He extended his hand. "It was a pleasure doing business with you, Brad. I wish you and the firm continued success."

The older man got to his feet and firmly gripped Brighton's hand. "If you need anything at all, please do not hesitate to call. I'd be happy to supply references for you."

"Thank you, Brad. That means a lot to me."

When Brad exited the office, Brighton briefly questioned his decision to leave. From the hall, he heard Flatley's distinctive laugh and all reluctance evaporated.

"There is no way I would stay here with that moron as partner," he thought.

After his shower, he grabbed a long neck out of the refrigerator and plopped on the sofa. He turned on the news. A snow storm was on its way due to arrive on Thanksgiving. The weatherman threatened five to ten inches in the city. Brighton closed his eyes for a moment. His head leaned back and the bottle in his hand nearly full as his body relaxed. A chill swept over him.

"Did you enjoy watching?" a voice asked. "Is it as much of a rush for you as it is for me?"

His hands felt warm and sticky.

"Brighton? Brighton, wake up?"

He sat straight up and stared at Cecelia. He recognized his name but her other words were like a foreign language.

"Are you all right?" she knelt before him. "Brighton, it's me, Cecelia. You were having a bad dream."

"What? I..."

"Brighton?"

He blinked several times. Then he inhaled deeply. "I guess I dozed off. What time is it?"

"Six thirty. I just got home." She put a hand to his cheek. "Do you want to tell me about it?"

"No, I do not," he said. He put a hand over hers and closed his eyes again. A moment later he looked at her and smiled. "I'm glad you're home. Let's eat then we can turn in."

Chapter Twenty

Detectives Shaw and Brooks were in an interrogation room with Brent Clay. There were discrepancies in his story with regard to the victims.

"OK Brent, we have identified five of the seven fingers. Who are the others?"

"I don't know their names. I told you. Sometimes she picked random women."

"Were you following Brighton the night Harmony Blake was murdered?"

"Who is Harmony Blake?"

"She was the first body we found, the actress."

"I don't know who you're talking about."

Detective Shaw pushed a head shot of Harmony across the wooden table.

"I've never seen her before. Maybe Lydia had someone else kill her."

"And you think we believe that?" Brooks spat.

"I have been honest with you about all the other women. I told you there were six, not counting Rachel. Now you bring this woman in? Why would I tell you we killed six women and lie about the identity of one?"

The two police men glanced at each other.

"Are you sure you haven't seen this woman before?" Shaw asked.

"I swear to you on my mother's grave."

After they had finished questioning Brent, Shaw and Brooks sat at their desks talking.

"No matter how many times he tells this story it does not make any sense unless Lydia had someone else help in her killing spree. Remember Brent saying Lydia would talk to someone else on the phone and he never knew who it was? That has to be the other culprit."

"Yeah, but how do we find out who that was? Lydia ain't talking."

Shaw shook his head. "I have no idea. The techs who examined the bodies found no DNA, no stray threads or hair, and no fingerprints. The bleach washed away evidence. We're still missing bodies. Lydia was damn good at covering her tracks."

"If Brent isn't lying, and there were seven women not counting Harmony, where is the other body? And why don't we have a finger?"

"Let's map out where all the women were picked up and see if we can find a pattern. And we should check for any new missing person's reports. Who knows? Maybe the other woman was from out of town and her family didn't realize she was missing."

Brighton had seen the psychiatrist a couple of times. He had received a prescription, filled it, and begun taking the medication. The doctor said it could take two weeks or maybe more for the pills to take full effect. It had only been nine days but he noticed a difference in his sleep patterns. He fell asleep faster and was not as restless. He still mumbled to himself. It came out like gibberish although once in a while he uttered a familiar name.

One Saturday morning, Cecelia woke up to the sound of the shower being turned on. She peered at the clock. She tossed the covers aside and made her way to the bathroom.

"Bri?"

"I'm sorry; did I wake you?"

"I don't know, maybe. Are you OK?"

He stuck his head out of the shower and smiled at her. "I'm better now that I see you. Do you want to join me?"

"I thought you'd never ask."

Cecelia pulled her nightie over her head and tossed it aside. Brighton stepped back allowed her to enter the stall.

"I was thinking," he said as he put his hands on her waist and pulled her into him. "Do you want to take a ride today?"

"You can ride me all day."

He nipped at her neck. "I would love to do that but what I meant was would you like to see the house in Long Island?"

Her head fell back in response to his lips on her flesh. "Uh, yes, that sounds... mm."

His right hand gently massaged her breast as the other slid down her side, over her hip, and to her backside. He turned their bodies and pressed her against the side wall of the shower. He lifted one leg to his hip. Cecelia grabbed his shoulders and wrapped her other leg around his waist. She gasped as he thrust into her.

"I love you," he said accenting each word with a deep hard penetration.

Brighton leaned his forehead against hers. His movements were frantic as if this would be the last time he would make love to her. Cecelia's body barely had time to react before he felt his climax explode inside her. His body shivered.

"Um, I'm sorry. I..."

"It's OK, Bri."

"You didn't..."

"No, but it's OK."

"Give me a few minutes to recover and then I'll make you come like there's no tomorrow."

Brighton's house was a sprawling ranch on more than two acres located on a quiet cul-de-sac. There was an eat-in kitchen with marble tiled floors, stainless appliances, and white wood cabinets decorated with ornate handles. The other rooms had had light hardwood floors. In the back yard there was a stone patio, fire-pit, and a huge resort-like salt water pool. The last room he showed to his fiancée was the luxurious master suite which had an attached sitting room and beautiful en suite bath.

"Oh Bri, I have no words. This place is beyond beautiful."

"I thought you might like it." He gestured to the California king sized bed. "Care to christen the place?"

She told herself not to think too much. "Every room."

"Should we begin here?" he asked, taking her hands in his and leading her to the bed. His legs came in contact with the edge of the mattress.

"I think we should talk."

He put a hand to her cheek. "What's wrong?"

"Did you? I mean, of course you did but..."

With a tilt of his head he said, "You're wondering about Lydia."

She nodded.

"Sit." She obeyed. "Yes, Lydia and I spent time here. I bought the house with her in mind. We were going to spend the weekends here and live in the city during the week. We decorated the place together. If you're not comfortable here, we can sell if and find another house." He tried to make light of the situation but adding, "Or we could tent the house and have it bombed for bugs."

Cecelia had to laugh. "It is a lovely house. I doubt you could find another like it."

"We could sell all the furniture, paint, re-tile, and make it all new inside."

"That would cost a lot of money."

"I'm selling the brownstone and with all the work I did on it, I should turn a nice profit. And in the meantime, I can get a home equity line of credit on this place to get started with making it our home. We could use that money to redesign this place."

"It is a nice neighborhood. I like that it's at the end of the street."

"So we're good then?"

"Um, I hate to ask this but did you and she..?" Cecelia glanced back at the bed.

"We never did it in the loft."

Cecelia stood and in a playful tone said, "Last one there has to be on the bottom," then she took off.

Laughing, he ran after her.

Later Saturday afternoon, Brighton and Cecelia picked up an air mattress, sheets, blankets, and pillows. They spent the night at the house watching the living room television from the loft and making love. On Sunday they looked at new furniture and stopped at the hardware store to check out paint samples.

Brighton made dinner on Sunday. He noticed she was a bit distracted and poking at her food.

"You don't like my cooking?"

"It's fine. I guess I have a lot on my mind."

"Are you sure you don't want to sell the house and pick out a place together?"

"Actually, I was thinking about something else."

Brighton put his fork down and said, "Tell me what's troubling you."

"Well, it's not really troubling. It's two things really. I love the yard. I was thinking it would be a great place to get married. But we'd have to wait at least until spring. I really want my family there. When we talked about going to Vegas I was all for it, but now I'm not so sure. And I didn't think you'd want to wait."

He reached over and took her hand. "We can get married whenever or however you want. There's no rush. I don't want to pressure you."

"Which brings up my next point. If we're waiting to get married, I think we should hold off on the baby making as well."

"That's probably for the best," he admitted. Lately, he had also been thinking they should wait to have children.

"So you're all right with waiting on the wedding and having children?"

"Absolutely, I told you, no rush."

She smiled at him. "I'm glad we talked. I was worried you might be upset putting things off."

"I feel like we're married already. Getting a legal document is just a formality."

"I feel the same way."

Brighton and Cecelia stayed at the house that night and headed home early Monday morning.

One Saturday morning, Cecelia was standing in front of the full length mirror in the bedroom. She was thinking about her parents. With the holidays approaching, she asked Brighton if he would go with her to upstate New York to her family's home for Christmas.

"I was hoping we could go to Palm Springs," he said wrapping his arms around her waist from behind. He drew his lips along her shoulder.

She looked at his reflection. "Oh."

"I haven't bought the tickets yet. Why don't we do your family for Christmas and fly to Palm Springs for New Year's to see my grandparents?"

She turned around and said, "That sounds like a nice compromise. I'll call my mom and let her know we're coming."

"Are you sure you want them to meet me?"

"We're getting married. Of course I want my parents to meet you."

"Is there anything I need to know?"

She shook her head. "They're normal everyday people. And they are going to love you. Trust me."

"I do, with my life."

December twenty second, they were on their way to North Tonawanda. Cecelia's parents lived so close to Niagara Falls that they visited the tourist trap often. It was a seven hour ride from New York City if you obeyed the speed limit. Brighton tended to go a bit faster, especially in his Mercedes. As he drove he let his hand wander up and down his fiancée's thigh. He asked about her family and she told him what life had been like growing up and how she and her sister had been in competition for everything.

"My sister was the pretty one. I was better in school."

"Wait, she is prettier than you? That cannot possibly be."

"I was an awkward teen. Luckily the braces were removed, my skin cleared up, and I got contacts. She had the perfect complexion, straight teeth, and 20/20 vision."

"But she's fat and ugly now though."

"I wish. She never spent Valentine's Day alone and her phone rang constantly. On the other hand, she rarely went out with the same guy more than a few times until recently."

Brighton shifted in his seat. His fingers traveled a little further up her skirt. She pushed his hand away.

"Eyes on the road, hands on the wheel."

"Having my hand on your thigh never bothered you before."

"You never drove quite this fast."

"We're on the highway," he explained slightly easing up on the accelerator. The gauge dropped a few miles per hour but not enough to be noticeable. He reached over once more and pushed up the hem of her skirt.

"If you're really that desirous, perhaps we should pull over."

"My thoughts exactly," he smirked. He checked the rear and side view mirrors and moved from the fast lane, to the middle, then to the right.

"You can't wait a couple of hours?" she asked.

"In a couple of hours we'll be at your parents' home. What do you think they'd say if we walked into their house and I hiked up your skirt and took you right there in the doorway?"

"I swear you have the hormones of a sixteen year old boy," Cecelia remarked yet she could not prevent her lips from curling up. "I ought to take you over my knee."

"Wow, kinky... I like that."

"I'm sure you do."

Brighton turned off at the next exit. He pulled into the first parking lot he saw.

"You're not seriously thinking we're going to do it in the car out in broad daylight?"

"Aw, c'mon. Where's your sense of adventure?"

He drove to the far side of the lot which was lined with trees.

"I'm not so sure about this."

"You don't even have to get undressed. Just tug up your skirt."

"What? And climb on top? What if someone sees us?"

He threw the car in park and raised an eyebrow at her. "We can go in the back."

She shook her head. Brighton unzipped his slacks. "You know you want to touch him," he said waving his length at her. She hesitated.

"Fine, I'll take care of him myself."

He slowly stroked his erection. "You know this would feel so much better if it was your hand."

Cecelia looked out the side window. "I am not watching you play with yourself."

"Then why don't you play with me. Please," he whined.

"Damn it," she muttered through a grin. "If we get caught, I am leaving you right here and now." Although her tone was slightly aggravated, her eyes were shimmering. "You are such a horn-dog."

"You love me this way."

Brighton pushed the seat back as Cecelia went down on him. He moaned feeling the warmth of her mouth. Brighton stroked her hair.

"That's it. Mm, I love you.'"

Brighton felt the blood rush to his head. He felt mentally hazy. Cecelia knew exactly how to manipulate and tease him. Within minutes he was panting, his hips thrusting up as his body begged for released. A slow burn spread through his groin.

Brighton grabbed the back of her head and forced it down as he let out a stream of obscenities. His powerful released wracked his entire being blocking out all sense of time and place.

Nearly a minute passed and he did not loosen the hold he had on her. Cecelia could barely breathe as she tried to escape his grasp. With one hand on the back of her neck and the other atop her head, he held her in position so tightly fear welled in her heart. Her whimpers and thrashing arms brought him back to reality and he eventually let go.

She jumped away from him so that her back hit the passenger door with a thud.

"What the hell, Brighton?"

"Oh God, Ce, I'm sorry. It just felt so good. I guess I got carried away."

She wiped her mouth with the palm of her hand. "Carried away?" she repeated. "Shit, you almost choked me to death."

He said "I'm sorry," several more times as he took her hands in his. "It won't happen again; I promise."

"I need to get away from you for a minute," she told him as she smoothed her hair and exited the car.

Brighton felt sick. An intense nausea filled his stomach. He watched as she paced back and forth in front of the car for nearly ten minutes. Finally she paused and looked at him, wondering what had happened to him and why had he changed.

What if he got worse? What if he really hurts me next time?

She had no idea what he had been through. He never talked about it. As he peered through the windshield at her, there was a helpless look in his eyes. He mouthed, "I'm sorry."

She returned to the car. "Please don't take this the wrong way. I'm not trying to nag or act like your mother but... Have you been taking the medication the doctor prescribed for you?"

"I, um, missed a couple of days," he muttered sheepishly. "I promise to be more diligent at taking them. I love you. I don't want to lose you."

Cecelia took his hand in hers. "Look at me," she insisted. She waited until his gaze met hers before continuing. "I love you too. Whatever is bothering you, we will work through it. However, I will not be manipulated or abused..."

His eyes widened and his lips parted to object. His words were stopped by a finger to his mouth.

"Don't. Do not try to make light of what just happened. You held me down. I was choking. It continued longer than an accident, Brighton. There was no mistaking what you did. You hurt me. It was intentional."

A single tear streamed down his face. In a child-like voice he said he was sorry and that it would never happen again.

She put a hand to his cheek. "I'm going with you to your next session with Dr. Craig."

He leaned into her touch. "I'm not sure why you put up with me. Without you..."

"Sh," she whispered, pulling his head to her chest and running her fingers through his hair. "It's going to be OK."

Chapter Twenty-One

Mr. Jonathan Demure was nothing like one might expect of a man with that name. He was tall and broad shouldered and spoke in a very deep commanding voice. Although he was in his fifties, he had not one gray hair and was the fittest he had even been in his life. He shook Brighton's hand firmly and slapped him on his back.

"It's good to finally meet the man who has captured my daughter's heart. Now maybe she can quit that job of hers and do something more respectable."

"Oh, Dad. I have my certificate now. No more stripping for me I promise."

He released Brighton's hand and pulled Cecelia in for a hug. In her ear he breathed, "If he ever does anything to hurt you, I will kill him."

The sentence sent a shock wave through her body and made her stomach tighten.

"He's a good man, Daddy."

He leaned back enough to get a good look at his beautiful daughter. "You look fantastic as always. Your sister said you were in a bit of trouble. Is everything OK now?"

"She has a big mouth and yes, everything is just fine. There was no trouble. I just needed to get away for a while."

He regarded her expression for a moment then with a single nod, dismissed her. "Mother is in the kitchen. Brighton, follow me. You can put your things in the guest room."

Brighton grabbed the two suitcases and quickly caught up with Mr. Demure who was already halfway up the stairs occasionally taking two steps at a time. He was testing Brighton and the younger man knew it. Still, Brighton kept up with Jonathan and smiled confidently the entire time.

Brighton placed the bags on the bed then looked at his soon-to-be father-in-law.

"Do you like cigars?"

"Yes, I do, John."

"Let's go down to the den and chat, shall we? And don't call me John. I'm not a toilet."

"Yes, Sir."

"Jonathan would be just fine, Brighton. No need for formality."

The den was a room that was rarely visited by women other than to clean. It smelled of musk, cigars, and old books. One wall was completely shelved and held what Brighton estimated to be over two hundred books from psychology texts to hunting memoirs. Another wall was covered with trophies. In the center was a large moose-head flanked by two deer. Next to a humidor stood a weapon cabinet with double pane glass doors. Brighton saw several guns and hunting knives.

Jonathan opened a drawer in the roll top mahogany desk and took out a key. Then he moved to the humidor and selected two of his finest cigars. He clipped the first end and handed it to Brighton before clipping his own.

"Thanks, Jonathan."

The older man gestured to one of the leather chairs. "Sit."

Brighton obeyed yet he sat on the edge of the chair with perfect posture. He knew Jonathan Demure was trying to intimidate him and, at the same time, sizing him up to see if he was good enough for his eldest daughter.

"Do you hunt?"

"No, I have never hunted."

"Maybe Ce and I can take you while the two of you are here."

Brighton's eyebrow popped up.

"What? Does it surprise you that I taught my daughters how to use a gun?"

"Cecelia hardly strikes me as a hunter."

"Maybe you don't know her as well as you think," Jonathan said relaxing against the edge of his desk yet remaining on his feet. He took a moment to light his cigar. "My wife gave me two beautiful daughters. I am not complaining, mind you. I love them dearly. Next to my wife, they are the center of my world. On the other hand, I wanted a son. So, I compromised. My daughters dress and act like ladies but they also know how to handle a weapon, gut a fish, and they can knock a man twice their size on his ass if he looks at them the wrong way."

Brighton stood so he could look Mr. Demure straight in the eye. "Then you can trust that I would never hurt your daughter, sir. From what you said, she knows how to protect herself. I love her, Jonathan. I'll be there for her no matter what life brings."

"I saw the headlines, Brighton. I know you were under suspicion for those murders. And even though they caught and are trying someone else, you were in the center of things. I'm not so sure you had nothing to do with the case."

"If you read the stories, you know I was framed by my brother and ex-fiancée."

"That does not say much about you, Brighton. Usually when someone is the target of such a plot, he is not as innocent as he claims to be."

Brighton tugged on the cigar for a few minutes, holding Jonathan's gaze. "Sometimes people can turn on an innocent man, Sir. Just because I fell in love with a psychopath does not mean I am one. And as far as my brother goes, I didn't even know he existed until after the first bodies were discovered. We were separated at birth."

"Hm, time will tell, Brighton, whether you are worthy of my daughter. Make her happy and keep her safe and you will live a long and healthy life."

"That sounds an awful lot like a threat."

"You can take it however you like." Jonathan glanced back at the desk and stubbed out his cigar in a silver ashtray. He turned back to his daughter's fiancé and said, "I'm going to go check on dinner. You can finish that if you like."

Brighton watched Mr. Demure walk out of the den. He glanced around the very masculine room once more and wondered how Cecelia felt about her father. She had never discussed him, said her parents were totally "normal", and yet Mr. Demure seemed far from Brighton's idea of normal.

Brighton fell out of bed with a loud thud when Jonathan Demure banged on the guest room door at five in the morning. Cecelia laughed. Her father had told her they would be hunting that day, and she knew he liked to get up early.

"Good morning, Daddy," she said watching Brighton jump to his feet and grab the first piece of clothing he could find. "We'll be down in fifteen minutes."

"You know I hate to be kept waiting, especially for what I think you were doing in there." Jonathan's lips curled. He waited a moment, listening at the door.

"Jesus, is he always like this?" Brighton whispered.

"Like what?" Cecelia said trying desperately to curb her laughter.

"Like bang on the damn door at five o'clock in the morning and try to scare the shit out of me."

Outside the guest room, Jonathan snickered and headed for the stairs.

She shook her head and looking at his crotch said, "It's amazing how a knock can make that thing shrink."

"It wasn't the knock; it was his comment about what we were doing, which we weren't even doing."

"I'll make sure I tell him we were just sleeping. Go get in the shower," she commanded pointing toward the bathroom.

"Why don't you go first?" he asked, pulling off the boxers he had just tugged on.

Cecelia got out of bed. "Because if I make it down to the kitchen before you do, it will not be pretty," she smirked slapping his behind. "I'm going to brush my teeth and get my clothes ready."

Brighton quickly ran a razor over his skin and hopped into the shower. "Who the hell gets up at five freaking o'clock in the morning on the day before Christmas Eve to go hunting," he muttered to himself. "Normal my ass," he added.

"What are you grumbling about, darling?"

"Nothing, sweetheart."

A moment later, Cecelia stuck her head in the shower. "Are you almost done?"

"Yeah," he said rinsing the last of the soap off his chest. "C'mon in."

She kissed him as they switched positions so she was under the spray of the water.

"If he wasn't in so much of a hurry, I'd suggest a quickie."

"I don't think that's wise," Brighton admitted. "I was just dragged out of bed at the crack of dawn to shoot God knows what. I'm afraid if we get started..." He shook his head as he stepped out of the stall.

"We don't have to go. I can tell my father..."

"No, we are going. I just need a few minutes to collect my thoughts. The last thing I want to do is be angry when the three of us are armed."

"Brighton, he was joking."

"I know. I know. Still," he sighed wrapping a towel around his waist.

"I'll talk to him."

"No, don't Ce. I have to get used to his sense of humor; I suppose. I'll be fine." He exited the bathroom in search of what to wear for a trip to the woods.

When Cecelia returned to the bedroom she sat on the bed next to him. "Are you all right?"

He took her hand in his. "I'm fine. I didn't sleep well last night."

"I know. You were tossing and turning and talking in your sleep. Did you take your pill last night?"

"Yeah, but I bet because I missed a couple it might take a day or two to get back to the right level. I'll be fine." His demeanor changed and a grin crept across his face. "But you had better get dressed or we are going to be late. Your father does not like to be kept waiting. And if you're naked much longer I am going to have trouble zipping my jeans."

"We wouldn't want that now would we?"

Mr. Demure was part owner of the sporting facility, and his partner's son Raymond had been working at the front desk for several years, taking over when his father could no longer handle the position. Both Raymond and his father treated Mr. Demure with the utmost respect. Normally, the facility was open only on weekends, but they made an exception for owners.

"Good morning, Mr. Demure. How are you this morning?"

"I'm fine, Raymond."

"Everything is ready for you on the clay courses."

"Excellent. My soon-to-be son-in-law has not been hunting before so I think Cecelia and I will run the first course and show him how it's done."

"Hi, Cecelia," Raymond said looking down for a moment. His eyes wandered up and he said, "You look amazing as always."

"Thanks, Ray. How is your father?"

"He is good some days, not so good others. It depends on the weather. This time of year the arthritis really kicks in."

"Send him my love, would you?"

"Absolutely and tell your sister I said hello."

"I will."

Jonathan rolled his eyes at the exchange of pleasantries. Raymond asked, "Would you like an instructor on the course to assist?"

Jonathan glanced at Brighton who began, "I don't think..."

The older man interrupted as he looked at Raymond. "Who's on today?"

"Bethany is here. Shall I have her meet you at station one?" Bethany was Raymond's younger sister. Alongside Cecelia and her sister, Bethany and her brother had learned to handle weapons at a very young age under the tutelage of their father and Mr. Demure.

"That would be fine."

Bethany was a year younger than Cecelia. Her red curls were pulled back in a loose pony tail. She wore no make-up to cover her spattering of freckles.

"I hear you have never held a gun."

"Only a hand gun and well... my own."

Behind him he heard a click.

"DO NOT flirt with other women when your fiancée is holding a loaded weapon."

"Understood, darling," he replied with a tilt of his head.

She lowered the shotgun. Jonathan laughed at his daughter then patted her back.

"I told you Brighton, my daughters know how to handle their men."

"I'm beginning to comprehend the full meaning of that statement, Jonathan."

Bethany showed him how to load, unload, and aim the gun.

"Are you ready, newbie?" Jonathan snickered.

"I'm as ready as you are."

"Ce and I will take the lead."

Through the course, Bethany remained close to her student giving him tips and making sure he didn't shoot anyone by mistake. He got off a few shots most of which did not mortally wound any of the clay targets. By the end, he was a bit more confident in his ability.

"You pick things up quickly, kid."

"Must be all the video games I played as a teenager," he joked.

"Let's you and I take another run through," Jonathan suggested dryly. "I want to see how much you learned."

Cecelia kissed Brighton's cheek then whispered in his ear. "Be careful out there. He won't shoot you by accident; I can promise you that."

"That does not give me a warm fuzzy feeling."

The men set off on a second course while Cecelia helped Bethany reset the first one.

"He's adorable. How did you two meet?"

"He came into the club one night. He looked at me with those green eyes and I was hooked. I wagged my ass at him and he could not resist."

"You do have a fine ass. Not that I look at it, I'm just saying."

"Thanks. Ray said your dad is doing well most days."

"He gets around on his own a bit. Mom does a lot of the stuff around the house. Ray and I do our best to help. I think we may have to get them to an assisted living facility soon."

"Brighton's father has dementia. I'm not sure which is worse, losing your mind or your body."

"I think I would rather lose my mind. Seeing my dad in pain and knowing he is suffering so much... It's hard on my mom too. She tries to help but he hates being waited on. He was always so active, and now he can't do anything on some days."

While the ladies were catching up, other two were getting acquainted. The younger man was concentrating on hitting the targets as they arose. For Cecelia's father, who had done the course many times, he didn't even have to guess at the timing or placement of the targets. Occasionally there were course changes yet Jonathan knew the terrain like no other.

"Are you and Cecelia thinking about starting a family?"

"We've decided to wait until were settled in the new house." Brighton fired a round and hit a target dead on. "We have some redecorating to do. She told you we are moving to Long Island?"

"Yes, into a house where your former fiancée had lived."

Brighton thought, "Damn she tells him everything." Out loud he said, "We spent a few weekends there and she picked out a good deal of the furniture and adornments. I told Cecelia we could gut the place and make everything new if it would make her comfortable."

Jonathan hit the next clay. "She's not getting any younger. Don't wait too long."

"I'm sure we'll know when the time is right."

"You have family in Palm Springs, right?"

"Yes, my grandparents are there." Brighton took another shot and grazed the animal. "Damn it," he grumbled.

"But your father is in the city?" Jonathan hit the target that Brighton missed.

"Yes, and I am going to leave him where he is. With his dementia, he will not take well to moving. It's close enough so we can visit every weekend. He won't remember, but I will."

"You can tell what kind of a person one is by the way he takes care of his parents," Jonathan said as he took aim at the next target. After firing, he lowered his weapon and regarded the younger man. "Cecelia told me your mother passed away. May I ask what happened?"

"She had ovarian cancer. By the time they found it, she..," Brighton took a deep breath so he could gather his thoughts and not break down. He hated to discuss that period in his life. "She passed within a few months of her diagnosis."

"I'm sorry for your loss. And Mitchell Daniels was your adopted father?"

"Yes, but I never thought of him that way. He and my grandfather were the only adult men in my life when I was small. I called Mitch Dad, still do."

"Then I am doubly impressed, young man. C'mon, let's finish the course so we can pick up a tree to bring back to the house."

After the morning hunt, the family went to pick out a fresh tree for the living room. The women chose the perfect specimen. It wasn't exactly symmetrical nor was it full and lush yet it had a certain character. The men chopped down the tree and affixed it to the top of the SUV.

By the time they arrived home, Cecelia's sister and her boyfriend were at the house. Cecelia hugged Natalia and

Samuel then introduced Brighton. He extended his hand to Natalia. Instead, she pulled him into a tight hug and winked at her sister over his shoulder.

"It's so nice to finally meet you," Natalia beamed.

"I've heard a lot about you," Brighton lied as he squirmed out of her arms. He slipped his arm around Cecelia's waist. She put a hand on his chest. He could sense the tension between the two women.

"Natalia, come in the kitchen with me. I'm going to make some eggnog while the boys set up the tree and put on the lights. Then we can decorate."

Natalia shot her sister a look then followed her mother.

"Samuel, could you help Brighton and me with the tree? The girls picked a tall one this year."

"Sure thing, Jonathan."

Cecelia gave her beau a peck on the cheek. "I'm going to get the ornaments."

He watched as she disappeared down the hall.

"So Brighton, I hear you're a big city lawyer?" Samuel said.

"Yes, that's correct. How did you and Natalia meet?" Brighton asked as he held open the door.

"We were at the wedding of her friend. I was best man and she was the maid of honor. I think it was a set up but we hit if off so I suppose it worked out. How did you hook up with Cecelia?"

Brighton lifted an eyebrow at Samuel's choice of words. "We met at a club."

Jonathan glanced at Brighton for a moment. Samuel nodded. Natalia had told him Ce was a stripper. He didn't to press the issue.

Over the next few hours they placed hand-blown, blue, silver and gold glass ornaments on the tree and hung garland around the mantle. They drank eggnog and told stories of the sisters when they were young. Jonathan was quiet only interjecting a few comments.

Natalia complained about the tree. "It's crooked. And one side is fuller than the other. Ce, did you choose this one?"

"Mom and I picked it out together. It looked like it needed a good home."

"Who are you Charlie Brown? Should we put Linus' blanket around the bottom and swoosh..." She gestured with her hands, "...it becomes perfectly triangular? Daddy, how could you agree to this?"

Brighton watched the interaction between the sisters. The competitive nature of their relationship was obvious. Both looked to their father for acceptance yet Natalia seemed more desperate for his attention. Several times she patted her father's hand, squeezed his shoulder, or planted a kiss atop his head. Brighton noticed that Cecelia was more confident in her relationship with Mr. Demure. She did not need public displays of affection. A few times, Brighton caught Mr. Demure glancing at each daughter, and he could tell who his favorite was.

After dinner that evening, he men retired to the den for a cigar while the ladies cleared the dining room table and washed the dishes.

"He seems very nice, Cecelia, and very intelligent. He held your father's attention with all that lawyer talk. And those eyes are spectacular," Mrs. Demure observed.

"It was his lips that caught my attention first."

"Mm, he does have nice lips," Cecelia's mom giggled. "I bet you could kiss him forever."

Cecelia nearly dropped the casserole dish she was carrying toward the sink. "Mom!"

"What? I may be married and well into my forties, but I am not dead."

"Samuel has rock hard abs," Natalia interjected. "He works out five days a week."

"Are things getting serious between you?" her mother asked.

Natalia smiled shyly at her mother as she wrapped foil around the leftovers. "I think so."

"Well good, it's about time you settled down."

"Me? What about Ce? She's older."

"Only by fourteen months," Cecelia shot back. "Brighton and I are getting married in the spring. He has a beautiful house on Long Island with a fire pit and a pool. We're going to have the ceremony there."

"You're not having a church wedding?"

"Oh Mom, I haven't been to church in years. If I went into one it would crumble."

"It's never too late to go back to mass, dear."

"Maybe you're right. I'm just not comfortable with that. Perhaps when we have children, we will go back to church."

"So Brighton is an attorney, right?"

Cecelia nodded.

"Samuel just made partner at the accounting firm. He also teaches college courses two nights a week."

"And you're not worried about him having access to all those young college girls?" Cecelia quipped then immediately regretted her words. "I'm sorry. That came out wrong."

"I'm not worried at all. I give him everything he needs."

"Then why would he want to marry you, dear? You know what they say about milk and cows."

"He wants children, mother."

While rinsing dishes and placing them in the dishwasher, Mrs. Demure nodded. "I see. Well, you should discuss that more with him. You're not getting any younger."

"Women have babies into their forties now."

"But most of those go through fertility treatments. It's not an easy path."

"We'll figure things out. I'm in no rush."

Once the kitchen and dining room were cleaned up, Mrs. Demure said she was going up to her room. Cecelia told her sister she was going to the den.

"You're just going to waltz right in there?"

"Why not?"

"But that's Daddy's room. We're not supposed to go in there."

"Nat, I'm not a little girl anymore and neither are you," she said as she exited the kitchen.

Ce knocked on the door yet she did not wait for an answer. She walked directly over to her fiancé and sat on the arm of the leather chair he occupied.

"What are you boys talking about?"

"Women," Samuel smirked.

Natalia stood right outside the door waiting for an invitation to enter. Jonathan ignored her and Brighton noticed Natalia's annoyance. She tapped her foot and put her hands on her hips. When she eyed Samuel he stood and excused himself. As he left the den he closed the door behind him.

"So, what do you think of Samuel," Mr. Demure asked Brighton.

"He seems honest and well bred."

"Hm, that's a fair assessment. I wonder sometimes why he is with Natalia. She can be very demanding." Jonathan lifted a brow waiting for him to respond negatively.

"I think she knows what she wants and isn't afraid to ask for it. There's nothing wrong with that."

Jonathan smiled at his answer. "Natalia has become quite the beautiful woman."

Brighton looked at his fiancée. "Cecelia's visual appeal surpasses that of any woman I have ever met. However, I love her for her internal beauty. She is my everything."

"I'm going to turn in so you can charm my daughter some more. Mrs. Demure will be up early tomorrow."

"Good night, Dad."

Jonathan leaned down and kissed his daughter's head. "Good night sweetheart."

As soon she heard the door latch click, Cecelia straddled Brighton. "So?"

"So what?"

"Were you saying those things to please my father or to charm the pants off of me?"

"Yes, yes, and may I add that I meant every word and if it means your pants come off that is just a bonus."

Cecelia covered his mouth with hers. Brighton's hands landed on her hips. They remained in the den for a while making out like teenagers. When Cecelia began to unbutton Brighton's shirt he put his hands over hers.

"Let's go upstairs."

"Why? We have the room to ourselves and everyone is out of earshot."

"While that is true my love, I don't want to have sex; I want to make love slowly and enjoy every inch of you."

Cecelia's stomach flipped. "Oh my."

They casually made their way up to the guest room holding hands. He took his time removing her clothes kissing each patch of newly exposed skin. Her flesh tingled with goose bumps causing her to shiver. He grinned at her reaction.

"I love you, Cecelia," he breathed into her ear just before running the tip his tongue down her throat continuing to her right breast.

He guided her to the bed as he adeptly unfastened her jeans. He pushed the fabric over her hips letting his palms graze her backside.

"Um, when are your clothes coming off?" she purred.

"Soon, darling. Sit."

As she obeyed, Brighton knelt before her and removed her boots followed by her jeans and panties. He nipped her pink painted toes on each foot.

"I love every part of you."

He made a trail of warm wet kisses up her legs alternating between right and left. On the way, he gently nudged her legs open. Cecelia leaned back on one hand while running the fingers of the other through his hair. As he neared her center, her heart rate increased in anticipation. He saw her bite her lip as he took his first taste of her sweet elixir.

They spent the next hour reveling in each other. Every touch, each move, and all the sweet spoken words added to the tenderness and intensity of their love. Before they fell asleep, Brighton wrapped his arms around Cecelia.

"You and I were meant to be together, Ce. I can't wait to be your husband and start the rest of our lives together. You are my universe."

Chapter Twenty-Two

Christmas Eve morning Brighton woke up before Cecelia. He lay motionless listening to her breathe and pondering how lucky he was to have her. He was sure any other woman would have left him after the recent turbulence in his life. Cecelia had been shuffled around by two goons and then went into hiding on her own. It had disrupted her routine and yet she remained committed to him.

A smile passed his lips as she sighed in her sleep. He wasn't sure how long he could linger without waking her. He decided to slip out of bed, grab something to wear, and exit the room before he disturbed her. As he approached the top of the stairs, the aroma of cinnamon and spice made his tummy growl. He found Mrs. Demure in the kitchen making icing for the batch of cinnamon buns that were in the oven.

"Merry Christmas," she said cheerily. "You're up early."

"I bet the rest of the family will get up once they smell breakfast," he said putting an arm over her shoulders and giving her a gentle squeeze. "I remember my mother having to make several batches of cinnamon buns on holidays because my dad and I ate so many."

"Oh then perhaps I should whip up some more."

Brighton retrieved a mug and filled it with coffee. "Please don't. I can't eat as many as I used to; and if they're made, I will try."

"So you have no self-control," she teased.

He leaned against the counter. "Not when it comes to fine cooking or beautiful women, I don't."

Mrs. Demure smiled at him as she put the bowl of icing aside. She washed her hands and dried them on her apron. "I'm glad we have a few minutes alone, Brighton. I wanted to speak with you."

His curiosity made his brow furrow. Mrs. Demure laughed at his expression.

"It is nothing bad, dear. Why don't you have a seat?" She gestured to the chair at the end of the table.

The two sat adjacent each other and Mrs. Demure took a sip of coffee then began. "I know my husband can be a bit intimidating. I have lived with him for many years and still sometimes he gets to me."

Brighton's lips parted to interject yet Mrs. Demure continued.

"He likes you. I can tell by the way he teases you. He likes Samuel too but with you... You're engaged to his favorite daughter. If you repeat that, I will deny saying it."

"Understood."

"Good, because it is important that it doesn't get back to Natalia. It would break her heart. The two of them have been vying for his attention all their lives. I think Ce has backed off a bit. She knows how to play him a lot better than Nat. And she knows that Jonathan is not a man you can cross and get away with it."

"That is brutally apparent, Mrs. Demure."

She smiled and patted his hand. "You can call me Mom if you wish. Samuel does."

"OK, Mom," he replied turning his hand over and holing both her hands in his. "That means a lot to me. Ce told you my mother passed several years ago?"

"Yes and I'm so sorry. I know you must have loved her very much. She told me about your father as well. So sad."

"Sometimes I think it is sadder for the people around him. He thinks his main caregiver is my mom most of the time. He thinks I'm law school. He doesn't remember all the hard times."

"That is a blessing; I suppose."

One by one other family members found their way to the kitchen. Jonathan arrived first fully dressed in casual clothes. He kissed his wife and nodded once at his house guest.

Mrs. Demure pushed her chair back and stood. "I'll have your egg white omelet ready in a minute, dear."

Jonathan rubbed her behind and she giggled.

"Don't you just love it when your woman giggles?" he asked Brighton.

Brighton was enjoying the unguarded moment he was witnessing and remained quiet so he would not disturb Jonathan's good mood.

"What should we do today, Bri?"

"What is there to do on a holiday with snow falling heavily outside?"

"We could start a fire and watch sports all day while the women cook."

"Oh, I am sure the women would get a charge out of that... us sitting in the den and them stuck in here."

"My daughters tend to get along better when I'm not in the room."

Brighton took a big gulp of coffee so he would not have to respond to Jonathan's comment.

"I think you're imagining things, dear." he winked at Brighton behind her husband's back. "Do you want some fresh cantaloupe or strawberries with your omelet?"

"It's a holiday. I'll have a cinnamon bun. Besides, you wore me out last night. I need the carbs."

Cecelia came in at the exact moment when Mrs. Demure and Brighton blushed at Jonathan's remark.

"Insatiable appetites run in the family, hey Bri?"

"Yes, dear," he grinned as she greeted him with a kiss.

Jonathan tried to hide his smirk by giving his wife another peck on the cheek.

The air in the kitchen remained light. The humor continued even after Samuel joined them. They talked about the upcoming wedding, which lead to a story from Jonathan about their honeymoon. His words made his wife turn crimson yet she brushed it off as being warm from cooking. Natalia walked in and, hearing them all laugh, she asked what they were talking about.

"The family's predilection for voracious appetites," Jonathan explained.

"Hm tell me about it. I could eat anything."

Everyone chuckled knowing she had no idea what the subject of the conversation had been. Natalia seized a cinnamon bun and sat next to Samuel. He tucked a strand of hair behind her ear as she nibbled.

As the day wore on, Jonathan's idea of what everyone would do fell into place. The men wound up in the den watching sports, smoking cigars, and talking business. The women gathered in the kitchen and intermittently chatted about wedding plans while preparing for Christmas dinner the following day.

Mrs. Demure mixed up a batch of dough to make fresh pasta. Cecelia put tomatoes in the deep stainless steel sink then covered them with boiling water to make them easier to peel for the sauce. Natalia reluctantly shredded some mozzarella trying not to ruin her manicure. Working with the cheese would be less harmful than peeling the acidic tomatoes.

Christmas dinner was usually some form of stuffed pasta that the ladies prepared the day before the big feast. This year, Natalia had decided on manicotti filled with chopped broccoli and a mixture of Italian cheeses. Once she was done with the mozzarella, Natalia started on the asiago. The pungent aroma tickled her nose.

Cecelia was busy removing the skin from the tomatoes. She plucked one out of the scalding water with tongs, placed it on the cutting board and peeled it with care trying not to get burned. Then she scooped out any loosened seeds and cut the fruit into a pot.

"We want something simple, Ma. We're getting a JP and having the ceremony at his house on the island. I'm having a bouquet of wildflowers. I'll pick up a nice dress, nothing fancy."

"Oh dear, you could have the wedding of your dreams. Your father would pay for everything."

"A simple wedding is what I have always dreamed of. It's Natalia that wants the fairy tale wedding."

"Hell yeah," Nat agreed. "Dad can spend fortunes on me if Ce has a small shindig."

Cecelia and her mother exchanged a knowing glance.

Brighton left the den and silently passed the kitchen. He went out to his car and retrieved a few items he had hidden in the trunk. When he had placed everything inside, he entered the kitchen.

"How is everything going in here?"

"We're doing just fine. Do you men need anything? Maybe a snack or a beer?"

"I could use a soda if you have any. I'll check with Jonathan and Samuel." He patted Cecelia on the behind and said, "I'll be right back."

He returned with a few requests for food and drink. Mrs. Demure pulled out a tray and loaded it up then ushered Brighton out.

"Whatever you're making sure smells delicious," he said over his shoulder as his was shooed away.

In the den he handed out the refreshments. "I have no idea what they are brewing up, but suddenly I cannot wait for dinner."

"All of my girls are fabulous cooks. Put them together and amazing things can happen. That is, as long as I am not in the room. Nat seems to be too busy fawning over me to pay much attention to food preparation."

"She idolizes you Jonathan," Samuel interjected. "She would do anything to please you."

Jonathan nodded thoughtfully. "I'm not sure how I raised two girls exactly the same and yet they can be so different sometimes. I never wanted them to compete for my affection. I have no idea where I went wrong."

Touched by the man's honesty, Brighton thoughtfully said, "Sometimes it is not what a parent does in raising a child; it is how the child reacts. Maybe you need to talk to her one on one."

"I think you're right, Brighton," Jonathan agreed. "And there is no time like the present."

Later that evening, they all sat in the living room by the light of the Christmas tree and the warmth of the fire in the hearth. Mr. and Mrs. Demure were on the sofa. The youngest couple sat next to each other on the love seat. Brighton was in an overstuffed chair with his woman perched on the armrest.

"I think we should open one present each and save the rest for tomorrow," Natalia suggested.

Everyone agreed. Nat retrieved one of the packages from under the tree and handed it to her mother.

"I'm not sure who this is from, Ma."

Cecelia leaned down and whispered in Brighton's ear. "When did you have time to put those under the tree? I didn't even know you brought any gifts."

"How do you know it's from me?" he asked.

"I saw that wrapping paper at our place tucked in the back of the closet."

"We're you snooping?"

"Yes," she admitted.

"You're going to be punished tonight."

"I hope so."

"I heard that," Jonathan said in a firm tone.

"Oh, these are lovely," Mrs. Demure commented as she looked at the ruby earrings.

Jonathan's attention turned to the gift in his wife's hands. "Who bought my wife jewelry?" he chuckled.

"They're from Brighton."

"How did you know I like rubies?"

"I pay attention," he explained.

"OK, Cecelia, this is from Samuel and me."

"I have no idea what it is. Natalia did all the shopping this year."

Cecelia moved from the arm of the chair and sat on the floor in front of Brighton. She carefully unwrapped the box and lifted the lid. Brighton's eye lit up as Ce pulled out a pair of red, stiletto heeled, ankle high boots.

"I love them. Thanks, Nat."

Brighton felt a twinge in his groin and shifted in his seat. Cecelia glanced up at him as if she knew exactly what he was thinking.

"My sister has impeccable taste, doesn't she Bri?"

"Uh huh," was all he could manage past the visions in his head.

Jonathan cleared his throat. "Natalia, I think it's time for another present."

Once everyone had opened one gift, Natalia returned to her spot next to Samuel. Cecelia stood with a little help from Brighton.

"I think I'm going to turn in," she said picking up the boots. "Are you coming?" she asked waving the boots in front of her fiancé.

"Yes, I, um, I'm going to help Mom clean up then I'll be right behind you."

"Interesting choice of words," she purred causing his cheeks burn.

Brighton and Mrs. Demure disposed of the wrappings and brought the glassware into the kitchen.

"Go," she said to him. "I can finish."

He gave her a peck on the cheek and thanked her.

When Brighton opened the door to the guest room, Cecelia was in the attached bathroom.

"I'll be out in a minute."

"Don't wait too long or I'll start without you."

When she emerged a few minutes later, Cecelia was wearing nothing but the red stiletto boots and a seductive grin.

Christmas morning, both Brighton and Cecelia woke up well after everyone else. She was stiff and sore yet smiled at the reason. He grunted when she tried to get out of bed.

"Not yet," he mumbled.

"Bri, it's nearly ten am. I need a long hot shower if I am going to make it down the stairs."

"Are you complaining?"

He smile d as his lips brushed against the back of her neck.

"No, I'm not complaining. I am merely stating a fact that I need something to loosen up my tight muscles and ease the ache."

"You know how they say the best cure for a hangover is to never stop drinking..?"

"Are you saying we should never stop having sex?"

"Well, if we keep up the pace like last night, our bodies would adjust and we wouldn't be as sore the day after."

She had to laugh at his reasoning. "That makes perfect sense. I still think I need a hot shower. Would you care to join me?"

By the time the couple managed to find their way to the kitchen, any sign of breakfast had disappeared.

"I'll get you something to eat," Cecelia's mother said when she saw them.

"It's OK, Ma. I'll make breakfast for us. Sorry we slept late."

"There's no need to apologize. It's Christmas morning. I made French toast from Challah bread. There is some in the oven. All of the cooked bacon is gone but I have more to cook."

"Thanks. I'll fry up the bacon. Go sit."

"Please, you look exhausted. Let me make it for you two. Brighton, would you like some coffee?"

"Yes, please."

As Mom poured the coffee, her daughter removed the dish from the oven and placed it on the table along with two plates. She retrieved the bacon from the refrigerator and the pan from the dish drainer.

"I can do that, dear. You're going to be cooking for him for the rest of your life."

"Oh, hell no I won't be. We will share the cooking along with all the other chores."

"Absolutely," Brighton said as he piled his plate with French toast. "We'll take turns cooking and cleaning or I'll hire a maid. You don't have to make the bacon, Ce. What time is dinner?" he asked just before taking a bite. "Mm, this is so good. Is that nutmeg?"

"It sure is, Brighton. When you two weren't down here by eight, Jonathan suggested we move dinner to three so you have a few hours. Are you sure you don't want bacon?"

"I'm sure," he said after swallowing. "Do you have any cantaloupe left?"

"We do; I'll get it for you."

Brighton ate voraciously as if he hadn't eaten for days. Cecelia leaned against the counter and watched him for a minute. She glanced at her mother who responded with a wink.

"Make sure you feed him well," her mother said placing a bowl of fruit near him. On her way out of the kitchen she commented over her shoulder, "A full stomach and a sexy wife will keep a husband from wandering."

Cecelia tilted her head as her mother disappeared.

"I wonder why she said that."

"Don't worry, Babe. I am a one woman kind of guy."

"That's not what I was thinking at all," Ce said as she pulled out a chair and sat next to Brighton. "Could she have been...?"

"Talking about your father?" Brighton finished her sentence. "I doubt it. Your parents are so happy with each other."

"Hm," she replied taking Brighton's fork from him to try the French toast.

"Hey, get your own utensil," he smirked. "I don't share silverware."

"With everything we did last night, I don't think we need to worry about using the same fork."

"You loved every minute of it, don't lie."

She leaned closer and kissed his mouth. "It was fabulous even though I had to contain the vocalization of my pleasure."

"I should have bought your parents ear plugs so you didn't have to swallow your screams," he said wiggling his eyebrows at her.

When Brighton had his fill of breakfast, he and Cecelia went to the living room where the others had gathered. They exchanged the remaining gifts and talked about Christmases past. Brighton and Samuel enjoyed listening to more stories of Natalia and Cecelia when they were young.

Just as dinner was being placed on the dining room table, Brighton's cell phone rang. He reluctantly peaked at the caller id. He smiled when he saw his friend's name.

"What's up, Jas?"

"Nothing is going on here. We were checking to see how things are up there."

Brighton told his friend everything was fine and that Cecelia's family was great.

"I bet they're all standing right there."

"Uh huh, we were about to have dinner, homemade pasta."

"Awesome, I'll let you go. Tell Ce we said Merry Christmas. We'll see you two when you get back to New York."

A few moments later, the phone rang again. Brighton was about to ask Jason what he forgot when he realized it was not his friend calling. He pushed back his chair as he answered. The sound of the caller's voice made his stomach tighten. A call from the nursing home on Christmas Day was unusual. As he greeted the caller, Brighton stepped out of the room but not before Cecelia heard him say his father's caregiver's name.

"Brighton, I am so sorry to bother you but I thought you should know something."

"It's not a bother, Madge. You can call any time day or night."

Madge was in the small office on the wing for privacy. "I'm worried about your father. I had the attending doctor check him but the doc said he was fine."

"Tell me what is going on."

"He called me Madge. I know that seems like nothing but he hasn't called me my real name in so long. And, well, he has not been eating. He sort of rolls the food around in his mouth and pretends to eat. He's lost a few pounds and he really cannot afford that right now. He is so thin as it is."

Brighton heard the concern in her voice. She was not one to exaggerate her patient's condition. "Yet the doctor didn't think anything was wrong?"

"He said your father is healthy 'considering'." Madge rolled her eyes at the doctor's choice of words. "I'm almost thinking I should call his regular doctor. I mean; the attending is nice and all but I think if he knew your father he would understand my trepidation. I have seen this before, Brighton. When my patients start to go down, they tend to stop eating. And he is very sullen, not like his normal self at all."

Cecelia came up behind him as he looked out the window at the snow covered scenery while listening to Madge. She only heard his half of the conversation yet it was enough to know the call was not good news. She placed a hand lightly on his left arm and leaned her chin on his right shoulder.

"How long has he been behaving like this?"

"Two, maybe three days," she explained. "Brighton, sometimes they go fast. I think you need to come see him."

"I'm upstate right now. It's a seven hour drive."

"I knew you were away. I should have called you earlier." Madge moved the phone to her other ear. "I'm sorry."

"Don't apologize. Listen, I'll head down in the morning. If I drive home now it will be after ten before I can get there. I don't want to wake anyone up."

Madge nodded glumly. "OK, I'll see you then. I may call his own doctor in the morning depending on how he is."

"That is a good idea. Call me when he's there."

"I will. Drive carefully."

"I will Madge, thanks."

Brighton disconnected the call and tucked the phone in his pocket. He leaned back against Cecelia.

"I'm sorry," she whispered in his ear.

"I knew this day would come I just didn't think it would come so fast. He's not eating. Madge said he is not acting like himself. The attending physician didn't find anything wrong but I trust Madge's judgment."

"You know, maybe it would be better if we drive tonight. You could get there earlier in the morning."

"You wouldn't mind?" he asked turning to face her.

"Brighton, he's your father. I know how much you love him. And you would do the same for me."

He pulled her close and buried his face in her neck. "I'm not ready for this."

Cecelia stroked his back and whispered gentle loving words to him. Brighton took a few deep breaths and pulled back.

"Let's have dinner. We can pack up some for my Dad. Maybe if he has some home cooked food he might eat."

"That sounds like a good idea. Then we can hit the road. We can take turns driving. We'll get a good night's sleep at home then head to the facility in the morning."

He softly pressed his lips to hers. "Thanks, Ce. I love you so much."

"I love you too."

They returned to the dining room holding hands. Everyone seemed to know something was wrong. Brighton held out a chair for Ce.

"After dinner I'm afraid we have to head back home," he sighed. "My father is not feeling well."

The family expressed their well wishes for Mitch and said they understood. The rest of dinner was somber. Brighton did not eat much. He was too worried. Before he finished what was on his plate, he pushed his chair back and excused himself.

"I'm going to go pack."

"I'll be right there, Bri."

"That's OK, Ce. Spend some more time with your family."

Once alone in the guest room, Brighton felt his emotions begin to boil up to the surface. Mitchell Daniels had been the only father he had even known. Mitch was a part of Brighton's earliest memories. And with his grandparents living so far away, his father was the only connection he had left to his mother.

Tears streamed down his cheeks and he incessantly brushed them away with the back of his hand. He was having trouble seeing what he was doing. Finally, he sat on the edge of the bed and let it all out. A few minutes later, he went to the bathroom and washed his face. Then he resumed packing.

"How are you?" Cecelia asked as she joined him.

"I'm OK."

"Bri?"

"OK, I'm not. But I have to be. We have a long drive ahead of us. Maybe once I see my Dad it won't be as bad as Madge says. I'll have to call my grandmother. There is no way we can go to Palm Springs now. I won't leave him."

"She'll understand."

He zipped up the suitcase and placed it upright on the floor. "I think that's it. Do you want to take a look around and make sure I didn't miss anything?"

She wrapped her arms around his neck. "Whatever happens, I will always be here for you."

He leaned his forehead against hers. "I'm not sure how I would make it through this without you."

"You don't have to even think about that. I am with you every step of the way for the rest of our lives. OK?"

Mrs. Demure filled two travel mugs with coffee and put a few containers of food in a bag for them to take home. She also made two sandwiches and packed fruit so they would not have to stop to get something to eat. Samuel helped Brighton pack up the car. Natalia gave her sister a big hug and told her to call as soon as they arrived home.

By the time they were on the road it was after four. Brighton took the first leg of the trip. Cecelia kept an eye on him. She was concerned that he was hiding the way he was really feeling. She hoped that once they were at home he would be able to deal with his pain.

The city was still buzzing with activity when she pulled off the highway. She had convinced him to let her drive the last two hours and he had dozed off in the passenger seat. As she turned into the parking lot of her building, she gently squeezed his thigh.

"We're home. Wake up, my love."

"Hm, already? I'm sorry I fell asleep."

"It's OK. Let's leave everything but the food in the car. I have to call Nat; I promised."

By the time she hung up from speaking with Natalia, Brighton had curled up in bed. She slipped in behind him and put an arm over him.

"I love you," she murmured.

"I set the alarm for seven. Visiting hours start at eight but I think they'll let me in earlier."

She stroked his hand. "I'll be ready."

Both Brighton and Cecelia woke up well before the alarm sounded. She was wrapped around him as if she could protect him from all his pain and heartache. She kissed his hair.

"Would you like me to make you something for breakfast?" she asked softly.

"I'd rather you stay with me."

Cecelia brushed her lips against his shoulder as she whispered softly, "I love you, Bri."

They remained in bed for a while enjoying a few quiet moments before the difficult day began. Slowly he began to move. He stretched his legs down then pulled them back up. He placed his hand over hers and interlaced their fingers. He turned his head and she kissed his lips chastely.

Brighton inhaled deeply then rolled over to face her. "I hope you had a nice Christmas even though we had to leave early."

"It was wonderful Brighton. I am glad you and Dad seemed to hit it off."

Grinning he thought about Jonathan. "I was worried for a little bit. He warmed up to me eventually."

"I wanted to thank you for talking to him about Natalia. I'm not sure what words you used but things changed noticeably."

"I didn't like the way she treated you or your father. Family should get along. And he said he thought he had done something wrong in raising the two of you and that maybe he had fostered the competition. I told him that it isn't necessarily what a parent does but how the child interprets the actions. Whatever he said to Natalia was all his doing."

Brighton cupped her cheek. "I was lucky. My mother married a man who took me in as his own. He was strict sometimes but he always made sure I knew he acted out of love. And he never raised his voice to me. Mitch was the embodiment of what a true parent should be."

He swallowed hard and closed his eyes for a moment. When his eyes opened he continued, "You have a wonderful family. I'm glad they have welcomed me. If Mitch..." A sigh escaped his lips. "Now I have a whole new family and I consider myself blessed."

As they were talking, Brighton noticed the light seeping in between the curtains made Cecelia's skin glow. He ran his thumb along her lips. He moved so that his entire body pressed against hers. He wanted to forget the fear of losing the only man who had been there for him as a child. Brighton wanted to get lost in Cecelia.

He pressed his lips to hers. She was like a delicate sweet pastry. He wanted to savor her, melt into her, become one with her.

His kiss turned urgent. She felt his need growing. Painstakingly slow, he moved his hand from her face, down the front of her throat to her breast. She moaned into him as her fingers tangled in his hair. Cecelia's head fell back as his open mouth moved down her neck. For the next hour, they were lost in each other. Reality was nowhere in sight. Every touch was tender. Each kiss seemed brand new. Their bodies harmonized like a fine piece of music.

The alarm rang at seven shattering the peace. Brighton's eyes flew open as he realized it was time to go see his father. As he sat up, Cecelia asked if he wanted coffee. He reached for her hand placing his lips to her palm.

"If you're making it for you, I'll have some but don't go to any trouble."

"It's no trouble. Go take a shower and I'll have your coffee by the time you're done."

When Brighton and Cecelia approached the sitting room in the home, Madge was trying to get Mitch to eat. His tray had scrambled eggs, oatmeal, and yogurt. Madge ordered all soft foods so he would have an easier time swallowing. Mitch didn't want any of it. Each time she held up the spoon he shook his head and tightened his lips.

"Mitch, you have to have something. I could get you a milkshake."

"I am not a child, Madge. And I am not hungry."

"You didn't eat last night."

Mitch pushed the tray at her. "Leave me alone!" he snarled.

Brighton entered the room and softly greeted his father hoping to change his demeanor.

"What the hell are you doing here?" Mitch snapped.

Brighton kept an even calm tone. "Dad, this is my fiancée, Cecelia." Brighton stepped aside and put his arm around her waist.

The edge in Mitch's features seemed so smooth. His face took on a tenderness that touched all of them.

"Hello, beautiful," his words seemed replete with charm. "Why haven't you come to see me sooner?"

"Perhaps Brighton was afraid such a good looking man as yourself might steal me away from him."

Madge stood and, after mouthing a greeting to Brighton, she quietly moved out of her patient's line of sight.

"You're are probably right, Cecelia." He gestured toward the chair next to him. "Sit here next to me and I'll tell you some stories about my boy."

"I'll make you a deal, Mitch. If you eat at least one thing on your tray, I'll sit next to you."

"Two bites," he bargained.

"Nope, you have to finish at least one dish. So, what will it be?" she asked taking a seat. "The yogurt, the eggs, or the oatmeal?"

"Are you a lawyer too?"

Brighton took a chair opposite Ce. He put the bag they brought on the end of the table.

Cecelia laughed. "No, I am going to be a physician's assistant as soon as we get settled in the house."

"Hm, well maybe you should go into politics or something. I bet you could beguile all the men in the city."

Cecelia picked up the spoon and put it too Mitch's lips. "The only man I am interested in beguiling is your son."

"You have already stolen my heart, Ce."

Mitch accepted the yogurt Cecelia offered him. Madge's eyes widened. Brighton glanced at Madge and shrugged. He waited a few minutes, watching Cecelia and his father talk. Then he stood and motioned for Madge to step out into the hall.

Once out of earshot, Madge gave Brighton a hug and thanked him for coming.

"Does he always get like that?"

"More and more, unfortunately. It's the way it goes sometimes. Some patients turn the pain inward, others lash out. Cecelia's doing well with him. Maybe it's because she is a new face. Something different can alter his personality." She paused and glanced into the room.

"I have been through this so many times, Brighton. It is never easy. Somehow..," she wiped a tear that escaped down her cheek. "Mitch has been a favorite of mine." She smiled. "When he calls me by your mother's name it hits me right here," she added placing her hand over her chest.

"You mean a lot to both of us, Madge. Don't ever forget that."

She was teary and on the verge of breaking down. Not wanting to lose control in front of him, she changed the subject.

"Dr. Helm will be here this morning. I told him what was going on. He may do some tests."

"We're staying until the doctor takes a look at him. We were supposed to fly out to Palm Springs but I'm going to call my grandmother and let her know we're not going."

"I'm sorry you have to change your plans."

He lightly touched her arm. "Don't be. I need to be here with him. He should have his family with him now."

Mitch ate more than anyone expected. He was so busy telling stories to Cecelia; he didn't seem to notice she was coaxing him to eat. Soon the yogurt was gone, only a nibble of eggs was left and there was barely any oatmeal in the bowl.

After breakfast, Mitch led his guests back to his room. The older man showed Cecelia some pictures he had of his son.

"He was a good boy, very smart, and rarely talked back to his mother or me. Did he tell you he used to be in all the school plays and sang in glee club?"

Ce grinned and glanced at Brighton. "Really? Well, I guess I'll have to insist on a little concert sometime, huh Bri?"

"I don't sing anymore. Maybe when we have babies I will sing them to sleep."

"You two are dating?" Mitch asked.

"We're getting married in the spring."

"What happened to Linda?"

"Lydia," Brighton corrected. "She moved on."

"Never quite liked her," Mitch admitted. "Not sure why, she rubbed me the wrong way."

A short while later Dr. Helm came to check on Mr. Daniels. Cecelia escaped out into the hall while the doctor examined his patient. She walked down to the front desk and found Madge completing some paperwork.

"I wanted to thank you for taking such good care of Brighton's dad. I'm glad you called."

"I knew Brighton would want to know what was going on. I heard you say you were a PA?"

"I will be; I hope. I just finished school."

"What kind of office do you want to work in?"

"Originally I was thinking a general physician because they see all types of people." Cecelia looked toward Mitch's room. "Now I'm thinking geriatric medicine might be an interesting field."

"It can be difficult at times especially if you work in a place like this where the only way your patient leaves is if something goes wrong or the inevitable happens."

Cecelia nodded thoughtfully. "It takes a special person; I'm sure."

Meanwhile, the doctor was talking to his patient and assessing his health. He asked Mitch questions to see if he knew what year it was, where he lived, and other everyday things. Some questions he answered correctly, others he did not. He told Dr. Helm he was in a nursing home then a few minutes later Mitch looked at his son and asked, "Why did the doctor have to come to my house? Couldn't you have taken me to his office?"

"Dad, you're in a convalescent home."

"Oh, what the hell am I doing here?"

The doctor listened to his patient's heart and lungs. He checked his pulse and looked at his throat, ears and nose. In addition, he did a few neurological tests to evaluate Mitch.

"I hear you're not eating very well, Mitch. Why is that?"

"I'm not hungry. I'm tired of the crap they try to pass off as food here."

Dr. Helm chuckled. "Maybe your son can sneak some homemade food in for you. Would you eat that?"

"If that pretty lady who fed me breakfast brings it in I will."

"You're getting homemade manicotti for lunch," Brighton told his father. "Cecelia and her mom and sister made it."

"Who is Cecelia?"

"She's my fiancée."

"What happened to Lucy?"

"Lydia and I broke up."

"Oh, right, you told me that. I wish I could remember things better. Is your mother here?"

"No, Dad, she's not here."

Mitch sighed.

"Can you stand up?" the doctor asked.

Mitch obliged.

"Close your eyes and just stand still for a minute."

Mitch swayed slightly but quickly regained his balance.

"Now, put your arms out to the side and touch your nose alternating hands."

Mr. Daniels passed that test.

"Great, now try to balance on one leg."

Brighton and the doctor stood on opposite sides in case he fell.

"Awesome, now switch to the other."

A moment later, the doctor looked at his patient and said, "Well, you look good, Mitch. You need to eat though. If you don't, I will have to put you on an IV. You don't want that; trust me. So, I'll make you a deal if it is all right with Brighton.

You have to eat at least one meal a day. Brighton can bring you anything you want as long as you eat it."

"Get Donna to cook for me and I'll eat."

Dr. Helm glanced at Brighton. He knew Mr. Daniels often referred to his caregiver by his deceased wife's name.

"Brighton will make sure your food is prepared to your liking."

Before the doctor left, Brighton pulled him aside.

"Is his behavior just a natural progression or is something else going on?"

"He is in amazing physical health considering his age. This may be a phase but it can be a sign that he is giving up. I'm going to order some blood work just to rule out a few things and check for any nutritional deficiencies. If he won't eat, he at least needs to drink and stay hydrated. I'll add some supplements to his meds. Other than that, it's a wait and see situation. I know that is not what you want to hear."

"I understand, Doctor. My fiancée and I were planning to move to Long Island. If we do, I can't come every day and feed him." He shook his head. "I don't want to move him from here. His relationship with his caregiver has been a blessing. Without Madge, I don't think my father would have lasted this long."

"She is very gifted and caring. And you're right, moving him would not be a good idea. Let's see what the test results are and then we can chat more."

Brighton thanked the doctor and returned to his father's room. Cecelia was perched on the edge of the bed. Mitch sat in a chair across from her and the two were discussing Brighton's visit to Boy Scout summer camp.

"The first night he called his mother saying how much he missed her. They talked for twenty minutes. The second night he spoke to her for half that time. Then the third night he didn't call at all. By the time the week was over, he told us he wanted to stay the rest of the summer."

"It was the first time I had stayed away from my family for that long. And, in my defense, I was only ten."

"I bet you were adorable. Did you go the following summer?"

"I sure did and four years later I was a counselor in training."

Cecelia and Mitch both laughed.

"I bet you were chasing girls by then."

"They were chasing him, Lydia."

"Dad, this is Cecelia."

"What did I say?"

"It doesn't matter, Dad. Listen, we brought some food for you. When it gets a little closer to lunch, I'll have Madge warm it up."

"I'm not hungry."

"Mitch, I made it. Please at least try some."

He smiled at Cecelia. "Well, I suppose I don't want to disappoint you, Donna."

"Tell me what you want and I'll make it every day if you promise to eat it."

Chapter Twenty-Three

Brighton and Cecelia spent the whole day at the convalescent home. At lunch time, Madge warmed the pasta for Mitch. Her patient had a few bites then said he didn't want anymore. She glanced at Brighton.

"He had a good breakfast. We can save the rest for later."

Brighton and Cecelia walked Mitch down to the courtyard to get some fresh air. Mitch told Cecelia stories about when he first met Donna and more tales of his as a young boy. She was thoroughly enjoying their conversation. She felt like she was getting a bit of payback after the stories her family told Brighton about her.

While they walked, Brighton noticed his father was a little unsteady. He tried twice to help him but the stubborn older man pushed him away. He tried not to take his father's actions personally.

"Maneuvering this snowy path in heels is not easy," Cecelia sighed. "Do you mind if I hold your arm, Mitch?"

"Not at all, beautiful," Mitch beamed letting Cecelia slip her hand into the crook of his arm. He patted her hand and added, "Anything for you, my dear."

Brighton knew exactly what she was doing. She had a way of getting people to do what they didn't want to do or helping when they did not want to be helped. Her behavior was endearing. The skill would help her in the career she chose.

Mitch refused dinner. He said he was tired and wanted to go to bed. Cecelia convinced him to drink a nutritional substitute by telling him it was a milkshake. When Mitch was settled in for the night, they headed back to her apartment making a quick stop at the market.

While Brighton grilled some chicken on the deck, Cecelia whipped up a salad and made some Spanish rice. As he set the meat on the table, she put the rice in a bowl. He grabbed a bottle of wine out of the refrigerator and opened it.

"When are you going to call your grandmother?"

"I'll call after dinner. She wasn't expecting us yet. I wish I had more definitive answer as to what is really going on other than it is the natural progression for people in his condition. I mean, my grandparents are like twenty years older than Mitch. They're in better health. How the hell does that happen?"

"Unfortunately, the medical profession does not have all the answers. Aging is not an exact science. There is no set expiration date on human life. As his brain deteriorates, his body does too. And sometimes geriatric patients give up whether consciously or not. There is not much that can be done other then be there for the patient."

Brighton felt his eyes begin to well up. Quietly he said, "You are so good with him, so incredibly patient. I probably would have gotten frustrated with him." He shook his head. "No, I definitely would have been frustrated."

"It's easier when the person isn't your own parent. Don't be hard on yourself," she added reaching for his hands. "We can do this together. Through thick and thin I am here for you and your father." She stressed the word "and".

Brighton stepped closer to her and slipped his arms around her waist. "I think my mother is watching over me. She brought you to me, so that you could help me get through all this. Without you I would be lost."

"I doubt that, Brighton but you never have to worry about it. OK?"

He kissed her softly. "Let's eat so I can call my grandmother," he suggested.

During dinner, they discussed meals they could make and bring to the home. He knew a few of his father's favorite foods items that his mother used to cook for him. Madge had said if they prepared a few things, she could keep them in the refrigerator. She explained that giving him smaller portions more often might be helpful.

They finished eating and cleaned up the kitchen. He was procrastinating. When the food was put away and the dishes were done, he asked if she wanted another glass of wine.

"We can have more wine after you make your call. C'mon. Let's go sit on the sofa."

He sighed as she took his hand and tugged him toward the living room. They took a seat on the sofa next to each other. Brighton dialed and put the receiver to his ear. Cecelia put an arm around his shoulders.

"Brighton? You're home. I thought you were spending a few days with Cecelia's family."

"We had a change of plans, Gran. Madge called from the home. Mitch hadn't been eating. She was worried about him so we came home."

Brighton told his grandmother what the doctor had said. She listened intently. He explained that he did not want to fly out to Palm Springs and leave his father.

"I'm the only family he has left. His parents are gone. He had no siblings. It's just me."

"I'm so sorry, Brighton. I know how difficult this must be for you. I was looking forward to meeting Cecelia. What are you going to do about the tickets?"

"I guess I'll just have to forfeit them."

"Can you change the dates or the names? Could your grandfather and I use them to fly to New York?"

"Hm, I hadn't thought of that. I will definitely check that out. We would love to see you guys and then you two could stop by the convalescent home while you're here. Mitch would love to see you both."

"OK, well let me know tomorrow. If you can't switch the tickets, Carl and I will buy our own."

Brighton felt relief wash over him knowing that his grandparents were coming. They had known Mitch for a long time. Maybe they could help.

"I can probably call the airline now. I'll call you in the morning."

The airline was sympathetic to Brighton's situation. Instead of changing the tickets, the representative suggested they process a credit and purchase new tickets.

"Changes to tickets can be expensive. If there was a death in the family, it would be different, unfortunately. I don't know why they have those rules. I see you have the trip insurance. You can apply to get at least a partial refund. That's really the best I can do."

"I understand. After I speak with my grandmother I can call and purchase the tickets."

While Brighton talked to the airline, Cecelia poured two glasses of wine. As she left one glass on the coffee table, she signaled to Brighton that she was heading to the bedroom. Once in the room, she turned down the bed clothes and then went to the bathroom to get ready for bed. She washed her face, removed her clothing and pulled on one of his cotton shirts. As she crawled in bed, she could see him watching her from the doorway.

"Do you have any idea how sexy you are in my shirt?"

"Why don't you come over here and show me?"

"Can I stand here for a moment and just memorize the way you look?"

"You get seventy five seconds starting... now."

They spent the next two days at the home with Mitch. Cecelia prepared his meals. Every couple of hours, she sat with a small plate of food for him. He never seemed to remember how often she tried to feed him. There were times when he accepted the food without question. Other times he pushed the plate away. Cecelia remained calm and composed, never batting an eyelash when Mitch turned grumpy. Her smile continued no matter what he said or did.

Brighton watched his fiancée with amazement. She had a gift. Of course her beauty was a plus. Mitch seemed to hang on her every word and get lost in her sultry voice. She reminded Brighton of his mother in temperament and style.

His grandparents arrived on December twenty ninth. He picked them up at the airport and drove straight to the convalescent home. On the way he talked about Mitch. Some of the test results had come back and most showed results within normal parameters. He had some nutritional deficiencies, yet that was to be expected.

"Madge does the best she can. She has other patients."

"I'm sure Madge is great with him. Your grandmother told me about her. I find it interesting that Mitch calls her Donna and she doesn't mind. I would think that might be disconcerting."

"She's been working with geriatric patients for a long time." Brighton told his grandfather. "I suppose a person gets used to being called other names."

As they pulled into the parking lot, Brighton noticed the coroners' vehicle in front of the building. He felt his insides tighten. He tried to tell himself their presence had nothing to do his father. He pulled into a spot close to the door so his grandparents would not have to walk too far. His hand shook as he tugged the keys out of the ignition.

Carl Clay opened the door for his wife. Brighton's eyes were fixed on the entrance. Before they reached the door, it slid open. Two well-dressed men emerged with a gurney. The sheet on top completely covered a body. Right behind them, a teary elderly woman came out. Brighton recognized her and felt a little guilty about the relief that washed over him knowing it wasn't Mitch being taken out.

"Thank God," Mrs. Clay whispered.

They were silent as Brighton led them into the facility, down the hall, and up the elevator to the Alzheimer's wing. Brighton entered the code and opened the door when the buzzer sounded. He gestured for Carl and Marie to enter then made sure the door closed tightly. Brighton heard a crash and took off down the hall. Mitch's voice boomed from his room.

"I said I don't want anymore!"

"OK, Mitch," Cecelia said quietly. "Would you like to take a walk through the garden?" She ignored the standing tray that had been shoved to the floor. "C'mon. Look, your son is here and I bet if we step out into the hall he has brought some people to see you."

"Is Donna here? Can she take me home?"

As Mitch turned toward the door he saw his son. Madge was standing right behind Brighton.

"Donna, can you please take me home? I hate this place."

"You have visitors, Mitch. Why don't you go into the sitting room and chat for a while. I have some cleaning to do," Madge said with a smile.

When he saw who was there to see him, his demeanor changed.

"Marie, Carl, how nice of you to come. Let's go have a seat. We can catch up."

There was a small room across from where Mitch stayed. It was used for residents to visit with their family members. There were two sofas and a few chairs as well as a television on the wall.

"You look great," Carl said cheerily shaking his son-in-law's hand.

"Nice tan, Carl. You must be out on the green every day."

They all entered the sitting room.

"I go five or six days a week now that I'm retired. It keeps me out of trouble."

Carl and Marie sat on the larger of the two sofas. Mitch sat on the other and patted the spot next to him as he grinned at Cecelia. Instead of sitting, she asked if anyone wanted coffee.

"That would be lovely, dear," Mrs. Clay said. "Do you need any help?"

"Brighton can help me. Stay and talk to Mitch."

Once in the hall, Brighton asked her if she was all right.

"I'm fine. I think the newness of me has worn off. Maybe because I have been here several days in a row he has gotten used to me. And I think he really didn't like the way I prepared his food today."

"I am sure it is nothing you did, Ce."

They went into Mitch's room. Madge had asked one of the cleaning people to pick up the tray and discard the uneaten food.

"I'll be out of your way in a minute," the young girl said quietly.

Brighton reached down and righted the table. "Can we help?"

"No Sir, I have it."

He nodded and yet both he and Cecelia helped the girl.

"Your father is one of Madge's favorite patients. On good days he is a very sweet man. On bad days he can be quite ornery. Of course, that is how they all are on this wing. You can't blame them. Most can't remember what they said five minutes ago. That has to be frustrating as heck."

"I can't imagine being here every day for so many hours. It takes a strong person to deal with this day in and day out," Brighton replied.

"You need to have patience and understanding as well as a good imagination. If you keep them occupied, they are less likely to lash out."

"How long have you worked here?"

"I started about a year ago. My great-grandmother had Alzheimer's. I grew up repeating everything I said," she said with a sad laugh. "I suppose it made me immune to the bad moods."

Madge returned moments later with a tray of coffee.

"I heard someone mention drinks?"

Brighton smiled. "I think you read minds, Madge."

She laughed. "I'm glad I don't around here. I would go from caregiver to care-needer pretty darn quickly."

The Clay's remained in the sitting room for nearly an hour reminiscing with Mitch. His mood remained positive although he asked Madge and Cecelia several times if one of them was taking him home.

At three, Marie announced she was hungry.

Cecelia spoke up. "Bri, let's run across the street and pick up something for your grandparents to eat. We can have dinner here. Then I can take them back to the apartment to get settled."

"That sounds wonderful. Are you hungry Mitch?" Marie asked.

"That depends on the menu."

"They make some amazing minestrone soup at the deli, Mitch," Cecelia told him. "How does that sound?"

"Perfect," he said with a big grin.

Brighton stayed at the home until his father had gone to sleep. When he returned to the apartment, his grandparents had turned in for the night. Cecelia was reading in the living room. She sat up and patted the sofa. He flopped down next to her.

Turning toward him, she ran a hand through his hair and kissed his cheek.

"I was talking with your grandmother. We think maybe you should take a break. She and your grandfather can spend the day at the home tomorrow. Maybe you and I can do something."

"I don't know. I feel weird leaving him," he sighed.

"You cannot be there all day every day. It's going to take its toll on you. Besides, maybe having Carl and Marie there instead of us will change his attitude. We can take turns going. Mix things up for him."

"Madge said changing his routine can make him agitated."

"We're not changing his routine, Brighton, just the faces he sees. He enjoyed talking to Marie and Carl today. I know you want to spend as much time with him as you can right now. I understand that. Really, I do. On the other hand, you can't put life on hold for him. I know Madge said he is..." She tried to choose her words carefully. "Deterioration is inevitable. Being there with him will not halt the process. You have to take care of your needs too. I think while your grandparents are here, we should take turns visiting."

"Don't think of this as turning your back on Mitch. You're not. Marie and Carl are family too. Let them have some time with him. OK?"

"If we don't go to the home, what do you want to do tomorrow?"

"Well, I was thinking. I could lend Carl my car so they can go on their own. Then you and I can take a drive to the house and work on a list of what we're keeping, what we're getting rid of, and things we need to do before the wedding."

"We may have to postpone..."

She squeezed his hand. "I know; I was thinking that too. That doesn't mean we can't plan, right? And tomorrow is Saturday. Let's call Jason. I bet Molly would love to get out of the house. She can supervise." His mood began to change. "What do you say? Can we?"

"Sure, I suppose we can do that."

"Great. Are you hungry? I can make you something to eat."

Brighton leaned forward and pulled off his boots. "I'm fine."

"How about a nice hot bubble bath before we go to bed?"

"For you or for me?" he asked.

"Both," she replied.

"I like the way you think. Let me call Jason and I'll meet you in there."

His watched her backside walk away as he dialed. "How is your dad?"

"There's no change really. He's been eating a bit more; I guess. My grandparents are here now. He had a good day for the most part although he yelled at Ce and tossed his tray."

"I'm sorry. Did the doctor say anything?"

"Nothing is abnormal."

Jason tried to be positive. "That's good, right?"

"I almost wish they found something so that they could fix it."

"It must be frustrating for you."

Brighton nodded switching the phone to his other ear. "Cecelia wanted to go to the house tomorrow," he said to change the subject. "Do you and Molly want to come along for the ride? We can do lunch."

"You're not going to see Mitch?"

"Ce thought Gran and Gramps could keep him occupied."

"Good idea, change things up a bit."

"She said I needed a break too."

"Molly, do you want to take a drive to Brighton's house tomorrow?" Jason asked his wife who was sitting on the bed next to him.

"Absolutely, I need to get out of here. I'm feeling claustrophobic."

"What time are we leaving, Bri?"

"We'll call in the morning. I'm thinking around nine."

"Sounds good, we'll be ready."

After removing his clothes, Brighton entered the bathroom and saw his fiancée leaning over to test the water temperature.

"You are beautiful from any angle."

"And you like looking at my bare behind." She straightened up then stepped into the tub and slipped down under the bubbles. "Are you coming?"

"Not yet," he smirked. "Move forward."

"Come here in front of me."

"Have I taught you nothing?" he teased.

"C'mon, I'll wash your back and then we'll switch."

Brighton sank into the water between her legs. Cecelia squirted the body wash onto a sponge and began to wash him. He closed his eyes and enjoyed the attention. His muscles relaxed and his breathing deepened.

"This is what life is all about," he said quietly. "These little crystal moments when you're with the one you love."

"I love you, Brighton," she whispered placing soft kisses on his shoulder.

She wrapped her legs around him and let the sponge travel his upper arms and chest. He leaned his head back as she washed away all his worry and tension. When his breathing began to slow, she suggested that they go to bed. She emptied the tub and rinsed it out while Brighton settled in. When she joined him, she slid between the sheets and placed her head on his chest.

"Should we set the alarm?" he asked.

"That depends on what time you want to leave. I gave Carl the key to my car so they can go when they're ready."

"Do you think he can find his way to the home?"

"I gave him the address for the GPS. I am sure they can get there."

"I told Jason we'd leave around nine so I think we'll wake up in time."

She moved as close as she could to him. She placed one leg over his. As she rubbed his abdomen she asked if he was comfortable.

"I always am when I'm in bed with you," he replied stroking her hair. "Are you sleepy?"

"Not at all, are you?"

He pushed her hand down. "Does that feel like I'm tired?"

"No," she answered as she repositioned her body over his. "But you were nodding off in the tub so maybe I should take the lead tonight."

Brighton tucked his hands behind his head. "Please me."

Carl and Marie were in the kitchen when their grandson went downstairs in the morning.

"There's coffee made. I'm bringing macaroni and cheese for Mitch's lunch. There's another pan on the stove if you want to bring it with you today. You'll just have to heat it up."

Brighton ran a hand through his rumpled hair. "You must have been up early."

"Your grandfather always gets up at five. It's hard to stay in bed long anyway." She patted his cheek. "Call me when you get there, OK?"

"It's not like we're going across the country, Gran."

"Humor me, Brighton."

He gave her a hug as he agreed to her request. "Promise you'll call if you need anything."

"I will, dear."

Mitch was finishing up breakfast when his in-laws arrived. He hadn't eaten much; they could tell by what remained on the tray. Since Mitch seemed in good spirits, Madge removed the tray and told him he had done well.

"Hey Mom, what are you doing here?"

"Carl and I came to spend some time with our favorite son-in-law."

Mitch laughed. "I'm your only son-in-law, Mom. So Carl, have you checked out any of the local courses yet?"

"There's snow on the ground, Mitch."

"Oh, well when spring gets here maybe we can go together."

Brighton and Ce picked up their friends around nine and headed to Long Island. The ladies sat in the back seat. They talked about the baby and the upcoming wedding. The conversation turned to the house. Molly made some decorating suggestions.

"You know Jason and I have been considering moving out of the city too. After the baby is born we're going to talk to a realtor. He has been scoping out firms to see if anyone is hiring."

Brighton glanced at Jason. "I thought we were going to go into business together?"

"I'm exploring options. I, um, had another idea. Have you ever considered changing careers completely?"

"Not particularly. What did you have in mind?"

"You know that bar on New York Avenue. It's up for sale. We could run it together."

Cecelia looked at Molly.

"Mid-life crisis," Molly whispered.

"What do you think, Ce?"

"I'm not sure. What do the two of you know about running a bar?"

"What's there to know?" Jason remarked. "We hire a couple of bartenders, a chef and kitchen staff for making a few appetizers and light meals, and a manager. We know all the legal stuff."

"You're serious about this; aren't you?" Brighton asked incredulously.

"Sure, why not?"

Brighton looked at Cecelia in the rear view mirror. She smiled with a shrug. "It will be will hard work running a dining establishment. I could help interview staff."

"I've already started a business plan," Jason interjected turning toward his friend. "We can do this Bri. It will be a huge change but I know we can do it. And when we get it up and running we can spend more time with our wives. Sure, we'll be at the bar a lot but they can come hang with us sometimes. Once we get a good manager we can take turns hanging out there. I think it will be amazing."

Molly reached forward and patted Brighton's shoulder. "He is really into this. I'm not sure if you're interested but you should look at the plan. He has done so much research. He even talked to a banker about getting a startup loan."

"And when were you planning on telling me this?"

"I was going to talk to you after you came home from Palm Springs. Then all this stuff happened with your dad so I wasn't sure you wanted to leave the city. I can get things started. You can come once in a while until things get more settled with Mitch."

"I need some time to think about all this, Jas. You kind of just threw this on me."

The discussion continued until they reached the house. They spent the day cleaning, moving furniture, and planning. They had the food that Marie had made for lunch. Molly went to take a nap and the others took a ride to the bar that Jason was considering as his next career choice.

"Did you like the mac and cheese, Mitch?"

"You know I love your cooking, Mom. I'm just not hungry."

"It's fine. I'll put what's left in the refrigerator. Maybe you can have some more later."

Marie covered the dish and walked down the hall to the small kitchen. On the way back, she noticed a man in a lab coat by the nurses' station. She assumed he was a doctor. When he looked over his shoulder at her, he quickly turned his entire body away. In seconds, Marie sensed a familiarity about the man. His shock of gray hair made her shake her head and dismiss the thought.

Carl saw the look on his wife's face as she reentered the sitting room.

"Are you all right, dear? You look like you saw a ghost."

"Maybe I did. I guess everything that has gone on has made me suspicious."

Chapter Twenty-Four

The following day, Marie convinced Cecelia to start dress shopping. Ce had wanted her friend to join them yet Molly was not up to it. Being at Brighton's house the day before had tuckered her out.

"OK, Molly, I understand. I'll tell you what. If I find something I like, I'll send you a pic."

"I'd like that, Ce. Thanks."

Carl went with his grandson to the home to visit with Mitch. The weather was a bit warmer so the three men walked down to the courtyard. Madge had found a walker for Mitch. He was becoming more unsteady on his feet.

The walkways on the courtyard had been completely cleared of ice and snow. They traveled around the small area a few times and then sat on one of the stone benches. A few minutes of sitting made Mitch a bit anxious so they repeated the walk. The fresh air changed Mitch's whole countenance. Anyone hearing the conversation would not know Mitch suffered from dementia.

"How is that girlfriend of yours, son?"

"She is my fiancée, Dad. She and Gran went dress shopping today."

"When are you getting married?"

"We haven't set a date yet. We were thinking once the weather gets warm we would have a backyard wedding at the house on Long Island."

"When are you going to bring Lydia to see me?" Mitch inquired.

"Cecelia will stop by tomorrow."

Mitch nodded. "We should head inside. Your mom has probably cooked up a big lunch for us."

"OK Dad, let's go in."

"Oh, Ce, that is beautiful," Molly said over the speaker phone.

"It is but I'm thinking it's not right for a spring wedding in the yard. I mean long lacy sleeves on a full length gown... I don't think so. I want you to see it though. I like the way the neckline is cut."

"Try on the tea length white one with the turquoise accent around the waist."

Cecelia smiled. "I liked that one too. Give me a few minutes to change. Talk to Marie."

Brighton's grandmother was sitting on a small padded bench in the corner of the large dressing room. She turned the cell phone so Molly wasn't watching Cecelia change.

"In my day, you wore white. That was it. No one would have thought of wearing black or turquoise. And if your dress wasn't pure white that meant you weren't a virgin. Of course, hardly anyone waits until they're married anymore."

Cecelia and Molly were both smiling as Mrs. Clay chattered on about wedding dresses and virgins. Finally, Cecelia finished changing and asked Marie to turn the phone.

"That is definitely the one, Ce. Brighton is going to trip over his own tongue. It is so perfect!"

"Thanks Molly. That's why I wanted you to see the other one on me first." She twirled slowly so Molly could see from each angle. "And it fits like it was made for me. I doubt I'll need any alterations."

Marie stood and approached Cecelia. "I like it too, Ce. Too bad your mom isn't here to see it."

"We can take a picture with the cell and email it to her. I'll send it to my sister too."

Ce showed Marie how to use the camera and she took three different shots. Then Cecelia forwarded the images to her mother and sister. Within seconds of sending a text to her sister, the cell pinged with a reply.

OMG! Love it!

The cell rang and Ce rolled her eyes before she hit accept.

"Hey Nat, so you like it huh?"

"It looks amazing. I just love the turquoise accent. I should have texted you a pic of mine. It's floor length with a wonderfully modest train. It was like seven grand but it is totally worth it. Oh, we set a date for September. I didn't want to upstage your wedding although mine will be totally different. I am not doing simple by any stretch of the imagination."

"Nat..."

"I think that dress suits the whole backyard wedding thing you're doing. You don't need a long gown. It's not like you're going to be dancing with Dad on the patio or anything like that. And the place we booked for the wedding has this long staircase that I'm going to walk down and..."

"Natalia," Ce said trying to get a word in.

"Oh, I'm sorry; I'm babbling. It's lovely, Ce. Really. Did you email a pic to Mom?"

"Yes, I did. I'm sure I'll be hearing from her later."

"OK, well, I should go. Oh, how is Brighton's father?"

"He's the same."

"Tell Brighton we're all praying for him. I'll talk to you later, sis."

After finishing nearly half of his lunch, Mitch pushed his tray aside and began to get up.

"Where are you going, Dad?"

"Do you have to know everything? I have to take a leak. Satisfied?"

"Do you need..?"

"I'm not an invalid. I can remember how to use the damn toilet."

Brighton glanced at Carl who shrugged back. Both of them watched Mitch make his way to the door. Brighton stood to follow but stayed far enough behind so his father didn't see him. Mitch's room was only a few doors down from the sitting room where they had been eating. All the patients had private baths in their rooms. Brighton stood right outside the door listening in case Mitch had any troubles. A few minutes passed and just as he was about to knock on the restroom door, a gentleman in a white coat stepped up to him.

"Is Mr. Daniels around?"

"He's in there," Brighton explained gesturing to the small bathroom. "He should be out any minute."

The man extended his hand. "Dr. Silverman. I don't think we've met."

Brighton shook the doctor's hand. "Brighton Clay, Mitch's son."

"Yes, Madge has told me about you. It's nice to meet you. How is he doing?"

The door to the bathroom opened. "I can hear you know. I'm not deaf."

"Good afternoon, Mitch. You look well."

"Pft. I suppose you want to check me out."

"I'll be quick, Mitch; I promise."

Dr. Silverman spent only a few minutes with Mitchell. He listened to his heart and lungs then asked a few questions.

Mitch was agitated. He had been all day and having the doctor examine him only irritated him more.

"Are you done yet?"

"I think we're all set, Mitch. Do you mind if I chat with your son a bit?"

"It's a free country," Mitchell mumbled as he got to his feet. "I'm going back to the sitting room."

Once his patient had exited the room, Dr. Silverman turned to the younger man.

"Madge told me you have been here quite a bit lately. That's good for him. If his mind is more active, the progression of the dementia might be kept in check. Unfortunately, we don't really know for sure."

"Yeah, I know. I've done my research and Madge is a great source of knowledge. She's worked with patients like my dad for a long time."

Dr. Silverman seemed to stare at him for a moment making Bri a bit uncomfortable. In response, he tilted his head and lifted a brow.

"I'm sorry; you don't really look like Mr. Daniels."

"I guess I take after my mother."

"You mean Donna?"

"How do you know my mother's name?"

"Mitch calls Madge Donna all the time so I assumed..."

"Oh, right, he does," Brighton snickered.

Dr. Silverman nodded. "You said your last name was Clay?"

"It's my mother's maiden name. Mitch married my mother after I was born."

"So you're not his blood relative?"

"He's my father nonetheless. He was there for me whenever I needed him." He was a bit perturbed by the inquisition. "How long have you been working here?"

"I normally work at the hospital. I visit here a few times a month when the other doctors are unavailable. I guess you can say I'm a fill in," he chuckled.

"Why haven't I run into you before?"

Dr. Silverman gestured toward the hall. "I guess I haven't been here when you are."

They walked toward the nurses' station which was just past the sitting room where Mitch and Carl were. As they wandered by the windowed wall, Dr. Silverman seemed to angle his body away from the room. Brighton thought it was odd.

"I suppose I will be seeing more of you."

"Well, I have been here more so I assume you're right."

"It was nice to meet you, Brighton. Your father is a wonderful man."

"I know he is."

They shook hands once more and Brighton returned to the sitting room.

Upon returning home, Brighton found Cecelia in the living room with her computer in her lap and the phone pressed to her ear. Carl heard his wife in the kitchen and went to see what she was cooking.

"I know it's not as fancy as Natalia's."

Brighton kissed the top of Ce's head before sitting next to her. He figured by her comment, she had found a wedding gown. As he sat, she closed her laptop so he could not see her dress.

Brighton whispered, "Are you hiding something from me?"

"Its simplicity is its beauty, dear. Sometimes more is less. Besides, the gown you chose is looks like it was designed with you in mind."

"Thanks, Ma. You always make me feel better. After speaking with Nat I was a bit... bothered." Cecelia covered the receiver for a moment and said, "You can't see my gown until our wedding day." Then she kissed him softly on the lips.

"Don't let her get to you. She's trying to change but she has been competing with you all her life and old habits are hard to break."

"I know; so are mine. I take her words to heart instead of brushing them off. I have to change too."

"Your father said you look absolutely stunning."

"I bet he said the exact same thing to Natalia."

"And he meant it both times. It sounds like Brighton is home. Send him my best. I'll talk to you soon."

"I love you."

"Love you too, dear."

Cecelia moved the computer to the coffee table and settled back into her fiancé's arms.

"So your trip today was successful?"

"Very," she replied. "I even found shoes and something special for the wedding night."

"Do I get to see it before then?"

"Nope."

"Tease."

"Yup."

"I missed you today," he breathed into her ear as he gave her a little squeeze.

"I missed you too. My sister and mother both sent their regards. Nat asked about your dad. How was he today?"

"He was edgy. Some new doctor came to see him and Mitch didn't seem to like him very much. I didn't particularly care for him either. He was a bit nosy. He mentioned I had a different last name then Mitch and said I don't look like him."

"You don't have the same features but you both have mischief in your eyes."

"I don't think Dr. Silverman saw that," Bri chortled. "To be honest, I felt like he was interrogating me. Maybe I am too guarded and he was just making conversation."

"It is totally understandable, but Brent and Lydia are still locked away. They were the instigators of that whole mess. I doubt either of them has the wherewithal to have someone else after you."

"I'm worried about Mitch, though. We know Lydia had other people helping her like the cop who took me from the warehouse. And then there is Flatley. He could still..."

Cecelia pulled back so she could look at him. "You cannot spend the rest of your life looking over your shoulder. Let's put all the mess behind us and get on with life. You're not at the firm anymore. Flatley can have the damn partnership. Who cares?"

"You know what, my love. You are absolutely right. And I am about to get started on the rest of our lives. Let's set a date. How about the first weekend in May? It will be warm enough for a cookout but not too hot to be dressed up. We'll do everything simple and easy. No muss, no fuss. We can spend the weekend at the Plaza. I'm sure Gran and Gramps will watch Mitch for a couple of days. I don't want to be too far away or for too long."

As he spoke, Cecelia's lips curled up and her eyes sparkled. "Really? May? You mean it?"

"I absolutely do. Let's get the invitations out."

"We don't need formal invitations, Bri, unless you plan on inviting a bunch of people. I was thinking Mom and Dad, Samuel and Nat, Molly and Jason, and your grandparents and the JP or a minister, whatever we decide."

"OK, then, let's email them all."

"Close your eyes for a minute."

"Why?"

"Just do it."

He complied. She opened her laptop and closed the picture of her gown. "OK, you can open them. Let's compose the email."

Dear Friends and Family:

It is with great joy that Brighton and I invite you to our wedding to be held on the first weekend in May pending us finding an available minister or JP. Please join us at our house on Long Island for a very private ceremony and barbeque. Please, no gifts.

Chapter Twenty-Five

Carl and Marie stayed in New York through mid-January. While in the city, they took turns visiting the convalescent home. As the days went by, Mitch seemed more like himself. The blood cultures came back revealing an infection and he was given antibiotics. Madge told Brighton that when a patient is sick, he can unconsciously shut down. Once the medication began to work, Mitch was eating better and his attitude improved. He was back to joking and laughing.

Brighton and Cecelia were busy planning the wedding. They visited the house on the island several times to clean and redecorate. She called florists and caterers. He asked Jason to be his best man and the two went to a men's shop to order custom made tuxedos. Molly decided to wait a few weeks before dress shopping.

Baby Jackson Campbell decided to make his appearance two weeks early. He was a bit small but otherwise healthy. His parents were thrilled and totally enamored with their son. For a few nights, the baby slept in a bassinet in his parents' room. Then Brighton helped his friend set up the nursery and put together the crib a few days after the baby came home from the hospital.

About a month after the baby was born, the Campbells started looking for a house on the island so they would be close to Brighton and Cecelia. They found a Garrison colonial not too far from Brighton's home. The backyard was completely fenced and big enough for a swing set. The grass was lush and a few small shrubs decorated the front of the building. Each of the three bedrooms had abundant closet space and there was a full bath at the top of the stairs. The previous owners had moved so the house was ready for a new family. Once the bid was accepted, Jason took his friends on a tour.

"I love how the laundry is on the first floor," Cecelia commented. "And the kitchen is pristine. The wife must have spent a good deal of time cooking and cleaning."

Jason told Brighton the basement was finished. "Come take a look," he suggested opening the door to the stairwell. "I have my own man-cave. I'm going to get a huge flat screen and surround sound. We can have poker night with the guys."

"Do you think you'll be able to move in before the wedding?"

"Probably not," Jason replied. "You know how these things go. We need to set up the inspection then the closing. It could take several weeks. I've listed the condo in the city. It should go pretty fast."

Brighton nodded as he squatted down to get a closer look at the furnace underneath the stairs. "This is so clean. It doesn't look half as old as the repair sticker says it is."

"The owner did regular maintenance on everything. I know our price was high but with the condition this place is in, it will be worth it in the long run. The inspection should go well."

Brighton straightened up and wiped his hands on the backside of his jeans.

His friend said, "You're worried about something. I can tell."

"There's a new doctor that's been stopping by to see Mitch. Call it intuition or paranoia but I don't like him. The first time we met he asked me why I didn't look like Mitch. Maybe Ce was right; I am suspicious of everyone now."

"You have every right to be cautious. We could have Johnson run a background check on him if it would ease your mind."

"Do it. I don't want anyone screwing around with Mitch."

Jason called the detective and asked him to get any information he could on Dr. Silverman.

"Be discreet."

"I always am, Jason. I'll get back to you soon."

After he disconnected the call, he looked at Bri and said, "Done. Is there anything else bothering you?"

Brighton stuffed his hands in his pockets. "We're you serious about buying that bar? Because I've been thinking about it and I think we should go for it. I don't want to defend scumbags anymore. I know it will be a lot of work but it will be a good change of pace. It would be fun to call the cops if anyone gets drunk and disorderly," he laughed.

"Did you read the business plan?"

"I did and I have to say I am quite impressed. You've been thinking about this for a while."

"C'mon, let's go back upstairs and tell the ladies we're going to do it. I can get things rolling and we can open up for business after you get back from your honeymoon."

Later that afternoon, the four went out to an early dinner to celebrate new beginnings. Brighton was happier than he had been in a long time. The improvement in his father's health and the prospect of a new career had a positive effect on his attitude.

On the ride back to the city, the ladies sat in the back of the new SUV Jason had purchased. The baby fell asleep almost as soon as the engine started.

"Let's go dress shopping tomorrow," Molly whispered. "I think I'm almost at my pre-pregnancy weight. Do you have any idea what you want me to wear?"

"You can choose something you can use again. As long as it doesn't clash with the accents on mine, I'll be happy. It is not like I am having a whole wedding party that has to match."

"Do you have a color scheme for the decorations or flowers?"

"My bouquet will be champagne colored roses. I ordered a few table arrangements with various complimentary colors. It is all simple, nothing flashy."

"Sounds lovely," Molly sighed. "Our wedding was a big to-do that I had no say in, huh Jason?"

"Your mother wanted to be in charge," he smirked. "You would have thought she was the one getting married."

"My parents eloped. Mom never had a lavish reception. I sort of gave in to her, let her run the show. I didn't mind as long as she didn't come on the honeymoon. Speaking of which, where are you two going?"

"Bri hasn't told me. I've been snooping around but I found nothing. He is very tight-lipped."

"That's too bad," Molly said giving Ce a knowing glance.

"You're so bad Molly."

A few days passed before Johnson called with information about Dr. Silverman. He decided to skip Jason and speak directly to Brighton.

"Hey Bri, how are the wedding plans coming along?"

"Things are falling into place. Are you coming?"

"Absolutely, I love happy endings. Although I am not sure this is all over. I hear Lydia is still in the psych ward. They haven't cracked through her shell and I am not sure they ever will."

"As long as she's locked away somewhere, I am not going to worry about her. What about Brent?"

"I'm sure he will have his day in court. Don't know if a jury is going to believe him that she was in control the whole time."

"So did you find out anything about Silverman?"

"He is a bona fide doctor for sure. He was born in La Jolla California and went to school out West. He was married and has two teenage girls. He moved to New York eight months after the divorce was finalized."

"La Jolla, huh?"

"Yeah, why? Any significance to that?"

"Promise me this goes no farther unless something happens."

"Sure Bri, what's up with La Jolla?"

"That's where I was born."

"I see some more investigation in my future. I'll get back to you."

Brighton tried not to dwell on the thoughts running through his head. He could talk to his grandmother yet he did not want to worry her. He wondered if she had seen the new doctor. If she had, why would she not have said something to him? Would she recognize a man she had not seen in over thirty years?

Brighton and Jason reviewed the business plan together for the bar before setting up a meeting at the bank. The loan officer was impressed with the work Jason had put into his plan. The loan was approved quickly and a closing was arranged. The process was relatively painless and both men could barely wait to redesign the bar and open their joint venture.

Buying the house was almost as easy as getting the loan for the bar. The inspection went smoothly. The closing on the new Campbell house was only a few days before the Clay wedding. Jason decided to have the movers pack everything up the following weekend. In the meantime, he and Molly would have time to clean the house top to bottom before the furniture arrived.

Chapter Twenty-Six

Brighton's grandparents returned to New York two days before the wedding. They visited Mitch and spent the first night at the Plaza. Friday they followed Brighton to the house in the island. Ce had made the hotel arrangements for all the guests coming from out of town. Although it was no Plaza, it was more posh than other accommodations she had researched.

The Demures and Samuel arrived on Friday. Jonathan walked into the suite and glanced at his wife. She smiled back and patted his shoulder as he placed the suitcases aside.

"This is nice," Natalia said.

"It will do for a couple of days," her father replied.

Once Jonathan and his wife were in the larger of the two bedrooms, Mrs. Demure spoke. "I know it's not quite what you're accustomed to but this is a small community. Please do not complain to your daughter. Promise me?"

"I won't darling. This is her weekend. I will not ruin it for her."

She patted his arm again. "Let's get settled then call Ce and see if they are ready for dinner."

Natalia crossed the living area to the other bedroom of the suite. As she closed the door, Samuel pulled her into his arms.

"Why are we sharing a suite with your parents?"

"I told Ce we could make our own reservations. She insisted. I said it would be all right if we were in a suite instead of her paying for two rooms."

"This might be a little awkward."

"It's only for two nights, Samuel. Sunday we will be heading back home."

"I think I can manage until then." Samuel squeezed her a bit tighter. "But you're going to have to put a sock in your mouth tonight."

"You reserved one suite for them?" Brighton asked as he dressed for dinner.

"Bri, that place is so small. None of the other rooms would have been adequate for my father and they only had one suite available. They could have slept here or worse, at the local no-tell motel."

"Maybe you and I should have stayed at the hotel so your family could stay here."

"It will be fine, Brighton."

"As long as your father doesn't rip me up one side and down the other everything will be fine."

Cecelia laughed at Brighton's comment. She kissed his cheek. "I'll protect you from my big bad father."

Jonathan drove his Mercedes to the restaurant. Carl followed in the sedan he had rented at the airport. Brighton, Cecelia, Jason, and Molly had been seated only minutes earlier at a large table in a private room. They two men rose to greet Cecelia's family. Both Bri and Jonathan reached to hold out Mrs. Demure's chair. Jonathan raised a teasing eyebrow at the younger man.

"Thank you both," Mrs. Demure laughed.

"You worked at the firm with Brighton," Jonathan asked Jason as he sat beside his wife.

"Yes, we went to law school together as well. We both graduated top of our class."

The baby cooed in Molly's arms.

"He's adorable, Molly."

"Thank you, Mrs. Demure. He's a good baby. After a tense pregnancy, I feel blessed that he is healthy and happy."

"My pregnancy with Natalia was difficult and she was two weeks early. Cecelia was stubbornly late. She has proven to have a mind of her own ever since."

Ce heard Brighton stifle a laugh and she elbowed him.

"What are you poking me for? There is nothing wrong with knowing what you want out of life."

"I know exactly what I want." She placed a soft kiss on his lips.

The waitress appeared and took drink orders.

"Can I get you any appetizers while you look at the menu?"

Everyone glanced around the table.

"I think we're good," Brighton told her.

After a single nod she disappeared.

Brighton looked at his fiancée. "What are you getting, my love?"

"It's a tossup between the Shrimp on Horseback and the crab cakes."

Molly said, "I'm looking at the Carbonara with wild mushrooms and asparagus."

"I saw that too," Ce said to her friend. "I thought it might be too heavy."

Dinner conversation centered mainly about the wedding. When that topic was thoroughly discussed, Cecelia's mom asked how soon she could expect grandchildren. Cecelia squeezed Brighton's hand under the table.

"We won't make you wait too long, Mom. We were going to start trying soon."

"Samuel and I are going to hold off for a year. He has a few things going on right now at work."

Jonathan looked at Brighton. "Cecelia tells me you and Jason are starting a business."

Brighton took a sip of his wine. "That's right. Jason wrote up a great business plan and we have already secured financing."

"Running a bar will take up a good deal of your time. What if it fails? How will you support your family?"

"Daddy!"

"I'm just making sure you are well cared for, sweetheart."

"I can take care of myself. The doctor's office where I applied to be an assistant called earlier this week. I start a week from Monday. We'll be fine even if the bar doesn't do well. You don't need to worry."

"It's my privilege as your father to worry, Cecelia. Don't take that away from me." He smirked when he said it. "You will understand when you have children of your own. How many are children are you planning to have?"

"We'd like a boy and a girl. I know it doesn't always happen that way. Maybe we will try for a third if we have two boys or two girls. It all depends."

"Jason is happy he has a son," Molly said looking at her husband. "I think we might go for one more but even if it is another boy, I am done."

Jason leaned back in his chair. "No more than two, that's our deal. One for you and one for me."

The following morning, Brighton was up at the crack of dawn. He slipped quietly out of bed and went into the bathroom. The sound of the water echoed into the bedroom. She smiled as her eyes fluttered open. She sauntered toward the sound of her soon-to-be husband humming as he shaved.

"Well you're up early," she purred.

"I wanted to get out of your way."

"Do you think it will take me four hours to prepare for our big day?"

"Not at all, my love." His eyes wandered down her naked form them returned to her lips. He tilted his head calling her closer. After a quick kiss he told her she needed no preparation to be beautiful.

"You are way too charming this early in the morning." She ran her hand along his arm and took the razor from him. "Shall I assist?"

"Should I trust you with a sharp object?"

"You trusted me with a firearm, remember?"

She carefully shaved around the edge of his beard along his jaw. Occasionally, her eyes would flick up to his. He remained as still as he could yet his lips kept wanting to curl. She rinsed the razor a few times and made sure her work was done well. When she was finished, she placed his razor down and picked up her own.

"Wanna do me?"

"Legs or landing strip?"

"Both. I want to be perfect for our wedding night."

Under the fall of warm water, Brighton shaved her legs. When he was done, he moved his hand toward her special place. She grabbed his wrist.

"Don't. I waxed last night."

He shivered slightly.

"It's not as bad as you think. I could show you some time if you like."

"Oh hell no, you are not shaving anywhere near my boys."

She removed the razor from his hand and put it on the edge of the tub. They spent close to an hour in the shower enjoying the last of their time before the guests arrived. When they emerged from the bathroom, Cecelia pulled on a thick terry robe and went down to the kitchen to make coffee. Brighton moved his clothes for the day to another bedroom. Just as he exited the room, he heard the doorbell. He jogged down the stairs and opened the door.

"C'mon in," he said to Cecelia's parents. "Ce is in the kitchen making coffee."

"I'm sorry we're so early Brighton."

"It's no bother, Mrs. Demure. We expected you to come around this time. Where are Nat and Samuel?"

"Still in bed," Jonathan grumbled.

The house was buzzing all morning long. Cecelia had made a few dishes of her own for the barbeque. Molly brought pasta salad and deviled eggs. Brighton had purchased steaks and kielbasa and had asked one of the cooks they had hired for the bar to tend the grill.

Cecelia went to get dressed shortly after ten. Her mother, sister and Molly joined her in the master bedroom. Marie remained downstairs and supervised the final preparations. The men set up two tables in the yard. Marie covered the tables and arranged plates, napkins, and plastic silverware.

The weather that day was picture perfect. There was a gentle breeze coming from the nearby ocean. Puffy clouds floated overhead. No one could have wished for a better day.

When Nick Johnson arrived, Brighton pulled him aside.

"Have you found out anything more since we talked?"

"Dr. Silverman's past is clean, Bri. If he is connected to you in some way, I haven't connected the dots yet but I will. I promise you."

Brighton blew out a long breath. "I've been debating asking my grandmother about him, I'm not sure she saw Dr. Silverman at the home. I think if she knew who he was she would have said something. Maybe if I talk to her I can spark a memory."

"Do yourself a favor. Enjoy the day. Have a nice honeymoon with your bride. We'll talk in a few days and decide where to go from here."

"I need to know, Nick."

"I understand. This is your wedding day. Concentrate on that." To change the subject, Johnson asked where they were going on their honeymoon.

"It's a secret but we are not going far. You have my cell. You can call me any time day or night."

"If I find something that needs immediate attention, I will."

The doorbell rang and Brighton turned to see Carl greet the Justice of the Peace.

"I guess it is just about that time," he said to the detective. "I'd better get ready."

Natalia and her mother came down to the living room to see if everything was set to go. Molly kept her friend company as they waited for the signal.

The ceremony lasted only a few minutes with the couple reciting their own simple vows. Jason's cheering was heard above the others when the JP pronounced the couple man and wife and everyone applauded.

Just after they kissed, Brighton whispered in his wife's ear. "I love you and although you look amazing in that dress all I can think about is tearing it off you."

"Don't get me started. We have our friends and family watching us."

"Can we sneak upstairs for a bit?"

"Down boy. You'll have me all night."

Everyone enjoyed the food, conversation, and the glorious spring weather. Johnson was the first to leave stating that he had work to do. Brighton walked with him through the house to the front door.

"Thanks for coming. Let me know if you find out anything else. We're not going far. My grandparents will be around to check in on Mitch. You can call the cell any time."

"I told you, if I found something I think needs you immediate attention, I will. Otherwise, enjoy your honeymoon." He clapped Brighton's shoulder. "Take a break from reality."

"Thanks, I'll do that."

Brighton returned to his wife's side, slipping his arm around her waist. She excused herself from the discussion she was having with Jason and the two moved away from the others.

"It was nice of you to invite Nick. He's done so much for you. Seems to me he is still on the job."

"I can't hide anything from you, can I?"

"If you don't want to talk about it…"

"I asked him to check out that new doctor. I wasn't going to say anything until my suspicions were confirmed."

"Do you think he is working for Lydia?"

Brighton shook his head. "I hope not."

"Then what?"

"The guy makes me uneasy. I didn't like the questions he asked. He was a bit too interested in my relationship with Mitch."

"I'm not sure what you're getting at."

"We'll talk about it later. I don't want my grandparents overhearing."

Cecelia placed a gentle kiss on his mouth. She pulled back slightly and gazed into his eyes. He pulled her tightly against him and with a hand placed on her cheek, he kissed her back. For a few moments, they were lost in each other.

She broke the kiss and put a finger to his lips. "Hold that thought for later. I don't want you getting all hot and bothered yet."

"Too late," he muttered.

Shortly after three, Brighton took his wife by the hand. "We should go change. It will take us a couple of hours to get where we're going tonight."

"And where would that be?"

"You'll find out soon enough."

"You're not going to tell me until we get there, huh?"

"I think you'll figure it out on the way."

Brighton had already packed two suitcases and placed them in the trunk of the car. She removed her gown and pulled a t-shirt dress over her head. She slipped into a comfortable pair of sandals for the ride.

"Did you pack my swimsuit?"

"As a matter of fact, I packed two."

"Always be prepared," she teased. "Did you pack one for you?"

"I certainly did."

"What about shampoo, conditioner, face cream..?"

He held up a hand. "I thought of everything, darling. And if I missed anything, we can buy it."

"I think I'll like this honeymoon."

When they returned to the living room, the couple said their good-byes to everyone. Ce helped Molly put the baby in the car seat.

"Call us when you get to where you are going so I know you're safe," Molly said.

"I will. I wish I knew where we were going. I know he didn't pack too many clothes, not much was missing."

"Who needs clothes when you're going to spend three days in bed?"

"That's true."

A few feet away, Jason shook his friend's hand and patted him on the shoulder. "You did it. Now, treat her well. She deserves it."

"Don't worry, Jas. She is going to get whatever she wants. I'm going to spoil her beyond all expectations."

Jason glanced back at the ladies then quietly asked, "What's up with Johnson? I saw you two talking earlier."

"He's looking into something for me."

"And you don't want to tell me?"

"Not yet, not until I know more. Just do me a favor and keep an eye on Mitch. My grandparents are sticking around until I get back but I don't want them involved in this if they aren't already."

"I'll check in on them as well. Don't worry. I'll call if anything strange goes on."

"Thanks. They're spending the night here in town and heading back to the city in the morning."

"I'll follow them; make sure they get there safely."

Brighton gave his friend a hug. "Thanks, man."

"Hey, you're like the brother I never had. I mean, not like..."

"I know what you mean."

After the remaining family had left, the newlyweds climbed into his Mercedes. During the ride, she watched the signs and scenery. When they crossed the state line she was surprised. Still, she did not ask where they were going.

"Part of me thought you might whisk me away to the Plaza but we passed that a while ago."

He opened his mouth. She raised her hand.

"No, don't tell me."

As they neared a city, Brighton reached over and took her hand. He brought it to his lips. "It's not the Plaza. However, they have a spa, five heated pools, in-room dining, and a fully stocked mini-bar. We could spend 80 or so hours without leaving the room which, by the way, has a fantastic view from what I've heard. On the other hand, we could go out every night dancing or hang in the casinos. It's all up to you. The only thing I have scheduled is a couples' massage on Monday afternoon. Everything else is spur of the moment, spontaneous, and all your choice."

"Have you been to Atlantic City before?" she asked.

"No but Jason took Molly here and he said the service and amenities are superb. You will be pampered and spoiled the entire time we're here."

"Sounds perfect."

The room was larger than any Cecelia had ever seen. The king size bed was piled high with pillows. She walked across the room and looked out over the water. Brighton gave a hefty tip to the young bellhop who had assisted with their bags.

"Your dinner shall be ready at seven thirty as requested, Sir. Please enjoy your stay."

"We will."

The bellhop leaned in and whispered, "You're a very lucky man. She's hot."

"Yes, I am and she certainly is."

Brighton closed the door and placed the key cards on the side table.

"What do you want to do first my beautiful bride?" he asked wrapping his arms around her.

She leaned her head back against his shoulder. "Well, we have about forty minutes before dinner arrives. I hope you didn't order too much."

"I thought you might be hungry by the time we got here. Don't worry; it's just enough to give us energy for the night."

"How thoughtful." She turned around and put her hands on his chest. "Perhaps we should test the king size bed."

He shook his head. "I don't think so. I want to take my time tonight. I'm going to please you from head to toe and back again. By sunrise tomorrow, you will be breathless and completely spent."

Ce bit her lip for a moment. "Um, well then I am going to go take a hot shower so I can warm my muscles for the long night ahead of us."

As she sauntered toward the bathroom, she tugged her dress up over her head and tossed it aside. She slipped her panties down, swung them around the tip of her index finger, and then shot them back at her husband.

"Care to join me?"

A growl emanated from deep inside his chest. "You are hard to resist."

"Don't try. Come play."

Dinner that evening included two simple green salads with a light sherry vinaigrette, shrimp cocktails, and a Mediterranean platter which included hummus, baba ganoush, olives, grilled pita bread, and tabbouleh. The couple sat in hotel robes at a small table in the corner of the room.

"This is amazing. Did you choose the menu?"

"Yes I did. I thought we could try something different. I'm so used to eating steaks I thought skipping the red meat might be an interesting change. And, if we're going to be trying to get pregnant, we should both eat healthier."

"Who are you?" she laughed.

Brighton placed a hand on his chest. "You offend me, dear wife. And not everything here is good for you." He lifted one of the lids to reveal a dish of profiteroles. "The sauce is dark chocolate."

"If you would like to pour that all over me you can," she purred.

Brighton and Cecelia finished eating and he pushed the dinner cart out in the hall. He hung the "do not disturb" sign on the door. When he turned he saw his wife had shed her robe and was propped up on the fluffy bed pillows. He approached her like prey tossing aside his robe. He crawled from the end of the bed over her.

Brighton placed a gentle kiss on her lips then asked if she was ready for a ride to heaven.

Chapter Twenty-Seven

Brighton's grandparents spent Monday at the home with Mitch. They brought him breakfast which he thoroughly enjoyed. Afterward, the three went downstairs to the courtyard. The weather was warm and sunny and a few birds chirped in the trees.

"When are you and I going golfing?" Mitch asked his father-in-law.

"I'll call the club and set up a tee time for next week."

Mitch nodded. "Do you think Brighton would join us?"

"We can sure ask."

"Do you know anyone else who can make it a foursome?"

"What about Brighton's friend Jason?"

"He'll do; I suppose. Where is Brighton today?"

"He's on his honeymoon," Marie told him.

"Finally married that Lydia girl?"

"No, he married Cecelia. You remember her; don't you?"

"Yeah, sure. The pretty one who always wants me to eat."

When they returned to the floor, Mrs. Clay noticed Madge talking to Nick Johnson. Madge saw the Clays and tugged on Nick's shirt sleeve. The detective looked over his shoulder then gestured to Madge. The two of them disappeared into the office behind the desk.

After lunch, Mitch fell asleep in his wheelchair. The Clays stayed in the sitting room talking and watching the television.

"Marie, why does that doctor look so familiar? I can't place him but I feel like I know him."

Marie glanced in the direction her husband was facing. "If I told you who he looks like I'm afraid of what you might do."

She turned back toward Carl. "I've only seen his profile. If I saw him straight on I would know for sure but he turns every time I get near. I feel like he does it on purpose which makes me think he is..."

Carl got to his feet. "I'm going to go talk to him."

Marie touched his arm. "Don't. Please. When Brighton comes back tomorrow, we can talk to him and I'll tell you who I think he looks like, all right?"

Carl inhaled sharply. His hands tightened into fists.

"You're too old to fight for her honor now, Carl."

Although the honeymoon was short, the couple enjoyed every minute of their time together. As Brighton put the last of the bags into his car on Tuesday morning, he told Cecelia he wanted to stop to see his father before heading home.

"I thought you might say that. We should get there about lunch time, right?"

He nodded as he closed the trunk. "Maybe we can stop at the deli across the street and get him some of that soup he likes."

"When we get close I'll call your grandmother and let her know."

Cecelia slid into the front seat. Brighton got in behind the wheel and slipped the key into the ignition.

"I know we only had a couple of days but the honeymoon doesn't really have to end here." He took her hand in his. "I love you, Ce."

"Ditto."

She put on some quiet music and hummed along as she watched the scenery whip by the window. Being away had given them a chance to connect on a new level. They had discussed her career and his new venture with Jason. With the turmoil of the past behind them, the two could concentrate on life as a married couple.

Cecelia watched the time. She was about to call Mrs. Clay when Brighton's cell chirped. She smiled looking at the caller ID.

"Hi Mrs. Clay. I was just thinking of you. Are you with Mitch?"

"Yes we are. I assume my grandson is driving."

"I'll put you on speaker." She hit the button. "Now we can both hear you. Bri and I were going to stop at the deli and bring Mitch some soup. Would you two like anything?"

"That would be lovely. When you get close, call me and I can order everything so it is ready when you get there."

"Will do."

"Gran, how is Dad?'

"He's well, Brighton. He asked about you a couple of times. I told him you were on your honeymoon but he keeps forgetting. Listen, Detective Johnson came by here yesterday morning. He spoke privately with Madge. Is there something I should know?"

"Let me talk to Nick when I get home. He was looking into something for me. Once I have some answers we'll chat, all right?"

"I don't like being kept in the dark."

"I know, Gran. But at this point, all I have is suspicions. Let me get the facts."

Mrs. Clay conceded.

After the call was over, Cecelia reached over and squeezed his hand. "Is there anything you would like to tell me now, or do I have to wait too?"

"I think Silverman is my birth father."

"Your what..?"

"He's from La Jolla where I was born. And the way he grilled me about Mitch made me uneasy. I'm having Johnson check him out but my gut tells me I'm right."

"Do you think he would harm Mitch?"

"Somehow I don't think he would. He's had ample opportunity and nothing has occurred. And he is a real doctor."

"Why is he in New York? Do you think he knows who you are?"

"I believe he does know. Why else would he have asked me about how I was related to Mitch?"

"Hopefully Nick had found some proof one way or the other."

"He will. He's good at what he does."

The family decided to have lunch out in the courtyard. Cecelia set Mitch's soup on a tray borrowed from the sitting room. She gave him a chunk of French bread to eat as well.

"You get prettier every time I see you," he said as she placed the food in front of him.

"And you get more charming."

"Brighton, you should marry this woman before she falls for some silver-tongued devil like me."

"We already are married, Dad. And she is not going anywhere."

Cecelia tilted her head toward her husband. "Bri is my silver-tongued devil."

Everyone laughed at her comment.

"So you married my son. Does he treat you well?"

"Oh most definitely he does."

"Good. Because if he ever mistreats you, I want you to come see me and I'll give him a firm talking to."

After Mitch finished eating, Cecelia took him inside. Marie and Carl glanced at each other than at their grandson.

"Brighton, I don't need proof from your detective to know that the new doctor is your father. I didn't recognize him at first and Carl only met him a couple of times many years ago. I would have said something sooner but yesterday was the first time we both had a real good look at him. Then I asked Madge his name. Neither of us told him we know. I'm leaving that up to you. If you want nothing to do with him it is your choice." Marie patted her grandson's hand. "We love you, Brighton. And getting to know your real father would not be disrespectful to Mitch or your mother. We're not sure why he left other than he was young and impetuous and perhaps he has realized he made a mistake leaving your mother."

Brighton drew a breath. "I'm not sure if I want to know him. Mitch is my father. That man was just a donor."

Carl said, "We can certainly understand that Brighton. You know nothing about him other than he took off. And to be honest, I'd like nothing more than to beat the tar out of him for devastating Donna the way he did. It's because of him that she had to give up your brother which is what may have led to Brent's downfall. Who knows what kind of family adopted Brent or what he may have suffered as a child?"

"I never told you Bri but Brent came looking for you several years back. You were still in school. It was just before your grandfather and I moved to Palm Springs. I suppose I should have told your mother. I feel like I made a huge mistake and if I hadn't perhaps things would have turned out differently."

"You never told me that, Marie."

"You were at work when he came by the house. I was stunned. He looked so much like Brighton except his eyes were empty like he had no soul. It scared me. I told him to stay away from Donna."

Brighton rubbed the back of his neck and tilted his head back and forth as if to loosen his thoughts. He straightened up then slouched down once more. "All of us made decisions that we regret. Maybe it is time to right a few wrongs. I should give Lance Silverman the chance to explain what happened. I think that's what mom would have wanted." He paused for a moment. "Mitch would have no idea who Silverman is, right?"

"I don't think your mother ever mentioned his name and, as far as I know, she had no pictures of Lance. I doubt Mitch would know."

"Good. Even though his mind is not all there, I don't want any chance that he will find out. Mitch has been through enough. I don't want him thinking I will abandon him"

Marie moved closer to her grandson and hugged him. "Mitch would never think that of you, darling. He knows how much you truly love him."

When they arrived home, he put in a load of laundry, she examined the contents of the refrigerator and made a list of items they needed. After a quick trip to the store and putting away the groceries, Cecelia settled on the sofa to make a few phone calls. Brighton retreated to the bedroom and dialed Johnson's number.

"My grandmother confirmed the doctor is my birth father. Have you found anything else?"

"His record is pretty clean other than a couple of traffic violations in California. He visited Brent last week. The guard said he was there for thirty minutes talking to your brother."

"Did he overhear anything?"

"Nothing of consequence was discussed, or so he said."

"Then Silverman didn't have anything to do with Brent's plan?"

"I don't believe so, Brighton. I think he saw your name in the media and moved up here to find you and your brother. I talked to Silverman's previous employer and had only positive comments. Told me he gave the good doctor one heck of a reference when he left."

Brighton blew out a long breath.

"You sound disappointed."

"I'm not, Nick. I'm glad he isn't here to mess with Mitch. I'd have to kill him if he was."

"Don't tell any cops that."

"I won't. Well, thanks for your help. If you do come across anything else, let me know."

"You betcha. Hey, how was the honeymoon?"

"Too short but otherwise perfect."

"That's good to hear. Give that beautiful bride a hug for me. And Bri?"

"Yeah?"

"I don't want to have to do any more work for you and Jason. Have a happy life."

"Thanks Nick. You too."

Brighton fell back onto the pillows relieved that Dr. Silverman was not up to something nefarious. Now the question in his head was whether or not to confront his father. Should he ask why he left? Did he really want to know?

Brighton went down to check on the laundry. The first load was done so he tossed it in the dryer and started a second. He headed up to the living room and saw that his wife was still on her cell. He leaned against the door frame and watched her for a moment. She had her back to him and showed no signs of knowing he was there. He wished they had met under different circumstances and that she had not suffered through being shuffled around from place to place to keep her safe.

"It was absolutely fabulous, Dad. I couldn't have asked for a more wonderful honeymoon."

Brighton smiled at her words then turned and went to the kitchen. He removed a pork loin from the fridge and prepared it for cooking sprinkling it with a mixture of herbs. He cut up three medium sized potatoes, coated them with olive oil and rosemary and placed them around the roast. Once the baking pan was in the oven, he chopped up the broccoli and placed it in the steamer with water so that when the meat was almost finished he could start the vegetables. Finally, he washed some baby greens and tossed them in a bowl along with cherry tomatoes, radishes, shredded carrots, and green peppers.

"You could have waited. I would have helped."

"I like cooking," he confessed, "especially for my gorgeous wife."

He wiped his hands off on a rag and then pulled her into a warm embraced.

"The roast will take a while. What shall we do while we wait?"

"Put in another load of laundry?"

"I did that already."

"Fool around?"

"Haven't you had enough of me yet?"

"Never," she replied.

Brighton lifted the roast out of the pan and placed it on a platter. As he began to slice the meat, Cecelia transferred the potatoes to a serving dish.

"Johnson doesn't think my father is up to anything. He still makes me uncomfortable though. I know I should talk to him or at least tell him I know who he is. He visited Brent."

"He did?"

"I'm not sure why he wouldn't tell me straight out who he was yet he visited my brother in prison."

"Perhaps he figured there was no way Brent could slug him or run away. And I agree; the way he has been hanging around gives me the creeps too. Instead of getting a job where Mitch is, he should have contacted you directly. Maybe he is hiding something. Or maybe he has something to tell you and he isn't quite sure how to do it." While she spoke, she placed the food on the table.

"What would I possibly need to know after all this time? I was perfectly happy not knowing who he was."

"You will never know why he came back unless you talk to him."

He placed the two pieces of pork on each of their plates. "I know and I plan to talk to him soon. But I may tell him to stay away from Mitch. He doesn't need to see my father at all."

"Are you going to say anything to Madge?" she asked putting potatoes and broccoli on his plate.

"I haven't decided yet." Brighton sat down adjacent his wife. "Let's talk about something else."

"Have you talked to Jason about when you're opening the bar?"

"Not yet but I should call him tonight."

"Since you cooked, I'll clean up while you talk to him."

"It's a deal."

After they ate, he followed her into the kitchen and leaned against the counter while she worked. Jason picked up the receiver on the second ring.

"How was the hotel?"

"It was superb my friend. Thanks for the suggestion. We were waited on hand and foot. The food was out of this world."

"You had time to eat? I thought you'd be spending the entire three days in bed."

"I have two words for you. Room. Service."

"Excellent."

"I was wondering what we're naming our new venture and when we're going to open."

"The permits say Captain Jack's. You know, like the Billy Joel song."

"And your son."

"Yeah, but that's not the reason."

"Do you think we can open in a couple of weeks?"

"If we interview staff this week then we can have our grand opening a week from Friday." As he spoke, Jason stood from the sofa and went down the hall to his home office. "All the permits have been filed. The whole place is cleaned up and redecorated. And I have a pile of resumes on my desk. How about we meet up at the bar tomorrow and start calling people?"

"What time do you want me there?"

"Is eight too early?"

"Not at all, I'm bringing my wife."

"I'll bring mine too. And the kid."

Brighton laughed. "I wouldn't expect you to leave him home. Molly would disown you."

"You're right about that. He comes first in her world."

"As he should, Jason. Hey, I have a hot babe in my kitchen who needs some assistance with her buns. We'll be at Captain Jack's at eight with coffee. Don't be late."

"Are you kidding? Jackson has us up every two hours."

"It won't last forever. Enjoy this time Jason. They grow up way too fast."

"Indeed they do. See you in the am."

As Brighton hung up, Cecelia stepped in front of him.

"Captain Jack, huh?"

"You know that song?"

"What girl who grew up in New York doesn't? So um, what do you think Captain Jack is?"

"Come upstairs and I'll demonstrate."

Most of the day on Wednesday, Jason and Brighton reviewed applications and set up appointments to meet with potential staff. Molly and Cecelia left right after lunch so Jackson could take a nap at home. By Thursday evening, the owners of Captain Jack's had hired nearly a full complement of waitpersons, bartenders, cooks, and bouncers. They set up a schedule for training. Jason had purchased a computer system for tracking food and drink and it was fully installed.

Friday the two men spent the day at the bar. They reviewed the final proofs of the menu and told the printer to have them ready by the following Wednesday. Jason showed his friend how to use the computer program for customer orders, tracking inventory, and running reports.

"This system can run spreadsheets that we can give to the accountant to do the taxes. Actually, he recommended it. He specializes in food services."

"You did an awful lot without me."

"You had things going on in your life that needed your attention. We'll split all the work from here on out."

"Awesome. And thanks for doing all of this. We wouldn't be opening next week if it wasn't for you."

"It's no problem, Bro. How's your dad doing?"

Brighton lifted a brow.

"What?"

"There's a doctor that has been hanging around the home. He's my birth father."

"No shit. Really? What the hell does he want with Mitch?"

"I think he was trying to find me but I haven't told him I know who he is yet. My grandmother saw him the other day and she confirmed my suspicions."

"Are you going to talk to him?"

"I don't think I have a choice. Johnson told me he visited Brent in lockup."

"No way, what the hell for?"

"I guess he wanted to meet him; I'm not sure."

"That's messed up. He talked to Brent first? Why not talk to you?"

"That is one question I am definitely going to ask."

Jason patted his friend on the shoulder. "If you want me to be there when you talk to him, let me know. I can be moral support or I can hold him down while you beat the tar out of him for leaving your mother hanging."

"I'm not planning to do much of anything to him other than find out why he left and why he came back. I don't need revenge. My mother had a great life with Mitch. I know she didn't have any regrets so I'm good."

"Still, I'm here for whatever you need."

Chapter Twenty-Eight

Brighton asked Madge to let him know when Dr. Silverman was at the home. She didn't ask why. Thursday morning, Madge called.

"The doctor is here today. He's not on the floor at the moment but I am sure he will stop by."

"Thanks, Madge. I'm heading over. If he comes to see Mitch, please ask him to wait."

"I will."

"Ce," he hollered down the hall. "I have to go to the home. Madge called."

"Do you want me to come with you?"

"If you want to, you can. We can grab dinner in the city."

"Can I get five minutes to change?"

"Absolutely."

The drive from Long Island seemed longer than normal. Brighton drummed his fingers on the steering wheel. He sighed and grumbled.

"Try to relax," she said to him. "He's just a man and if you decide you never want to see him again, then so be it."

"I know I shouldn't be nervous. He walked out on my mother and is nothing to me. Still..."

She placed a hand on his thigh. "Everything will be fine."

When they reached their destination, Brighton parked the car and turned off the ignition. He remained motionless for a few seconds.

"I'm not sure what I'll say to him."

"Simply tell him you know who he is and you would like an explanation as to why he was being so secretive."

"Won't that put him on the defensive?"

"He is the one hiding his identity, Bri. Not you."

"You're right. Head on, that's the way to deal with this. Let's go inside."

They found Mitch in the sun-room chatting with his friends. He was discussing golf and how his father-in-law and son were going to plan a day on the green soon. He saw Brighton and beamed.

"There's my son now and his beautiful wife, Lydia."

"It's Cecelia, Dad."

"Oh, what happened to Lydia?"

Brighton shook his father's hand and Cecelia leaned over to hug the older man.

"It's a long story," Bri sighed.

"How was the honeymoon?"

They were surprised Mitch remembered.

"It was wonderful," Cecelia remarked. "Brighton spoiled me."

"I taught him well."

"Have you seen the doctor today?"

"I think so but every day here is the same so maybe it was yesterday. I don't know."

"I'm going to go find Madge."

"Who's Madge?"

"Don't worry about it, Dad. I'll be right back."

Madge was down the hall distributing medication to her patients. She saw him approach and she hung her clipboard on the side of the cart.

"Dr. Silverman was here a short while ago. He had rounds on other floors but I asked him to come back." She checked her watch. "He should be back in forty five minutes or so. I reserved the sitting room for you so you would have privacy."

"Thanks. Did you tell him I wanted to talk to him?"

"I told him you were coming but I had no idea what you wanted to discuss."

"What do you think of him?"

Madge shifted her stance. "He is very good with the patients, competent, and polite. He and Dr. Helm work well together; they generally agree on treatment."

Brighton nodded as he listened.

"Is there something else you wanted to know?" she asked.

"No, not really."

"I know it is none of my business." She picked up her meds list and began to pull out what she needed. "I don't think you need to be concerned with the care your father is receiving. His not eating was a phase and it may come and go over time. The closer he gets to," she swallowed hard. "He may show other signs of failing. Unfortunately, it is a long process. Involuntary bodily functions begin to not work properly."

Madge lightly touched his arm.

"I know you're worried about him. There was nothing anyone did, Brighton. It just was."

"I'll be with my father until Dr. Silverman comes back."

"I'll ask him to come see you."

"Thanks, Madge. For everything."

Nearly an hour later, Dr. Silverman entered the sun-room. Brighton stood and absentmindedly smoothed his jeans. The doctor greeted him with an extended hand. As they shook hands, the younger man gestured toward the door. Dr. Silverman nodded and followed Brighton across the hall.

"I bet they're going to talk about me," Mitch said to Ce.

Cecelia simply smiled and patted his hand.

Brighton closed the door as the doctor turned toward him.

"Is there something you wanted to discuss about Mitch's health?" Lance Silverman asked.

"No actually, I wanted to discuss you."

The two men stood only a few feet apart. Being the same height, Brighton could look the doctor directly in the eye.

"I'd like an explanation of why you're here, Dr. Silverman." Brighton began.

The older man glanced to the right where the sunlight filtered in through the blinds. "When did you know?"

"I've had my suspicions for some time now. My grandmother figured it out while I was in Jersey on my honeymoon but even before then I had someone investigating you."

Lance turned back to his son. "I see." He blew out a long breath. "When I decided to come looking for you I thought it would all turn out differently. All I wanted to do was make sure you were all right and then I was going to disappear. I had no idea I would be working in the same convalescent where your step-father was living."

"He's my father."

"Yes, he is. Much more than I ever was which is why I was going to just leave once I knew you were OK. I had seen photos of you and Brent in the press. Serial murders tend to be publicized nationwide."

Lance could not hold Brighton's gaze. His eyes wandered.

"So you came back because of a news report? If that all had not happened you would never have searched for us?"

"Through old friends I had kept track of you while you were in school. I didn't want to interfere. I knew Donna had married and that Daniels was a good provider. I lost track of Brent as soon as he was adopted." Lance frowned. "I should have looked harder. Maybe I could have prevented..."

"Lydia was the mastermind behind the plot. I'm sure Brent wanted to screw with me but Lydia was the catalyst to the murders."

The silence following was deafening. The younger man felt some relief knowing that Dr. Silverman had not showed up to cause trouble for Mitch. Yet the question of why this man had walked out on his mother weighed heavy on Brighton. He shifted from one leg to the other.

Lance stuffed his hands in his pockets. "Your mother was a wonderful woman. I was young and selfish. When she told me she was pregnant all I thought about was how it would ruin my chances of becoming a doctor. I had almost convinced myself that things would work out. I called your mother to tell her maybe we could work things out. That's when she told me she was having twins and I freaked. With one child I might have had the guts to stay but two?" He stepped slightly closer to his son. "At eighteen, what would you have done?"

"I would have stayed even if it meant giving up law school. Anyway, it doesn't matter now. Too much has happened. It has been too long. Mitch is my father. He was there for me. He took me to baseball games, encouraged me to take risks, and he stood by me as if I were his own flesh and blood. Without him, I would not be the man I am today."

"If you want me to walk out of your life I will. I can ask that I not be assigned here."

"I'm not sure it makes much difference. Madge said you're a good doctor. But if I ever find out you did anything to put his health in jeopardy, you will pay."

"I would never hurt a patient."

Brighton asked why he had gone to see Brent before telling him who he was.

"Honestly, I wasn't going to tell you. You were obviously doing well. I didn't want to stir anything up. I wanted to make sure Brent was surviving as best he could under the circumstances."

"I haven't visited him. I often wonder if I should."

"He really is sorry for all he put you through. He went through some tough years when he was young, not that it excuses what he did."

"So he blames me for his difficulties?"

"Not any more, he doesn't. I think he has learned a few things lately."

"So he is all right?"

Lance nodded. "At the moment he is doing as well as can be expected. It's no picnic where he is."

"He had a choice. He made the wrong one."

"I understand how you feel. Still, he is your brother."

"No more than you are my father."

Lance winced as if he were punched. "I'll ask to be unassigned to the home," he said and stepped toward the door.

"Wait. I'm sorry. I spent my whole life hating you for leaving us. It's going to take some time to reprogram."

"I'll let you have your space. Madge knows how to get in touch with me should you want to talk more."

Brighton watched as his father exited the room and turned down the hall away from the sun-room where Mitch and Cecelia were. He wondered if he could ever forgive Lance Silverman for deserting his family.

Over dinner, Brighton told his wife about the conversation he had with the doctor.

"He seemed genuine."

"At least now you know he wasn't planning to cause trouble for you or Mitch. Are you going to talk to him again?"

"I haven't decided. It would be nice to find out more about my mother. I'm sure he knows things that my grandmother doesn't."

"I bet he does. What did he say about Brent?"

"He thought I should go see him. I'm not sure I'm ready for that yet."

Cecelia took his hand in hers. "You don't ever have to see him. But if you do decide to go, I can come with you."

"Thanks but if I take anyone, it will be Jason. I don't want you anywhere near Brent even if he is behind bars."

"I could wait in the car."

He brought her hand to his lips. "No way. I am not leaving you in the car outside a prison. I'm not taking any chances with you."

"I love you. And I would go to the end of the world for you."

"I love you too. Let's finish dinner so we can go home and do some baby making."

"I like the sound of that."

While she drove home, he called his grandmother and told her about the conversation he had with his birth father.

"I think I'd like to get to know him better but I wanted to talk to you first. I don't want you to feel betrayed in any way."

"People change, Brighton. He is probably not the man who walked out on your mother. It is up to you whether you want a relationship with him or not. Don't let my feelings interfere."

"Thanks, Gran. I was afraid you might be upset with me."

"Not at all. You do what you believe is right."

When he hung up Cecelia took his hand. "That went well."

"I was a little concerned but she seemed cool with me talking to Lance."

"Your grandmother is one great lady. I bet your Mom was too."

"She was the best mom ever. Well, yours is too."

"Agreed. So, are you excited about tomorrow?"

"I'm sure we'll get a good turnout with all the advertising you did for us."

"I didn't do that much."

"Are you kidding? You must have posted a hundred posters and put ads in the local papers. The website you set up is fabulous. We've gotten tons of hits and requests for reservations."

"It was my pleasure to assist my husband in his new business adventure. I just wish I could be there tomorrow."

"I don't expect the lunch crowd to be too big. And you're coming after work, right?"

"I should be there about six but something tells me I'll be coming sooner."

"That's all you want me for, isn't it?"

"It's near the top of the list."

He raised a brow at her. "So sex is not number one?"

"I love you Brighton Clay. For more reasons than I can count. I love your smile and the way your eyes sparkle when you're happy. When you say my name my knees get weak. And do not even get me started on your cooking."

"Really? You're that impressed with my kitchen acumen over my sexual prowess?"

"Mm, now you have me thinking..."

He grinned at her. "I accept your challenge, woman. I'm going to prove to you that expertise in here far exceeds my culinary proficiency."

Friday morning Brighton met Jason at Captain Jack's. Three of the other employees arrived early as well to assist with last minute details and food preparations. The remaining staff came in before nine and by ten they were ready for the lunch crowd.

Captain Jack's was located in a prime spot. There were a few businesses nearby. The building was close to a large intersection and less than a mile from the highway. When they opened the doors, there were a few people waiting. The staff took turns seating people in different areas of the dining room. Both of the owners visited tables and thanked their guests for coming. By noon the place was humming with activity. Background music played just loud enough to provide a relaxing atmosphere. Enticing aromas wafted from the large kitchen. Diners raved about the food.

"This Monte Cristo is fabulous," one customer told Jason.

"I'm glad you like it. You'll have to stop by and check out our late night menu sometime."

"Oh we will," another diner at the table said enthusiastically.

"If there is anything else you require I'm Jason. Just give me or my partner Brighton a shout." He gestured across the room to his friend.

The door seemed to move constantly as a steady stream of customers came and went throughout lunchtime. Close to two in the afternoon, things quieted down and the staff was able to take intermittent breaks. Brighton was in the kitchen speaking with the head chef when Jason approached and slapped him on the shoulder.

"Hey partner. With a crowd like that at lunch, I bet we'll be packed to capacity tonight."

"Thanks to your insight and Cecelia's advertising we are a hit."

"In a couple of weeks you should invite a food critic," the chef suggested. "A good review will really boost our reputation."

"Why not sooner?" Bri asked.

"It will give the kitchen staff a chance to perfect the dishes and there will already be people talking about us."

"All right then, I defer to your judgment. You know the business better than I."

The crowd picked up again a short time before five. In the afternoon, people stopped by for appetizers and drinks. The music was a bit louder and faster. The customers were more energetic and a tad less civilized. The owners were thrilled with the turn out.

Molly came by with the baby. Brighton told his friend to have dinner with his family and he would tend to the customers. He didn't see Cecelia enter the bar yet nearly every male head turned. The skin-toned dress she wore exposed the right amount of teaser cleavage and hugged her in all her perfect curves. When he spun around to see what everyone was staring at his mouth fell open. She walked toward him with purpose, tossed her arms around his neck, and crashed her lips into his.

When the kiss broke, he said, "Damn woman, you know how to make an entrance. When did you get this dress? I don't remember seeing this before."

"I purchased this sexy little number expressly for tonight. I thought you might want to show off your beautiful wife."

"Every man in this place just became instantly hard."

"Perhaps, but you're the one who gets to nail me later."

"If this wasn't my bar, I would take you in a back room and fuck you so hard right now," he growled in her ear.

"Good. Then the dress is doing its job."

The rest of the night, he kept one eye on her. She moved from table to table greeting guests and bragging about her husband. She enchanted men without making their women jealous. Brighton was sure their opening would not have been as successful had his wife not been there.

Molly left shortly after having dinner with her husband. She needed to get Jackson down for the night. Jason had urged her to stay until she confessed she was the one who needed rest. He walked her out to the car and buckled his son into his car seat. He waited until she was out of the parking lot before he went inside.

Having recently moved to the area, the partners knew very few of the clientele. Their banker stopped by for a quick drink as did the attorney who attended the closing on the business loan. Some of the lunch crowd returned to sample the evening fare before heading home.

The head chef stayed for the entire day. He wanted to supervise everyone for the first week or so to make sure everything was prepared properly and the kitchen ran smoothly. He had many years of experience in food services and came with glorious recommendations from previous employers. Just before one a.m., Brighton suggested to the chef that he call it a day.

"There's only an hour to go. The night staff can clean up and set up for tomorrow. Jason and I will make sure everything is done."

"Thanks, Mr. Clay. I'll be here at nine in the morning."

"Have a good night."

"You too, Sir."

Slowly the crowd dwindled. As the last few customers left, Cecelia pulled her husband aside.

"You won't be here much longer, will you?"

"I don't think so. We have to clean up but it should go quickly with all of us working together. You can go if you'd like. I know you had a long day." He stroked her backside. "I hate to let you go." His eyes trailed down her form. "Damn. I'm going to make sure we get done real fast."

"I'll be ready for you," she purred in his ear.

Brighton watched her hips sway as she walked toward the door. Before she exited, she turned back and blew him a kiss.

Seeing the interaction between his friends, Jason approached Brighton. "Let's clean up and lock down this place so you can get home to your wife. Oh, and make sure she comes here as often as possible. She's great for business. All the men were salivating. They needed to replenish their bodily fluids."

Captain Jack's doors closed to customers at two and ten minutes later Brighton was sliding into his Mercedes after Jason told him he would take care of things at the restaurant.

In the wee hours of the morning, very few cars were on the road. He managed to hit all the green lights and soon he was pulling into the garage. He kicked off his shoes and dashed up the stairs.

Two steps into the bedroom he stop dead in his tracks.

"Ce? Where are you?"

Chapter Twenty-Nine

Fear gripped his heart as he hollered her name again. His eyes darted around the room then he checked the master bathroom. Her car had been in the garage so he knew she had made it to the house.

"Ce..."

He whirled around when he heard a noise coming from downstairs.

"Brighton, I'm here," she replied as she dashed up the stairs. "I was in the basement."

As she reached the landing on the second floor he pulled her into his arms.

"Why are you shaking? C'mon, let's go sit." She guided him over to the bed.

"Don't ever do that again. You scared the hell out of me. I thought..."

"Oh, Bri, all those bad things are behind us now. I'm not going anywhere."

She knelt down speaking soothing words and stroking his cheek.

"All I could think was that someone took you. I couldn't bear to live without you."

"Sh, I'm right here. I was just folding the laundry I did this morning. I didn't know you would be home so soon."

His tears began to flow and she kissed both of his cheeks.

"It's all right. I'm fine. Nothing happened." She stood and added, "Let's get you undressed and into bed."

Captain Jack's opened at eleven on the weekends. The staff was there early to prepare for the day. The partners were in the small office reviewing the previous day's receipts.

"We made a killing yesterday," Jason beamed. "If we keep up like this, you and I can retire in a few years."

"Hm."

"Guess you're exhausted from last night. You've hardly said five words."

"Yeah."

"Is everything all right with Cecelia?"

"Huh? Yeah, she's fine."

"Talk to me, Bri."

Brighton leaned back in his chair and rubbed his eyes. "I didn't sleep well. When I got home, I couldn't find her. I freaked until I heard her coming up the stairs. You have no idea the kind of things I had running through my head like maybe one of the people working with Lydia took her."

"Do you really think that could happen?"

"Logically, no I don't. After everything she did, I wouldn't put it past her to do something like that."

"Bri, she has no contact with the outside world. There is no way she could have put that kind of thing in motion. You need to stop worrying and get all that shit behind you."

"I know. I will. It's just going to take some time. Let's go over the numbers again. I wasn't paying attention the first time."

An hour later they emerged from the office to find the dining area even more packed than it had been during the Friday lunch hour. There was a short line waiting to be seated. Every bar stool was occupied. Wait staff buzzed in and out of the kitchen carrying trays of food or empty plates.

Brighton's eye caught Cecelia as she rounded tables chatting with the guests. She was wearing a violet silk blouse and a pencil skirt which hung just above the knee showing off her finely muscled calves. As if she felt the heat of his gaze, she glanced over at him with raised brow and a mischievous grin. She tilted chin up toward the door. He nodded once and winked.

"Hey, Jas. Do you think you can hold the fort for an hour or so?"

Jason followed his friend's line of sight then replied, "What are partners for?"

By the time they returned to the restaurant, the line was gone and there were a few empty tables.

Jason smacked his friend on the shoulder.

"You look a hell of a lot better then you did earlier. Molly is here, Ce." He pointed to a corner table.

She thanked him and went to sit with Molly and the baby.

"I expect you to pay back that favor."

"Any time you need a break Jason, let me know."

"Oh I will. Count on it."

"Did anything happen while I was gone?"

"Nothing out of the ordinary, why? Were you expecting something?"

"No, I was just checking."

Brighton watched as Cecelia took Jackson from Molly's arms.

"When are you two going to start a family?"

"We're at the not-preventing stage. If we don't get pregnant in a few months, we may get a little more serious about it. Honestly, I'd like some time for us to be a couple first."

"That's probably a good idea given everything you guys have been through lately."

The bell attached to the front door clanged and the partners glanced over at the same time.

"If you want to go hide in the office, I wouldn't blame you," Jason said.

Bri patted his arm then walked toward the customer. Lance saw his son approaching and smiled.

"I, um, if you don't want me here, I understand. I wanted to see how things were going."

"How did you know about the restaurant?"

"I overheard. I wasn't eavesdropping or stalking you; I promise."

"Given you're track record..."

"I know. I'm done hiding in the shadows."

Brighton told the hostess he would seat Lance and she stepped back.

"Are you alone?"

The older man nodded.

"My partner's wife is with Cecelia. Would you like to sit with us?"

"I would like that very much."

As they crossed the floor to the table, Lance asked, "Is that your baby?"

"No, that's Jason's son. Cecelia and I don't have any children yet."

"Yet?"

"Someday we will."

When they got to the corner table, Brighton introduced him to Molly as Dr. Lance Silverman.

"He works at the home where Mitch stays. I was wondering if you wouldn't mind keeping him company for a bit."

As the men sat, a waitress appeared.

"Can I get you something to drink?"

"We have a couple of local brews, Lance."

"I'll have coffee, please."

"Make that two," Brighton said to the server. He turned back to Lance. "Did you come for lunch or to check up on us?"

"A little of both I suppose."

"We have an excellent assortment of appetizers, salads, and sandwiches as well as some damn good burgers."

"Try the Captain Jack's burger," Ce suggested. "It has a Jack Daniels glaze, smoked bacon, and New York sharp cheddar."

"I can hear my arteries hardening already."

"So skip the bacon and have a side salad with it," Molly suggested.

Jason cruised the restaurant while Brighton had lunch. He waited until they were done eating before he pulled up a chair and joined them.

"Lance, this is my partner in crime, Jason Campbell."

"It's a pleasure. How did you two meet?"

"Jason and I went to law school together and worked at the same firm. He used to steal all my girlfriends until he met Molly."

"I'm sure there were plenty of women chasing after both of you."

"Can we not talk about this in front of our wives?" Jason grumbled.

"It's okay, darling. Ce and I know you had lives before us. So Lance, what about you? Are you married?"

"Divorced," he replied sadly.

"I'm sorry," she whispered and patted his hand.

"It was my own fault. I worked long hours and didn't take enough time to spend with my family."

"You have children?"

"Two daughters, Leslie and Lindsay. I figured out too late how much I had missed of their lives."

"You can start over. Do it right this time."

"I'm too old for that."

"Men can make babies late in life, Lance. All you need to do is find the right woman. You're a good looking doctor and you seem really nice. What woman wouldn't want to start a family with you?"

Cecelia squeezed her husband's hand under the table.

"That's very kind of you to say, Molly." Lance looked quickly at his son. He glanced at his watch. "Perhaps I should be going. It's been nice meeting you all."

"I think I'm going to take Jackson home as well. I need to feed him."

"You can do it in the office," Jason suggested.

"I know but he'll probably fall asleep. I'd rather put him down in his crib so I can get a little nap too."

Brighton walked his father out to the car.

"It was good seeing you," the older man said.

"You can stop by any time although it's kind of a drive for you."

Shrugging he replied, "I don't mind." He unlocked then opened the driver's side door. "You have a great place here."

"Thanks. Most of it was Jason's idea."

"Don't get wrapped up in work. You and Jason can take turns running the business so you have time to be with your families. Life has a way of passing you by."

"I'll keep that in mind."

Lance got into the car and turned over the engine. As he drove off, he waved at his son. Brighton watched until the car was out of sight. Inside the restaurant, he told Jason to take the afternoon off so he could be with his wife.

Chapter Thirty

As the months passed, the volume of people threading through the door at Captain Jack's slowed somewhat as with any new business. Daily receipts remained fairly steady after a couple of weeks. With start-up cost they had yet to turn a decent profit. The owners were not discouraged in the least. They knew at the beginning the financial statements would be far from stellar.

The partners alternated working weekends to allow them time with their families. Brighton traveled to the city no less than twice a week to see Mitch. During the week, he would leave early in the morning and bring his father coffee and something sweet from the bakery down the street from the home. After breakfast with Mitch, he would head back to the island. On the weekends, Cecelia joined her husband.

It was difficult for Brighton to watch Mitch's health deteriorate. Some days, the older man was positive and alert. During other visits, he had mood swings and refused to eat. By October, his body had become less responsive to stimuli and he could no longer walk. Because sitting up was difficult, Mitch was secured by safety belts in a wheelchair during the day. A fall-risk sign was posted on his door.

Carl and Marie Clay came to New York for Thanksgiving. When they went to visit their son-in-law, he didn't recognize them at first. They had been chatting for several minutes when Mitch asked who they were.

"I'm Marie and this is Carl."

"Do you live here?"

"No, we live in Palm Springs."

"Where are we?"

"You're in New York," Carl told him.

"Oh, are you friends with Donna?"

"We're her parents."

Mitch was silent for a moment. Then he nodded and asked Carl when their tee time was.

Later that evening, Carl and Marie were at Captain Jack's having dinner with their grandson.

"His memory has gotten worse," Marie said to Brighton. "He doesn't focus as well. He barely ate his lunch."

"I know, Gran. He's failing. It was inevitable. And, although it is difficult to watch, think of how he must feel on the days when he is coherent."

"The worst part of it is that there is nothing anyone can do," Carl added. "There is no antidote, no magic potion to undo the memory loss or reverse or halt the aging process."

Christmas was approaching fast. When Brighton wasn't worrying about Mitch, much of his time was spent tending to the restaurant. Cecelia's thoughts were centered on something else. They had been married for seven months. She decided to make an appointment.

Thursday evening after dinner, Ce told Brighton she was taking Friday off.

"Nat is meeting me in the city for lunch. Would you like me to check in on Mitch?"

"If you have time, you can. I'm sure he would like the company. When are you coming back home?"

"I'm not sure. My sister wants to do some shopping too. I figured I would leave about nine tomorrow. I can stop by and see Mitch then meet up with Nat."

"Sounds like a good plan. Do you need any money for lunch?"

"You know I would never turn that down."

Brighton pulled a few bills out of his wallet. "That should do it."

"Hm, should I stop by Victoria's?"

He took out a few more. "Get something for me too."

"Silk boxers?"

"In your favorite color."

"See through it is."

At eleven o'clock, Cecelia drove across the city to her appointment. She entered the familiar office and greeted the receptionist.

"The nurse will be out to get you in a few minutes. Has anything changed?"

"Everything has changed."

The receptionist pulled out a clipboard and handed it to her. "This might take a while to complete then."

"It probably will."

Cecelia was still filling out forms when the nurse called her name. After the nurse had done a preliminary check, Cecelia finished the paperwork while waiting for the doctor. The knock on the door surprised her.

"Come in."

"Hello, Cecelia. How are things with you?"

"I'm well but I thought I would come in for a checkup."

"It hasn't been a year yet. Is there something on your mind?"

"Well, yes there is. We got married last May and since then have not been preventing but I'm still not pregnant."

"Have you been tracking your cycle?"

"I started about three months ago. I've been doing some research online when I get the chance. I thought I would come in and make sure everything is all right."

Dr. Harvey asked a few more questions then proceeded with the exam. When she was done, she made a few notes in the chart.

"While I don't see anything wrong, there are a few tests we can do. I'd like to start with some blood work to see how your hormone levels are. I see you moved. If you are planning to get pregnant, you might want to find a doctor and hospital closer to home. Would you like me to forward a copy of your records to you?" As she spoke, Dr. Harvey pulled out a lab slip.

"That would be great. Do you know any doctors on the island?"

"I'll check around and give you some names. In the meantime, there is a lab right down stairs. You can stop by on your way out. I'll forward the results with the rest of your records. For now, try to have intercourse during your fertile days. Do you know when those are?"

"Yes, I signed up for a website that helps track the best days for conception."

"Good. I think with all the changes in your life over the past year, maybe it might be stress that's preventing conception. Try to take some time to relax. Don't put too much pressure on conceiving. When we get the blood work back, if there are any issues, we can have you see a specialist. And let's start you on some prenatal vitamins. Does that sound doable?"

"You don't see any reason for concern?"

"Not at all, Cecelia. Getting pregnant isn't as easy as it may seem. And, the older a woman gets, the more difficult conception can be."

"I had a feeling the age factor would come into play."

"It stinks; I know. We're only born with so many eggs and they age along with us. Your hormone levels will tell us a few things. Let's keep our fingers crossed."

"I'll be rubbing my rabbit's foot too."

Cecelia left the office feeling a bit disheartened. Natalia was meeting her at two so she decided to do some shopping before meeting up with her sister. A few minutes before two, she was sitting in a small cafe where they had agreed to meet. She ordered herbal tea and awaited her sister's arrival. As expected, Natalia was late. She buzzed in and flopped down in the chair across from Ce.

"I had to drop Samuel off at the office. He figured since I was coming into the city he would stop by and see the city crew. I think he wishes he worked here instead of the other office but whatever. How are you? You look fantastic. How's married life? Do you like Long Island? How is Brighton's father?"

"Nat, take a breath."

"Phew. Sorry. I guess I'm a little hyper today."

"Everything is great except Mitch. I'm not sure how much longer he will be around."

"That sucks."

The waitress came over and Natalia asked for water and a Cobb salad.

"I'll have the salad too."

"Would you like a bread basket while you wait on the salads?"

"That sounds wonderful."

"Okay, I'll be right back with that."

"So, how do you like the new job at the doctor's office?"

Cecelia told her sister all about her work. Then she talked about Captain Jack's.

"Maybe Samuel and I can stop by some day."

During lunch, Natalia poked at her salad. About half way through she put her fork down and folded her hands in her lap.

"I have some news but you have to keep it a secret. Don't tell Mom and Dad. I want them to think they're the first to know."

Cecelia swallowed hard. She had a feeling she knew exactly what her sister was thinking. She listened, smiled and wished her sister well. She wanted to speak to her sister about her doctor appointment yet now was not the time.

Cecelia left the city shortly after three. She told Nat she wanted to beat the afternoon traffic. They hugged goodbye. As soon as Ce was out of the city, tears began to trickle down her cheeks. She pulled over and broke down. She was on the side of the highway for several minutes when her attention was drawn to the rear view mirror.

"Great," she said aloud. Wondering why she was being stopped, she took out her license and registration then rolled down the window.

"Ma'am, are you all right?"

"Yes, officer, I just pulled over for a minute."

"A passer-by said you pulled over fairly quickly. She was concerned for your safety but was afraid to stop."

"I'm fine. I, um, just needed a minute to gather my thoughts."

"This is not a good place to be at this hour with all the cars. Would you like me to escort you to the next exit?"

"No, I'm okay now."

"All right then. When you're ready to pull out, put your signal on and I'll make sure you do so safely."

"Thank you, officer."

"You're welcome, ma'am."

She headed straight to the house. She took a long hot shower then pulled on her skinny jeans and an emerald green cashmere sweater. A few drops removed the redness in her eyes and makeup covered any other signs she had been crying.

Cecelia drove to the restaurant trying to concentrate on anything other than the appointment and her sister's news. By the time she reached Captain Jack's, the parking lot was practically full. She parked on the street around the corner and went in the staff entrance. Everyone in the kitchen greeted her kindly. The head chef told her Brighton was playing bartender.

"Nicholas had a family emergency."

"Is everything all right?"

"His wife was having contractions. She's not due for a couple of weeks but this is their third."

"Well, let me know if anyone hears anything. I'd like to send them something when the baby comes."

As she passed through the door to the main dining area, Ce mumbled, "What the hell? Is everyone else freaking pregnant?"

She spotted Brighton tossing bottles in the air and mixing concoctions. She froze in her tracks and smiled. "You know what?" she thought. "I have the best husband in the world. Nothing else should matter."

Brighton glanced up for a second and saw her standing there. His eyes traveled over her form as she glided toward him. He nearly dropped a bottle of whiskey as he watched her hips sway. Not one stool was open so she moved behind the bar. As she passed by him, she patted his rear end.

"Would you like some assistance? I used to sub at the night club. I can make anything without having to consult the book you have propped open there."

"Be my guest, beautiful." He gave her a quick peck on the cheek. Looking at the other men watching her from their seats he said, "This is my wife for those of you who don't know. You can think about her all you want but she belongs to me."

"I belong to no man, Bri. We are partners."

"Okay, so maybe I should have said I'm the one who gets to take you home."

"That's a little better."

They worked side by side for a few hours until another bartender arrived to relieve them. Jason had already left so Brighton had to stay until closing. Cecelia remained with him until Captain Jack's was closed. Then he followed her home.

As they turned in for the night, Brighton pulled her close and asked how her day in the city went. She told him about seeing Mitch and shopping before meeting up with Natalia.

"How is your sister doing?"

"She's pregnant. They just found out a few weeks ago. She hasn't told my parents yet so we have to keep it quiet." Cecelia avoided his eyes.

He kissed her forehead then placed a finger on her chin lifting her face. "What's wrong?"

"I'm worried about your father."

He shook his head. "No, it's something else. You can tell me anything, Ce."

She rolled over and pushed her back against him. "It's nothing really."

"When you're ready to talk, I'm here."

A moment later she swept her hand across her face. He sat up and turned on the light. "Now I know there's something on your mind. Please don't cry. C'mere."

She rolled over and put her head in his lap. "I love you. Maybe it's PMS or something."

"Did your sister say something to upset you?"

"They got married in freaking September and she is pregnant already. Didn't she say they were going to wait? Does he have super human sperm or does she pop like a thousand eggs a month?"

"Is that what this about? You're upset that they didn't wait?"

"She said it was an accident, for cripes' sake. One night they forgot to use a condom and she gets pregnant."

"I see."

"I think there's something wrong with me."

"Darling, there is nothing wrong with you. Nat is what, four years younger than you? I know it's not much but it makes a difference. And you have been busy with work. I've been wrapped up in the restaurant. We haven't even been trying."

"I know. I'm being irrational, emotional, and illogical. But damn it, I wanted to be the one first."

"You were first with everything else: the first to drive, the first to get married. Maybe it was her time to be first."

"That sucks."

He brushed away the tears that lingered on her cheeks. "Ce, no matter what, we have each other."

She quickly looked up at him. "Are you saying you don't want children?"

"No, I'm only saying that if for some reason we can't conceive on our own, we can decide together what to do. We can look into adoption or fertility treatments. We'll discuss our options. In the end though, since you will be the one to endure any medical procedures, it is ultimately your choice to make. I'll be here to support you in that decision. And who knows, maybe by spring we'll be pregnant and we'll look back and think, 'What were we so worried about?'"

"I hope you're right. And I'm sorry I didn't talk to you sooner. I went to see Dr. Harvey this morning. She's not worried at all. I saw Natalie and her news sent me over the edge. Then to hear that Nicholas' wife is in labor. It all is a bit too much. I know I shouldn't be worried, at least not yet. She is sending my medical records so I can find a doctor closer to home. And I did some blood work."

"I think if the doctor has no concerns then we shouldn't yet either. But I do understand. Seeing others having what you want and wondering if you'll ever have it is very difficult. We'll work through this together. Don't ever be afraid to talk to me."

"I didn't say anything because with Mitch and the new business I knew you had a lot on your mind. I didn't want to complicate things."

"I'll always make time for you no matter what else is going on."

"I'll try to remember that."

"Now get some sleep," he said reaching for the light. "Tomorrow is my day off. We can do whatever you want even if that means spending the day with my arms wrapped tightly around you."

"What if I said I want to practice baby making all day?"

"I would make that sacrifice for you."

Chapter Thirty-One

Because Brighton didn't want to travel too far from Mitch, Ce's family came to the island to celebrate Christmas arriving a few days before the holiday. Everyone went to Captain Jack's that first evening. Brighton invited Jonathan into the office to review the financial statements. Jonathan was impressed with the way the partners were handling the business.

"I am pleasantly surprised," he said. "I knew you were determined to make this work. You've done an amazing job."

"Thank you. I wish we were doing even better but things are coming along. Most new businesses collapse in the first year. I think we're going to be in the minority."

"You've had a couple of profitable months in a row. Keep this up and maybe you can start a franchise."

"In a few years we might think about that. Right now I am happy with the one restaurant. I need to be home for Cecelia."

Jonathan froze. "Is something wrong?"

"No, nothing is wrong. We're trying to get pregnant. When we do, I don't want to be over burdened by work. I need to be around, involved."

Jonathan relaxed and nodded. "I'm surprised Natalia is pregnant. She seemed adamant that they were going to wait."

"Yeah well, these things happen." Brighton shifted his stance. "After the holidays we're going to try more consistently. We've had too much going on to concentrate on conception. How many life changes are you supposed to do in a year?"

"Do you feel odd talking with me about this?"

"Honestly Jonathan, I do. I shouldn't. But she's your daughter."

"Well we all know where babies come from and you are married."

"Guys don't usually talk to their fathers-in-law about impregnating their wives. Wait. That came out wrong. You know what I mean."

Jonathan laughed. "I'm not old fashioned or out of touch. What you and my daughter do behind closed doors is none of my business. As long as you treat her right and from where I stand I have no complaints."

While they were in the office, Jason was showing Samuel around the restaurant and the ladies were seated at a large table. Natalia was telling her sister about her pregnancy.

"I am exhausted all the time. The doctor said that was normal." She patted her belly as if she were nine months along. "I can't wait to feel her kick around in there."

"Do you know it's a girl?"

"They say you can tell at about sixteen weeks but I think we are going to wait until she is born. I may change my mind. He says it doesn't matter as long as the baby is healthy. I know every guy wants a son. We're going to have two probably so I hope it will be one boy and one girl."

"How is work going, Cecelia?" Mrs. Demure asked.

"It's great. I love the doctors in the group and the nurses are nice as well. We see many different maladies and injuries since it is a general practice. The majority of the clientele are older. Some don't speak English very well. One of the doctors is from Cuba so he handles the Spanish speaking patients. I've picked up some of the Spanish medical terms."

"Your father is happy you're not doing what you used to do."

"I think Brighton is too, for the most part."

Nat chimed in, "Men want their cake and to eat it too. I bet he asks you to dance for him."

"Well you would lose that bet. He has never asked me to. If he did, I would not hesitate to please him."

Nat looked at her sister for a moment then glanced around the room. She saw Samuel and Jason talking at the bar.

"This really is a nice place, Sis. Did you help with the décor?"

"A few things were my idea but Jason took the lead. I did more of the advertising side. I set up the web page and designed the posters and print ads."

"The website is cool. I like how you can order on there. If we lived closer I would do that a lot."

"We have a couple of regulars who order their food online then eat it here especially at lunch. It saves them time."

In the afternoon on Christmas Eve, everyone went to the home where Mitch resided. Even Natalia and Samuel joined them. They gathered in the largest of the sitting rooms. There was a small tree atop a table in the corner decorated with tiny lights and ornaments. Underneath it there were a few small gifts Brighton brought as well as two others from the Demures.

Cecelia made lasagna with her mother's help. They also had homemade bread and salad. It was a simple holiday celebration. The big family dinner would be at the Clay house the following day.

Mitch was a little confused by the new faces. He continually asked his son who all the people were. Brighton replied pretending each question was new. For most people, the constant repetitive questions would be frustrating. Brighton had learned to be patient with his father because he had no idea how much time he had left.

After everyone had something to eat, Cecelia sat next to her father-in-law and helped him open his presents. She held up each item for everyone to see. Most of the packages contained clothes. Bri also wrapped a small frame with a picture of his parents.

"Oh this is lovely, Mitch. You can put this on your nightstand," Cecelia remarked.

He stared at the picture for several minutes. His eyes slowly lifted. "This is me and your mother. I remember that dress. This was the day I asked her to marry me."

Tears welled in nearly everyone's eyes as Mitch continued.

"She was so beautiful and smart. I fell in love instantaneously." He glanced at the photo then back to his son. "And you. You were a brilliant little boy. She adored you. She said 'Maybe' when I popped the question adding that she had to ask you first."

Brighton had to laugh. "That sounds like Mom. Gran found that picture."

The older man searched the room. "Where is Donna? Why isn't she here?"

Cecelia saw her husband's face and calmly said to Mitch, "She's in the kitchen. I'm sure she'll be back in a minute or two. Let's open another gift in the meantime."

Molly gave in to her husband's request to hire a nanny occasionally. The woman came highly recommended from the babysitting service. The woman agreed to spend the night at their house on New Year's Eve so the couple could go out.

Jason had planned a big New Year's celebration at Captain Jack's. He hired a small local band to play and arranged for extra staff to be on hand. Posters had been put up in the windows of a few stores in the area and Jason put an ad designed by Cecelia in the local papers. The restaurant was booked to capacity.

"Do you mind if I go to Jack's a little later," Ce asked her husband before he left for work. "If I'm going to stay up all night, I'll to need a nap."

"What time are you coming?"

"I was thinking nine or so."

"Okay," he said giving her a quick kiss.

"Do you need to leave right now?"

"Why?"

"I may need some help relaxing," she replied letting her hand travel down his chest.

"Why don't you take a long hot shower or a nice bubble bath?"

She began to unbuckle his belt. "A bath sounds nice. Would you care to join me?"

"I suppose I have enough time for that."

An hour later, Brighton walked into Captain Jack's grinning ear to ear. Jason asked where his wife was.

"I wore her out. She's resting."

"No one likes a bragger."

"I'm not bragging; I'm simply stating the truth."

"Molly is coming later too. Do you think Cecelia could pick her up?"

"I'll call Ce and ask. She said she'll be here around nine."

"Nine should be good."

The men were so busy that evening neither saw their wives when they arrived. The hostess led the two women to a reserved table. As they slid into the booth, the waitress asked what they would like to drink.

"Just herbal tea for me," Molly said.

"I'll have the same."

"Coming right up. Oh, and you both look fantastic tonight."

"Thank you, Morgan."

When the waitress was gone, Molly leaned across the table. "I feel like I am stuffed into this thing. My boobs have doubled in size."

"I'm sure Jason loves that."

Molly giggled. "That's so true but it can be a little uncomfortable. In any case, you do look incredible. Where do you find dresses like that?"

Cecelia was wearing a midi dress embellished with graduated silver and blue sequins. The form fitting garment had a diamond cut-out revealing a good deal of her finely tanned back. Molly wore a basic little black dress with a sweetheart neckline.

"Usually I have to go to specialty shops," Cecelia confessed. "My shoulders are very broad probably to carry the girls. And my waist is not proportionate."

"You have the perfect hourglass figure, Ce. Women have surgery to look like you."

"Too bad they don't make clothes that way. I think they purposely make clothes that won't fit anyone. If you're tall, short, thin, heavy or anything unusual, it's hard to find the right fit."

"We should start a clothing line of our own. We could call it The Un-Perfect Fit. We'd carry sizes you can't normally find."

"That sounds like fun but I think one new business is enough to handle right now."

"You're right. And if you two are trying to have a baby, you don't need the added stress."

"Who's causing you stress, my love?" Brighton asked as he slid in next to his wife and kissed her cheek.

"No one is; we were just talking."

"Sorry we were busy when you arrived," Jason told Molly. "This place is crazy tonight. Do you two want something to eat?"

"Let's get a few appetizers to share," Molly suggested. "I feel like pigging out."

They all agreed and Jason signaled to the waitress. He ordered Oysters Oreganata, Texas Chili Fries, Fried Calamari, and Salmon Sliders.

"Can I have a side salad?"

"Good idea, Ce, I'll have one too," Molly said. "I have to offset the bad with the good."

As the evening continued, people ordered less food but more to drink. The owners had to call rides for a couple of customers to make sure they arrived home safely. A few of the party-goers asked if they could move some tables to enlarge the modest dance floor area. The staff assisted and as the midnight hour approached, nearly every person at Captain Jack's was on his or her feet.

One of the bartenders had called Brighton aside to talk to him. When he was done, Bri searched the restaurant for his wife. He moved behind her and wrapped his arms around her waist. She placed her hands atop his.

"This is going to be our year, my love," he breathed in her ear. "I can feel it."

She pressed her body against his and replied, "I can feel it too."

Making sure everything was in order and the security staff was in place, Jason found Molly and the two moved near their friends. The four stood watching the crowd and the band. Sounds of music and laughter filled the air. The room was warm from all the bodies yet no one seemed to mind. Most of the remaining clientele were business people with their significant others or small groups of friends. Many had visited the restaurant before and the owners knew them by name.

The lead singer began the countdown. Brighton whirled his wife around and put his hands on either side of her face. Her lips moved close to his yet he made sure they did not touch until he heard the singer shout out, "One!"

What began as a simple brush of smiling lips with open eyes morphed to a deeper kiss growing with passionate hunger. One of his hands slid up into her hair and the other down her neck. Hers traveled down his chest and around his waist. One found a home on the small of his back and the other on his behind as she pulled him as close as possible. His mouth moved to the hollow of her neck causing her head to fall back and a moan to escape from deep inside her. Her knees weakened.

"Get a room," Jason laughed.

Brighton huskily replied, "It's your turn to close. We're heading home."

"You know you need to let the guys build up down there. If you do it too often, you're gonna be shooting blanks."

A few days after the New Year began; Cecelia received a call from her doctor.

"I have your blood work results. Your FSH was low but not so much that you can't conceive naturally. It may take a little longer. You're a good candidate for other options if you want to increase your chances. Personally, I would wait a few months. There's no point in jumping into treatments if you don't need them. The only thing I might suggest is having your husband do a sperm analysis just to rule out any issues there. You said Brighton has not fathered any children, correct?"

"He never told me he did. It's not something I've asked him though."

"It might be a tough topic to discuss. You two can come in for a consult if you wish."

"No, that's okay. I'll ask. I'm sure he would have told me but I'll find out."

The next Saturday that Brighton wasn't working, he and Cecelia decided to have a romantic evening at home. In the afternoon they took a trip to the market to buy everything they needed for a candlelit dinner. The main course was French onion beef tenderloin for two smothered with sweet caramelized onions and topped by a crispy Swiss cheese-covered crostini. As a side, Ce suggested orecchiette with broccoli rabe, chickpeas and a sprinkling of asiago cheese. She had seen the chef at Jack's make it and called him for the recipe.

They worked together well in the kitchen. She seasoned the meat with salt, pepper, and dried onion while he heated the skillet with a small amount of olive oil. She placed the steaks in the skillet. He kept an eye on the steaks while she sliced an onion. As she walked around him to retrieve the large pot for the pasta, she ran her hand over his backside. He was wearing one of her favorite pairs of jeans that were butter soft and fit as if made for him.

"Hey, no fondling the cook while he's at the stove."

"That was hardly fondling. When I start fondling, you'll know it. Are those done?"

"If you like them rare they are."

"Sounds good, put them on the plate and tent them."

Ce checked the positioning of the oven rack and turned on the broiler. Then she tossed the onion in the skillet where the meat had been cooked and added a dash of cooking sherry. Brighton went to work on the pasta as she finished caramelizing the onions.

"Stand back for a second; I need to put the pasta in the water and I don't want you to get splashed."

She took two steps away and he put the orecchiette in the pot. She returned to the stove and sprinkled some flour over the onions. He chopped some fresh thyme and tossed it in with the onions along with beef broth.

The pasta was fresh and needed only a few minutes to cook. After two minutes, he added the broccoli rabe to the pot. She put the skillet aside for a moment and prepared the sauce for the pasta. She heated chicken broth and whisked in some flour to thicken it. Then she added garlic and rosemary and continued heating the mixture for about a minute before adding the chickpeas, vinegar, salt and pepper. When the pasta and broccoli rabe were tender, Brighton drained the water and dumped the orecchiette and broccoli rabe into the sauce.

Ce topped the steaks with the onions and a baguette slice and covered them with Swiss cheese. She slid the pan into the oven for two minutes until the cheese was bubbling and melted.

Over dinner, Cecelia told her husband about the results of her blood work.

"I told you there was nothing to worry about."

"He asked if you had any children."

Brighton put down his fork and reached for her hand. She bit her lip anticipating his response. He took a deep breath before speaking.

"Senior year in college I was dating a woman who was in pre-med. We were careful most of the time but..."

"Where is the child now?"

His eyes closed momentarily. "It was her decision. I supported her. We both had promising careers and – we were young, Ce. I drove her to the clinic. Waited for her. Took her home afterward. We broke up about a month later. She mourned the decision and had a hard time dealing with it. She never looked at me the same way."

"I'm so sorry. I didn't mean to open old wounds."

"No one knows except Jason. I never even told Lydia."

Cecelia moved closer to him and caressed his cheek. "I love you. You both did what you thought was right at the time."

"I know. I wish I had talked to her more, maybe suggested she talk to a counselor before actually having the procedure. I had no idea what kind of affect it would have on her."

A tear rolled down his cheek and she brushed it away with her thumb. He leaned toward her and kissed her softly.

"I love you, Ce. I'm sorry I didn't tell you before. I didn't think it mattered."

"It doesn't matter to me. I think the doctor was only asking because he mentioned having you tested for fertility. I'm not sure it's necessary at this point."

He nodded. "Boy, I know how to change the mood, don't I?"

"I brought it up."

"Let's clean up and have dessert."

"Which kind of dessert are you thinking we should have first?"

Brighton started a pot of decaf coffee then put the dishes in the dish washer and washed the pot and skillet while Ce prepared dessert. She had chosen to make something fun but low calorie. At the market, they had picked up some strawberries, a carambola, low fat vanilla ice cream, and low fat chocolate muffins. She scooped out two ice cream balls, placed them on a plate and returned them to the freezer. Next, she cut the muffins in half and placed a small indentation in the bottom halves with a spoon then dusted the tops with confectioner's sugar.

When he was finished cleaning up, Bri sliced the strawberries and the star fruit. She melted a small amount of ice cream in the microwave. When it was done, she placed the muffin bottoms on two plates, put one of the frozen pearls of ice cream on each and rested the muffin tops against the pearls. He garnished the plates with the fruit and she poured the sauce on top.

"Shall we eat in the living room?"

"That sounds lovely."

"I'll get the coffee. Just milk in yours, right?"

"Yes please."

A few days later, Brighton was at work when he received a call from Madge. He sent a quick text to Jason asking him to come in so he could head to the home in the city. He called Cecelia from the car phone. He told the receptionist he needed to speak to his wife immediately. He was put on hold for only a brief time.

"What's wrong?" she asked before even saying hello.

"It's Dad. He's not well. Can you leave work?"

"Do you want to pick me up here or should I meet you at home?"

"I'll meet you at the house. Love you."

"Love you too."

Cecelia told the physician she had a family emergency and she would call if she would be out the following day. She went home and quickly packed a change of clothes for both of them. She rushed downstairs when she heard the front door close.

"How bad is he?"

"Madge called the doctor before she called me. She said to get there as fast as I could. I texted Jas and left."

He took the small bag from her and they went out to the car. He tossed the bag in the trunk and climbed into the driver's seat. After she buckled in, Cecelia reached for his hand.

The traffic on the ride to the city was heavy due to the time of day. Brighton's heart was pounding in his chest. Several times he sighed. She fidgeted in her seat.

As they neared the home, he whispered, "This is it."

"You don't know that."

"Madge would not have called the doctor first unless he was really bad. She wasn't specific. She just said come now."

"Maybe she was short because she wanted to be with Mitch so he wasn't alone."

"I should have stayed in the city. I could have gotten to him faster."

"It would not have made a difference."

"He would know I was there."

"Maybe he might not have. Madge is there and most days he thinks she is your mother."

He shook his head.

"Don't make yourself sick over this, Brighton. Do not feel guilty."

"Easier said than done."

When he pulled into the driveway, Cecelia told him to stop at the door. "I'll park the car. Just go in and be with your father."

Her hand shook as she punched in the code to let her in the unit where Mitch lived. As she walked hurriedly down the hall she saw Madge weeping just outside of Mitch's room. Her feet moved faster until she froze in the doorway. Brighton was holding his father's hand against his cheek. His eyes were closed. Dr. Silverman stood behind his son resting his hand on Brighton's shoulder. When he saw Cecelia, Lance stepped back. Bri felt the doctor move away and he looked up. He blinked away the tears.

"I wasn't here."

Cecelia entered the room and moved closer to her husband. "I'm so sorry."

He looked at Mitch then up at his wife. "He's with my mother now and he's at peace."

A few hours later, Cecelia called Jason and let him know they would be staying in the city for a couple of days to make arrangements. "The funeral will be in Palm Springs so he can be buried with his wife. We'll probably have a memorial service in a couple of weeks back home. I'm not sure when."

"How's Brighton doing?"

"He's handling things as well as can be expected. He called his grandmother first. She's going to take care of things there."

"Give Brighton our best. I'll hold down the fort. Tell him not to worry."

"I will Jason. Thanks."

It was after five when she called her office so she left a message. Then she called her parents. Brighton stepped into the sitting room while she was speaking with her mother. He wrapped his arms around her from behind and put his chin on her shoulder.

"Hi Mrs. Demure."

Cecelia handed him her cell.

"How are you?" he asked his mother-in-law.

"Brighton, I'm sorry for your loss. Mitch is in a much better place now."

"I know; he's with my mother and they are probably catching up."

"I bet you're right. I never met your mother but she raised an incredible son. Let us know when the services are so we can come down."

"It will be in a few weeks." Brighton explained everything then returned the telephone to his wife after saying good-bye. When she disconnected the call, he asked if she was hungry.

"Not really," she replied, "but I think we should both eat."

He nodded. "Let's stop by the deli and get something to go. Then we can stop by the drugstore and find a hotel room for the night."

"Why are we going to the drugstore?"

"Because you are four days late. I've been checking the calendar."

"We can wait to..."

"No, I want to know."

Chapter Thirty-Two

Cecelia tugged open the top drawer of the small bureau and removed a red sweater vest and a green tie. Next, she went to the closet and took out a white shirt and black dress slacks.

"Mommy, do we have to stay at Grandpa J's tonight?"

"Yes, Mitchell, we do. It's a long drive and we can't do it all in one day."

"But we're going so early. And how will Santa know where to leave our presents?"

"Santa knows all," she told her two year old son as she placed his dress clothes in a miniature backpack. "Which pajamas do you want to bring? Superman or Spiderman?"

"I want the ones like Daddy's."

"Okay, red plaid it is. Good thing I packed his already. Now, what do you want to wear for the drive up?"

"Nothing," he giggled as he scrambled off his sports car shaped toddler bed and dashed out of the room.

"Mitchell Daniel Clay, you get back her," she hollered after him. She could not hold back her laughter. "You're just like your father."

Brighton stepped out of another bedroom just as Mitch ran by. "Whoa little man. Where do you think you're going with no clothes on?" With one hand he tousled his son's hair.

"I'm going to Grandpa J's with you and Mommy."

Cecelia covered her still grinning mouth. A second later she said, "You were supposed to deal with the boys, I'm supposed to handle the girls."

"I wish you had reminded me of that before I changed princess's diaper. I'm still gagging," he joked handing his ten month old daughter to his wife. "She just gets through pooping and then she pees all over me."

"You have to keep her covered."

Brighton rubbed Cecelia's tummy. "Are you going to be okay on the drive upstate?"

"As long as we stop every hour so I can pee I'll be just fine. Do you think you can finish getting him dressed and packed? I still need a shower."

"I'd rather help you shower."

"I would rather you do that too but we have no one to watch your son."

"What are you going to do with her?"

"I'll put her in the bouncy seat in the room. She'll be fine for fifteen minutes. When I'm done I'll nurse her so we can get on the road. What time are we picking up Lance?"

"Grandpa Lance is coming too?"

Mitchell asked running around his father's legs.

"He sure is," Brighton said. "I told him between seven and seven thirty. We have plenty of time."

"Maybe we shouldn't have spent an extra hour in bed," she said patting her husband's behind.

He watched as she sauntered down the hall to the master bedroom.

"I'm ready again if you want me to tie this kid down for twenty minutes or so."

"Tie me down. Tie me down," the little boy chanted. "Whoa ho, tie me down."

"C'mon buddy. Let's find you something to wear."

"Mommy said she packed your plaid pajamas like mine."

"She did? Well, it's a good thing Mommy packed for me. I would have forgotten them."

"Mommy remembers everything."

They returned to the boy's room and Brighton dressed his son then checked his backpack. "She even remembered your toothbrush."

"I hate brushing my teeth."

"I know but it's important. You don't want to get cavities."

While they discussed the details of dental care, Brighton and Mitchell made their way down stairs and finished packing the car.

"Before we leave do you need to use the potty?"

"I got my pull-ups on Daddy."

"Those are for accidents only. You should use the potty whenever you can, okay?"

The little boy nodded and ran to the bathroom. Brighton made sure the house was locked up. Then he went upstairs to check on the rest of his family with Mitchell only a few steps behind.

Ce was on the bed nursing Donatella when her guys entered the room. Mitchell crawled up on the bed and told her they were ready to go.

"As soon as your sister is done, we can leave."

The boy softly touched his sister's head. "She's going to be pretty like you, Mommy."

"And you're going to be as handsome as Daddy."

"Yup. And smart like him too."

"You already are smart little man. Bri, maybe you should call Lance and let him know we'll be leaving soon."

"Will do. Is there anything else I need to put in the car?"

"You can take the makeup case on the bureau and the bag on the floor there."

"Mommy have I told you how much I love you today?"

"Yes, you have my sweet boy." She looked at her husband and said, "He's been listening to you. I bet were going to have to keep him on a short leash when he's old enough to date."

Brighton laughed. "Hopefully he will find someone as perfect for him as you are for me."

"There's no one as perfect as Mommy."

Lance had spent the night in a local hotel so his son wouldn't have to drive into the city in the morning. He was waiting outside when Brighton pulled into the parking lot.

As Brighton took Lance's duffel he said, "I hope you weren't waiting too long. Are you checked out?"

"I just finished settling the bill. Thank you for inviting me Brighton."

"I know your daughters are with their mother this year. I didn't think you should spend Christmas alone and you're part of our family too."

"You have no idea how much that means to me."

"C'mon, we have a long drive and we'll probably have to stop a few times along the way."

The front passenger side door opened. Lance walked toward it and said, "Ce, stay in the front. You'll be more comfortable there."

"Are you sure, Lance? There's more leg room in the front for you."

"I'll make do."

As he slid in to the back seat, he said hello to Mitchell.

"Hi Grandpa. Wanna play I spy with me?"

"Okay, you go first."

Donatella was quiet for the first couple of hours. Lance kept his grandson occupied with games and talking about baseball. When Ce began to shift in her seat, Brighton asked how she was feeling.

"I'm fine. I just get a little stiff sitting still. If I wasn't so big I could rearrange myself."

"We can stop if you like."

"Let's wait a bit longer. Dona is going to wake up soon to nurse."

"All right, just say the word."

Not long after that, Mitchell said, "Mommy, I have to go potty and Daddy said the pull-ups are only for accidents. Can we find a potty?"

"I'll get off at the next exit, buddy."

As if on cue, Donatella started to stir. Her eyes fluttered open.

"Hi baby Dona," her brother said. "We're not there yet. Go back to sleep. Mommy she smiled at me."

"She loves you."

"I love you too baby."

They went to a small restaurant right off the highway. Brighton took his son to the bathroom while Cecelia went to the ladies room with the baby. Lance ordered two cups of coffee, an herbal tea and a milk to go. The boys sat at a table waiting for Cecelia to finish nursing Donatella. Not long after they were back on the road, both children were asleep.

"I'm going to close my eyes for a bit Bri."

"Okay, my love, I'll wake you when it's time for lunch."

Although it had snowed the day before, the roads were clear. The sun was out and white fluffy clouds hung sparingly in the sky. Brighton set the cruise control and relaxed. He glanced into the rear view mirror and asked his father how work was going.

"Things are good. I'm cutting back my hours. We hired a new doctor who will take over my patients. In six months or so I'll be retiring."

"Will you stay in New York?"

"My eldest girl will be starting at NYU next fall. She chose the school for a few reasons but I think having me here is a plus. It's a long way from La Jolla."

"Cecelia and I would love to meet her. Maybe you could bring her by for a home cooked meal some Sunday. That is if you told her about me."

"I told them both about you and Brent. It wasn't an easy topic of discussion. They're very forgiving kids."

"I suppose that runs in the family."

Lance chuckled.

"I went to see my brother last week. He is doing all right, all things considered. I think he is genuinely sorry. His therapy seems to be helping him deal with his past. He hasn't had any contact with her."

"Have you heard anything about her since they transferred her to a higher security facility?"

"No I haven't. The threatening letters stopped and they found the guy who was helping her send them. He's been locked up as well but probably not for long."

"Do you feel like that chapter in your life is closed?"

"I hope so."

"How are Jason and Molly?"

"They're doing well. Molly has been helping out at Jack's a few times a week. It gives her a chance to have adult conversations. Usually when she works, Ce sits with the four kids and when Ce works Molly watches them."

"They must be a handful and you have another on the way."

"Jackson is very well behaved and he helps with the younger ones."

"He's going to be four in the spring, right?"

Brighton nodded.

The family stopped for a light lunch at twelve thirty. For the remainder of the trip to North Tonawanda, Mitchell was talking non-stop. He told his grandfather all about his play group, Saturday morning trips to the library, and how to build the perfect snowman.

"Mommy said they get lots of snow up where Grandpa J lives. Maybe we can make a snow fort tomorrow."

"That would be fun," Lance said to the wide-eyed boy.

Mitchell rubbed his hands together. "Mommy, did you pack my snowsuit?"

"I sure did."

"And extra mittens too?"

"I have everything you need, sweetheart."

The closer they came to Tonawanda, the higher the piles of snow were on the side of the highway. This was the children's first visit to upstate New York. Cecelia's parents had traveled south a few times to see their grandchildren over the past two years.

As Brighton threw the car in park in the driveway of the Demure house, Mitchell almost crawled over Lance to get out.

"Hold your horses, young man. Give me a minute."

Brighton opened the driver's side passenger door and his daughter giggled while he tried to release her car seat.

"Ce, how the heck do you..? Never mind, I got it. You think Daddy is funny, huh princess?"

"I can take her," Ce said as she rounded the front of the car.

"No you don't. Go inside. It's cold out here."

"I'm fine. I have my own personal heater." She rubbed her swollen abdomen.

Both Jonathan and Samuel emerged from the house to help Brighton with the luggage. Jonathan kissed his daughter as she passed.

"You look amazing."

"My cheeks are probably pink from the cold air."

"It suits you."

Mitchell was dragging Lance by the hand. "C'mon. I wanna go see my cousins."

Once everyone was inside and their belongings delivered to the bedrooms, the family congregated in the living room. Mr.

Demure greeted Lance. "Brighton speaks very highly of you. I'm so glad you could join us for the holiday."

"Thank you, Jonathan. You have a charming home and a beautiful daughter."

The room was abuzz with activity. Mitchell was chatting with his older cousin James and his brother William. Brighton and Samuel were catching up. Natalia hugged her sister and asked how she was feeling.

"I can't complain. I love being pregnant."

"Are you having twins? You're big this time."

Cecelia spied her mother coming and ignored the comment. "Hi Ma. How are you?" She gave her mother a big hug.

"You look marvelous Cecelia. How are you feeling?"

"I'm great. This little one keeps me up at night though always moving around. I don't remember the others being as active at this stage."

"I think the more times you are pregnant the easier it is to feel the movements. Dinner is almost ready. I put the pizza in a couple of minutes ago. Come and sit down."

Jonathan had borrowed a folding table so they would have enough room for everyone to sit without being crowded together. The three boys sat at the end of the smaller table with Cecelia next to Mitchell and Natalia beside James. Brighton took the spot next to his wife. He held on to his daughter so Ce could help Mitchell with his food.

Nat and her mother brought out the homemade pizza. One pizza was cheese for the children. Another was covered in Italian sausage and pepperoni. Roasted vegetables adorned the third. Mrs. Demure also made a small dish of plain pasta for the baby.

As the ladies sat, Brighton stood from his chair.

"If no one minds, I'd like to say a few words before we enjoy the meal."

"Go ahead Brighton," Jonathan said with a nod.

Little Dona looked up at her father and stroked his beard.

"When Cecelia and I first met, my life was a mess."

Ce smiled.

"Still, she stood by me, believed in me, and put up with a myriad of difficulties. Without her, I would not have survived. And then, she introduced me to her family. You welcomed me with open arms and a loaded rifle," he laughed. "I learned once more what being a part of a family was. Losing Mitch was not easy. He was the only man I ever called father. But somehow, that change became a blessing because I got to know my birth father."

Lance straightened in his seat.

"Each and every one of you holds a special place in here," he continued, putting his hand over his chest. "I have never felt so complete as I do today surrounded by my family, my beautiful wife and our two soon-to-be three children. I know we will continue to be blessed. I thank you all for accepting me regardless of the turmoil my life was when I came into the family."

Brighton took a deep breath and before he could say another word, Mitchell asked, "Can we eat now?"

Did you love *Feat of Clay*? Then you should read *Beautiful Anomaly* by Mary-ellen DeLeon!

After a brutal attack, a Texas woman decides to move to LA and reinvent herself as Serafina Divine. She opens a studio specializing in photographing animals. During the week, she works diligently to grow her business and soon she hires Martha Blake as her assistant. Serafina keeps her private weekend activities from Martha for as long as she can.

Blaze Hunter is a reckless rock star who has alienated nearly everyone in the music industry with his demands for perfection. His loyal fans toss flowers and other items on the stage when he performs and the paparazzi follow him relentlessly seeking juicy tidbits of information about the rock

God. When at the last minute, the photographer for his soon to be released album falls ill, no one wants to work with Blaze to finish the cover.

Blaze's assistant, Terry Smithers is at his wits end trying to find a photographer for the cover. He has called every well-known lens-man in the book. The last studio he calls accepts the job, but only if Terry can get his boss to the studio early on Sunday morning.

Terry's decision to employ Divine Photography for the cover pictures changes the life of all of them... forever.

Read more at wp.me/3DDdp.

Also by Mary-ellen DeLeon

Beautiful Anomaly
Family Secrets
Transcendent Love
Feat of Clay
Get Revenge
When Demons Hide

Watch for more at wp.me/3DDdp.

About the Author

Mary-ellen DeLeon lives in Connecticut with her teenage daughter. She has a passion for writing. Her books deal with difficult yet timely issues of today's society. Her favorite writers include F. Scott Fitzgerald, Robert Parker, Nicolette Gianni, Gillian Flynn, Lauren Kate, and Nicholas Sparks.

Writing is an escape, a way to live someone else's life and take control of destiny. Travel into one of Mary-ellen's books and visit a world of love and tragedy, suspense and survival. See who comes out winning in the end.

https://www.facebook.com/MDeLeonAuthor/
@MagnoliaWriter2
Read more at wp.me/3DDdp.